FOR ALL THE RIGHT REASONS

FOR ALL THE RIGHT REASONS

MAUREEN HARTMAN

PROBABLY A BEAR
PRESS

PART 1

PORTLAND, OREGON
—FALL, 2004

CHAPTER ONE

Lorenzo

Lorenzo gazed out his office window in disgust as a team of reporters encroached on the central police station like hyenas coming in for the kill. The arraignment had come in for the thirteen-year-old arsonist who'd burned down his school. Now the kid had *this* to contend with. Lorenzo knew how it felt to have the worst day of your life publicly exposed—stripped naked for a juicy headline.

Behind him, station business carried on as usual—fingers on keypads, laughter, banter, and heated conversations provided a comforting familiarity amid his darker thoughts.

"Detective, line 3. Can you take this?"

It was Buddy, Lorenzo's young counterpart, from across their shared cubicle wall.

Lorenzo took a deep breath, turning away from the window. "Press?" Lorenzo had a rule about speaking with the press. *Don't. It never ends well.*

"No, someone from the port. A request for collaboration. Interested?"

"Sure." Lorenzo reached across his desk and picked up the line. "Detective Rotondo. Who am I speaking with?" His Italian accent bled through, despite three decades in the US.

"Detective, this is Officer Klein. Port of Portland Police."

"What can I do for you, Officer?" Lorenzo slipped his moleskin from his breast pocket, turned to a blank page, and wrote the man's name across the top.

"Had an unexpected visitor today, and frankly, he made me nervous. I'd look into it myself, but the thing is . . . we're shorthanded here, and I could use some help."

"I'll do what I can. Could you give me a breakdown? What happened?" Lorenzo waited with the tip of his pen already pressed to the paper.

"He said the freight company confirmed his shipment's arrival from Genoa, Italy," Officer Klein said, "but it hadn't been delivered to its destination. What's worrisome is the guy had nothing to prove his legitimacy. No shipping documents, proof of delivery, or bill of entry—just bluster about how the Italian embassy could vouch for him."

"The *Italian* embassy?" Lorenzo watched gratefully as Buddy set a steaming cup of fresh coffee on his desk.

"Yeah. I turned him away, and he went berserk like he was accustomed to getting his own way. I mean, I have a four-year-old at home who's better behaved. Anyway, I called for the guards to escort him off the property. I have the feeling that wasn't the end of it, you know? Like he'd be back with guns blazing."

"I'm sorry, I don't know how to help you," Lorenzo said. But he was still taking notes. *International Freight. Genoa. Missing documents. Warehouse.*

"Detective, I don't have the right men to deal with this."

"Um, okay—let's start with a name."

"That's the thing, detective. There were no documents. No ID. All I got for you is a short, fat guy with a bad comb-over. Think of a well-dressed Danny DeVito with enough cologne to choke a horse."

"Anything else?"

"Well, he had this lapel pin with a stone that looked like a robin's egg." Officer Klein paused. "Ah! That's it! His name was Robini."

Robini. Lorenzo shoved his moleskin away as if it were on fire, dropping his pen and inadvertently spilling his coffee across his desk like a Stumptown tsunami.

"What the fuck?" cried Buddy. But Lorenzo just stared blankly as the coffee bled into a stack of folders, soaking his notebook.

"Detective?" said Officer Klein.

Lorenzo held the phone away from his face and slowly counted to three. "Could we meet tomorrow, Officer Klein?" Lorenzo needed to get off the phone. He needed to pull himself together. "I'd like to see any video footage you have." He could scarcely hear himself speak over the ringing in his ears. He hardly noticed Buddy blotting up the spilled coffee with a stack of paper towels.

They set a time to meet at the port's cargo center. Retrieving his pen, Lorenzo scribbled the appointment into his Word-A-Day desk calendar. October 16, 2004. *Motivate*: verb. To stimulate interest in or enthusiasm for doing something.

Lorenzo packed his things, pulled his wool blazer tight against the autumn chill, and walked home from the station under the glow of a quickly setting sun. He climbed the flight of stairs to his apartment and locked the door behind him.

He stepped into the living room and turned on CNN announcing poll numbers for the upcoming presidential election, then peeled off his holster and laid it on the kitchen counter, his fingers lingering on the soft, worn leather. It reminded him of happier days.

Lorenzo wandered into his bedroom. With a trembling hand, he reached for a tin box buried deep on a closet shelf and pulled off the lid, revealing a small collection of artifacts from his previous life.

On top was the note his sister had tucked into his jacket the day he left Italy. It had since been heavily creased and crumpled. He'd memorized it—but he was a glutton for punishment, and he unfolded it to read again.

May 15, 1974

Enzo,

My dear brother. Although I will never understand your grief, my heart still aches for you. I realize you need to get away, but do not forget your family. Don't worry about your little Emilio. He will be in excellent hands with his grandparents and doting aunts. Please remember that we will keep you with us through stories and photographs. Your young son will know you through us until your return.

I love you, and we will all miss you terribly. Please stay in touch.

Muriel

He tucked the note behind a stack of envelopes, stamped *Posta Aerea, Italia*. Then he opened the first letter. There was a photo of his son tucked inside, his wavy jet-black hair neatly combed, a concentrated furrow across his brow. Lorenzo flipped the picture over. In her flowery penmanship, Muriel had scrawled, "Emilio, age 7." The letter promised Emilio was well cared for. That boy would be thirty-one now. He wasn't that kid anymore. But Lorenzo wasn't the frightened twenty-two-year-old he'd been back then either. Now, at fifty-two, Lorenzo wondered if he'd ever hold another infant in his arms again.

The other letters, all lovingly written, contained details of his son's milestones, updates on the family, their health, marriages, children. Though intended for his benefit, these details only heightened his guilt as he thought of his aging parents.

Lorenzo searched deeper into the box. He found a tan leather wallet, brittle with age. His police ID slipped out, and he stared at the photo taken on his first day with the Liguria Municipal Police in La Spezia. The gold buttons of his crisp new uniform gleamed, and the shiny brim of his cap sat low over his eyes. Lorenzo remembered how he had shaved that morning, trimming his long trendy sideburns to regulation length. He put the wallet down with a heavy sigh.

And then he saw it. What he'd been searching for. At the bottom of the box: a photo of him and Ella on their wedding day.

He'd long exhausted the tears shed for this past life, and for his youthful ignorance. But the oppressive guilt and shame remained. He sometimes wondered if it was too late to return—but mostly he believed it was too soon. He'd maintained his Italian citizenship, but worried about what he'd find back there in his little coastal village. Heartache? Reminders of a life unlived? His failure to face reality like a man? Today, those possibilities stood front and center.

Robini.

Lorenzo had worked side by side with Marco Robini. The family were notorious crooks, but Marco seemed different. He'd called himself the white sheep of the family, flaunting his badge as proof.

That was decades ago. A lifetime.

Clutching the box, Lorenzo sat on the side of his bed and closed his eyes, remembering the incident that changed his life forever.

That afternoon so long ago, while the rest of the village celebrated the annual feast day, Lorenzo and Ella had sneaked away to explore the abandoned farmhouse on Via Rosa—intending to buy it, fix it up, and raise a dozen children under its roof despite the stigma of the Robini's suspected fascist ties, and a local superstition that bad luck came to whomever passed through its door.

The sun felt hot on their backs. Ella could hardly contain her excitement as they waded through the tall grass and skirted past a stand of overgrown rose bushes. But when Lorenzo heard voices at the back door, he shushed her and approached on his own.

"Lorenzo, my friend," said the handsome young man, opening the door from the inside. "What are you doing here? You're missing the party."

At first, Lorenzo felt relief at the familiar face. "As are you, Marco," he said. Marco stood several inches taller than Lorenzo. He was uncommonly handsome and a charismatic ladies' man.

An older gentleman with thinning black hair stepped out of the house then, leaving the door ajar, his mouth set in a fierce scowl. "Who are you, and what are you doing here?" he said curtly. Lorenzo thought Marco and his companion seemed out of place at the ramshackle house, clad neatly in dress slacks and crisp white shirts, though Marco's sleeves were rolled up.

"Uncle Carlo, this is Lorenzo Rotondo, my compatriot with the *polizi*." Marco straightened his tie and gazed over Lorenzo's shoulder. "And this is his beautiful bride." He leered at Ella as she stepped bashfully out of the shadows. She gazed up at Lorenzo, tugging at a loose braid over her shoulder, her face flush from the August heat.

"We're looking to move out of my parents' house," Lorenzo said, taking Ella's arm and drawing her close beside him. Perhaps that made him appear territorial, but Marco had a reputation, and Lorenzo wanted it clear that Ella was off-limits. "Is this old place for sale?" He knew the farmhouse belonged to the Robini family, but it hadn't been lived in for several decades.

Without taking his eyes from Ella, Marco reached back and closed the farmhouse door.

Uncle Carlo locked his steely gaze on Lorenzo. "The house has been in our family for generations, and we have no intention of selling it."

Ella's shoulders sagged. "But no one lives here," she said softly. "It's such a waste with so little on the market." She looked from Uncle Carlo to Marco, then glanced at the crumbling barn beyond the house.

"I said it's not for sale," Uncle Carlo said. "Marco, get these people out of here." He stormed off toward his black Mercedes.

"Sorry, folks," said Marco. "See you at the celebration tonight?" Lorenzo took Ella's hand and turned to leave when Marco added, "Ella, sweetheart, save a dance for me." His grin sent chills up Lorenzo's spine.

That night, as the festivities ended and strings of colorful lights glowed in the piazza, Marco appeared at Lorenzo's side and whispered in his ear. "Come anywhere near that house again, and your family will pay." Then he winked at Ella and disappeared into the crowd. Marco was *not* the white sheep in the family, Lorenzo decided, but a wolf in sheep's clothing.

Lorenzo kept his concerns from Ella, but confided the incident to his superior, Comissario Santos, at the police station the following day. He was pushed aside as if there was nothing to Marco's warning.

"Then why would he warn me away?" said Lorenzo. "What is he hiding?"

"What makes you think he's hiding anything?" said Santos.

Lorenzo's suspicions were sealed when Comissario Santos glanced outside his office, where Marco stood with his hands in his pockets and a smirk fixed on his face. These suspicions festered for a year until, finally, Lorenzo could wait no longer.

One day after work, he took it upon himself to explore the old farmhouse. Cautiously, he approached from the rear and peered in through a cracked window. His discovery took his breath away. Art in every shape and form—standing on pedestals, leaning on easels, and hanging on the walls. It seemed as out of place as Marco and his uncle had a year earlier.

Lorenzo entered the house with the foreboding one gets when in a forbidden place. He reached for a beautiful statuette, artfully crafted from white marble. He admired the artist's attention to detail, like the figure's delicate toes and a wisp of hair framing the side of her face.

A thump on the floor above jolted him to attention. Lorenzo

waited a moment, heart thumping wildly in his chest, then drew his gun, reset the clip, and climbed the first few steps. The fourth step creaked beneath his feet, and he froze, holding his breath, listening. Silence.

Reaching the landing, he glanced down the hall, and then treaded further toward the open door at the other end, advancing slowly and deliberately, pausing outside before entering. In the room, a fair-haired woman sat calmly in a ladder-backed chair by the window, an unfinished painting before her. Beside it was the original she was reproducing. It featured a young girl in a white dress sitting primly on an ornately carved chair.

The woman's brush barely touched the canvas before she turned her head. Lorenzo trained his pistol on her.

"Can I help you?" she asked, setting down her brush.

He kept the gun steady, his eyes scanning the room—he feared they were not alone.

"Hello, Lorenzo," said Marco, stepping forward, grinning as if he'd known all along this would happen.

"Your family will pay," Marco had said. But it was Ella who'd paid. Lorenzo placed the lid back on the tin box and returned it to the closet with the familiar stir of unresolved grief in the pit of his stomach. He'd lost track of time. The room had grown dark.

The television was still on when he returned to the living room. "More on Mount St. Helens' growing dome," the announcer droned, "and the latest in the Scott Peterson trial, after the break."

Lorenzo stood transfixed through an ad for Kerry, an ad for Bush, and an ad for erectile dysfunction medication. Before they could convince him he needed a late-night visit to Taco Bell, he switched the television off and went to bed, tormented by memories he thought he'd buried long ago.

CHAPTER TWO

Kate ignored the insistent rap on her door for a full minute before setting down her wrench and squirming out from beneath the kitchen sink with a mixture of annoyance and dread. It was George—she knew by the knock.

She pictured her pasty-faced ex-husband standing on the front porch in the drizzly October rain with his pinched, self-entitled smirk and slicked-back hair. She'd hoped he'd grow impatient and storm off into the night in his brand-new Audi. But alas, he'd found the forbearance to wait. She gritted her teeth, took a deep breath, and opened the door.

"Jesus Christ, what took you so long!" George blew past her and hung his dripping umbrella on the flimsy coatrack beside the door, then hung his sport coat alongside the umbrella and kicked off his Armani shoes. The wood floor creaked beneath his stocking feet as he crossed the living room and stretched out on the black leather sofa. It was one of two furniture pieces he'd left behind. The other was the antique bed.

Thanks to the generosity of Kate's friends and one-of-a-kind thrift-store gems, she'd collected a few other odds and ends—but the house still lacked more than it held. In the year since her divorce had been finalized, she'd been too broke and too busy to do much about that. All in good time, she reminded herself regularly.

"What are you doing here, George?" Kate said nervously, combing her fingers through her black shoulder-length curls. She hiked up her old button-fly jeans and straightened the faded T-shirt, suddenly aware of her unkempt appearance.

"It's about the house. If you'd read my emails, you would have ..."

Kate stopped listening. George's emails, like his phone messages, provoked the same reflex—delete. She returned to the sanctuary of her unfinished task in the kitchen.

"So, did you get that promotion you were after?" George called from the other room. Since the divorce, they seldom spoke to one another—but the conversations they did have usually dealt with the ambiguous alimony agreement and Kate's tenuous position at the newspaper.

Kate cringed. For a hot second, she considered lying—but that wasn't who she was. "Um, no," she said meekly. She'd been turned down for the last two promotions. It was a heavy blow, but Kate knew she'd need to earn the position and was prepared to put in the necessary time and hard work.

She heard him enter the kitchen. "Christ, Katie, how did you screw this one up?" She hated it when he called her Katie. That name was reserved for friends; people who actually loved her. "You always do this. So weak. No follow-through. You always give up before the race is over." Kate held up her middle finger in the privacy of the cabinet as he went on. "You know what you should do, don't you? You should storm into that asshole's office and demand a raise."

"And get fired?"

"See what I mean? You always give up. No confidence. I suppose you'd have to have skills for that, though, huh? You should have chosen a different career—like, I don't know, goat farmer." He laughed. Kate had heard the same message a hundred different ways over the years. Goat farmer. Sheep herder. Combine operator. He had a way of turning her childhood into a joke—something to be ashamed of.

She'd never replied to his jabs before and wasn't going to start now, lying captive beneath the sink. Being there seemed appropriate. George had a way of making her feel trapped while she blindly made space for his moods and demands.

He rifled through the refrigerator until she heard a *pfft* and the tink and rattle of a bottle cap skipping across the countertop. She'd finished with her task but remained hidden under the sink, avoiding eye contact, her grimy hands gripped the heavy pipe wrench.

"Get out of there," George said. "We need to talk."

"Hmm?"

"The house. Half of it is still mine until we either sell it or you buy me out."

"Where would I get the money for that?"

"I don't care. Get a loan." George guzzled the beer. "What the hell are you doing under there, anyway?"

"Replacing the disposal." She winced, waiting for the expected censure.

"What the hell do you know about garbage disposals? Why don't you call a damn plumber, for Christ's sake?"

Equal share in the house was the judge's idea. She would be allowed to stay for the first year of their divorce, then they'd make the final decision to sell. It suited her at first. She had nowhere to go, and he was paying half the mortgage for a year. She supposed it was the judge's concession to the otherwise raw deal she'd gotten in the settlement. But now her year was up, and George seemed eager to move on.

She thought about George in the early days of their relationship: attentive, flirtatious, charismatic. She'd fallen hard for him. He took pleasure in her journalistic aspirations and wooed her with boasts of his success as an insurance broker. The youngest one in the firm, apparently. But after the honeymoon blush faded, he seemed bent on shattering the moxie he'd said he loved about her, revealing his own weak self-esteem. By the time she realized what had happened, it was too late.

Finally, after seven years of quiet resentment, Kate had recognized him for the bully he was and pulled the plug.

"Leave me alone, George. Please?"

His tone softened. "Will you at least think about it? You could swing the payments if you got the raise. The best of both." He slugged back the beer and left the bottle in the sink, nudging her bottom with his stocking foot before leaving the room. "Or better yet, let's just sell it." His voice trailed off into the other room.

Only after she heard the front door open and close did Kate clamber out from beneath the sink. Suddenly in need of a friend, she wiped her hands and headed next door.

Megan opened the door, holding a dripping head of romaine lettuce. She looked radiant. Pregnancy suited her. "Get in here, you crazy lady!" she said. The house felt warm and inviting, with magnificent homey aromas wafting from the kitchen and Steely Dan's *Aja* spinning on the turntable. Megan's brows furrowed. "You okay?"

"I'm sorry to barge in on you like this," Kate said. "You're getting dinner on."

"Don't think about it. I'll set another place at the table."

Briley, Megan's four-year-old son, stretched out two fists. "Yes, no, or maybe so?" he asked. Kate looked at Megan.

"It's from a show he watches. Just go along with it."

"Yes," she said. Briley opened his fists to reveal a rubber band bracelet.

"I made it," he said proudly, placing it in Kate's hand. "You can keep it."

"I love your gifts, Briley. Thank you." She crouched low and kissed him on the cheek, feeling his soft dark curls brush against her face.

Kate recalled the day Megan told her she was pregnant with Briley. She'd stood at Kate's kitchen door in a pool of tears, crying, "I'm not ready for this!" Kate swallowed her envy then, as she did now.

"Off you go, Briley. Daddy's getting your bath ready." Megan smiled tenderly down at the boy, then turned to Kate. "Thomas just got home a minute ago and I've already put him to work."

"Taskmaster," Kate said, grinning.

"He loves it."

"Briley, get your butt down here!" called Thomas from the hall. Briley's eyes widened, and he took off running.

Megan led Kate into the kitchen and bellied up to the sink to shake out the lettuce. "What gives?" she asked.

"George stopped by." Kate took the lettuce from her friend and began tearing it into a bowl on the counter as she downloaded the brief exchange with her ex-husband.

"It's been a year since he cleaned you out in the divorce. So now he's broke and needs you to bail *him* out?" Megan huffed.

"A deal's a deal."

"He left you with nothing!" Megan waved a thick carrot through the air like a maestro's baton.

"I got the sofa, the bed, and half a house for a year. It's more than I expected." Kate was prepared to lose everything to be out from under him.

"The bed was already yours, sweetheart," said Megan, rinsing the carrot and laying it on the cutting board.

Kate shrugged, thinking of the antique bed from her childhood that had sat in the basement unused because George couldn't possibly share anything so small. He'd needed his space. Now, that prized possession was where she laid her head each night.

"Maybe he needs the money. The insurance business isn't what it used to be," said Kate, marveling that, even now, she could find excuses for George.

Megan raised her knife. "Listen, Mary Katheryn Noonan, you are a winner." *Chop, chop.* "A winner does not give in." *Chop.* "A winner comes away from a fight with more power than she went in with." Megan had all but neutered George by the time she tossed the carrot's little stub into the sink.

Kate shook her head. "Feels more like George won tonight, waltzing in like he still owned the place. Well, I guess he does."

"Yeah, well, you'll get him next time—right, slugger?" Megan laughed. "Screw him."

Kate looked at the pathetic remains in the sink. "I'd rather not," she said, reaching for a dishtowel to pat the lettuce dry.

Megan wiped crumbs from the table where Briley had just eaten, then laid out an extra place setting. "You still working on the St. Helens story?" A peel of laughter rang from the hall, and she glanced out the kitchen door.

"Yeah." Kate folded the towel and laid it on the counter, feeling grateful for the newspaper's trust in her. "I'm going camping up there in a couple of days to check out the growing dome. The staff photographer, too. We're working on a piece for the Sunday edition. If all goes well, it could be a regular series."

"*Camping?*" Megan turned away from the table to face Kate. "Are you serious? When was the last time you did that?"

"Years. Thanks to George, I don't even have any decent gear left. He doesn't even *like* the outdoors."

"Thomas and I have all the gear you need. I'll dig it out for you after dinner." Megan pulled the pot roast from the oven, lifted the lid off the Dutch oven, and inhaled approvingly.

Backpacking had been one of Kate's favorite pastimes—she'd taken it up in college and it was part of her rationale for moving to Oregon. Unfortunately, it became a *former* pastime after she met George. His intolerance of her hiking friends put a quick end to it— and the sad part was that she let him.

Suddenly, little Briley thundered down the hallway in his birthday suit. Thomas followed close behind with his sleeves rolled up and shirtfront dampened, then swept the boy up in his arms and gave him a spin. Finally, he handed him off to his mother. "Your turn, Princess," he said.

Megan smiled up at her husband and went to settle Briley down with a bedtime story.

Kate felt a tug at her heart. She'd had her chance years ago to be a mother. A college indiscretion followed by a trip to the clinic. *Quitter*, she thought—but it was George's voice in her head again. When she was married, motherhood became less of an option than a challenge. But fertility treatments? Forget it. She wasn't going to do that to her body. *Quitter*, she thought again.

Thomas reached into the cabinet for a pair of wine glasses. "It's hard to believe there are only four more months until round two," he said.

"Four months? It's going so fast." Kate glanced up at the recent family portrait on the wall.

"Don't tell Megan that. It's not fast enough for her." Thomas smiled, deepening his endearing crow's feet. "Did she show you the ultrasound?"

"Not yet. You guys don't want to know the gender?"

"She doesn't. I do. We'll work it out." Thomas filled their glasses, and they settled in at the kitchen table.

"How are things at the port?" she asked, sipping the wine.

"Kinda weird, really. You know, with the more stringent Homeland Security rules, I've never been busier. We're finding holes everywhere, and there's not enough of us to deal with them." He shook his head. "This morning, some guy wanted a tour of the warehouse. He said his shipment from Italy never arrived."

"He thought you would let him wander the warehouse to find it?"

"Yeah. Exactly. Everything about this guy was odd—from his powerful cologne to the high-end suit he wore. He was so confident that I'd bend the rules for him. I couldn't, and now he's pissed, right?

So, I have to post an alert for him on the docks and all over the whole flippin' terminal, and I have no goddamned extra personnel. The newest batch of Homeland Security rules stretched the whole damn budget to the breaking point with the new screening equipment and daily policy changes. There's only so much I can do here at the cargo center." Thomas took a deep breath. "This country sucks right now, you know?"

"Maybe things will change after the election."

"You think a new president will change anything? I'll tell you, Katie, I would vote for John Kerry—but, hell, Dubya got us into this mess. He's going to have to get us out."

"Or make a bigger mess." Kate thought about the soldiers fighting in Iraq and Afghanistan, doing their best to stomp out the Taliban. Their minor victories always led to more attacks, and more attacks led to more death and destruction.

"I asked for backup from PPB," said Thomas. Kate didn't work the police beat but knew that PPB stood for the Portland Police Bureau and operated independently from the Port of Portland Police.

Thomas took a long draw from his wineglass as Kate stood to check the roast. She loved playing house at Megan's. It made her feel connected, like being back home on the farm in Colorado.

"I dunno, Kate, maybe something will come of it. Or not." Thomas chuckled. "They're on a shoestring too."

"Did I miss anything?" asked Megan, entering the room. Her shirt looked wrinkled—Briley must have been sitting on her lap and resting his freshly bathed head against her. She had a dreamy look— as if she could have crawled into bed with her son and fallen asleep too.

Another reminder of that absence in Kate's life.

That night, Kate carried her boombox upstairs, where she ran a hot bath and slipped one of her favorite CDs into the tray. She undressed to the prelude of *La Traviata* and emerged an hour later, prune-fingered and shivering, but contented.

She'd seen the opera in Portland three years earlier with George, who'd acted like he was doing her a monumental favor. Despite his sour mood, Kate enjoyed the performance thanks to the handsome, blue-eyed Italian gentleman sitting to her left, who had not needed the synopsis provided at the door. She remembered admiring his corduroy sport coat. It made him look professorial, especially with the sprinkle of gray at his temples. Everything else about him seemed youthful, from the twinkle in his eyes to his playful smile. His date was a young blond who kept touching his knee, as if reminding him she was still there. He didn't hesitate to answer whenever Kate had a question about the storyline. He looked her in the eye when she spoke, hanging onto every word. In fact, he seemed to enjoy her attention very much, laughing with a subtle *mm-hm-hm*, or *heh-heh-heh*. George grew so jealous, he dragged her out before the last act.

This wasn't unusual for George. He'd taken her home from Megan and Thomas's wedding before the dancing even started, and he'd skipped out on her brother's visit altogether.

As Kate lay back on her pillow now, she thought about the odd encounter Thomas had shared with her that evening. What did the man want from the warehouse, and why couldn't he provide documentation? Was there a story here? She kicked herself for not asking more questions at dinner. Maybe George was right, and she lacked the skills and confidence she needed to get ahead.

"Ugh!" She punched her pillow, trying to purge George from her head.

CHAPTER THREE

Lorenzo

Lorenzo met with Officer Klein at the Port of Portland security office the following day.

"Have a seat, detective," Officer Klein said, easing behind a desk surrounded by monitors and dotted with photos of a pre-school-aged boy with dark curls. A small square window offered some natural light, while a fluorescent fixture buzzed and flickered overhead.

Lorenzo took it all in as he sat down in the orange plastic chair across from Officer Klein and opened his recently coffee-stained notebook. "They've informed me this is a priority case," Lorenzo said, suppressing the queasy feeling in his stomach.

Officer Klein laughed and leaned back in his chair with a grin, revealing deep-set smile lines fanning out from each eye. "Is that so? I'm flattered."

"Heh. Well, I've been thinking about the international freight element of your dilemma. Could step on some federal toes." A part of Lorenzo hoped the case skipped right to the feds.

"Called the feds. They passed. Besides, I'm more concerned with that guy who showed up to collect it."

Lorenzo swallowed hard, but the lump in his throat remained. "You said you have surveillance." Lorenzo braced himself as Officer Klein leaned forward to load the DVD.

On the screen, they watched the visitor approach the building, stop for a moment to straighten his suit jacket, then open the door. He walked with a confident stride that Lorenzo recognized—the sort of strut used by professional criminals to conceal their intentions.

"Stop—there. Go back a bit. Okay, freeze that." Lorenzo examined the grainy image but couldn't identify the face. *Who are you? What are you up to?*

"I seriously don't even know how he got through the terminal gate," Officer Klein said. "For all I know, he's a terrorist."

"You said he received confirmation from the freight company. Which one?"

"No idea."

Lorenzo tapped his pen on the open notebook. "Could I have a look around?" He hoped the warehouse held the key. Perhaps *hope* wasn't the right word, given his suspicions, but the warehouse would either confirm or dispel his fears. Which side of hope would he find?

The door squeaked, and Lorenzo turned. A woman stood in the doorway wearing a jean jacket and black turtleneck. Her face, warmed to a rosy blush across freckled cheeks, was framed in large black looping curls. Lorenzo's heart skipped a beat. It had been years, but he recognized her immediately.

Officer Klein's face lit up. "Katie! I wasn't expecting you."

Lorenzo looked sharply from one to the other, registering their familiarity with one another.

"Hey," she said, smiling. "Got a minute to answer a few questions about your mystery man?" she said.

"Mystery man?"

"Yeah, the guy from yesterday . . . you mentioned him at

dinner . . ." Her voice trailed off when she noticed Lorenzo. They held each other's gaze, and he watched with delight as her face blossomed with recognition.

Lorenzo stood, pushing his hair back from his face.

"Detective Lorenzo Rotondo, meet my next-door neighbor, Katie Noonan." She threw Officer Klein a look, and he went on. "Excuse me. *Kate* Noonan. She's only Katie to a select few."

Lorenzo smiled. "Very nice to meet you, Kate, not Katie—though I believe we've met before."

Her blush brightened, as did the full lips of her broad smile. "Yes! The opera, right? This is going to sound weird—but I was just thinking about you last night."

Now it was Lorenzo's turn to blush. Had he made an impression? He was almost afraid to believe it. But he was also amused at the look of surprise on Officer Klein's face.

Lorenzo recalled how she'd scoured the program for a synopsis. "That's it?" she'd mumbled, flipping to the back page for more and finding only advertisements for high-end jewelry and expensive furniture. "Boy meets girl, boy loses girl."

"Girl also loses boy," he'd volunteered, turning to look at her, "then dies just as they reunite."

"No! How awful!" She'd turned to him so sharply that her silky black curls took a moment to catch up.

"A tragedy," he'd said, gazing into eyes as blue as the sea on a summer day and accentuated by thick black lashes.

"Is that what *La Traviata* means? The Tragedy?"

"No. It means 'the fallen woman,' like . . ."

"A prostitute?" she interrupted.

"Not exactly. You see, Violetta and Alfonso were deeply in love, then she ran off with another man."

Her eyes widened. "Why would she *do* that?"

"She was told to. It was all part of a twisted plot. That's the tragedy. They missed their chance at love because of a lie. Have you ever seen *Carmen*?"

The woman sitting in front of them turned and glared as the lights dimmed, a finger to her lips. Lorenzo mimicked her, and Kate broke into the most delighted smile. They had many interactions throughout that performance—strangers in the dark. If anyone had guessed, they might have believed them to be on a date, though his date sat to his left, and her date sat to her right, growing more irritated with every passing minute. It had pleased Lorenzo, though, to entertain her with whispered insights to the unfolding story while irritating her companion. Of course, he'd annoyed his date as well, but felt it worth the risk. If not for the ring on her finger, he would have asked for a phone number.

Where was that ring now? Lorenzo grinned.

He'd thought of her often since the opera. For months, he watched for her on the off chance they'd meet again. How remarkable it felt to see her now.

"What a delightful surprise," he said.

"Wait," said Officer Klein. "You've met before?"

"A few years ago, yes," Lorenzo said.

"Such a small world, isn't it? Kate's a writer for the *Oregonian*. Are you familiar with her work?"

Lorenzo raised his eyebrows. He hadn't seen her on the police beat. He would have remembered that.

"I'm doing a piece on Mount St. Helens," she said as if it wasn't special. As if she never expected it to see the light of day.

"Is that so?" Lorenzo said, not taking his eyes from her. "I look forward to reading it."

"And, if Thomas is game, I'd like to learn more about this mystery man." She glanced at Officer Klein, her blue eyes pleading. "Yes?"

"That's up to this guy," said Officer Klein, nodding at Lorenzo.

Lorenzo considered his rule about not talking to the press—their hunger for the sensational, violating the privacy of strangers, and the point that it never ends well. But seeing Kate's disarming face, he happily set his prejudice aside—for now.

"It would be a pleasure, officer."

"Call me Thomas," Officer Klein said, the smile lines deepening. "Mutual friends and all."

Mutual friends, thought Lorenzo. "Certainly."

Thomas filled Kate in on the few knowns as they walked across the expansive parking lot to a warehouse resembling an airplane hangar filled six rows deep and twelve across with pallets of unclaimed cargo.

"Is there any order to this?" Lorenzo asked, his voice amplified in the large space.

"Not really, they get shuffled around a lot as freight comes and goes," Thomas said.

Lorenzo meandered to the first pallet and checked the stamp on the packing slip.

"What happens if no one claims it?" Kate asked.

"It will be considered abandoned and auctioned off," Thomas said from two rows down. Lorenzo peeled open the packing slip on a pallet, checked the date, and moved on. Kate joined him at the next pallet.

"What if it's valuable?" said Kate and Lorenzo in unison.

"What? Well, tough luck, I suppose."

Lorenzo studied label after label before he found something that looked worthwhile. "Thomas! Over here!" Three crates from Italy were stacked side by side. The first came from Rome, the second from Florence, and the third and smallest from Genoa. Lorenzo examined the label fastened to the latter crate and removed the packing slip.

Three stamps mapped the crate's route. Departed September 8, 2004, from Porto di Genova. Arrived October 4 in New York. Boarded American Air Freight for Portland the following day. Arrived the same day. *Nearly a week ago.* Lorenzo unfolded the packing slip, his palms sweaty.

Shipper: Fondazione d'arte Italiana
    Via Amata 7, 22647

Genova, Italia
Destination: Robi__ Nes____
91_ NW Lovej__
Portland, Ore___. USA.

The heavily smudged address explained why the crate had never arrived. On closer examination, Lorenzo noticed a small signature stamp at the bottom of the sheet. He fumbled in his breast pocket for his reading glasses and puzzled out the ornate handwriting. *Marco Robini.*

Lorenzo lost all feeling in his limbs. "*Dio Santo.*"

"Should we open it?" asked Thomas, approaching the crate with a crowbar. Lorenzo nodded but said nothing. Did he *want* to know? Did he even have the authority? Kate stepped close to him and placed a light hand on his arm.

"Lorenzo?" she said, staring up into his face.

"Open it."

Pressure mounted in Lorenzo's chest as Thomas pried open the crate. It was filled with six canisters of various sizes and what looked to be a 3x6 wooden box, tightly bound in bubble wrap. Lorenzo popped the top off one canister. He slipped out a yellowed canvas rolled loosely between sheets of protective paper and laid it across the top of the neighboring crate, then peeled the top protective sheet back to reveal a portrait of a young girl sitting primly on an ornately carved chair—her white dress contrasting with her pursed red lips and dark brown eyes.

Lorenzo stared, transfixed. He'd seen this painting before.

"It's beautiful," said Kate, leaning in for a closer look. Lorenzo struggled for breath, his mind retreating to the day he'd entered the farmhouse on Via Rosa.

It cost him everything he loved.

Lorenzo returned to the station that afternoon and knocked on Sergeant Monroe's office door, holding the packing slip. Monroe looked up from his computer.

"Remember the call I told you about from the Port of Portland?

"Let me see that." Monroe took it from Lorenzo's hand. "What's this?" He pointed at the shipper, *Fondazione d'arte Italiana*.

"Italian Art Foundation."

"The destination, Northwest Lovejoy?" Monroe tossed the slip of paper on his desk.

"It's a gallery called the Robin's Nest. I'll stop in and get a closer look."

"Your thoughts?" asked Monroe.

Lorenzo pointed to Marco's signature. "I know this man—or *knew* him. And I'd like to verify the authenticity of the crate's contents."

"You think they're forgeries."

"I do," said Lorenzo.

"Okay. We'll confiscate and have them tested, but you'd better be right."

Lorenzo had fled Italy hoping to get away from Marco. But he was beginning to think there would never be peace for him—and this crate merely rubbed that sorry possibility in his face. Trying to push the thought aside, he returned to his desk and flipped open the case file, scanning it for any detail he might have missed. At least the chance meeting with Kate was a nice distraction. He tapped his pen on his desk, thinking of her bright eyes, her freckled cheeks, and her smile when she'd recognized him in Thomas's office. He smiled, too— pleased she'd been thinking of him the night before.

Someday, life will give you a second chance. When that time comes, take it. It was a line he used whenever he made an arrest. Today it seemed particularly poignant.

———

As soon as Lorenzo got home, he slipped into his running shoes and hit the Portland streets to clear his head. Three blocks in, he found his rhythm. Four blocks in, he found his train of thought.

The Robini name was enough to make Lorenzo ill, but he pushed past the rising bile as he jogged past St. Mary's Cathedral toward the West Hills with its gated driveways and million-dollar homes. A crunch of leaves underfoot accompanied the comforting peal of church bells that filtered through the surrounding streets, reminding him of his home village and the church up the road from his parents' house. A pang of heartache needled at his chest. Thirty years. It seemed unbelievable.

Lorenzo steered his thoughts to the label on the crate, *Fondazione d'arte Italiana*—Italian Art Foundation—and the packing slip, signed by Marco Robini. With the church bells behind him, Lorenzo picked up his pace and focused on the painting he'd unwrapped from the crate. It was the same picture, real or fake. The girl in the white dress. A house full of art one day and empty the next. He suspected the worst. And if Marco and his family ran a forgery operation, they would stop at nothing to protect it. And now, at fifty-two, Lorenzo felt like he'd walked right back into that fateful farmhouse in the tiny Mediterranean village of Manarola that he hadn't seen in decades.

The following day, Lorenzo visited the Robin's Nest gallery, tucked into the heart of Portland's trendy Pearl District. It had been a couple of years since he'd toured the galleries as part of the neighborhood's First Thursday event sipping free wine and listening to snippets of critical conversations about up-and-coming artists, some more promising than others. He'd never heard of the Robin's Nest, however. He parked his Ford Bronco right out front and peeked in the picture window where a floor lamp caught his eye. According to the tag, the exquisite piece was hand-carved from Oregon-coast manzanita. Delicate dragonflies made of polished sea glass decorated the shade. It was a collaboration between two local artists that cost enough to yield each of them rent money for half the year.

Lorenzo found equally expensive pieces of handcrafted furniture inside the oddly quiet gallery. A coffee table fashioned from a slice of redwood, shellacked and polished to a mirror finish, sat beside a chest of drawers with ornately carved trim and cut-glass pulls that caught the light and cast it about the room in a rainbow of colors.

A young woman emerged from a curtained door at the rear of the gallery. She wore her dyed-green hair pinned back, and a flannel shirt untucked with the sleeves rolled up. Her eyes grew wide when she saw him.

"Do you work here?" Lorenzo asked, trying not to alarm her more than she already was.

"Uh, yeah," she said. A clatter sounded from the back room and the clerk froze. "Sorry. My boyfriend. Don't tell anyone, all right? The owner would literally murder me if she knew."

"Your secret's safe with me," Lorenzo said with a charming smile. "I'm looking for the owner, actually."

"She's hardly ever here except for a surprise visit now and then. I thought you were her." The clerk laughed nervously.

"I'm sorry to have alarmed you." Lorenzo nodded to the boyfriend peeking through the curtain, then turned back to the clerk. "A rather valuable collection here."

"Right? It's ridiculous. I've never sold a thing. Can't imagine how this place stays in business."

"Who's the owner here, if you don't mind my asking?"

"I don't mind. Her name is Monica Bower."

Lorenzo glanced at the stack of brochures at the register. "May I take one of those?"

"Take two," she said with a mischievous smile. "They're free."

Lorenzo slipped a brochure into his pocket and left, shutting the door behind him.

A café across the street boasted authentic Italian espresso on its window banner. He strolled over, entered, and took a table at the window, where he studied the gallery pamphlet for anything that might be useful.

"*Ciao*, what are you having?" asked the young server in a thick Italian accent.

He gazed up into the large brown eyes of a lovely girl. "*Ciao, avrò espresso per favore.*" Lorenzo grinned at her stunned reaction. The look and smell of the café took him momentarily back in time. "It's been years since I've spoken Italian," Lorenzo said, continuing in Italian.

"I've been here for one year, and my English is still so terrible." She giggled. "What part of Italy are you from?"

"The Northwest, down the coast from Genoa. You?"

"Salerno," she said excitedly. "But another man who has been coming in for the past few weeks is from Genoa."

Lorenzo wondered if it had been Marco, then nodded at the gallery across the street. "*Sei mai stato in quell negozio laggiu`?*" he asked, though he guessed that her coffee shop salary prevented her from shopping there.

"*Mai*," she said, shaking her head.

She glanced over her shoulder—her manager, standing at the pastry counter, had caught her lingering at Lorenzo's table. "I have to get to work—ciao." She returned shortly with his espresso and two complimentary biscotti.

Lorenzo took a sip from his tiny cup and referred to the trifold brochure. The Robin's Nest logo depicted an embossed image of a nest housing three perfect robin eggs. What is the nature of this gallery's relationship with the Italian Art Foundation, he wondered, and what role did Marco play? He couldn't put aside his suspicions about Marco, given his history. But what was that history, after all? A threat, a farmhouse filled with art, an artist caught creating a reproduction, and the evacuation of the whole collection once Lorenzo had discovered it. If it hadn't been for Marco making good on his threat, Lorenzo wouldn't be in the position he was now. He'd be in Italy with his beautiful wife, Emilio, and his family.

Scowling, he ran his thumb across the logo and left the café.

Lorenzo drove to the station to do more research. The website for the Robin's Nest offered little more than the brochure had. Beautiful photographs, hours of operation, address, and phone number. He called the number, but it went to an answering service. Did he want to leave a message? No, thank you. A quick search for Monica Bower in the PPB database revealed nothing more than a dozen outstanding parking tickets.

He scanned the website for the *Fondazione d'Arte Italiana*, looking for contact information, history, charities, and donors. The Genoa address and phone number matched the ones on the packing slip. Stock photos of well-dressed businesspeople shaking hands or sitting around a conference table inferred a legitimacy that nevertheless added to Lorenzo's suspicions. He scrolled down to a headshot of the foundation's president—a white-haired man with a pig-like face and tobacco-stained teeth. The photograph didn't fit with the others. The caption below the image read, Marco Robini. *Marco?* A bitter sting rose in Lorenzo's throat as he looked closer for a resemblance to the handsome man he'd known years ago.

The website touted a long list of donors, including C. Robini Property Insurance. C. Robini was Carlo Robini—the "Uncle Carlo" who'd been at the farmhouse when Lorenzo first inquired about buying it.

Lorenzo entered the insurance firm into the search bar. There, on the first page of the website, he read, *Since 1965, protecting your valuable possessions from damage, theft, or loss. Click here for an estimate on your valuable heirlooms or irreplaceable art.*

Alfonso, Carlo's son, now ran the firm. Marco had often referred to his cousin as a leech. "The idiot has nothing to offer," he'd say. "An elephant without tusks."

The insurance company was one more piece to the puzzle, but Lorenzo needed more information. Besides the packing slip, he still had no idea how the gallery fit in.

That night, sleep came sporadically, with splintered images of waves crashing against rocky bluffs, dense vineyards flanked by olive groves along terraced slopes . . . and finally, his dear Ella. A cherry-red scarf covered her black hair as she stood high on the bluff, her dress flapping wildly in the wind. The pleasant memory was fleeting, though—quickly replaced with a sense of panic, terror, and grief.

Sunday morning, Lorenzo settled back on his sofa, carefully unfolded his plain black reading glasses, and placed them on his nose. He skimmed each section of the newspaper, glancing over headlines and captions until he set eyes on a stunning photo of Mount St. Helens with its growing dome emerging from inside the crater that had formed two decades earlier. Then he recognized the author's byline— Mary Katheryn Noonan—and a slow grin spread across his face. Kate. The grayscale image didn't do her justice.

"A gradual extrusion of magma along the south side of Mount St. Helens, first detected on October 1, 2004, gives rise to cracks on the newly formed snowy dome, emitting an occasional puff of volcanic ash and steam. It's early yet, according to forest service geologist, Jeffery Davis, but the crew is still on high alert." She used words like *majestic* and *inspiring* as if to counter the potential repetition of the death and destruction experienced in 1981. Lorenzo had been in Portland then and remembered the city coated in gray-brown ash.

Lorenzo turned back to the front page to learn more about the newly released video from Osama bin Laden. This elusive man and his kind were a genuine menace to the United States. How could it be that bin Laden could still threaten this country three years after

September 11? Lorenzo shook his head, flipped back to Kate's photo, and laid the paper on the counter while he readied himself for a morning run.

That afternoon, Lorenzo continued his research into the Portland art scene. After visiting galleries and interviewing dealers for a couple of hours with no new leads to help his investigation, he stopped at the Virginia Café on Park Avenue for a late lunch and made himself comfortable in a booth by the window. He needed a lead that could break the case wide open, but today wasn't his day. So, he ordered coffee and threw open his leather satchel to review his notes.

He flipped open his moleskin and jotted down a few questions. Who is the Italian visitor? Is the art from the crate authentic? If so, was it stolen or purchased legally? The test result Sergeant Monroe requested would be helpful. But Lorenzo still had no idea who the Italian visitor was, or who to blame when the test result arrived.

The melodic ring tone of Lorenzo's new phone interrupted his thoughts.

"Thomas? I'm glad you called. Have you heard anything from your visitor?"

"Not a peep. But the art foundation emailed the documents this morning. I'll forward them to you."

"Excellent." Lorenzo felt as though a weight had been lifted. He'd been afraid that Thomas would ask him to call the art foundation. What if he'd have to speak with Marco? He simply was not prepared for that.

A hip young waiter leaned over Lorenzo. "More coffee? Lorenzo nodded and pushed his empty cup toward the edge of the table while pointing to the grilled cheese sandwich on the menu.

Lorenzo set aside his phone and checked his watch. It was going on three, and the sun he'd enjoyed on his morning run now hid behind a blanket of clouds.

Tap-tap-tap. He looked sharply up at the window, and his heart skipped a beat.

It was Kate. She smiled and hurried to the door, throwing it open with such gusto it made him laugh.

"Small world," she said, removing her denim jacket and laying it beside her on the bench.

"Isn't it?" Lorenzo grinned, collecting the loose papers from the table. The server laid a thick grilled cheese in front of him, and Lorenzo set it to one side. "I read your article this morning," he said. "You have a tremendous grasp of the situation on Mount St. Helens." Instantly, he wanted to kick himself. Had he really said that? As if he knew anything about the volcano.

"Thank you kindly, detective." Kate tugged at the soft blue scarf around her neck. It matched the color of her eyes. "I've gone through a crash course in geology and wasn't sure if it was paying off." The server placed a large mug before her, filled it, and topped off Lorenzo's. "I actually camped out up there with a staff photographer to get that piece."

"Yes, the photo is memorable." Lorenzo pushed the plate toward her, his heart racing like a fourteen-year-old.

"So was the trip." Kate lifted a fry from the plate and bit off the end. "I used to camp all the time with my hiking club, but I've grown a little too used to the comforts of home. Alex, though, he was a total rookie."

"Alex?" Lorenzo asked. Was there a man in her life?

"The photographer." She ate the rest of the fry and snitched another. "Thanks," she said with a sweet grin, gazing at the short stack of gallery brochures he'd set aside. "Anything new on Thomas's mystery man?"

Lorenzo considered the question, suddenly fearing that Kate's involvement in the case would jeopardize the possibility of a relationship. It was already trouble, being attracted to a journalist. But Kate was different, right?

Her eyes drifted over the Robin's Nest brochure peeking out

from the bottom of the stack. She picked it up and turned it over in her hand.

"Did you go?" Kate asked. Lorenzo nodded, and she went on. "I've been there. It's all furniture, right? Nothing on the walls—which is odd, considering the shipment of oil paintings." Kate picked up another fry and pushed the plate back toward him. "That piece we saw looked like it belongs in a museum."

Lorenzo gently took the brochure back and tucked it in his satchel. "I thought the same. In fact, it would fit right in with this month's Renaissance exhibit at the Portland Art Museum."

"Would any of that be Italian, by chance?" she asked. Lorenzo caught a glimmer of mischief in her eyes. Ella used to smile like that.

"Quite a bit, actually," he said, grinning more broadly in response to her smile. "Would you like to see it? It's only a few blocks up the road."

"Now?"

"Well—sure," said Lorenzo, picking at the crust on his sandwich. "Unless you're busy."

Kate beamed. "Not busy." She stood and pulled on her jean jacket while Lorenzo packed his bag and, remembering his hunger, grabbed the sandwich too.

***

A young couple sat on a bench inside the museum doors, holding hands and whispering to one another as Kate followed Lorenzo around the corner and down a corridor flanked with landscape paintings on loan from Charles K. Pinchot III. Lorenzo took her hand and guided her into the Renaissance exhibit he'd told her about.

"Take a deep breath," he said, his voice resonating off the walls. Kate played along.

He led her to *The Virgin Holding the Sleeping Child* by Bernardino Luini. Kate sat down on a bench opposite the painting. Her eyes drifted from the mother to the sleeping child, the precious infant's head fitting snugly beneath his mother's chin as she prepared to lay him on a cloth proffered by a joyful child angel as other angels looked on.

Lorenzo felt a rise of emotion as he gazed at the painting. It reminded him of his own infant son. So innocent, so pure. How anyone could choose abortion was beyond him.

"My mother hung a framed print of this in our sitting room when I was a boy. It makes me a little homesick." Looking at the painting, Lorenzo felt calm—the calmest he'd been in days, even weeks. It was the kind of peace he felt in church. Though his attendance was spotty at best, when he went, he felt comforted by the ritual and familiarity.

"It's breathtaking," Kate said reverently. "The soft lines of their faces, their shoulders. Funny that you had to come halfway around the world to see the original." Her smile warmed his heart, as it had done three years ago at the opera.

They viewed the remaining collection while chatting in hushed voices about Portland's growing art scene. But the moment they left the warm, dry museum, a cloudburst hit. They skipped from doorway to doorway, through wet autumn leaves, to Kate's old white Volvo parked off Pioneer Square, where they took shelter from the wind and rain.

"I never have an umbrella when I need one," said Kate, combing her fingers through her damp curls.

"Me neither," said Lorenzo, peeling open the flap of his messenger bag to make sure his case notes and file hadn't gotten wet. He laughed softly, pulling out a small black umbrella. "Sorry, I completely forgot."

"It looks like the rain is here for a while. Can I take you home? Maybe back to your car?"

"I can walk." Lorenzo reached for the door, then hesitated. "I enjoyed myself today."

"Me too," Kate answered with a smile.

Lorenzo closed the door and walked away under his little black umbrella. He kicked himself for not getting her phone number, then cursed himself for not accepting the ride when he finally reached his Bronco—his shoes soaked, and his fingers numb from cold. When he got home, he ran up the steps two by two to his warm apartment, where the newspaper remained strewn across the kitchen island—Kate's byline image still looking up at him.

CHAPTER FOUR

Kate

Kate approached her editor's stuffy office Monday morning feeling giddy. She was about to propose a story on the art-filled crate at the port—the international aspect could put her on the journalism map. Though she was proud of the work she and Alex had done with the Mount St. Helens update, the fact that she had stood alongside news crews from across the country boosted her confidence toward a higher-profile story.

Camping with the staff photographer had been an adventure beyond anything provided by the volcano. Alex was no camper—he belonged behind a camera, not in a cheap tent pitched in a rustic campsite. But while he jumped at every noise outside his tent and shrieked when a curious squirrel found its way into his boot, Kate felt like she was twenty again. She reveled in the cozy sleeping bag, the cool mountain air, and the hot coffee kissed by smoke from the little campfire she'd built.

Miles Walker, Kate's editor, had suggested there could be a series. If so, she'd have to forget Thomas's mystery man. And Lorenzo? She couldn't forget him if she tried. The way he'd smiled when they recognized one another in Thomas's office. "Kate not Katie," he'd said. His whole demeanor shifted when he'd studied the shipping label. What had he seen? She needed to know.

At sixty, Miles Walker was the oldest editor on the staff and had the scars to prove it. He'd been through three divorces and suffered from high blood pressure and irritable bowel syndrome. He'd lost his hair and developed a paunch. He kept the Starbucks downstairs in business. Everyone under his stewardship understood that he always got his way, and that there was no point in arguing.

Kate barely understood this complex man and felt nervous about the meeting he'd set up the night before. After a deep, cleansing breath, she stepped into his office to find him licking his fingers, the dusty remains of a powdered doughnut flecked white against his blue oxford shirt. A reek of burned coffee filled the room. Kate spied a nicotine patch on his forearm and mentally wished him luck. She'd heard that every method Miles Walker had used to kick the habit had failed—even hypnotism.

"Sit down, sit down, for Pete's sake!" he blustered. Kate sat down in the armchair beside his desk, and he went on. "Your piece on St. Helens was excellent. I don't know how you came up with so much original material on this."

"Thank you, Mr. Walker. I enjoyed the research."

"Hang onto that. Sounds like we're on the cusp of a series, the way that dome keeps growing. I'll need your continued enthusiasm. Okay then. The reason you're here. I got a call from the University of Oregon about a rare painting that could be worth a fortune." Walker scratched his head, smoothing over his thinning hair. "An intern to some nutty professor said it was a gift to the department. It might be a decent story for you, or it might be nothing." Kate frantically scribbled the few details in the notebook on her lap, wondering if this might tie in with Lorenzo's case. She was about to lay down her story proposal when he said, "First, though, I need a scoop on the tight mayoral race for the Sunday edition."

"Mr. Walker, I'm not very political. Can someone else take that?"

Walker glared at her and his face went crimson. "You can feed pigeons all day if you like, but don't expect a paycheck without a story on the election."

The harsh words stung. The notion that Miles Walker held her future in his sticky fingers gripped Kate by the heart, but she'd do as he said. She couldn't afford to be out of a job.

The following week, Kate volunteered to stuff envelopes in both mayoral candidates' election offices, hoping she might glean enough information for a story. Back home, she settled into the wicker stool in front of the card table desk of her makeshift office and began to type.

"If stuffed envelopes spoke for the voters of Portland," she wrote, "I could tell you today who will win by the number of paper cuts I acquired in each office. If calluses spoke for the voters of Portland, I could tell you who will win by the fresh landscape of my hands. But I'll let the polls speak for my blisters and bloodshed, and . . ."

She worked hard, and finally, with fingers crossed, she submitted the piece just before seven that night. Thirty minutes later, Walker emailed back, "Brilliant!"

Kate jumped when she heard the first knock—but then recognized Megan's rhythmic shave and a haircut and opened the front door to Paddington Bear in a floppy red hat and blue jacket.

"Trick or treat," Briley chirped.

"Halloween, remember?" Megan said. "Your porch light is out." She ushered her son into the house.

"Uh, yeah. I've been working. Sorry." Kate glanced at Briley's plastic pumpkin. "Um. Give me a sec." She wasn't prepared for this. Halloween. A day she'd always celebrated as if it were her birthday.

"Working on Halloween should be a crime," Megan said as she and Briley followed Kate into the kitchen.

"Just a fluff piece, but I've got something more interesting in the wings."

"Something about that crate?"

"You heard?" Kate fished around the kitchen for a suitable treat. Even Old Mother Hubbard would be ashamed of the selection.

"And the detective?" Megan winked.

Kate smiled. "Detective?" She tossed a granola bar into the pumpkin bucket and watched Briley rifle through his meager haul.

"Thomas noticed some chemistry there."

Kate looked away, remembering the chance encounter in the office and again at the café. A twist of fate she never saw coming. She'd felt his eyes on her in the museum. While she was admiring the painting, he was admiring her. Or was that her imagination?

"Don't make too much of it, hey Megan? I'm not in any hurry to get involved—with anyone." Just a year out of her rocky marriage, Kate didn't feel ready for another relationship.

"Look at you," Megan said. "You're blushing."

Briley grabbed Kate's hand. "Yes, no, or maybe so?"

"I'll always say yes," Kate said, laughing.

"Happy Halloween!" he said, holding out a cellophane wrapped caramel.

She stooped to hug the boy. "You are the sweetest, Briley Bear. I love these."

After Megan and Briley left, Kate returned to her office and pushed aside her election notes, a notepad filled with her own shorthand—a blend of words and doodles that only *she* could understand, and a far cry from what she'd learned in college.

She took a deep breath, then googled the University of Oregon art department. Up popped several related options—U of O, U of O football, registration, event calendar . . . and a few that seemed so far off the mark that she wondered what brilliant algorithm wormed their way to her attention. Eventually, she found the staff page through the general university website, and looked up Dr. Wade Marshall, the "nutty professor" Mr. Walker had mentioned. She emailed him to set up an appointment.

To her surprise, a reply popped up minutes later. Apparently, Dr. Marshall had no plans this Halloween either.

> Ms. Noonan,
>
> Thank you for reaching out to the department regarding our recent acquisition. My schedule during the day is rather hectic, between instruction and tutoring. Would it be possible to meet in the evening, either Tuesday or Thursday?
>
> I look forward to sharing my exciting discovery.
>
> Dr. Wade Marshall
>
> University of Oregon, Department of Art and Design

Kate excitedly dashed off a reply. Though she hadn't even met Dr. Marshall or seen the painting, she now understood that the seed of her article had taken root when Lorenzo opened that crate.

The following Tuesday was election day. Kate dropped her ballot off at the library and drove down to Eugene to meet with the professor.

How long had it been since she'd walked the footpaths of her alma mater in Colorado? Twenty years? Before body piercing, pink hair, and cell phones. Before live-in boyfriends and reliable birth control. She frowned. She'd learned the hard way that the most unreliable birth control was crossed fingers and wishful thinking. Neither could turn back the clock on pregnancy, so she'd taken the matter into her own hands with a visit to the clinic. It was not her proudest moment.

"Stop your crying!" the doctor had said, but she hadn't been prepared for the pain. She hadn't expected to hear the roar of the vacuum. In recovery, Kate encountered one other woman, orange juice in hand, who boasted of her third "procedure"—as if that term made it all less awful.

Whenever the issue reared its head, Kate did her best to duck it. She would never wish that experience on anyone, much less face it again herself. She wondered if she looked like a hypocrite to those with no choice. With the gift of hindsight, would she have chosen differently? She shook the question off, as she'd done so often before, and climbed the flight of stairs to Dr. Marshall's office.

It surprised her to see students in the hall, given the hour. Their youth made her self-conscious, but when Dr. Marshall opened his office door, she suddenly felt young again. He was a pleasant-looking man with thick white hair and a contrasting black goatee.

"Dr. Marshall? I'm Kate Noonan."

He peered at her over smudged reading glasses perched on the end of his nose, then smiled enthusiastically, revealing a dimpled grin. "Pleased to meet you, Ms. Noonan." He removed his glasses and opened the door wider. "Please, come in. Would you like a coffee?"

She'd be up all night but didn't want to refuse him. "A coffee would be great. It's cold out there."

He laughed and rubbed his hands together. "November chill. Same every year."

Kate gazed after him as he moved across the cluttered room where stacks of books and papers littered tables and chairs in a mountain range of organized chaos. Leonardo DaVinci's bronze bust stared at her from beneath his dusty flat cap on a desk across the room. A pair of blank canvases leaned against a sturdy wall of bookshelves, packed tight with texts and references. A smaller canvas lay propped on a rickety easel, a tray of brushes and tubes of paint at the ready as if awaiting inspiration.

"Midterm essays were due today," Dr. Marshall said, lifting the glass pot from the coffee maker. "Art history." He pointed to a bulging manila folder sitting on a second desk in the corner where she guessed he'd been working before she'd arrived.

"That sounds fascinating," Kate said. "How far back do you go?"

"It depends on the semester," he said, handing her a mug and filling it. "That folder is the twentieth century."

"The painting you've acquired—is that twentieth century?" The stale coffee burned her lip as she sipped.

"Heavens no. It's the mid-nineteenth century. The 1860s or thereabouts. Are you familiar with Rossetti?" When Kate shook her head, the professor reached for two heavy books from the bookshelf and dropped them on his desk with a thud. "Please, sit," he said, massaging the cover of the first volume. Kate took the indicated chair beside his desk and set down her cup. "This one includes a beautiful illustration of our recent treasure," he said, opening the leather-bound tome to the center and clumsily flipping pages until he found the picture. He turned the book to face Kate and took a deep breath.

Kate pulled the book closer. "She's beautiful."

"Isn't she? Come."

He pulled a key from a desk drawer, and they walked into an adjoining room where he unlocked a six-foot-tall gray cabinet. After carefully pulling on a pair of white cotton gloves, he removed a large canister and popped off the plastic cap from one end before delicately spreading the coiled canvas across a long table. After removing the sheath of protective paper, he placed a weighted stick along one end to keep it from curling. Kate was absorbed by the ceremony.

She stepped cautiously toward the painting. A woman, lounging against a stack of colorful cushions, lay draped in a red cloak that fell open in the front, revealing her breast and the length of one leg stretching out toward the edge of the painting. The grass beneath her looked soft and cool, the sky above a brilliant blue. It was sensual and suggestive enough to make Kate blush.

"Dante Gabriel Rossetti had an affinity for painting sensual women. His lover, who later became his wife, was his favorite model." Dr. Marshall gazed down at the canvas. "He was also a poet. So, think how I felt when I peeled away the backing and discovered this." He delicately flipped the canvas over. "Here, in his own script, a poem dedicated to the subject of the masterpiece, his beloved wife." The dimples reappeared with his enormous grin, and he read, "The depths of my passion thrust all caution aside, bound by flesh and dew. I give my soul to the gods of desire, for there is nothing so fine as you, my love."

Kate took a moment to collect herself. She'd never heard such a testament to love and desire. Finally, she asked, "Is it valuable?"

Dr. Marshall grinned. "You just asked the million-dollar question. Originally, I believed it a fabrication. But once I saw this—well, I knew otherwise. In the blink of an eye, the value of the piece doubled —and not merely in dollars. It's a collector's dream."

"Who else knows about this?" Kate asked.

Dr. Marshall clasped his hands in front of him and cleared his throat. "I dropped a hint to one of my grad students, who undoubtedly was your tip. Other than him, no one."

"I'm flattered you agreed to meet with me, but a newspaper piece is rather—public."

"Yes, yes, but once the cat is out of the bag, I might get what I'm looking for."

"Which is?"

"Here's the rub. My gratitude is boundless. I feel compelled to write our benefactor with our most sincere thanks. But this individual, as it turns out, is anonymous."

"So, you don't know where to send your thanks," said Kate.

"Indeed."

"You know nothing of the benefactor?"

"Nothing." He frowned. "Well, that's not *exactly* true." He laid the protective paper over the painting and led Kate back into his office. From the top drawer of his battered antique desk, Dr. Marshall produced a card with the picture of a nest holding three robin's eggs— the Robin's Nest logo she'd seen on the brochure Lorenzo had taken from the gallery. Her pulse quickened. This meant a connection between the donation and Lorenzo's case, just as she'd hoped.

"This is a gallery in Portland," Kate said, looking at the professor.

"Is it? I didn't know. There's only a picture of a nest."

Kate accepted the card and flipped it over. Her heart sank. "Right. There's nothing here, no name, no address. Why would someone even bother with the card or donate such a valuable item without identifying themselves? There's no tax incentive or public recognition."

"That is a mystery to me, too, dear. *Why?*"

Whoever they were, they had ties with The Robin's Nest. Kate opened her notebook.

"Could I see those books again?"

CHAPTER FIVE

Lorenzo

Wednesday morning, Lorenzo woke before his alarm went off feeling more alert than his rough night's sleep would have suggested. With energy to burn, he skipped the coffee, and went for his running shoes. Soon, he was headed into the center of town. He took a lap around Pioneer Square followed by a grueling sprint up the Park Blocks where autumn had taken hold with a spattering of gold and orange leaves overhead. He stopped in front of the Portland Art Museum to catch his breath and recalled his visit with Kate. How her face softened before the *Madonna and Child*. He'd admired the painting too, but Kate seemed altogether transfixed. He wanted to see it through her eyes.

Many years ago, Lorenzo knew another woman who could alter his perception of the world with a single look. She would sigh, and it felt as if he had taken the breath himself. Ella was his first and only love. He'd pined for her since the age of seven and longed for her in unholy ways since adolescence. If she hadn't agreed to become his wife, he would have thought God a merciless trickster.

He'd had only one lasting relationship since her death. Six years invested in a complicated relationship doomed to failure. Was it his fault? Had it been too soon after Ella? He'd never know. And now there was Kate. He still needed her phone number. Maybe he could get it from Thomas. Better yet, he'd call the newspaper. Yes. More direct.

A light drizzle began to fall, as Lorenzo set off again at a steady pace toward Burnside Boulevard, thinking of the night he met Kate at the opera. Lorenzo's date had been someone he'd met in a night class at Portland State University—a class he'd taken to beat the unrelenting boredom of single life. As it turned out, urban planning was a dull subject. But he'd struck up a lively conversation with the pretty woman sitting in front of him about the future of Portland and its suburbs. He'd feigned interest long enough to ask her out, but the opera was not what she'd expected—especially since he'd spent most of it talking with someone else.

Lorenzo checked his watch as he climbed the stairs to his apartment. There would be plenty of time to get ready for work. He was also pleased to see that the newspaper had arrived while he was out.

After putting on the coffee, he poured over the headlines for election results. Former police chief Tom Potter had become Portland's new mayor. Bush would remain president, and the levy, feeding much-needed revenue into the Portland schools and police bureau, passed with a resounding majority. These were the issues Lorenzo had followed the closest. And although he hadn't become a citizen, and couldn't vote, he had some definite opinions that did not include Bush being reelected. With a heavy sigh, he folded the paper and set it aside while he poured his coffee.

Lorenzo had been raised Catholic—an old-world religion with pagan rituals that teaches its followers fundamental Christian ideals like healing the sick, feeding the hungry, clothing the poor, and not discriminating against your fellow human beings. George Bush called himself a Christian, yet Lorenzo thought his politics fell short of the faith's most elementary principles. This war in Iraq was particularly troubling—there was no firm logic to support it. In fact, Americans were expected to take the president's word on faith—any opposition was either silenced by the fervent right-wing or those unwilling to put their necks on the line. Moreover, neighbors and citizens didn't communicate their concerns for fear of being judged or misunderstood. It was assumed that critique of the war implied critique of the soldiers fighting it—which was ridiculous, in Lorenzo's opinion.

In Italy, these issues were freely and passionately debated in every coffeehouse and gathering place. Sometimes a sound argument might persuade someone. More often the point was to expose oneself to criticism for the sake of community well-being. Italians saw bending to popular opinion as a sign of weakness. This, in Lorenzo's view, had been John Kerry's flaw.

The station was a riot of activity when Lorenzo arrived later that morning. The election results had everyone fired up with the prospect of a new police chief to fill Potter's position, and a bigger budget.

Lorenzo pushed through the throng to his desk. He hadn't been seated more than a minute before his phone rang.

"Rotondo," he said. Silence followed. "Hello?"

"I heard you were asking around about the Robin's Nest," said the caller.

"Yes. That's right." Lorenzo whipped out his moleskin notebook and grabbed a pen. "Could I get your name?" Lorenzo asked. The caller answered with a laugh.

"Do you know the owner?" said Lorenzo, adding *Anonymous* to his notes.

The caller went on to describe Monica as a vixen—a tall, curvaceous brunette who oozed sensuality and whose flirtations accounted for much of her success.

"And how do you know her?" Lorenzo asked.

The caller paused before answering. "I met her at a gallery opening in Seattle."

"Her gallery?" Lorenzo wondered if there was a network.

"No, a place called the Heron's Perch. It closed a couple years ago."

The caller couldn't say enough about Monica Bower and her underground clientele. The missing shipment left a path of unhappy customers in its wake, the caller among them. Lorenzo rubbed his forehead in frustration. He needed more.

"Does she work alone?"

"I don't think so." The caller said he'd attended the opening of the Robin's Nest two years earlier where he'd met her Italian counterpart. "The clown fell all over himself, trying to impress her. It was positively embarrassing."

"Was his name Robini?"

"Yes, that's it. Alfonso Robini. You could smell the guy from a block away."

"Did he wear a lapel pin shaped like an egg?"

"We all did. Monica handed one out to everyone at the opening."

"Is there anything else you can add? Another name? Collector or supplier?" Lorenzo asked.

"Um, well, I remember her talking about this guy. I think his name is Maximo Corta. He has something to do with the export arrangements."

"He's with the Italian Art Foundation?" Lorenzo asked, trying to make the link.

"She didn't say."

Lorenzo drew a circle around *anonymous* in his notebook. "I didn't catch your name."

The caller laughed and hung up the phone. It was worth a shot.

Lorenzo reviewed his notes—details written in his shorthand, which was part Italian, part English, and part something that only he could understand.

He wished he'd pushed for more details, like who owned the

Heron's Perch gallery? And wondered if it's closing two years ago in tandem with the Robin's Nest gallery opening was simply a coincidence? He thought about Monica Bower and Alfonso Robini. Were they a couple? That would make sense. How else . . .

"Lorenzo. Hey, Lorenzo. Dude, snap out of it, will ya? Your phone's ringin'." Lorenzo jumped to attention, seeing Buddy standing nearby, as his thoughts concerning the anonymous caller were replaced by the office clatter he'd completely tuned out. "Are you with us today, partner? I'm worried about you." Buddy said.

"I'm fine." Lorenzo reached for the phone, speaking into the receiver while Buddy quietly returned to his desk. "Detective Rotondo."

"Good morning, detective. This is Kate. Kate Noonan. Remember me?"

His heart leapt. He suddenly longed to have a private office with a door that closed. "Yes, of course!"

"I think I have a lead relating to your case. That guy from Italy?"

"Yes?"

"I'm working on a story about a donated painting at The University of Oregon and was hoping, well . . ." She sounded nervous. "I'd like to share what I've found, maybe compare notes."

Lorenzo looked around at the general madness of the station. "Here?" he asked.

"Well, I was thinking . . . *here*, actually. My place. I'll make dinner."

Had he heard her right? He thought she'd said dinner at her house, but it might have been wishful thinking. "Excuse me, could you repeat that?"

"I know this is weird. You don't have to say yes. I just thought it would be easier to talk." She waited for him to speak. "I'm a pretty good cook. Promise I won't poison you."

She had a lead. The invitation was professional. "Sure, of course," he said. "I'm sorry for being so clumsy. My mind has been elsewhere today."

"Is that a yes?" Lorenzo heard the smile in her voice.

"Only if I can contribute."

"An appetizer would be nice," she said.

"Where and when?" He scribbled the details on the back of that day's page from his Word-a-Day desk calendar and stuffed it in his jacket pocket, wondering what had gotten hold of him. She was a journalist of all things.

Buddy looked up from his desk and grinned as Lorenzo hung up. "Business or pleasure?"

Lorenzo didn't answer. He wasn't entirely sure. On his way home that afternoon, Lorenzo stopped at a nearby market to pick up the ingredients for the antipasti he'd offered to bring. He considered the funnel-shaped bucket filled with floral bouquets, well-positioned beside the register. *Two for $5.* He nearly made the impulse buy but resisted.

Once he stepped into his apartment, Lorenzo got busy fixing his appetizer and poured himself a glass of wine to calm down, checking the clock from time to time. Then, finally, he put the food in the refrigerator, corked the wine, and sat on the couch to watch Peter Jennings impart the daily details of a chaotic Iraq.

Sometime later, his ringing phone woke him out of a sound sleep. Shaking off his exhaustion, he crossed the room, glimpsing the clock on the way. Damn it. He was going to be late.

"Rotondo," he said.

It was Buddy. "Hey, man—you all right? You were really checked out this afternoon."

"I'm fine. Just—distracted by the case. You know how it gets." Buddy's concern warmed Lorenzo. They'd never been friends exactly, but they shared some history and understood one another.

"Take some time off. I can handle things here. When was your last vacation?" Lorenzo couldn't remember. Two, three years ago? No, it had been much longer.

"Perhaps you're right about the vacation." Lorenzo stared at the clock. "Thanks for checking in, Buddy. I need to get going, though."

"Ah, that's right. You've got a date tonight. Fraternizing with the enemy," Buddy said with a boyish giggle.

"It's not a date," Lorenzo said, rethinking his reluctance to pursue a personal-professional relationship.

"Right, Lorenzo. Enjoy your *meeting*, then. Catch ya later."

Lorenzo glanced at the clock again. He had planned to take a shower, change his clothes, and have another glass of wine. No dice. He looked down at his wrinkled pants and shirt. It's not a date, he reminded himself.

He had an address but no phone number. There was no way of letting her know he was running late. He snatched the antipasti from the refrigerator and pulled the piece of paper from his pocket to check the address. "Ugh," he groaned, reading the word of the day. Expeditious: *adj*. Acting or done with speed and efficiency.

***

"Come in, come in, it's freezing out here," Kate said when she opened her door. "I actually built a fire in the fireplace—can't remember the last time I did that." She laughed her soft, joyful laugh—Lorenzo enjoyed that more each time he heard it. "The house will probably go up in flames, but at least we'll be warm." She took the platter from his hands and disappeared into the kitchen.

Lorenzo noted the black leather sofa facing the fireplace, and a framed Carol Grigg print on the wall leading into an empty dining room. Diana Krall's warm, laid-back voice flowed from a boombox sitting on the bare wood floor. He set his satchel beside the sofa and was hanging his jacket on the coat rack when Kate returned with two wine glasses and a bottle of Cabernet. Lorenzo glanced at his satchel. Work could wait. He took the open bottle and filled the glasses.

"*Cin cin*."

Kate lifted her glass. "Chin chin to you. Have a seat." She sat down in the center of the sofa and nodded at the boom box. "Is the music all right?"

Lorenzo was familiar with the artist and her rise as one of the finest jazz voices in a generation. "It's lovely."

"I love that she sings the classics. My parents had a huge album collection at home when I was a kid. Jazz, mostly." Kate sipped her wine and smiled. "It's one of those comfort things for me, like gingerbread cookies. Are you a fan?"

Lorenzo grinned. "Of gingerbread?" Kate laughed.

The crackling fire, the delicious wine, and Diana Krall's evocative music filled the room; if this had been a date, he would have asked Kate to dance.

They visited briefly with some talk of the weather and the challenges ahead for Portland's newly elected mayor. Kate topped off his glass, then her own. She sipped, he sipped, the music played, and the fire burned through an awkward extended silence.

"I hope you're hungry. I'm making lamb chops. Is that all right?"

"Yes, perfect."

"Would you like to get started on your appetizer? It looks wonderful. Antipasti, right? It's Italian?" Her short, breathless questions implied she was likely as nervous as he was.

Kate stood and ambled to the kitchen. Lorenzo followed her through the empty dining room, dodging the light fixture hanging from the ceiling on the way. "Did you move in here recently?" he asked as they entered the kitchen.

"Ha! Looks that way, doesn't it?" She held out the platter filled with cheese, cured meats, and a selection of olives. "Remember the opera?"

Lorenzo nodded. Three years ago, almost to the day. "I remember it well."

"That was my husband who dragged me out before the last act. Ex-husband now. We lived in this house for seven years before the divorce." Kate looked past Lorenzo into the dining room. "He took nearly everything." She held her glass high. "So, here's to starting over."

Lorenzo smiled as they clinked their glasses. He knew all about starting over. He hoped she'd have better luck than he did. Kate peeled a slice of cheese off the platter, folded it, and popped it into her mouth. He looked from Kate to his platter and the fixings for the meal beside it. She lit the burner under a cast-iron skillet. The chops sizzled when they hit the pan.

A light flickered on in the house next door, catching Lorenzo's attention. "Is that Officer Klein's house there?"

"Thomas? Yeah. They moved in right after we did. Megan's my best friend."

"His wife?"

"Mm-hmm," said Kate, flipping the chops. "So, where in Italy are you from?"

"Manarola. It's part of the Cinque Terre," he said. Kate plucked up some olives and a slice of prosciutto, then stepped aside so he could reach the platter. He smelled the delicate scent of something sweet. Her perfume? Shampoo? Talc? He couldn't place it. Lay off the wine, he told himself.

"I'm sorry—can you say that again?"

"Cinque Terre. It's a chain of five villages along the Mediterranean Sea that can only be accessed by train or by boat."

"No roads?"

"Through town, yes. But only for walking."

"Sounds wonderful. Must have been a great place to grow up." She eased open the oven to peek inside. A steamy, fragrant waft spurred Lorenzo's appetite.

"Well, it's a small village," he said. "Everyone knows everyone. Which means everyone knows everyone's business."

Kate closed the oven door. "I get it. I'm from a small community too."

"In Oregon?"

"Colorado. I'm a foreigner, like you." She winked.

Lorenzo laughed and plucked a stuffed olive off the plate.

They ate in the living room, balancing their plates on their laps. After, Lorenzo helped clear the dishes and put away the leftovers, getting a feel for the kitchen. She washed. He dried. They spoke of mundane things. The weather—Colorado winters, Mediterranean summers. Finally, they got to work on the case.

Kate knelt on the living room floor and popped in another CD. Soon, the steady beat of an upright bass was joined by the warm vibes of a tenor sax.

Kate lowered the volume and sat down on the sofa. "I'm afraid there's no dessert. I meant to hit the bakery this afternoon, but time got away from me."

"I had no expectations." Lorenzo grinned, recalling her phone call and dinner invitation. Business or pleasure, Buddy had asked. "I discovered an excellent Italian bakery across from the Robin's Nest the other day."

Kate smiled. "Yes, I've been there a couple of times. Their pastry is dangerously delicious—especially the panettone. Wish I could pull off anything half as good."

"Panettone? My mother ran a bakery out of our home. Her specialty was sweetbread like panettone. You don't grow up in a home like that without learning a few things about baking."

"You bake? I can't picture you in an apron, detective."

Lorenzo wondered if she was flirting. Had he read her invitation all wrong? He should have showered. He should have changed his clothes.

"Wait here." Kate jumped up and scurried down the hall to the back of the house.

The embers burned low in the fireplace, so he poked them to life and added some wood before Kate returned with a small notebook. She glanced at the flames and grinned, then pulled a business card from her book and handed it to him. Lorenzo stared down at the calling card. The nest. The eggs.

"Where did you get this?"

"I went to Eugene for a story on a painting the university received as a gift. The painting arrived with that card."

"The Robin's Nest?"

"That's why I called you."

Remembering the reason for his visit, Lorenzo reached over the arm of the sofa for his satchel and removed the brochure. Yes, it was the same logo.

"What else did you learn?" he asked, excited about the lead.

"This professor had two textbooks with the piece listed, so I tracked down the publishers and located the painting's previous owner." Lorenzo was impressed. She handed him a printed email. "It's in Italian."

Lorenzo reached back into his satchel for his reading glasses. The crumpled note with Kate's address fell out and onto the floor. She picked it up, noticing the word of the day.

"Expeditious?" She grinned. "Let's hope that's a good omen."

"Yes, well . . ." He placed his glasses on his nose and read the email she'd handed him. "The previous owner is still in possession of the piece and regrets to inform you of the apparent counterfeit you have acquired."

Kate's voice wavered as Lorenzo stared at her. "The professor was certain it was authentic because of the writing on the back of the canvas. It was a handwritten poem intended for the model in the painting." Blushing, she produced two more sheets of paper, front and back photocopies of the painting from one of the professor's textbooks that she laid out between them on the sofa.

Lorenzo glanced at the photocopies then read the poem. *Depths of my passion . . . gods of desire.* He removed his glasses. Clearly the painter had been smitten.

"What I saw at the port looked original too, but there are dubious characters out there, Kate." Dubious: *adj.* Causing doubt, uncertainty, or suspicion. "I wouldn't put money on any of the paintings being real. Nor would I put money on any being fake. I don't have enough evidence to prove either," Lorenzo tapped the calling card. "I had an interesting caller this morning. He knows Monica Bower, the owner of the Robin's Nest. He mentioned Monica's contact—Alfonso Robini." Lorenzo took a long, thoughtful draw from his wine, wondering how much, if anything, he should share with Kate about his history with the Robini family.

"Alfonso Robini? Well, now we're getting somewhere," said Kate. She flipped open her notebook and searched through the mess of papers for her pen, then scribbled *Alfonso* in the corner of a page. "Wanna know what I think?" Kate sat up straight and brought her wineglass to her flushed lips. She had his attention. "I think he's selling stolen goods, and I think he's fencing them through Monica Bower's gallery."

"Ah, I've thought the same, but . . . it's tricky. No proof, you see. The department ordered tests for the paintings, but there are no results yet."

"What will you do with the paintings once the results come in?" Kate asked.

"Return the crate to the port," Lorenzo said.

"Really? But if the art is stolen, wouldn't the police just hold it?"

"We haven't proven that it's stolen yet. It's just a theory at this point."

"But you're pretty sure," Kate said with a grin.

"Yes. I'm pretty sure." Lorenzo smiled back. "And this," he tapped on Kate's photocopies and the printed email set between them on the sofa, "is exactly what I needed." The email and a statement from the professor might be enough to bring Monica in for questioning.

Lorenzo excused himself to use the bathroom. When he returned to the living room, he stopped suddenly in the doorway.

He couldn't believe it. Kate was going through his notebook. The sight brought a sudden ache to his chest. *Why?*

"You realize the police only talk to the press grudgingly, right?" he said, refusing to make eye contact. Quickly, he stepped over to the couch and began grabbing his things, stuffing them back in his bag. It was hard to control his voice. "I broke my rule because I . . . because I trusted you."

Kate jumped to her feet. "No, Lorenzo. You've misunderstood. I just saw your writing. It's . . ."

Lorenzo turned for the door as Kate scrambled for her own pad.

"It's just that—look at *my* notes. They're . . . they're . . ." He paused, wanting so badly to believe her. "Look!" She held out the open notebook. He squinted down at the open page, hard-pressed to understand any of it without his reading glasses, though he could distinguish words from arrows and doodles. Her face flushed crimson. Her lips burned deep red. "See what I mean?"

He did. He thought of his own cryptic notes.

"Yes . . . I see," he said, looking into her pleading eyes. "My apologies, Kate. I'm exhausted, and this case is leading me into some difficult territory." He turned to go, feeling embarrassed.

"I shouldn't have pried, Lorenzo," Kate said as he reached for the door. "It was your shorthand that got my attention, that's all."

She laid a hand on his arm. He paused, wondering if he should explain about the farmhouse, Marco's threat, and Ella's murder, then decided against it. "I'm—I'm sorry if I've upset you. Thank you for dinner." Once outside, Lorenzo turned around to see her standing at the open door. "You were right; you are a pretty good cook."

He smiled, hoping that would undo some of the damage he'd caused to their young friendship. Then he walked away.

The following morning, a blare of sirens whizzed past Lorenzo's apartment building as he dialed Sergeant Monroe about the painting at the university. He wanted that tested as well.

"There's a link?" asked Monroe.

"It's flimsy, but yes." Lorenzo explained what Kate had discovered. The Robin's Nest calling card and the email suggesting the original Rossetti painting was replaced with a reproduction.

"Let me get this straight. You think the painting at the university is the original, and the Italian has a fake?"

"Exactly," Lorenzo said. "But she believes she still has the original."

"We're talking fraud, forgery, and the sale of stolen goods."

"Yes, and if I can prove the connection between the Rossetti and the Robin's Nest, then the items in the crate are also stolen."

"Would the university release the painting to us?" Monroe asked.

"I think so." Lorenzo rubbed his shoulder. "How much longer till we get lab results on the rest of it?"

"Don't know. I'll give them a ring this afternoon," Monroe said.

"It's not enough to bring her in, though."

"Right, but if they're real, and your link to the painting at U of O pans out, you've got your probable cause," Monroe said. Lorenzo felt the tension in his shoulders ease.

Next, Lorenzo called Thomas to let him know the department would return the crate as soon as the lab results came in.

"All right, but what if they've scheduled a pickup before that?"

"*Have* they?" asked Lorenzo, his heart raced at the thought.

"Not yet. I wanted to be sure the bases were covered. Oh, hey, I saw you leaving Kate's last night. So—what's the deal there, hmm? You two seeing each other now?"

Lorenzo cringed, remembering how he'd left things the night before. "A professional visit, Thomas. Nothing more. Kate had some information that might help the case."

Thomas laughed. "Progress, eh?"

"Goodbye, Thomas. I have work to do," Lorenzo said curtly, snapping his phone closed.

He drove his Bronco down to the Robin's Nest where he noticed a dark-haired beauty dressed in a snug twill suit exit and lock the door. Monica Bower. It *had* to be. He parked his car and followed her into the Italian cafe intending to confront her about Alfonso—but he stopped short when she sat down beside a balding man with an ample spare tire around his middle, picking nervously at a paper napkin on the table and stacking the tiny bits into a precarious mountain.

Change of plan. Lorenzo turned away, taking a table with a

peripheral view of theirs. He watched as the server from the other day took Monica's order.

When the server arrived at Lorenzo's table, she greeted him in Italian. Immediately Lorenzo shushed her.

"English today, eh?" he said quietly, revealing a glimpse of his badge with a nod to Monica's table. Her eyes widened, staring at the badge. Lorenzo went on. "Do you know that man? Is he the one you saw earlier?"

She glanced at the balding man and then turned back to Lorenzo, nodding again.

"What will you have, *signore*—sir?"

"Espresso, please." He gazed up into her big brown eyes and smiled. "And if you can, would you wrap up a slice of panettone?" He wanted a peace offering after embarrassing himself at Kate's.

"Right away," she said, hustling off to the kitchen.

There were others in the cafe, speaking in hushed tones or sitting alone with a book or newspaper. "Please Forgive Me" by David Gray played in the background—but quiet enough that Lorenzo could hear Monica's conversation.

"It was supposed to be yesterday," she hissed. "Today at the latest. We can't wait too long." Her companion added to his paper mountain. "How did this happen, Alfonso? Your men had the documents all along. This should *not* have been an issue."

Lorenzo jerked to attention. So, *that's* Alfonso, he thought, barely able to contain the years of anguish and anger he'd been harboring for the Robini's. Gripping the edge of his table, he homed in on the conversation.

"What issue? You worry too much, *gattino mio*."

"Something's not right. I can feel it," Monica said. "I think we need to change the venue."

"Don't be ridiculous. It's all decided." Alfonso said.

The server set his espresso down on the table beside a lovingly wrapped panettone. "Is this everything, sir?"

Lorenzo looked up at her and grinned. "This is perfect, thank you."

Alfonso raised his voice. "Where is our *caffe*? What's taking so long?"

"*Scusami, signore*." The server dashed off to get their order.

"You hardly need another coffee, Alfonso," Monica said. "You're already a nervous wreck."

"Hush, love. I'm fine."

"Well, *I'm* not fine. *I* have clients waiting for their orders, and they are *not* happy. There's a lot at stake for me." Monica huffed, scattering the paper mountain across the table. The fragments drifted to the floor like snowflakes.

Alfonso lost his patience. "You don't have the first idea what *I* have at stake." He glared at her and wiped the table clean of his mess. "This is not merely a *job* for me, Monica. My neck is on the line here." Alfonso lowered his voice, and Lorenzo struggled to hear what he said next. "We share this risk, you and me. Remember that."

It wasn't quite the gotcha Lorenzo had hoped for, but it was damning.

Their order finally arrived, and Monica snatched her latte. "Tomorrow, Alfonso. That's final." She stood and stormed out of the cafe. Alfonso dropped some cash on the table and ran after her.

"Monica! *Amore!*" he shouted, hurrying to catch up to her.

Leaving more than enough to cover the bill, and tucking the cake into his bag, Lorenzo followed them out the door.

He tracked the couple two blocks to a black Mercedes, and then jumped into his Bronco parked nearby and pulled into traffic behind them.

The Mercedes turned off on 19th. He lost them briefly in traffic, then spotted them several blocks down.

Southbound on Burnside, the Mercedes swerved into the right lane—then, just past the iconic Powell's Books, they turned right and pulled over in front of the Benson Hotel where Alfonso got out, slamming the door behind him, and charged past the doorman who did a double take as Alfonso entered the building.

Alfonso remained on Lorenzo's mind long into another sleepless night. "My neck is on the line here," he'd said. On the line to whom? Marco? Or was there a more extensive network?

Lorenzo was convinced Marco was at the heart of this case. Wasn't the name on the packing slip proof enough? Would there ever be enough? Thirty years ago, Lorenzo had given up everything he'd known—his job, his family, and his infant son, Emilio—rather than putting his loved ones at further risk by pursuing Marco and his corrupt family. The barrier between past and present grew thinner with every new revelation. The demons Lorenzo never entirely suppressed haunted him more with each passing day. Though exhausted, sleep eluded him as his thoughts skipped from 1974 to the present, splitting open his grief, heartache, anger, and shame. At the center of it all—Ella.

Sometime in the early morning—as he felt himself drifting off—a loud cry came from the hall outside his apartment. His body tensed, fully awake, his eyes wide as he listened further. A door opened, then slammed. He didn't know his neighbors well, but imagined it was the Iraqi war vet at the end of the hall. The man kept odd hours and talked to himself. Lorenzo felt a kind of kinship, identifying with the tormented man as he pulled his blankets back, surrendering any hope of rest. The clock read 5:03 a.m. He made his bed with military precision and stumbled barefoot into the kitchen to start the coffee. It would help clear the fog left by his lack of sleep. He heard the morning paper hit his doormat with a thud and was moving to fetch it when his cell phone rang.

"Lorenzo, they're on their way to the port." Thomas cleared his throat. "I'm on my way to meet them."

"Them?"

"The Italians. You know, the crate? The Art Foundation is sending over a van," Thomas said.

Lorenzo shook his head. "But the crate is still with the police."

"Nope, they dropped it off last night." Thomas said. So, the lab results were in. Lorenzo remembered Monica suggesting a change of venue. He quickly hung up the phone and dialed Monroe.

"The lab results are in?"

"Late yesterday. We released the art soon after," Monroe said.

"I heard. Officer Klein phoned a moment ago. A driver is on his way to pick it up."

"What did the lab determine?"

"They're real," Monroe said.

"And the Rossetti?" Lorenzo asked, heart racing. His case hinged on its authenticity.

"Too soon to tell."

Lorenzo glanced at his watch. "I'm going to meet Thomas at the port, then track the delivery in case they have other plans for it."

"I'll post Buddy at the Robin's Nest," Monroe said.

Fifteen minutes later, Lorenzo hit the road with an insulated mug of hot coffee, a racing heart, and his pistol and holster in the glove box. He pulled up to the port office soon after. Thomas, who'd been waiting outside, jogged down the handicap ramp to meet him. Lorenzo rolled down the window.

"I wasn't expecting you," Thomas said.

"After what you said, I wanted to make sure they *are* taking the crate to the Robin's Nest."

They watched as a black van rolled slowly past the office doors and parked alongside the building about fifty feet from Lorenzo's Bronco. Two men jumped out—one with a mustache and a Portland Trail Blazers sweatshirt, the other in a gray driving cap and baggy striped coveralls, two sizes too big.

"Wait here. I need to check their documents and get a signature before I can release the crate to them."

"Got it." Lorenzo wrapped a hand around the travel mug, welcoming its warmth.

The sweatshirt followed Thomas into the building while the coveralls stood with his back to Lorenzo, fists stuffed deep into his pockets. Lorenzo's phone buzzed from the empty cup holder.

"What do you have, Buddy?" Lorenzo focused on the coveralls climbing back into the van. *Show your face.*

"Monica Bower. She just pulled up to the Robin's Nest, and she's not alone." Lorenzo checked his watch. 6:08.

"Alfonso with her?"

"No, he's still back at the hotel. But I see three cars waiting in the alley." Seems like Monica's sticking to the plan, thought Lorenzo. Buddy cleared his throat. "Your friend is at the hotel, too."

"My friend?" Lorenzo noticed the man in coveralls staring at him through the van's side mirror, the cap pulled low over his forehead. Their eyes locked for a second or two before the coveralls turned away.

"Yeah, the chick from the paper. Kate? She's been there all night. Thinks she's got the story of the century. She calls Alfonso 'mystery man.'"

"She's at the hotel? And you *left* her there?" He hadn't known what to expect after the evening at Kate's house, but evidently, she hadn't let go of the story, and now she'd exposed herself to a potentially dangerous man.

No, not potentially. Alfonso was a Robini.

"Well, yeah. She volunteered to watch the elevator."

"She *what?*" Thomas and the sweatshirt emerged from the building. "I'm at the port," Lorenzo said. "There's a van here to collect the crate. Two men. It won't be long now. Are you ready?"

"Got a whole crew here. We're ready," Buddy said.

"Send a man to the hotel. Kate shouldn't be there alone." Lorenzo considered going to the hotel himself but wasn't comfortable leaving the arrests to Buddy.

"Will do," Buddy said to Lorenzo's great relief.

Lorenzo hung up, watching the van follow Thomas around the corner toward the warehouse while sorting out his emotions about Kate's proximity to Alfonso Robini. It was insane. She was too close to this. His own words about the press came back to him. *It never ends well.*

When the van came back into view, Lorenzo put the Bronco in gear and followed it down the interstate through rush hour traffic into town. The delay only gave him more time to worry about Kate. Why had she gotten herself mixed up in this? Was she trying to be some kind of hero? She had no business anywhere near Alfonso Robini. Lorenzo's gut ached as he imagined everything that could go wrong.

When they arrived at the gallery, Lorenzo parked as inconspicuously as he could, about a block down. He noticed Buddy's car and strapped on his holster as he watched sweatshirt and coveralls lug the crate inside. Then he got out and walked over to Buddy's car.

Buddy rolled down his window. "Forensics says they're the real deal, man," he said. "We got our proof."

"Proof that they're real—we need proof that they're stolen." Lorenzo prayed the professor's painting had similar results. Otherwise, he didn't have a case. He barely had enough to make an arrest.

A light drizzle began to fall. Lorenzo climbed into the passenger seat of Buddy's car.

"You sent a man to the hotel, right?" Lorenzo said, still worried about Kate.

"Relax, she'll be fine." Buddy said with a reassuring grin. "Your friend's pretty cool. Not my type—but cool, you know?"

"She's not my friend, Buddy," Lorenzo said, believing he'd ruined any chance of friendship when he'd confronted her the other night.

"That's not what she said."

Lorenzo had just begun to process that when an officer waved from the alley. "Okay, here we go. Let's make it quick."

Lorenzo entered the gallery, and the police poured in behind him. The crate lay open in the center of the showroom. Monica glanced at Lorenzo and turned for the back office.

"Monica Bower," he called after her, "you are under arrest for possession and sales of stolen property."

Monica glanced back at him without missing a step in her pencil-heeled stilettos. "You have *got* to be kidding me!"

Lorenzo caught up to her, exposing the badge at his hip. "You have the right to remain silent. Anything you say . . ." He continued reading Monica her rights, pulling her along with him to the alley where three men in custody were being loaded into waiting police cars. "Buddy!" Lorenzo shouted, handing Monica off to another officer. "Any sign of Alfonso?"

Buddy looked over the hood of a police cruiser with two men in the back and shook his head. Lorenzo wasted no time. He *had* to get to the Benson Hotel.

When Lorenzo entered the hotel, Kate waltzed up behind him. "He's on the fifth floor," she said.

"How do you know?"

"I followed Monica to a suite there last night, then asked the front desk who had booked the room. I said they'd helped me out earlier in the day, and I wanted to thank them. They gave me his name and offered to order flowers for me."

"You didn't!"

"The flowers? Of course not."

"You were here all night?"

Kate pointed to a straight-backed wing chair and smiled. "It's not as comfortable as it looks." They both looked up when the elevator doors slid open. "Speak of the devil." Kate pointed. "That's him."

Alfonso emerged from the elevator, a blue roller bag at his side like an obedient pet. Deep creases lined his furrowed brow as he scowled, eyes darting this way and that. Then he hurried out the door to a cab waiting at the curb. A doorman rushed out to help him, holding an umbrella overhead.

Careful not to let Alfonso see him, Lorenzo rushed to his Bronco across the street. He looked up as Kate reached for the door.

"Where do you think you're going?" said Lorenzo.

"The story, remember?" she said, meeting his eyes, her face dampened by the rain.

Of course he remembered. He looked into her eyes, recalling the last time he'd seen her, regretting his emotional exit.

"It's too dangerous," he said.

Kate pulled her shoulders back defiantly. "I need this, Lorenzo. The *whole* story."

Lorenzo frowned and checked his watch. They were wasting time. Alfonso's cab was already disappearing down the street. "Get in."

Once they'd pulled into the morning traffic and located the yellow cab, Lorenzo called Sergeant Monroe.

"We're tailing his cab. I think it's bound for the airport." Lorenzo flipped on the windshield wipers. *Bump-a-dump.*

"The reporter was watching for him."

"Yes, she's here with me now."

"Are you nuts? The paper will have a field day if anything happens to her."

Lorenzo clenched the steering wheel. "Yes, sir, I understand."

"Good. Now, we're holding Monica Bower and the others from the raid. Buddy's going back to the gallery to see if they missed anything. He said you'd want Monica's computer, or any paper trail she might have left behind."

"Excellent." Lorenzo set down his phone and focused on the road ahead as the cab turned onto the interstate on-ramp.

Kate stared at him. "What was that all about?"

"Nothing." Lorenzo pulled onto the highway and headed east in heavy rush-hour traffic. His windshield wipers bounced—*bump-a-*

dump, bump-a-dump, back and forth in a futile attempt to keep pace with the rain.

"Are you going to arrest him?"

"No," Lorenzo snapped. His scalp prickled with the onset of a headache.

"Why not?"

"I'm not after him," Lorenzo said curtly.

"Who *are* you after?"

Lorenzo said nothing. Eventually the cab made its way to the airport, and he followed it up to the doors in front of Delta Airlines. They watched as Alfonso slipped out of the cab and disappeared through the revolving door. Cursing, Lorenzo quickly drove past and down the ramp behind a green Prius whose driver seemed in no particular hurry.

"Lorenzo—*who are you after?*" Kate repeated as he sped past the Prius.

He frowned at her as he drove, looking desperately for a place to park, and wishing more than ever that he'd left her behind. Why wouldn't she stop with the questions? Where would he even begin with an answer? The farmhouse? The funeral? The tragedy that had become his life because of one man? Lorenzo turned sharply into the short-term lot and grabbed the first open spot. "Stay put. I'll be right back."

"Hey!"

He got out and jogged across the sky bridge.

"Hey!" she called again, following him.

She stepped up beside him outside the entrance doors. "Get back in the car," he insisted, pointing to the parking garage.

"I won't." She stood her ground, scowling. Her freckled cheeks flushed red as she braced for whatever he'd say next.

"Then stay behind me," he grumbled, turning away, but acutely aware of her presence.

CHAPTER SIX

Kate

Kate wondered how close to stand. When Lorenzo moved, she moved. His body blocked her from view. She tried to get his attention by touching his back and felt the ridge of something beneath her fingers. Of course. A shoulder strap. The holster shouldn't have surprised her, but it did.

"What?" he snapped.

"I'm going to go sit by the window."

"Good."

Kate sat in a plastic chair by the window with her back to the ticket counter. She used the window's reflection to watch for Alfonso —but Lorenzo turned and met her eyes in the glass. She felt put in her place—it was the sort of look George had given her when she disagreed with him or said something he disapproved of. She'd spent the better part of her marriage trying to navigate his arbitrary rules and holding her tongue as his moods shifted from love to hate, approval to disapproval.

Lorenzo had his moods as well. How quickly he'd turned on her the other night. Friend to foe. Where did she stand now? How was he any different from George?

No. Stop. She couldn't go there. The two men were *completely* different.

Kate held her hands in her lap and stared at her sorry reflection. *Be a good girl*, she thought. *Keep your mouth shut, don't stir the pot, and mind your own business.*

Then, with shoulders back and chin up, Kate scanned the crowd for Lorenzo, who'd left his post while she was busy pouting.

She turned from the window, spotting Lorenzo at the ticket counter. She wanted to run over to him, but instead—wait! Alfonso —*there!* He vanished around the corner to his gate, his phone pressed to his ear. As she took her first step in that direction, Lorenzo grabbed her wrist and led her up the escalator to the sky bridge—back the way they had come.

So were they going to let Alfonso go?

"What did the ticket agent say? Where are we going?" Kate took a quick breath, pulling away from Lorenzo's grip, but still following closely. Squealing tires echoed throughout the garage. "Why aren't you *talking* to me? What the hell is going *on?*" A couple, emerging from their car, looked back over their shoulders at her.

"Not here," Lorenzo said, as they neared his Bronco. He got in and slammed his door shut. Kate got in too, listening intently as he called Sergeant Monroe—her pouting now replaced with indignation and resolve.

"Sergeant," said Lorenzo. There was a long pause. "Milan. Direct flight, but likely on his way to Genoa." Lorenzo put the Bronco in gear and drove toward the exit.

Kate watched him—his phone in one hand, his other navigating the pay station and his irritation, as he fumbled around in the console for his wallet.

"What was that about the Feds?" he asked, still speaking into the phone. The barricade lifted and the Bronco surged forward. "Do I have a say in this?" Lorenzo tightened his grip on the wheel and looked over at Kate as if realizing she was still there. "I'll be there soon," he told the sergeant. "Just pulling onto the highway."

With that, he flipped his phone closed and chucked it in the empty cup holder beside a dinged-up travel mug.

"The lab is going to test the professor's painting. Thought you'd like to know."

Kate scrambled to retrieve her notebook from her backpack. "What about the paintings in the crate?" She stared at him, waiting with her notebook on her lap and a pen pinched between her fingers.

Lorenzo frowned. "Authentic." His phone rang, but he ignored it.

"Why didn't you arrest Alfonso? How could you let him go so easily?" Lorenzo's glare confirmed Kate had pushed her luck again.

"Because he'll lead us to the people who oversee this operation." Lorenzo's voice was flat, emotionless. His eyes locked on the road ahead. It had stopped raining, but the wipers still thumped back and forth periodically, clearing road spray off the windshield.

"What happens to Monica and the collectors? Are they off the hook too?"

"Monica's been charged with possession and sales of stolen goods. The collectors with intent to purchase stolen goods."

"Intent? You mean they didn't pay in advance?"

Lorenzo raised an eyebrow. "Not that I could prove, but I'll know more after questioning them. And Alfonso is *not* off the hook," he corrected her.

"Questioned by whom?"

"Me."

Kate waited patiently for an invitation. She'd do anything to listen in. But Lorenzo turned off the highway into city traffic without a peep.

Finally, she had to ask. "Could I . . . come with you?" She held her breath.

"No."

"Could we meet? After?" *Don't be so needy*, she told herself.

"It'll be late." He pulled the Bronco behind her Volvo across from the hotel and shut off the engine.

Kate turned to him. "Lorenzo, are you still angry with me about looking at your notes? You know that was innocent, don't you? I would never . . ."

"Listen, Kate, this is not a game for me." He met her eyes then looked away. "You don't know—you don't know what this means to me." He lowered his voice. "This case dug up some old demons. It's a long, dark story. Maybe, someday, I'll tell you. But right now, I am going to sit down with Monica and the others." He cleared his throat and straightened his back. "I'll call you after I wrap up the interviews. How's that?" He smiled weakly.

Some old demons? Kate had no idea what he could be talking about—but she saw the sadness in his eyes, heard the tremble in his voice, and dropped the subject. She could wait for the results from the interviews. But waiting for whatever long, dark story he was referring to . . . she sensed that would be more difficult.

"It's fine." She dug into her pack for a business card and held it out to him. "I'm sorry for tagging along. Sometimes I . . ."

"Don't be sorry. We're both simply doing our jobs." His eyes didn't leave her face as he took the card from her fingers. "I'm not angry."

She stepped out of the Bronco onto the sidewalk and waited for Lorenzo to drive off before calling Mr. Walker.

"So? Whadayagot?" he said.

Kate had already shared details of her evolving story. Her boss knew about the Rossetti, the crate at the port, and their unproven connection. She didn't have much else to add yet.

"I know the identity of the mystery man that I told you about from the port, but he's on his way to Italy as we speak." Kate climbed into the driver's seat. "I also know that the lab is testing the professor's Rossetti to verify its authenticity, but I still don't know who the donor was. There were several arrests at the Robin's Nest this morning, but I don't have everyone's name—"

"What are you telling me?" asked Walker. "Where's the story?"

"Until they complete the interviews, I don't have a story. I need more time."

She braced herself.

"If you don't have something by midnight, you'll be back to the old beat. Is that what you want? Dog shows and art fairs?"

"No, sir." The cramp in her throat prevented her from saying more.

Kate sat at her card table desk, her laptop screen saver image of Mount St. Helens beaming back at her as she mulled over her options. She could call Lorenzo and insist on meeting him. She could walk right into the station like she belonged there. She could go behind his back and speak with Buddy. Or she could bang out a simple piece about the University of Oregon's good fortune, high-lighting Dante Gabriel Rossetti's works.

It wasn't what Walker wanted, but it might hold off a demotion. She chose door number three—the path of least resistance. She began with Dr. Marshall's words: "Imagine how I felt when I discovered, in his own script, a poem dedicated to the subject of the masterpiece, his beloved wife." She recalled the moment she'd set eyes on the piece and added, "The sensual painting itself evoked Rossetti's ardor, but the poem drew me into their private sphere of love and passion." Kate read over the last bit. Was this their fantasy or hers? She scrapped the whole thing and started over.

This time she tied the Rossetti's original owner in Italy and the calling card with the Robin's Nest logo. In another version, she worked on an angle using the Italian Art Foundation's relationship with the gallery and the crate at the port. Each attempt at the story seemed more inadequate than the last.

Kate gazed out her office window, considering her predicament. She'd hoped that with Lorenzo's help, she could tie the Rossetti together with the crate at the port, the Italian mystery man, and the

Robin's Nest gallery. Unfortunately, without the details from Lorenzo's interview, there were too many loose ends. And she refused to go the route of "allegedly this" or "allegedly that" to make a story out of nothing.

As midnight approached, she still hadn't heard from Lorenzo. She thought back to his hesitation at the cargo center, and then his hint at a long dark story. "This case dug up some old demons," he'd said. It still made no sense.

Worried that she'd never make her deadline, she called the station, but there was no answer. Finally, with the deadline looming, she set fingertips to keypad, dashed off the only story she was prepared to write, her original draft about the professor's discovery, and pushed send. A few minutes later, her phone rang.

"This is it?" Miles Walker said.

"I'll know more in the morning, but the deadline . . ."

"The deadline stands," he blustered.

"Perhaps a follow-up?"

"No, this is it. I shouldn't have expected more from you, honestly. So, what's happening on St. Helens?"

"Excuse me?" Kate's neck and shoulders ached. She felt tired. She didn't want to hear Walker's stupid constraints.

"Get me an update."

"But the art story isn't over! There's so much more!"

"Not my fault."

Kate felt the heat rise to her face. "Not mine either. Just one more day. It's all I need. Please."

"No."

Kate suppressed the urge to scream. Walker's unreasonable stance did not compute. She wasn't asking for much—just a few hours. "Then I'm done."

"What?"

"I quit."

"Don't be ridiculous," Walker said. But in her head, she heard George's voice, and hung up the phone.

CHAPTER SEVEN

Lorenzo

Lorenzo wrapped up the interviews, knowing that the charge of intent to purchase stolen goods would likely never stick since, apparently, no one believed the art was stolen. But Lorenzo would leave that to the district attorney to determine. As for Monica, he had nothing to hold her on. Not without the Rossetti lab results. But at least he now knew the identity of the donor, who was at the gallery that morning.

He glanced at the wall clock before closing the door to the interview room and plodded down the hall. It was nearly midnight. He was famished. The last thing he'd had to eat was an apple and a small bag of potato chips Buddy had given him partway through the interviews.

The halls of the station were quiet, but Lorenzo noticed light spilling from Sergeant Monroe's office. He knocked softly on the open door. Two other men were with him. One was Captain Frazier, who stood immediately as Lorenzo entered the room.

"Have a seat, detective," said Captain Frazier. Lorenzo sat in the empty chair between the two men. Sergeant Monroe remained seated behind his desk. "First, let me congratulate you on pulling this all together."

"It's not settled, sir. I still have some loose ends." Lorenzo thought of the Rossetti's owner. He thought of Alfonso, en route to Milan. He thought of Marco.

"Which reminds me," said the captain. "The Rossetti result came in a few minutes ago. It's authentic."

The captain turned toward the third man in the room. He was dressed in street clothes, and his blond hair was combed back away from his face, revealing a kidney-shaped mole on his temple. "Allow me to introduce Agent Fogarty with the FBI," Captain Frazier said. "He'll be taking over from here."

Lorenzo shot a look at Monroe. *What the hell?*

Fogarty stood and leaned across the desk—his arm outstretched for a handshake.

"A pleasure to meet you, detective. We have a man on the ground in Italy. He'll be filling in the AISI. Once I have a better grasp of the case, I'll pass on the details to him."

Lorenzo was familiar with Italy's Internal Investigation Service. They were based out of Rome and thought themselves superior to every other branch of Italian law enforcement.

"But . . ." Lorenzo burned with rage. Monica's computer revealed emails and records of sales agreements leading back six months. The emails between Monica and Alfonso were damaging, but they never mentioned where the pieces came from. Lorenzo believed more than ever that the deception led back to Marco.

"I'd like to stay involved."

"No can do," answered Agent Fogarty. "I'm nothing more than a simple go-between."

Unbelievable. Dismissed, Lorenzo held his tongue and returned to his desk to sort through his notes, files, and collected documents for Agent Fogarty. Was this all he had to show for the past month's work? It was over? Though he understood the protocols of the bureau, he couldn't shake his dissatisfaction. What about Alfonso, Marco, the art foundation, and everything else? He needed closure.

Lorenzo pushed aside the case file. He'd have to leave that, but tucked his notebook into his breast pocket, wondering what he'd tell Kate in the morning. It reminded him of the way he'd left things when he'd dropped her off at the hotel. The intensity in her eyes when he hinted at his personal connection to the case. Should he call her now? He ran his fingers through his hair. No, too late, and he had a lot of processing to do after his fateful conversation with Captain Frazier and Agent Fogarty.

Lorenzo glanced back at the file on his desk, tasting the bitter pill he'd been forced to swallow.

The short drive home gave Lorenzo little time to unwind. He anticipated another rough night's sleep. Now, as he walked toward his apartment door, he noticed the broken latch and cursed.

Reaching for his gun, he stepped inside and gasped at the sight.

The intruder had spared nothing. Lorenzo's dresser drawers had been dumped unceremoniously onto the living room floor amid sofa cushions, books, and magazines. The contents of his bedroom closet lay strewn across the bed.

Lorenzo felt sick to his stomach. But nausea gave way to rage, and he turned and ran back to the empty street. Though instinct told him the intruder was long gone, he dared to hope. Surely this had something to do with the case. A message from Marco, perhaps.

After a quick search of the neighborhood turned up nothing, he returned to his apartment and stumbled through the mayhem, his nerves as shattered as the destroyed latch on the door.

He flipped open his phone with trembling hands and dialed 911. Lorenzo described the scene, trying to remain calm. Trying to disconnect from the personal and relay the facts as if this were any other crime scene.

He returned to the bedroom where the old wallet and letters lay scattered across the floor among his clothes, shoes, and the shards of a broken lamp. Ella's photo lay at the foot of the bed. He knew better than to touch anything, but he picked it up and flattened it, his thumb brushing across her smiling face. Lorenzo swallowed hard. Then, one by one, he returned the cherished items to the tin box and dropped it into his suitcase with some clothes, his running shoes, and a few other odds and ends before driving off into the night—numb with shock and exhaustion and no notion of where to go.

He circled the Park blocks then drove toward the river looking for a hotel. But he didn't stop at any of the hotels he saw—driving on as an inner compass led him to someone who would truly understand him. At half past one, Lorenzo pulled his Bronco in front of Kate's house. Once he'd gotten up the nerve to knock, she eased open the door, eyes wide and questioning, no doubt wary of her late-night visitor. He must have been a sight. But when she realized who it was, she let him in without a word, made up the sofa, and tucked him in with a warm cup of tea before disappearing into her own room.

Lorenzo woke before sunrise. The house was quiet, and Kate was still asleep as he pulled on his running shoes. Today, of all days, he needed a run. He needed to purge the toxins his body had stored up over the past weeks of stress and anxiety. He needed to clear his head and figure out his next move.

The front door groaned shut behind him as he stepped onto the porch, his breath visible in the cool, damp air. A golden sunrise crested above the house across the street. He walked through the wet grass, dappled yellow and orange with the season's fallen leaves, and set off at an easy jog, then ran several blocks down to Ladd's Addition, circling the heavily pruned rose gardens, his heart pounding. His mind raced with thoughts of Marco, Monica, stolen art, and the FBI. He tried to block the vision of his ransacked apartment. He didn't know who'd done it, but guessed it had something to do with Monica's arrest. A warning, he supposed, or a threat.

A car rumbled past, and he stopped to let it by, taking a beat to map his next move. His shadow on the pavement vanished as a cloud passed overhead. Then, like his darkest memories, it suddenly came back into view.

With an internal scream, Lorenzo bolted up Hawthorne Boulevard, feeling as if his heart would burst from the exertion—but also from anguish, anger, and fear. His feet slapped rhythmically against the pavement—one-two, one-two, like the pounding of his heart. The street was quiet. The shops were still closed. He doubled back down Hawthorne, slowing his pace, allowing his mind to settle on more pleasant thoughts, like the expression on Kate's face when she'd opened the door to him the night before. Surprised at first, then her face softened when she'd recognized him. She'd taken his hand and led him inside. They barely knew each other. But somehow, he knew she'd take him in. He was grateful that she didn't push for an explanation that he couldn't yet give.

Damp with sweat, he slowed to a walk, arriving at the Safeway store, with a plan to repay Kate's kindness the way his mother might have. That morning he'd found the panettone from the coffee shop flattened in his bag, still wrapped in the purple wax paper. He could do better than that. He emerged from the store with a sack of flour, fruit, eggs, and milk, intent on fixing a beautiful Italian breakfast.

The short walk back was pleasant. The sun had dried the streets and fallen leaves, which somersaulted past in the gentle breeze. As Lorenzo approached Kate's house, he looked up into the picture window of the house next door at a small boy in fuzzy blue pajamas.

This was Thomas's house, Lorenzo recalled Kate telling him so the night she'd invited him to dinner.

Thomas appeared beside the boy and swept him up in his arms, his face aglow with love. The scene tugged at Lorenzo's heart. He'd missed that with Emilio. He'd missed it all. Then Thomas looked out the window, set the boy down, and opened the door.

"Lorenzo! What brings you by?" Lorenzo pointed toward Kate's house, and Thomas looked at the bag of groceries with a sly grin. "Ah! I see. For a second there, I thought you were here to see me." He laughed. A woman emerged from the house wearing a flannel bathrobe and carrying the small boy on her hip. She was pretty, with long dark hair and copper skin.

"Megan, this is Lorenzo. I told you about him, right?"

"Yes, good morning, Lorenzo." She glanced at the groceries, then across the shared driveway to Kate's, and smiled.

A breeze passed through Lorenzo's sweat-dampened shirt, sending a shiver up his spine. "Good morning," he said with a nod. "I don't want you to get the wrong idea, Thomas," said Lorenzo. "After the raid yesterday, someone trashed my apartment. Kate let me sleep on her sofa."

Megan's jaw dropped open. Thomas's grin evaporated. "Lorenzo. My God! Are you all right?"

Lorenzo waved him off. "I'm fine," he said. The standard reply. But he still felt last night's aftershocks. "I'll call you later." He turned to go.

"Interesting, though," Thomas called after him. "Of all the places you could have landed last night, you chose Kate's."

———

Back at Kate's front door, Lorenzo fumbled for the key he'd found that morning in a clay dish on the counter, a silver heart dangled from the chain. He unlocked the door and entered Kate's house, expecting to see her waiting for him—hoping, perhaps. But all was quiet. She must have been sleeping in. So, after a hot, rejuvenating shower, he set to work in the kitchen. Measuring and mixing—two cups of this, a quarter teaspoon of that. He sliced and diced a selection of fruit. He held a bowl in one hand, filled with egg custard he'd just whipped up.

"Well, you've been busy."

Kate's voice nearly made Lorenzo drop the custard. She stood in the doorway, wearing a thin gray T-shirt and pink cotton pajama bottoms, her hair tousled about her smiling face.

"*Buongiorno*," he said, grinning, feeling genuinely delighted to see her.

"Is that my word of the day?" she said.

Lorenzo laughed. "*Assolutamente.*"

"How'd you sleep?"

"Very well," he said. But truthfully, he'd slept very little, plagued by thoughts of Marco Robini, his meeting with the captain, and the scene in his apartment. Lorenzo thought of telling her what had happened at the apartment but held off. It was too much information for now, and he didn't want to ruin the moment. "I hope you're hungry."

Kate looked around the kitchen, ogling the pan of caramelized baked pear and gushing over the toasted bruschetta with ricotta cheese and tomato jam.

"Here, taste this." He dipped a clean spoon into the custard. Kate stepped closer and opened her mouth.

"Oh, Lorenzo. This is positively orgasmic."

"That good, eh?" Lorenzo grinned, his face warming with embarrassment.

"Your mother would be proud."

"I don't know about that. My sister, Muriel, was always better. She has a gift." He poured Kate a fresh cup of coffee from the French press, then handed her a plate of bruschetta and a baked pear doused with custard.

The thought of Muriel comforted him. His sister had been his best friend growing up. The only one who knew what made him tick.

He put the sweetbread in the oven and set the timer, feeling so pleased with himself he'd nearly forgotten his troubles. Kate glanced over at him. She held her coffee cup to her lips, but even so, he could see the smile in her eyes. Of all the places I could have landed, I landed here.

Kate took a plateful of Lorenzo's handiwork through the dining room, dodging a light fixture dangling from a tarnished brass chain. "I really need a table." Her voice reverberated off the bare gray walls as Lorenzo stepped up beside her, sipping his coffee.

He nudged her with his elbow. "Well, you have a comfortable sofa." They laughed and sat together on the sofa beside a small tower of folded sheets and blankets. Kate sat with one leg tucked under the other and turned toward Lorenzo.

"I have no words for how delicious this is, detective." Kate smacked her lips while balancing the plate on one knee.

"It's the least I could do. And you can call me Lorenzo."

She looked down into her coffee. "I know. I just like calling you detective. It sounds, um—never mind." Lorenzo wondered what she meant. Official? Professional? Masculine? Or—hmm. He grinned and looked at his watch.

"Are you working today?" he asked. Kate shrugged, so he went on. "Ah! You're waiting for my report."

Kate looked away. "You can finish your coffee. No rush."

Lorenzo picked his coffee cup up off the floor and sipped—a delicate maneuver with his plate balanced precariously on his leg. "My interview with Monica wasn't much help. She denied everything. One collector admitted to donating the U of O painting."

She turned to face him. "Did he say why?"

"He was going to sell it, but said he'd had a funny feeling about its providence, so he donated it for the tax write off. Turns out even an anonymous donor can file for a write off."

"Funny." Kate unfolded her legs and reached down to set her plate and cup on the floor. Her shirt twisted, and Lorenzo couldn't help but notice the gentle curve of her back and the exposed flesh above her pajama bottoms. "So—if he had his doubts about the Rossetti, why did he go back to Monica yesterday?" She nestled back against the cushions. "What changed?"

"It was the painting we saw at the port. The girl in the chair, remember? He said it was worth the risk." He paused, wondering what else he could share from his interviews. "There's another name I can give you. Maximo Corta.

"He's important?"

"Supposedly, he's the man in charge of operations in Parma, something to do with a school, but I don't know how it ties in with the insurance company, or the art foundation." Lorenzo's gaze wandered to the corner of the room. "This isn't solely about stolen art, there's forgery too, but there are still so many unknowns. I know this isn't what you wanted to hear, Kate." He looked into her eyes. "And now I'm out of the loop because the captain turned everything over to the Feds."

Kate shifted awkwardly in her seat, breaking eye contact. Was she still upset about the day before? Why wasn't she pushing for more details?

"It's all right," she said.

"What about your story?"

She focused on the picture window and shrugged. "I just turned in some fluff about the university and Gabriel Rossetti, the artist. It's done. Not what I wanted, but there was a deadline."

"No! You should have said. Kate, I'm so sorry."

She looked back at him with a shy smile. "Seriously, it's okay," she said, licking tomato jam from her fingers. "This was delicious. Thank you."

"Thank you for taking me in last night."

"Do you want to talk about it?" she asked, her blue eyes wide and inquisitive.

"Hmm." The kitchen timer went off. Lorenzo excused himself to pull his bread out of the oven and set it aside to cool. He still felt gripped by the events from the night before. He returned and stood behind the sofa, resting his fingertips on the leather behind Kate's shoulders. "Someone broke into my apartment last night."

"Lorenzo!" Kate spun around to look at him.

"They trashed the place, and—I couldn't stay."

"Who would do that? Why?"

Calmly, he stepped around the sofa to face her. "This is what I meant yesterday. The long story."

Lorenzo sat down beside her. Kate nudged him. She wanted to hear the story, and he needed to tell it. He wanted her to know why this case was so important to him, and why he needed to see it through.

Lorenzo began his story with the Manarola feast day of San Lorenzo in 1973, when he and Ella hiked up to the abandoned farmhouse on Via Rosa. He told Kate about the awkward encounter with Marco and his uncle Carlo at the house and the threat in the piazza that followed. If you come anywhere near that farmhouse again, your family will pay.

Kate listened intently, looking slightly alarmed when he'd mentioned Ella, more so when he brought up his son, Emilio. He expected as much. Then he launched into what he'd seen at the farmhouse a year later when he'd ignored Marco's threat and went to the house alone to discover what Marco was hiding. He left nothing out as he described the scene in the room upstairs, the woman, the painting, and Marco poised on the other side of the room as if he'd been waiting for him.

Lorenzo leaned forward on the couch, meeting Kate's eyes. "Marco kept his promise," he said, his voice weak and shaking. "My family paid dearly." His throat clenched with guilt, grief, and painful memory. He envisioned Ella standing on the rocky cliffs over the harbor, her red scarf flapping wildly in the coastal breeze. He pictured himself climbing the stairs from the boat ramp and joining her, feeling her warm arms wrap around him. How he'd treasured her, his Ella.

"She was found dead the following day. He murdered her, Kate. Marco murdered Ella. I had no proof, but I knew it was him."

Lorenzo buried his face in his hands, then felt Kate's hand settle on his back, as soft and gentle as a feather.

He sensed her apprehension and sat up, but she took his hands in hers. Silent. Reverent. He would have allowed her closer. He would have welcomed her arms around him. Perhaps another time. A time when he was not grieving for a wife who'd died a lifetime ago.

"I was mad with grief and rage back then, insisting on pinning Marco down. I wanted to arrest him. None of the police took me seriously. One of our own? Why would he? Not Marco, they said. But when Marco didn't show up at the station, a few men went around to the farmhouse."

"So, they saw it all," Kate said, looking him in the eye.

"They saw nothing. The place was bare."

"All the art was gone? And Marco?"

"He vanished, too." Lorenzo groaned, blinking away the tears. "I should have gone after him, but he'd made sure there wasn't enough evidence. And I didn't have it in me. After the funeral, I packed my bags and left for the United States. I left my son. I left my family. I left everything I knew, thinking they'd be better off without me. Thinking I'd left all that agony behind me. But the US has been a prison to me—not the sanctuary I sought. Self-exiled from the country I loved and the family I . . . the family I cherished." Oh, the ache in his chest! He felt Kate's warm thigh pressed against his as she squeezed his hands.

"The Marco from your story," she said tenderly. He could see her making the connection. "That's Marco Robini."

Lorenzo nodded. "That's why this case is so difficult for me. It's taken me to the brink of the madness I'd run away from. It's as vivid today as the day I left." He looked down at their woven hands on his lap. "It's more than the miles of separation, Kate. It's . . ." He'd gone this far; why stop? "It's the shame I feel for running away. The guilt of leaving my son and shirking my responsibilities as a father. I left my *son*. What kind of man does that? Worst of all, I think of how I failed Ella." His eyes stung with the tears he struggled to hold back.

Before Lorenzo registered what was happening, Kate's arms were around him, her cheek pressed against his. She held him tight, like a child in her arms, and he clung to her as the dam broke, dampening her face and hair, spilling onto her shoulder. The wall he'd built up to protect himself crumbled to rubble. Kate melted into him, and it seemed she was crying as well. Lorenzo's arms tightened their hold as if she was his lifeline. He buried his face in her neck and inhaled the scent of her, feeling more liberated than he had in three decades.

Was there a future for him here? He couldn't yet see it clearly through the mire of his past.

It had been thirty years since Marco turned Lorenzo's world upside down. He couldn't turn back the clock on Ella's death, the abandonment of his son, or his emotional exodus from Italy. But he could vindicate Ella, shut down the Robini business, and mend fences with his family. It was his only path forward.

Then it hit him. "I have to go back to Italy."

Kate's soft lips brushed against his ear. "When do we leave?"

"We?" Lorenzo sat back, eyes still burning and cheeks wet with fallen tears. "No, no, no."

Kate wiped his tears away and grinned. "Every brave knight needs his Sancho Panza."

He could have kissed her right then. It would only be natural after sharing his deepest feelings. Her rose-bud lips were so close to his. He felt her warm fingertips gently wiping his tears away.

"Thank you, Sancho," he said.

Kate sat up straight and looked into his eyes, wiping their mingled tears from her freckled cheek with the back of her hand. "That's what friends are for."

CHAPTER EIGHT

Kate

"I'm overdue for a vacation," Lorenzo said as they wiped up the flour-dusted countertops and washed the mountain of bowls and pans left from his Italian breakfast. "They can't say no. How about you?"

"I'm fine."

Lorenzo laughed. "I know you're fine. Can you get the time off?"

"Already arranged." Kate refused to say anything of her conversation with Miles Walker the night before—she feared Lorenzo would feel responsible, and he didn't need that on top of everything else. But Kate had her own problems. She'd quit her job with bills to pay and her share of the house in the balance. Now there was the expense of traveling to Italy. But what choice did she have? The story was her only hope of keeping the house and establishing herself as a freelancer. It *had* to be great.

Kate started putting the dishes away, half-listening to Lorenzo when he said he'd need to go to the station to ask for the time off.

"It's always better in person," he said. Kate said nothing,

distracted by her own difficulties. Lorenzo laid a hand on her shoulder. "Are you all right?"

"Hmm? Yeah. Just—you know, digesting everything that's going on."

"It's a lot. I'm sorry."

"It's fine, really." Kate stacked the bowls and stooped to put them away into the cupboard.

"Is it?" He held out his hand to help her back up, and when she stood, he didn't budge, searching her face with his dark blue eyes.

After Lorenzo left the house to meet with Sergeant Monroe, Kate plugged Edie Brickell's *Volcano* CD into her boombox and stretched out on the sofa to take stock of her situation.

A trip to Italy and a blossoming affection for a man twelve years older—she had done the math.

Kate thought about how he'd arrived the night before. How, as she struggled to fall asleep after the call with Mr. Walker, she heard a soft tap-ta-tap at the front door. How she padded downstairs and peeked out the window. There was Lorenzo, standing on her porch with dark rings under his eyes and a small suitcase in hand. When she opened the door, she knew something terrible had happened—but what? She led him into the house, prickling with curiosity. But she respected his privacy too much to ask.

She still felt the lingering effects of Lorenzo's emotional embrace from that morning. How he'd clung to her after confiding his history with the Robini family, dropping nuggets along the way like a son he'd left behind and a murdered wife. Both earth-shattering revelations on their own—but to have been in the position to pursue Marco, and instead flee? Was Lorenzo protecting his family, or himself? It couldn't have been an easy decision, and though Kate wondered if she'd ever understand his rationale, her heart ached for him at the separation he's endured and the suffering he's kept hidden for decades.

Kate stared at the ceiling and sighed. "Maybe George should buy *me* out," she said aloud. But she wanted the house. It had become her sanctuary since George moved out, taking all the reminders of their marriage with him. The king-sized bed, the grandfather clock his parents had given them as a wedding present, and the Persian rug where they'd made love their first night after moving in. It was all gone now.

Kate drifted off to sleep and woke hours later, refreshed but hungry. She wandered into the kitchen and was picking at leftovers from breakfast and devising a plan to pay for the trip when Megan knocked on the kitchen door and let herself in.

"You alone?" she asked.

"Yes. Why?"

"I met your Italian this morning," Megan said. "He told us you put him up last night after his apartment was broken into. How's he doing?"

"He's fine, I think." Kate could only guess, but telling his story seemed to have unburdened him. "And before you get any big ideas, he slept on the sofa."

"So, the man shows up at your door looking for comfort, and you put him on the couch? What were you *thinking*?"

"Megan, stop. I'm not ready. You know that." Kate envisioned herself leading Lorenzo upstairs and wrapping herself around him. It had been a long time since she'd been with a man.

"I want you to be happy," Megan said.

"I thought I could be happy with George but look where that got me."

"Not a fair comparison, and you know it."

Kate sliced off a wedge of sweetbread. "Here, try this."

Megan laughed. "You bake now?"

"Lorenzo. His mother had a bakery where he grew up in Italy." Kate cut a slice for herself. "He's invited me to go back with him."

Kate thought again of Lorenzo's arms around her. That moment when she honestly believed he was about to kiss her and that part of her that wanted it. But not like that. Not when he was so vulnerable.

"He invited you to Italy?" Megan took a bite of the sweetbread. "God, this is amazing!"

"Well, I kind of invited myself. There's a big story here. I know there is. I just don't know how I'm going to be able to afford the trip to write it."

Megan wiped crumbs from her mouth. "The paper?"

"I quit last night."

"Holy shit! So, okay—this is big."

"I had no choice. When Walker told me I couldn't do a follow-up, I challenged him, and he promptly demoted me. I need this story, Megan. My career depends on it."

"Freelance?" Megan asked.

"Be honest—am I dreaming to think I can do this?" asked Kate. Confidence had never been part of her character.

"Someday, you'll be a household name like Maureen Dowd." Megan reached out with a hug, her pregnant belly pressing against Kate. "We can help. A loan, you know?"

"I couldn't."

"Think about it," Megan said, stuffing one last bite of sweetbread into her mouth.

"Where's Briley?"

"Preschool. I get a whole two hours to myself twice a week. Speaking of which," Megan checked her watch, "I gotta go." Kate glanced at the clock on the stove. It was after three. What's been taking Lorenzo so long?

She watched Megan dart across the shared driveway. She'd already rejected her offer. She had a little in savings and two credit cards. That should be enough. It had to be. And the story would be written, whether for The Oregonian or some other paper. It was an opportunity that was too good to pass up.

Kate went down the hall to her office and found her passport in a folder mingled with Polaroid pictures and postcards of white, sandy beaches and colorful umbrellas. Memories of an ill-fated Fijian honeymoon. With fingers crossed, she opened the passport. Not expired.

Her phone rang a moment later, and she grinned when she heard Lorenzo's voice. "Well, hello there, detective. Did you get everything sorted out?" She glanced over her shoulder at the digital clock on her desk.

"I swung by the apartment," Lorenzo said.

So that's what took so long. "That must have been hard."

"Yeah. What a mess. Buddy taped it off as a crime scene but let me slip by to grab a few things for the trip."

"The sergeant approved your—vacation?" said Kate.

"Heh," he laughed. "They couldn't refuse me."

"Will you be much longer? Should I get dinner started?"

"One night on your sofa, and we're playing house?" Lorenzo laughed. "I'm on my way, but let's go out."

"Yes, all right," Kate said, smiling. "I get it—table and chairs and all that."

A tea candle flickered between them at their table for two as Lorenzo explained how he'd gotten his leave of absence. "After they looked into the break-in, Monroe said it was mandatory, and that I should take all the time I need."

"I'll join you as long as my credit card holds out."

"Oh, Kate. If this is a burden . . ."

"You can't ditch me so quickly, detective. You don't know how thrifty I can be."

"I've been to your house, rummaged through your kitchen, and slept on your only piece of furniture. I know how thrifty you can be." Of course, it wasn't the *only* piece of furniture, but he hadn't seen her bed, so she let it go.

"So, detective, what's the plan? Where do we begin our search?"

"Everything seems to spring from Genoa. So how about we start there? We'll need to be careful, though. If Marco finds out I'm after him, he'll be more intent on getting me out of the picture for good." His eyes narrowed. "And you. He proved that with Ella." Lorenzo set his fork on his plate. "Maybe we need to rethink this."

Kate locked eyes with him. "Don't you dare, mister. I'm going, like it or not." Though he didn't need her to go with him, she allowed herself to hope he wanted her to.

"I . . ." Lorenzo shook his head, but Kate could see by his growing smile that she'd reached him. "I like it."

When they returned to the house, Lorenzo went to Kate's office to book their tickets. She went upstairs to sort through her clothes, setting aside a few items for the trip before joining him. She immediately noticed the answering machine's flashing light and pushed play.

"Kate! It's George. Why the fuck don't you answer my emails?" *Click*. Again: "Kate! Listen! What about the house?" *Click*. Again: "Katie, be reasonable. We need to talk about this!" She reached across Lorenzo and unplugged the answering machine.

"The office is *closed*!"

Kate turned and stomped into the hall. Then her cell phone rang. "Oh, for crying out loud!" she screamed. "Leave me alone!" Lorenzo took the phone from her and shut it off before she could smash it into tiny bits or chuck it out the window.

"It's none of my business, but George seems determined. Maybe you could—"

"Don't start." Kate crossed her arms and leaned back against the door frame in the narrow hall. She didn't want to talk about George. She didn't even want to *think* about him. "I can't wait to be out of his reach."

Lorenzo handed her phone back and stuffed his hands into his pockets. "I booked our tickets. We fly into Milan the day after tomorrow, then take the train into Genoa." A little grin tugged at his mouth. "Is that far enough?" There was something about the even tone of Lorenzo's voice and his steady gaze that soothed her.

Kate took a deep breath, feeling calmer now. "Thank you," she said, then winced. "How much?"

"Don't worry, it's not extravagant. We'll sort it out later."

"Milan, Italy. I can't believe it." She yawned and glanced up the stairs. Lorenzo followed her gaze. Kate remembered Megan's words. *So, the man shows up at your door looking for comfort and you put him on the couch?* Kate met Lorenzo's deep blue eyes, reconsidering her choice with more of an open mind. Not now. Maybe soon.

"Good night, Lorenzo."

"*Dormi bene*, Kate."

***

The next morning, Lorenzo had already been for a run and folded his blankets on the sofa when Kate walked in on him making coffee.

He lopped off a slice of the day-old sweet bread and handed it to her.

"I need to pick up a few more things."

"Back at your apartment?"

His brow furrowed into tow deep valleys. "No, I was so overwhelmed yesterday, I ..."

"Shopping, then? I'm in."

Kate soon learned that Lorenzo's idea of clothes shopping was a grab-and-go race to the finish line. "Meier and Frank is designed for lingering," she said, chasing behind him through the department store. "We have all day!" But he bounced from here to there—stopping only long enough to check the price tags.

As Lorenzo paid for his items, Kate tossed a pair of boxer shorts onto the sales counter. Lorenzo looked up from his wallet, noticing the unusual pattern.

"Windmills?" He shook his head with an embarrassed grin.

"Seemed appropriate." Kate looked around, seeking alternatives to the gray shirt and brown sweater combination he'd chosen.

"This is all I need," Lorenzo said. "Honestly."

Kate pulled the sweater from the counter and held it up to her own frame with a wink. Lorenzo took it from her and stuffed it in the bag, along with the other items.

***

That night, the pair sat companionably in front of the fireplace, listening to the local jazz station and sipping Merlot as Lorenzo described what he remembered of Genoa and his home in Manarola.

"Will we see your family?" she asked. He squirmed, and Kate turned to face him. "Your sister? Your son? Your . . ."

"Yes, yes, I know what a family is." He glared at her. "I'm struggling with that."

"Would you rather see them on your own?"

"It's not that. It's difficult, you know? It's been so long."

"Do they know you're coming?"

"No. I want to keep them out of it until I've dealt with Marco."

Kate looked at the empty wine glass in his hand, then drained the splash remaining in her own, trying to put herself in his shoes.

It wasn't hard. She hadn't seen her folks since the wedding. That was on her. She'd allowed George to ruin every good thing in her life, and it was past time to remedy that.

With a firm nod, she said, "It'll be fine." She took their wine glasses to the kitchen and returned to find him reaching for the bedding. "Lorenzo," she began, unsure how to broach another subject she'd been pondering. A subject that made her heart race.

"Yes?" he said, holding a folded blanket in his arms like a child's teddy bear. The boyish pose made him look even more endearing.

"You're sure you're comfortable here? I mean—did you have

something else in mind, you know, when you came here the other night?"

Yes?

He stared at her, his blue eyes searching, the slightest hint of a grin tugging at the corner of his mouth. "Well, honestly, I wasn't thinking at all that night."

"Okay—so," she said, turning away, and then back, while she burned with embarrassment. "It's not that I . . ." Wasn't interested? Eye contact was impossible. "Never mind." Why was this so difficult? She *was* interested.

The grin blossomed across his face, and it was his turn to blush. Now she felt more embarrassed about bringing it up. He'd been nothing but professional since they'd met. How could she assume he had any other motive? If it hadn't been for Megan's suggestion, she would never have mentioned it—but since then, it was all she could think about.

Lorenzo glanced at the sofa and shrugged. "This is fine." No?

Kate reached idly for his pillow. "Tomorrow will be plush hotel beds and Italian TV. Oh, Italian music, Italian *food*."

"Looking forward to that, are you?" He unfurled the blanket onto the sofa.

"I'm looking forward to *all* of it," Kate said, tossing Lorenzo's pillow at him. Did she realize what she was getting herself into? Yes, no, maybe so.

CHAPTER NINE

Lorenzo

It had been a hectic morning. Megan, Thomas, and Briley insisted on seeing them off at the curb, the cab waiting patiently while they said their goodbyes.

"It's a long flight," said Thomas. The statement of the obvious made Lorenzo smile. "You've got good company, though." *Also true,* Lorenzo thought, looking over at Kate in a stylish dress and overcoat. It was the first time since the opera he had seen her dressed up, wearing jewelry.

Briley bounded up to her with a hug that suggested he expected never to see her again. "I'll be back before you know it," she told him. Lorenzo felt a deep emotional tug. That pang of guilt or shame—the sting of self-reproach that lived right under the surface. The open wound he'd inflicted upon himself.

Suddenly, an Audi pulled in front of the cab. A man got out, red-faced and furious, storming up to Kate and grabbing her arm. Briley jumped back and ran to his mother.

"I've called my lawyer," George said, then glanced from her to the driver loading the suitcases into the back of the cab. "Where are you going?"

"Piss off, George," Kate hollered, pulling away. Lorenzo stepped up behind her in two strides.

George gawped at Lorenzo. "Who the fuck are you?"

"Detective Lorenzo Rotondo." He figured his full title held more authority. "I'm a friend of Kate's." He put an arm around her waist and gently drew her away from George toward the waiting cab. For the first time since knowing Kate, Lorenzo didn't worry about someone getting the wrong idea.

As George made for his car, he lofted a departing shot. "If you don't pay up, the house is mine. Got it?"

Kate fidgeted with the pale blue scarf draped around her neck while the plane taxied out onto the runway.

"Relax," Lorenzo said. "Remember what Thomas said? It's a long flight."

"Right." She released the scarf, then grabbed up the extra length of seat belt, repeatedly rolling it up and flattening it out as the flight attendants instructed them about using oxygen masks, floatation devices, and emergency exits.

The 747 sported two columns of two seats on either side and a bank of four through the center. It was a full flight, and the foul scent of jet fuel infused the air. Sitting in coach wasn't ideal. Lorenzo reached up and twisted the knob for more air, then took Kate's hand on the shared armrest and squeezed it. She looked at him and smiled weakly.

"I hate this part. I'll be fine in a bit." She flicked off her heels and pushed them to the side.

They were seated near the wing. The jet engines roared, the flaps tilting into position. As the plane sped up for takeoff, Kate gripped the armrests. Then they were airborne—and just as Kate had suggested, she began to calm.

The beverage cart arrived once the jet reached its cruising altitude. Lorenzo requested two bottles of water—then, at the last moment, asked about getting some wine.

"It's five o'clock somewhere," he joked, twisting open the miniature wine bottles and pouring them into their plastic cups. "*Salute.*" It wasn't as bad as he'd expected. He took another sip.

Kate did, too. "Thank you. I'm a nervous flyer anyway, but . . ."

"George?" said Lorenzo, thinking about the surprise visit that morning. "I get the feeling he still loves you." He sipped more wine.

Kate laughed in disbelief, then set down her cup and looked out the window at the snow-capped Cascade mountains below, with Mount St. Helens blowing off steam in the distance. Lorenzo nudged her knee, encouraging her to speak. She sighed. "George was everything I thought I wanted," she said, leaning back in her seat, her gaze still fixed on the landscape.

"It's like that when we're young," said Lorenzo. "We see only what we want to."

"I wasn't *that* young, detective. Just foolish. I wore that ring like it made me a better person—a different, more-important-than-that-other-girl person. I quickly learned that wedding rings do not hold superpowers. It did not make me more valuable or more relevant. And it certainly did *nothing* for George."

"What does that mean?" Lorenzo said, knowing the power of the oath he'd taken with Ella. He'd worn his wedding band for several years after her death before reluctantly abandoning it to his tin box of memories.

"I never seemed to meet his expectations. I was always on the wrong end of things. Even when I agreed with him, he'd find fault. He pulled me apart at the seams, Lorenzo—stitch by stitch, until there was nothing left. No love, and certainly no respect." Kate paused, sipping her wine. "Then one night, he came home very late, very drunk, stinking of cigarettes and cologne, and told me what a worthless piece of shit I was. I thought he wouldn't remember it in the morning—but he remembered. I thought he'd apologize, but nope, he just piled on—and I snapped. I told him to go to hell and . . ." A grin slowly spread across her face. "He left."

"George left *you?* I thought it was the other way around."

"You're teasing me."

"No. Those desperate phone calls and the stunt he pulled in front of your house this morning, literally crying out for your attention like a spurned lover."

Kate laughed. "Spurned lover?"

"Besides, with the way he treated you, you had every right to walk away."

Kate tilted her head as if realizing something for the first time. "I think he'd expected me to fight it, you know? Come to my senses and run after him. But I just watched him drive off." She took another sip of wine and retreated into her own thoughts. Lorenzo gazed past her out the window, where the Cascades had receded from view.

In his line of work, Lorenzo often encountered men like George. Men with low self-esteem found power in abusing others. Whether physical or psychological, domestic abuse takes its toll, and the kindest women get the brunt of it.

There was a hum of conversation from the seats behind them. A child's voice. "How much longer?"

"Go to sleep," the mother said. "Here's your bunny."

Lorenzo turned to Kate. "Tell me about your family."

"No, it's your turn."

"You already know too much about me, Sancho," he said, grinning.

"Ugh. All right. Well, I have an older brother. Glenn. He's an instructor at the naval academy in Maryland—happily married, two kids. One son's in high school, the other studies at Columbia. He's the ideal son, husband, father." Lorenzo heard the self-reproach in her voice. "My parents still live in Colorado."

"In a small town," Lorenzo added.

Kate smiled. "You remembered. Burton is an hour's drive from Denver, but it's not on the map." Lorenzo raised an eyebrow. "That's a long, weird story," she said.

"We have time." Lorenzo reclined his seat as far as it would go—not far enough. Kate did the same, trying to get comfortable before turning to face him.

"My parents lived in Chicago when they were young. They hung out in funky coffee houses—you know, reading poetry, playing music. A real Allen Ginsberg kind of thing. One night they talked a handful of their friends into pitching in to buy a 600-acre farm in Colorado." She looked at Lorenzo, but he didn't bat an eye. "They named it Burton."

"So, it's not actually a town, this Burton."

"Not actually, no. Just a Burt—my dad. There's ego for you." She glanced at him again and sipped her wine. "They built a barn and living quarters, plowed the fields, and started planning for harvest. Before they knew it, they had a commune."

"A farm?"

"Yes."

"There must have been a town nearby. Where did you go to school?" Lorenzo shifted in his seat, then lifted the armrest between them to get a little more space.

"Our parents taught us. Mom taught art. Dad taught science and history. Carla, another resident, taught us to write. It's because of her I became a journalist."

"So, how many families did the farm support? I mean, did you grow all your own food?" The novelty fascinated him.

Kate smiled. "You ask a lot of questions. Have you ever considered becoming a journalist?"

"Detectives also ask many questions." Lorenzo smiled and tapped his cup to hers.

Bump. "Excuse me," said a middle-aged woman navigating the aisle toward the rear of the plane. Lorenzo glanced up at her and pulled in his elbow.

"I know," Kate said. "The farm sounds idyllic, doesn't it? A community based on shared values, unrestricted by the powerful influences of a stress-filled society, yadda, yadda. We wanted for nothing. But . . ." Kate sipped her wine. "It didn't suit everyone. There were six families in the beginning. All the founders are still there and working the farm as best they can at their age. Some kids stayed. Some moved off—like Glenn and me. Others left, then returned with a partner or spouse. I'm guessing there are probably twelve couples now. I don't keep up as I should. I haven't been back since George and I were married."

"Not once?"

"You're not exactly in a position to criticize, detective." There was something sensuous about the way her teeth rested on her lower lip when she said *detective*, drawing his attention to her mouth.

"Fair enough." He sat up straight as the flight attendant passed by, asking them if they wanted more wine.

"Please. More water too." The attendant handed him two more single-serve bottles.

Lorenzo poured the wine. "You know why I haven't been home. What's your excuse?"

"My dad thought George was . . ." she began. Lorenzo raised an eyebrow, and Kate smirked. "He thought George was an ass. And he was right." She sipped her water, then drank the bottle half empty. "When I brought George home to meet the folks, he made fun of it all. The pigs, the hens, the hayfield that sent his allergies through the roof. Nothing was sacred, including me. I'd laughed it off, but my dad wanted to punch him. He said, '*That's* the guy you're going to grow old with?' I should have listened. Basically, George wasn't welcome on the farm, and I never returned simply to prove some stupid point." Kate turned to Lorenzo with an embarrassed grin. "Dad warned me the night before the wedding. He told me that marriage is for keeps. He said I needed to be sure I was marrying George for all the right reasons."

"What did he mean by that?"

Kate shrugged. "I was thirty-two. My friends were getting married and having kids. I felt like I needed to keep up and didn't think it through beyond that damn ring. Stupid." She paused. "I married George for all the *wrong* reasons."

"You haven't answered my question."

"Why I haven't been home?" Kate tugged at her scarf and looked over at Lorenzo. "Pride?"

"And?"

"And—judgment. I screwed up. My dad was right. I only have myself to blame."

"You should call him," Lorenzo said.

Kate frowned. "I know. I need to make peace with him, at least for my mom's sake."

"No, for *your* sake," Lorenzo said. "Take it from me." Kate grimaced, and he immediately wished he could take his words back. "I'm sorry," he added. "It's none of my business."

Across the aisle, Lorenzo noticed a young woman, twentyish, her baseball cap tilted low over her head. He could tell she was watching him—them. It made him wonder how he and Kate appeared to others. Did they look like a couple, despite the twelve years that separated them?

"If it makes you feel any better, I talk to my mom all the time," Kate said.

"What's she like?" Lorenzo stifled a yawn—he wasn't bored, but the wine was making him drowsy.

"She's beautiful, strong, generous to a fault, and creative. She sculpts, weaves, and paints beautiful watercolors that she used to sell at the art festival in Denver." Kate sipped her wine and emptied the last of her second bottle into her cup. "I miss her."

"Mm," said Lorenzo. He understood that kind of longing. He closed his eyes, thinking of his own mother; his sister, Muriel; and the unread letters that lived in the tin box he'd left at Kate's.

In the silence that followed, Lorenzo drifted off to sleep. The next thing he knew, Kate's soft curls were brushing against his face as she reached over him for their meals. Flustered awake, Lorenzo grabbed the trays, excited to see warm rolls included with the meal. He ripped his in half, then brought it to his nose and inhaled.

"Like the bread, do you?" said Kate, smiling as he took a mouthful.

Lorenzo grinned and nodded. "It's a sickness," he mumbled, chewing. "Even airline bread triggers wonderful memories for me."

He washed down his mouthful with a splash of wine, thinking of the warm, sweet scent of baking that had filled his childhood home. How to describe it to her? "We'd all pitch in on market day—Muriel, Antonio, and the others, loading the cart or setting up the stand."

"You have a big family?"

"I'm the oldest of eight."

"That's big, all right. You mentioned a sister?"

"Yes—Muriel. She's closest in age to me." He paused. "We were like a separate family, often enlisted as surrogate parents to the others. I think that's why we became so close."

"You must miss her," Kate said as if she'd reached in and pulled the most prominent thought from his head.

Lorenzo nodded. "We keep in touch some, but I've not held up my share." An understatement. He tore a bite from the roll and popped it into his mouth, then painstakingly brushed the crumbs away—as if that could remove the stain of guilt.

They took up more controversial issues while finishing their meal, like the politics of war and religion, the Taliban's grip on Islam, and how American politicians used Christianity as a tool.

"You can't equate the Taliban with American politics," said Lorenzo.

"No? Just look at the dismantling of social welfare and public health by politicians who tout their faith as their most valuable asset."

"*That's* how American politics is like the Taliban?"

"They use religion to manipulate the population. The Taliban use sharia law. We use the Ten Commandments, splitting hairs to suit our purposes. Take abortion, for example."

Lorenzo frowned. "Go on," he said, wondering where she was going with this.

"The Christian right took one issue and made it the cornerstone of their party. Abortion should be between a woman and her conscience, not a woman and her political leaders."

Lorenzo shook his head. "I have my own misgivings about the Catholic church, Kate, but I believe that life begins at conception. And this wouldn't even be an issue if more women held to a religious, moral code. The pro-abortion people—"

"No one is *pro*-abortion, Lorenzo. It's a choice—sometimes the best and only choice a woman has."

"It's a *false* choice," Lorenzo insisted, raising his voice. "There are risks and consequences. Lives are at stake."

"Yes—the life of a woman forced to raise and care for a child she is unprepared for or cannot afford. An unwanted child."

"God's child."

"And I suppose you go to church every Sunday to maintain your religious, moral code."

Her remark stung. At first, he wasn't sure how to respond.

"Not lately, no," he said, finally. "But I still go from time to time. It grounds me—reminds me of what's important in the world. I'm not merely referring to belief in a higher power, but community and fellowship. It's like—think about the way you grew up. Wouldn't you feel at home in a similar environment?"

"No. That's why I left."

"That's not why you left. You left to seek knowledge beyond what they could teach you. Knowledge of the world. You have that now."

"Perhaps you're right," she conceded.

"It was just a guess," he said, glancing away. He felt suddenly ashamed, wondering if he was becoming as bossy as George had been. What gave him the right?

They discussed the election with a more congenial spirit. For different reasons, both supported the Democrats—though Lorenzo couldn't vote.

"Lorenzo, you've chosen to live and work in the United States. Why not become a citizen?"

"It wouldn't change anything. Americans vote the way they vote. This Electoral College—it's ridiculous. My vote, your vote—they mean nothing."

"Well, when we're done with this trip, you can stay in Italy then," she said. Lorenzo shut her up with a piercing stare.

"Let's say *you* take a liking to my country and choose to stay," he said, trying a different approach. "Would you cease to be an American? Would you sever all ties with your identity? We never know these things. I believed I'd only be away for a few months. Then a year went by. I had a job, a lease, responsibilities. Two years, three, then four; it just got away from me."

"It's called putting down roots."

"Roots?" Lorenzo thought about his rented apartment, rented furniture, and his failure to form any lasting relationships. "No, just an excuse not to face the fact that my stay in the US was supposed to be temporary. And now that so much time has gone by, I dread the reception I'll get." He picked at the remaining food on his tray. "I'm realistic, Kate. Emilio has every reason to hate me. Muriel has every reason to resent me. And my parents have every reason to disown me."

"I'm sorry. This isn't easy for you."

The flight attendant pushed her cart up the aisle collecting trays and garbage.

"Next topic, Katie."

She frowned. "*Katie?*"

"All right. Kate." It had been worth a try.

"No, it's fine. I *like* how you say it." She grinned at him—and suddenly it was as if they hadn't been arguing at all. "Say it again."

He shook his head. "You're teasing me."

"No, really. The way you say my name. The way you say anything, actually."

"Katie," he said. "*Un bel nome per una bella donna.*" He smiled, then sat back and looked out the cabin window. Ella had had a beautiful name, too: *Isabella Martina Fiore. Fiore* means flower in Italian. Marco took that flower from him.

Lorenzo frowned. What would stop Marco from taking Kate as well?

PART 2

ITALY—WINTER, 2004

CHAPTER TEN

Kate

Kate felt grateful to have Lorenzo at her side as they navigated the Milan airport, caught a cab to the train station, and booked their tickets. All the signs were posted in English as well as Italian, but he zipped past them as if he did this every day.

They boarded the train alongside businessmen, tourists, and tradesmen. Their car was half full. A young family sat in front of them—their daughter so small Kate couldn't even see her head over the seatback, though she could hear the steady stream of questions. It reminded her of little Briley.

Lorenzo's head swiveled around as he took in their travel companions.

"Expecting someone?" Kate joked. But Lorenzo only nodded slightly.

"You never can be too careful," he said, with a grim expression.

Once underway to Genoa, Kate gazed out the window at the passing olive groves, vineyards, and farms between the small towns and villages. Though not flush with the green of growing season, the landscape, illuminated by the midday sun, captured her heart.

"It's beautiful," she said, removing her coat.

"Yes, this is okay—but there are more beautiful areas."

"Cinque Terre pride speaking?"

Lorenzo laughed. "*Si. Assolutamente.* Best wine. Best pasta. Best seafood."

"Are all Italians like that? My tomatoes are better than yours?"

"Tomatoes, cheese, wine, and oil. Compared to the US, it's a small country, but each region has its own dialect, holidays, and traditions. North versus south, and east versus west."

He went on to refer to someone or something making the competitiveness worse—Kate didn't catch the word, but it sounded like *gaucho*—and then mentioned soccer. Kare furrowed her brows and leaned forward.

"Wait—*gaucho* is soccer?"

"No, it's *calcio*," he said. "Cal-cho. Do you hear it?" It still sounded like *gaucho* to her.

When the train pulled into Genoa, Lorenzo looked down at her shoes. "Do you have something else you could wear?" Kate had chosen heels and a cream-colored dress for the journey, as if it were some kind of glamorous trans-Atlantic excursion. Who was she trying to impress?

She glanced at Lorenzo, and exchanged her heels for clean white Nikes, then followed him through the train station into the busy Genoa streets. Cars, vans, motorcycles, and delivery trucks all zoomed noisily past as they walked toward the port in search of a hotel.

They did not have to look far. Many beautiful, large, historic hotels lined the road on either side. None resembled anything as humble as a Holiday Inn. Given Kate's limited resources, economy mattered.

Lorenzo appeared to know where he was going as he guided her into the heart of the city, along the ancient narrow streets, dodging exceedingly compact cars as they navigated the confounding lefts and rights, passing under stone archways and dark alcoves until hitting upon a lively piazza. Here, musicians performed, children played, and lovers cuddled on benches with the afternoon sun warming their faces. The ancient city was colorful and alive.

"Are you hungry?" Lorenzo asked. She was hungry, and cold, and extremely tired. Neither of them had slept much on the flight. When Kate nodded, Lorenzo cleared a path through pigeons and seagulls across the piazza to a *ristorante* on the other side.

They were greeted by a waiter who introduced himself as Paulo. Kate almost mistook him for a young woman, with his lean body and his shoulder-length hair, tucked gracefully behind his ears. Paulo sat them at a booth near the rear of the restaurant, where Lorenzo had a full view of the front door and windows. Kate realized that he still suspected someone was following them. It made her uneasy to think that Alfonso would waltz in and—no, not Alfonso. It would be another man. The sort who would turn Lorenzo's apartment upside down. Or the sort who would lay in wait for them to let down their guard, and then, when they least expected it . . .

Her thoughts were interrupted when Lorenzo called the waiter over to their table.

Their friendly chit-chat was joined by several cooks and included grandiose gestures that escalated into something of an argument that ended in laughter. Kate understood none of it.

"I want to learn Italian," she said excitedly once they were left alone. Lorenzo laughed and said something that she couldn't understand. She protested. "I'm not joking."

"I wasn't either," he said, grinning and narrowing his eyes playfully. Kate scowled and opened her menu, then promptly closed it again.

"Paolo knows of an apartment available nearby," Lorenzo continued. "It belongs to his cousin, who rents it out when he's out of town. They assured me we would have privacy there for as long as we need it. And it's cheap."

"It sounds too good to be true."

"I told them this was a romantic rendezvous."

"You didn't!" Kate looked over her shoulder at Paulo, who winked at her. Lorenzo flashed a shy smile. If she'd blinked, she would have missed it.

Paulo reappeared at their table. Kate's stomach rumbled.

"Are you ready to order?" Lorenzo asked.

Kate reopened the menu and pointed to the one word she could recognize. Pasta.

It was midday in Genoa, and she tried to calculate the time difference from Portland. Was it nine hours or ten? Was this breakfast or lunch? It made no difference. When her entrée finally hit the table, she practically fell on it.

"This bread!" Kate moaned. "This sausage!"

Lorenzo laughed. "Pace yourself."

"Oh, and the pasta." She plunged her fork into the creamy bow-tie pasta.

"*Farfalle*," Lorenzo said. "It means butterfly."

"Farafala," Kate said.

Lorenzo grinned. "No, watch my lips, FAR-fall-e."

"Far-A-fall-e."

"You'll get it, eventually."

"Butterfly," she said with a firm nod.

Paulo reverently laid a pair of keys beside their bill and whispered something to Lorenzo. Maybe she couldn't understand the words, but she recognized the implication considering their supposed *romantic rendezvous*.

With bellies full and a complimentary bottle of wine from Paulo, Kate and Lorenzo headed out into the piazza and stopped to listen to a street musician playing in front of an open mandolin case. His leathered face turned to them with a beaming smile.

Lorenzo bowed his head to Kate's ear. "He's playing *Vieni al Mare*. My father loved this song. He was always singing or humming it. He played it on the old mandolin handed down from his father."

Kate smiled, thinking maybe his homecoming wouldn't be as difficult as he'd imagined.

When the song ended, Lorenzo turned the apartment keys over in his hand. "Ready to move on?" Kate turned up the collar of her trench coat, looked around at the piazza's carnival atmosphere, and nodded. As much as she wanted to stay, she was curious about the apartment and longed to lie down. Lorenzo tossed a coin into the open case and continued walking to the next street, which ran parallel to a long stretch of parkland along the harbor where docks jutted into the water like fingers on a glove, each with a variety of boats tied up in their slips.

Kate shivered. "I thought it would be warmer here," she said.

"In November? No." Lorenzo stuffed his hands into the pockets of his wool coat. Unlike her, he'd been prepared for the damp chill.

"You could have warned me," Kate said, pulling her coat tighter around her. He looked at her apologetically as they rounded the next corner. Then she stopped and pointed. "Look, you can see the ocean."

Lorenzo tilted his head. "Not exactly. What you see there is Porto Antico. Beyond that is the Mediterranean Sea, and if you're adventurous, you could thread the needle through the Strait of Gibraltar to the Atlantic Ocean."

Kate blushed. She'd known all this once, studying geography with her father, pouring over maps of exotic locales like the Mediterranean Sea, wondering if she'd ever get there.

They turned down the busy road flanking the harbor—the honking horns and squealing brakes grated on Kate in her sleep-deprived state—and walked another block to where Lorenzo said the apartment should have been. He stopped and rubbed his chin.

"I must have heard him wrong," Lorenzo said, staring into a bookstore window. Kate gazed up at the ornate windows above the shop and the thickly painted blue door to her right, blistered and flaking. She pulled on his sleeve.

Lorenzo nodded and opened the door. They lugged their suitcases up the stairs to another door at the top, which Lorenzo unlocked with the second key and pushed.

The small apartment smelled stagnant. The shades were closed, and the heat was off.

She left her roller bag at the door and laid her backpack on the countertop bar that separated the galley kitchen from the sitting room. There was a small red sofa at one end of the room, and a petite leather club chair with a side table polished to a gleaming shine. Kate stepped up to one of the two windows. She pulled the ring on the roll-up shade, and it snapped up. "Ahh. Lorenzo, look at this." He stepped up beside her as she stared fixedly at the boats in the harbor. Their sails and flags fixed to tall masts flapped wildly in the wind. Fishing boats boasted enormous nets sagging from their booms. Beyond the harbor, a blue sea sparkled in the sunlight beneath a cloudless azure sky.

Years ago, in Astoria, she used to watch ships and barges push through the mouth of the Columbia River. She'd walked along the commercial piers as fishing boats offloaded their catch. But Genoa was like that Oregon port city on steroids. Cruise ships, cargo ships, and hundreds of recreational craft dotted the many-fingered ports as far as the eye could see.

As Lorenzo inspected the apartment, Kate ducked into the bathroom. Shower, toilet, sink—everything within arm's reach. When she emerged, she found Lorenzo in the sitting room, standing with hands on hips, in front of an open bedroom door.

"Everything in this place is so *teeny*," she said, walking past him, and then swinging her suitcase onto the full-size bed beside a small chest of drawers. Just the one bed? Just the one room? She popped her head out of the bedroom to confirm it was the only one.

"Lorenzo?"

"Let's step out and explore," he said. "It's best to push through jet-lag." Exhausted, Kate looked longingly at the bed, but agreed, happy to postpone that awkward conversation.

CHAPTER ELEVEN

Lorenzo

That night, Lorenzo insisted Kate take the single bedroom. She didn't appear pleased about the arrangement—which confused him but also encouraged him, in a way that gave him a sliver of hope for future intimacy.

He insisted it was for her protection. He'd be closer to the door should they have an intruder—a grim possibility, considering what happened to his apartment in Portland.

Kate insisted they were adults and could share a bed platonically. He agreed it was possible, but he wasn't about to compromise their relationship—whatever sort of relationship it was. Just friends? He was still figuring that out.

She plucked a blanket off the bed with a huff and tossed Lorenzo the second pillow before her long-awaited shower. Unfortunately, his own shower did nothing to help him sleep—nor did the many hours he'd pushed through his jet lag.

He twisted on the love seat—his knees tucked up one moment,

his legs dangling over the side the next—thinking about their long walk to the outdoor market to grab a bit of the local scene and a few groceries for the apartment. On their return, they had stopped into the bookstore below their apartment, where he picked up the local newspaper and Kate bought an Italian phrase book.

There was no way around it—the love seat was uncomfortable. Lorenzo winced at the tingling in his arm and the stabbing pain between his shoulders, watching the shadow play on the stucco ceiling. Sounds of traffic and far-off sirens and boat horns joined occasional voices and laughter that filtered up from the sidewalk below.

He snatched up his pants and sweater from the floor and balled them up under his knees. It didn't help.

He closed his eyes and prayed for sleep, digesting the events of the last few days—the Robin's Nest, Monica Bower, and Alfonso Robini. Still, there were so many pieces missing. He'd felt great relief in telling his story to Kate—her deep compassion had soothed him. But what *had* he expected, when he'd gone to her house? If she'd taken him to her bed, he would have gone willingly. But she hadn't. Faced with the kind of truth that comes in the sleepless hours of the night, he concluded that he wanted more from her than she from him. He would respect that. That's why he was twisted up on a loveseat in a stranger's apartment.

Then his mind drifted to Ella. Her doe-like eyes, beautiful smile, and zest for life. Her lifeless body had looked like a stranger laid out in the coffin, with her hair parted on the wrong side and heavy rouge on her cheeks. Lorenzo twisted in the love seat, thinking of how he'd failed to keep Ella safe. He should have heeded Marco's warning. How he hated that man. How he longed for justice. Or was it revenge? *Sleep, damn it.* For hours, grief and loss haunted his dreams. A woman's voice called out, but he couldn't understand what she was saying. Ella?

He steered his thoughts back to Kate—so youthful, feisty, and intelligent. He pictured her soft blue eyes and thick lashes and her lips that burned whenever her freckled cheeks blushed with emotion.

In a moment of wakefulness, Lorenzo imagined her sleeping in the next room, the remaining cover tucked under her chin, her face at rest, breathing softly with her lips parted just so. Lorenzo wondered, not for the first time, what it would feel like to kiss those lips or run his fingers through her soft curls. He imagined her body pressed against his, as they made love in the dark.

The next morning, he woke drowsily, shielding his eyes from the sharp rays of sunlight beaming through the window. He rolled over to grab a few more minutes—and noticed Kate lying beside him in the bed.

He sat up with a jolt, wide-eyed. The *bed? Kate?*

"How did I get here?" he said, breathlessly trying to remember. Kate grinned and rose from the bed, wearing her pink pajama bottoms and a revealing T-shirt. As it was, the dream he'd awoken from had aroused him. Had she noticed? Now there she stood with the outline of her breasts as clear as if she wore nothing at all. Embarrassed, Lorenzo hastily covered his lap with an armload of bedding. It dawned on him that his pants were in the other room. "I'm sorry," he said. "This—well. I'm so sorry." Had he been sleepwalking? He hadn't done that since childhood.

Kate laughed. "Oh, Lorenzo, relax. I brought you in here."

"You did *what?*"

"I got up for a glass of water last night and saw you knotted up on that love seat. You looked miserable, so I whispered in your ear, and you followed me." It sounded innocent enough, but her grin was mischievous. "So, either we find another place to stay, or we have a friendly understanding." She came around to his side of the bed. "Personally, I like it here."

He looked away, avoiding her gaze. His dream—the memory of him with Kate, their bodies pressed together—was still fresh in his mind.

Kate left him to get the coffee started, and Lorenzo waited a few minutes to compose himself before leaving the relative privacy of the bedsheets to retrieve his pants from the living room, then disappeared into the bathroom without another word. He emerged to find Kate standing at the door with a tiny white cup of espresso. Still feeling embarrassed, Lorenzo accepted the cup and sipped, unable to meet her eyes.

Kate slipped past him into the bathroom as he crossed into the kitchen with his coffee. He picked at some sliced fruit on the counter and whatever remained of the spice cake they'd brought home from the market the day before. The kitchen clock read eleven-thirty. He checked it against his watch and reached for yesterday's paper, which Kate had stacked neatly on a bar stool at the kitchen counter, and began rifling through, looking for a hotel or bed-and-breakfast. If worse came to worst, they could split up. Although, like Kate, he did like the tiny apartment over the bookstore. It had charm, a great location, and cost them only 100 euros a night. Split two ways, it was something they could both afford, and the open-ended stay suited Lorenzo, since he had no idea how long they'd be in Genoa. "Just drop off the keys when you leave," Paulo had said. "We'll settle up then." It would be a lot to give up.

He'd eaten the bulk of the fruit and finished a second espresso by the time Kate entered the kitchen, looking fresh and alert, dressed in jeans and a white cotton blouse. The soft blue scarf draped over her shoulders drew his attention to her eyes.

"Well, today's the day," she said. "Where do we begin—the art foundation or the insurance company?"

"First, we'll find another place to stay."

"Oh, Lorenzo, stop. We won't find anything this nice. The view, a kitchen, privacy—it's perfect."

He agreed. But *thinking* about being in the same bed and *being* in the same bed were completely different. He was at a loss to convey his embarrassment. Flustered, he picked up his brown sweater, which had fallen to the floor beside the love seat. He struggled to push his arm into the inverted sleeve and tossed it onto the sofa in frustration. Kate picked it up and straightened it, then put it on.

She giggled. "A perfect fit." It hung on her like a flour sack. "I think I'll keep it."

"Suit yourself." Didn't she understand? Did he have to spell it out for her? Lorenzo snatched his jacket from a hook on the wall, flung open the door, and tramped down the stairs, furthering his embarrassment in a juvenile display.

Kate stood at the top of the stairs. "Lorenzo!" He stopped before reaching the bottom door and looked up at her. She peeled the sweater off and went back for her denim jacket. He waited for her outside the door, then locked it behind her.

"I'm sorry," she said, breathing hard, as they passed the bookstore. "I didn't realize that would upset you so much."

"It's not about the sweater." Lorenzo sighed. "It's about—how I woke up."

"Oh—*that*," Kate said. So, she *had* noticed.

"Apologies, Kate. I'm not handling this well. Could we start over?"

Kate smiled. "Good morning, detective."

"*Buongiorno.*"

They returned to the piazza, surrounded by delectable aromas from every corner of the square, where food carts promoted their *caffè*, panini, or heaping portions of gelato under a dome of blue sky. Lorenzo hungered for it all. He and started with a toasted panino with salami, fresh mozzarella, and a thick layer of tangy red sauce. Kate went for the deep-fried risotto balls.

"Mmm." Her eyes widened with each bite. "Oh, that's good." Lorenzo didn't enjoy his sandwich nearly as much as watching Kate savor each bite of her fried risotto, happy to share in her pleasure as she bit through the hard shell and discovered the melted burrata cheese. It was a childhood favorite of his.

"Save room for gelato."

"I'm going to outgrow my entire wardrobe if we keep eating like this."

She took that back once they were on foot, scouting the beautiful city for a hotel that wouldn't break the bank, or a B&B with privacy. A mile in from the harbor, Kate pointed to a quaint corner hotel that sparked her interest. It was stone, like most of Genoa's old town, with peaked arches over the floor-to-ceiling windows and inlaid stone-carved tiles above the door. Kate threw open the door, and they stepped across the marble floors to the counter.

"What's your credit limit?" Lorenzo asked, grinning.

"Not nearly enough, but *look* at this place," Kate said.

They waited while the concierge finished with another guest—a mustached man who spoke English. American English.

As Lorenzo tried to remember where he'd seen the man, Kate nudged him with her elbow, pointing to a photo of a standard room. "Queen beds." She beamed, eyes twinkling. "Television." Lorenzo smiled. "Only two hundred American dollars a night." More than twice as expensive as their apartment. Double that for two rooms.

Lorenzo turned to the guest when the concierge left to answer the phone. "Nice day. Are you vacationing?"

The man collected his black cap from the counter and placed it on his head. "Something like that," he said. He turned to face Lorenzo with a broad grin. In the center of the cap was the trademark red-and-white pinwheel of the Portland Trail Blazers.

Lorenzo pulled Kate aside. "We have to go."

"What is it?" she asked. He glanced back at the man at the counter, then grabbed her arm and hurried outside.

"He was one of the men who picked up the crate at the port." Lorenzo's grip tightened as he led her around the corner. "He may have recognized me."

"What's he doing here?"

Lorenzo looked up and down the street. "There—look." He

pointed at a building at the end of the block, three stories high, with large windows and the dubious charm of a suburban storage facility. The sign outside read, *C. Robini Compagnia di Assicurazioni sulla Proprietà.* "C. Robini Property Insurance."

Kate looked up at the sign. "Robini."

"Alfonso."

Lorenzo led Kate to a nearby coffee shop with a narrow view of the insurance building.

"So, Marco runs the foundation, and Alfonso runs the insurance company," Kate said, dipping a biscuit into her tea.

"And endowments from the insurance company fund the foundation," Lorenzo added.

"And the man from the hotel ties Alfonso to the art."

"*Esatto.*"

"There he is!" said Kate excitedly. Alfonso emerged from the building with a cell phone fixed to his ear. A leggy woman, wearing stiletto heels and enough makeup to rival RuPaul, chased after him with a Doberman straining its leash ahead of her. Alfonso shooed her away and climbed into a green Jaguar.

Kate sniggered. "It's like a Benny Hill rerun."

"Benny Hill?"

"Never mind." She grabbed her coat off the back of her chair. "Can we give up on the hotel search and get back to our little love nest?"

"You have the wrong idea," said Lorenzo. He picked up their empty cups.

"You started it," she said, grinning. "You're the one who told the waiter it was a romantic rendezvous."

"Heh. Well, that *wasn't* what I had in mind." He shook his head, still a little embarrassed. "I hope you don't think this was some ploy, because I'm not that man." He tossed the cups into the open bin by the door.

"It's fine. We're grown-ups, right? So, we'll work it out." Kate sighed and followed him out the door. "I have to warn you, though—I'm a bed hog."

"And I snore."

"I noticed." They laughed nervously.

"Well then, that's settled. Friends?" Kate offered her hand, and he shook it, relieved to have it behind them—mostly.

CHAPTER TWELVE

Kate

The next morning, Kate peeled one eye open and peeked over to the other side of the bed. Empty. She felt both disappointed and relieved. She wondered if sharing a bed was such a good idea after all, despite the comfort of having Lorenzo so close—his musky scent, his security. She could have done without the snoring. At least Lorenzo wasn't as bad as George. No, she was grateful.

She stood at the bedroom door and saw Lorenzo standing at the kitchen counter. "Have you been up long?" She asked, stepping into the kitchen.

Lorenzo turned around and smiled. "A while. I've been thinking about that painting, you know?"

"Painting?" Kate retrieved a cup from the cabinet, rubbing the sleep from her eyes. "Oh, the university painting." She glanced out the sitting-room window, noticing their usual Mediterranean view was fogged in that morning.

He set his empty cup beside hers. He'd already showered. Kate smelled the clean on him, but his face bristled with a two-day beard, and he wore the gray shirt from the previous day.

"Do you still have that email address to contact the Rossetti's original owner?" he said. "We could pay a visit today if you're up for it." He filled the portafilter on the espresso maker and tamped it.

"It was a forwarded message from the publisher. I'll find it." Kate pulled the email up on her laptop and waited as her espresso sputtered to an end. Once Lorenzo had the address, he dashed off a quick email. While they waited for a reply, she studied her phrase book. "*Mi chiamo Kate*," she murmured. "*Mi chiamo Kate*."

"Do you plan on introducing yourself often?" Lorenzo grinned, and she scowled at him.

"*Mi chiamo Kate. Sono felice di conoscerti*."

Lorenzo leaned over her shoulder with a tender smile. "I'm pleased to meet you too."

"Back up. You're making me nervous." She pushed him away and began working on the days of the week. "*Lunedì, martedì . . .*"

The eventual reply suggested Sylvia DiCapo was willing to meet that afternoon. It included her contact information. So, after a shower and a light lunch, they caught a taxi to the other side of town, where tall buildings gave way to tall trees and large homes.

Sylvia DiCapo waited for them in front of her white stucco house. She wore her hair tied up in a tight bun and sandals despite the cold, damp weather.

"*Mi chiamo Kate. Sono felice di conoscerti*."

"Hello, Kate. I'm fluent in English, but I appreciate the effort. You must be Lorenzo." Lorenzo nodded. "Come, I've made coffee." Sylvia led them down the driveway to the kitchen door.

From the tile floor to the pressed tin ceiling, Sylvia's kitchen was like something out of *Architectural Digest*. She led them through a butler's pantry to the dining room and onward to a large sitting room with cathedral ceilings and tall windows. Lorenzo and Kate sat together on the flowered chintz sofa while Sylvia poured coffee into china cups. She offered cake and candied fruit, then sat down across from them with a satisfied sigh. "Such a day."

"It's been ages since I've been to *Genova*," Lorenzo said. "Has the jazz museum been here long? I've seen signs all over town for some big event next week."

"That? Oh, I don't know. There is an excellent jazz club in that piazza, though. Have you been?"

"Not yet," Lorenzo said.

"Genoa is a lovely city," Kate said, feeling out of place in this grand house. "So much to see."

"Yes, yes, and you would like to see my Rossetti," Sylvia said, beaming.

"We would," Lorenzo said. "But I'm sure you've been told that they've deceived you. This is not the original."

"Oh, but it *is*. Signore Robini has assured me of its authenticity. The cost of insuring it alone tells me all I need to know."

Kate and Lorenzo exchanged glances.

"No one's called you?" asked Lorenzo. Sylvia looked confused, so he went on. "It's why we're here, actually. The original turned up in the US."

"What? That's ridiculous."

Kate fished in her bag for the reply she'd received through the publisher and handed it to Sylvia.

"Oh, *that* call. Yes. I told him it was a mistake."

"Are you aware of the poem on the back of your painting?" asked Kate.

"Of course. Truth is, that's the whole reason I had it assessed. It's unique to Rossetti." Sylvia looked over Lorenzo's head to the next room. "Should we have a look?" She stood and led them into a large home office with heavy drapes on the windows and a wall of books. The remarkable painting dominated the opposite wall.

"*Bellissimo*," said Lorenzo, moving closer to the sensual painting.

"How long ago did you insure it?" Kate stepped close beside him, marveling at the vibrant reds and vivid blues, like the painting in Dr. Marshall's office.

"I purchased it at an auction ten years ago," Sylvia answered. "It went directly to Robini for an official assessment and returned to us later. They took great care to examine it and assured us of its authenticity."

"Could we see the documents?" Lorenzo asked.

Kate watched Sylvia's fists tighten as she stepped between them and the painting. *She doesn't believe us.*

"I'm sorry—are you with the police?"

"I'm a detective with the Portland Police Bureau. I'm here unofficially on behalf of the . . . on behalf of the University of Oregon." Kate turned away so that Sylvia couldn't see her surprise at the blatant lie. Lorenzo showed Sylvia his badge. "I lived and worked in the Cinque Terre years ago." Sylvia crossed her arms, but her expression softened. "A team of experts tested the university painting. It was authentic."

"What about the poem?" Kate asked. "Could we have a look?"

Sylvia stood on one side of the picture. "Help me get this off the wall." Lorenzo did, and they flipped it around. Together they set it on the floor and leaned it against the wall. The poem was there. "Humph. What do you make of that?" Sylvia said.

Kate stepped closer and read, "The depths of my passion thrust all caution aside, bound by flesh and dew. I give my soul to the gods of desire, for there is nothing so fine as you." Something looked wrong. Kate looked from Lorenzo to Sylvia, then stepped out to the sitting room and returned with photocopies from Dr. Marshall's books. Kate read the last line, "I give my soul to the gods of desire, for there is nothing so fine as you, my love." Kate pointed to the last two words. "Now, look at yours." Both Lorenzo and Sylvia turned toward the poem on the back of her painting.

"My love," Lorenzo said, glancing at Kate. "It's missing."

"And the penmanship is too neat, compared to the photocopy," said Kate.

Lorenzo and Sylvia turned the painting back around and leaned it against the wall. Kate pointed below the signature. It was barely noticeable, but she saw a small *p*. Just the one letter, passed off as an errant brush stroke.

"The forger's signature, perhaps?" Lorenzo said. "A point of pride?" He stepped close behind Kate and whispered, "You're brilliant."

"Could I see your sheet of paper again?" asked Sylvia. She read Dr. Marshall's photocopy from the top, examined the picture on the page, and reread the poem. "It was tested, you say? The painting at the university?" Lorenzo nodded. "And how exactly did this university acquire it?"

"It was a donation," said Kate. "Anonymous. I know it seems crazy, but a whole shipment of paintings arrived in Portland. They were all tested. They were all original. We suspect they're stolen, the originals replaced with forgeries. We want to find the man—or business—responsible."

"And you have proof of these tests?"

"I do." Lorenzo left the room and returned with his own photocopy. "Here's a report of the full spectrum test of your painting and the firm who'd carried it out." He handed it to her.

Kate and Lorenzo stepped back while Sylvia read the report. "Where did you get *that*?" whispered Kate.

"I grabbed it when I went in to ask for time off," he whispered back, with a playful grin. "I was nearly caught."

"Brilliant," she said, nudging him with her elbow. Sylvia laid the report on her desk.

"How did you learn about the Robinis?" Lorenzo asked. "Did someone recommend them?"

"My late husband considered himself a collector. He had that authenticated by them too." She referred to a painting behind the desk—a gleaming black horse standing regally before a backdrop of mountains with thick fog swirling about its ankles. Kate stood closer and spotted a tiny letter *t* in the fog below the signature.

Sylvia began throwing open file drawers and rifling through. She picked out one file after another, opening them and pushing them aside until she found what she'd been after.

"This is my original agreement for the Rossetti. And the authentication." She laid the appraisal on the desk. It was signed by Alfonso and one other person—Kate couldn't make the signature out from where she stood. Lorenzo pulled his reading glasses from his shirt pocket.

"The Bolognese School of Art in Parma issued the authentication," he said, glancing at Kate. "It's signed by Maximo Corta."

It looked official enough to Kate's untrained eye, printed on school letterhead with an embossed gold seal at the bottom. Their logo was an easel bearing a canvas reading *Scuola d'arte Bolognese* in black and white with a glossy red three-legged stool placed before it.

"I know this is way out there," Kate said, looking hesitantly at Lorenzo. "But what if we set a trap?"

He frowned. "What kind of trap?"

"We choose a piece of art from Sylvia's collection, document it, then have her take it to Alfonso for appraisal. See where that takes us. See if they reproduce it and send back a forgery."

"That could take ages," Lorenzo said. "Maybe more time than we have."

Sylvia glanced back at her Rossetti, then laid her hand on a pink paperweight the size of a baseball. "This is *Il Gatto*. Pink opal—very rare. It's one of two. My sister has *Il Cane*, a black opal dog. They were handed down to us by our grandfather. The artist is Federico Gamberini from Turino. He's well respected. If you think it'll work, Alfonso is welcome to have it."

Kate picked it up, admiring the cat's graceful curve from neck to tail and the demure, downcast face. "Are you sure?" Sylvia nodded.

"Thank you, Sylvia. This is a great help," Lorenzo said.

On the way back to their apartment, Lorenzo asked the young cab driver to drive by the address listed for the Italian Art Foundation. The driver, eager to please, circled the industrial neighborhood, but there was no such organization—merely an auto shop with an abandoned '80s vintage Fiat out front and a white van parked cockeyed down the street. Lorenzo tapped the driver on the shoulder and pointed. "*Si fermi qui.*" The car pulled over. "I'm going to have a look around," said Lorenzo. Kate grabbed her bag and reached for the door, but he held up his hand. "No. You stay put. I won't be long."

Feeling rebuffed, she let him get as far as the gravel drive beside the building and then followed him to a back lot where a collection of junked cars waited to be cannibalized for parts.

"Go back to the cab," he said when he saw her, but she was already peering in one of the clouded windows of a roll-up door.

"It's just an auto garage." She stepped back and glanced up at the second story with its cracked walls and boarded-up windows, then pulled on the rusted metal door. It squealed open.

The garage stank of oil and gasoline. A truck with its hood up exposed the engine, a heavy blanket draped across the front as if someone had been working on it recently. It all seemed normal—for a garage. Kate watched as Lorenzo poked around the perimeter to a staircase where she caught up to him. His glare urged her to go back to the car. But she shook her head, eyes locked on his. He conceded with a subtle, reassuring smile. She had as much right to be here as he did, and he knew it.

The boarded windows dimmed the loft on the upper floor. Lorenzo pointed to a green tarp laying in a heap. Kate lifted it warily, imagining what lay beneath. A mouse? Spiders? She found only a scrap of paper—the stub from an Italian freight liner dated September 8, 2004.

"Look," Kate said excitedly, holding it out to Lorenzo. "The crate. It has to be." Lorenzo read it and nodded.

When they'd returned to the cab, the van was gone.

<hr>

That evening, Kate found the website for the Bolognese School of Art in Parma. She clicked around, and with Lorenzo's translation help, they visited pages for admissions, registration, faculty, curriculum, calendar. *Click, click, click.* On one page, he stopped her. "Founders," he said. "The original founder, Carlo Robini, opened the school in 1975 with funds from the Italian Art Foundation now operated by Marco." Lorenzo jotted down the address for the school.

Kate filled two wine glasses and slid one toward him. He looked at her with a warm smile and took a sip.

"Marco operates the National Art Foundation, and the foundation funds the school," said Kate, recalling what Lorenzo had told her the day before.

"And here's a list of donors." Lorenzo pointed to the topmost name: C. Robini Property Insurance. Kate recalled the art school logo from Sylvia's appraisal and immediately understood the three-legged stool as representing the art foundation, the insurance company, and the school in Parma. One, two, three.

CHAPTER THIRTEEN

Lorenzo

Lorenzo woke early the following day to Kate sprawled across the bed with her arms outstretched and pajama bottoms bunched up to her knees. He smiled, marveling at how he ever managed to get comfortable, with a bedmate like that.

He stepped into the sitting room and looked out the window past the harbor, where the morning's first light glinted off the sea like stars twinkling in the night. It was a perfect morning for a run.

Lorenzo always ran to sort out his thoughts, and today he had a lot to think about. After jogging across the street to the promenade, he picked up his pace as he turned toward the aquarium, trying to tie together the events in Portland with Maximo Corta and the art school in Parma, then the discovery of the cargo receipt in the auto shop. It finally dawned on him that he may have bitten off more than he could chew. All he'd wanted was Marco. But to do that, he'd need to take down the whole network.

Just before arriving at the aquarium, he dodged a delivery van and veered into the depths of the Caruggi district—Genoa's old town.

It's where he and Kate had spent most of their time so far—a beautiful place to show off the culture. His feet beat the pavement as the ancient city came to life and the early morning sun touched each rooftop, balcony, and steeple. The sight was exquisite. Lorenzo stopped to take it all in, heart thumping. A chill rolled across his sweat-dampened flesh like the sea rolling ashore along a sandy beach. He ran his hand over his thickening beard. The facial hair would take a while to get used to, but it would help disguise him. Finally, he took one last gulp of the crisp morning air before taking off around the corner toward the piazza with the jazz museum. He spotted the club Sylvia mentioned. Poor lady. He thought of her painting, a forgery—a particularly good one. It was a clever scheme to receive artwork for appraisal, then replace it with the fake and sell the original. This would never work without skilled forgers from the art school. It was all clear to Lorenzo. He just had to prove it.

She'd emailed him and Kate with a long list of other pieces in her husband's collection, with the small letters or other unique marks inserted near the artist's autograph. The nearly inconspicuous mark of the forger. It was a matter of pride that would ultimately do them in. What was he to make of *Il Gatto*? It was beautiful, but without the mate she mentioned, Alfonso might take a pass. He might want the pair.

Lorenzo resumed his run, reaching the outer limits of the Caruggi, where a scooter sputtered past, shattering his concentration. It disappeared around the next corner. Lorenzo imagined that the driver was en route to work, or school—something ordinary in this extraordinary city.

His mind skipped to Monica Bower as the streets came alive with traffic, exhaust, and noise. Had she gotten bail? Would Alfonso have taken that risk? Alfonso. The Benson Hotel. The Robin's Nest and sale of stolen art. With Sylvia's help, he believed he was on track to seal Monica's fate when her case came up in court. She was part of this—either as a dealer of stolen art or an accomplice to fraud.

Bong! Bong! Church bells rang out across the city, and Lorenzo stopped again to embrace the moment. It filled his heart with longing for his village of Manarola, and San Lorenzo church with its baptisms and weddings. He still remembered receiving those sacraments within its hallowed walls. He recalled his wedding day—April 1, 1973. A spring storm had been brewing to the south, blessing them with its strong breeze.

He still hadn't let his family know he was in the country. Partly because he wasn't ready for a hard-hitting rebuke. Partly because he wanted to deal with Marco first, or they'd all be in danger.

There was another reason, of course. Ella. As it was, his memory of her seemed unnaturally keen. He feared seeing her around every turn, particularly in Manarola. It was just too painful, being here.

The church bells quieted, and with a deep breath, Lorenzo began running once more, heading for the sea and the steady thrum of boat horns and barges, his heart pounding as he wove in and out between pedestrians. He wondered about the Italian federal agents assigned to Alfonso. Would the AISI take up the case as Agent Fogarty suggested?

Lorenzo passed back by the aquarium and down the promenade, where he began his cool down. Finally, he stopped at a kiosk on the other side of the harbor parking lot and looked down the busy street toward the apartment.

Kate would be up by now. The thought cheered him. He imagined her at the kitchen counter, laptop open, as she worked on her story. Or maybe she was stretched out on the sofa with her phrase book. That made him laugh. "*Sono felice di conoscerti,*" he said, thinking how happy he was to know her too. With that thought, he headed home.

By Lorenzo's calculations, it was after 11 p.m. in Portland. So, he waited till evening before calling Sergeant Monroe to get some of these issues off his mind.

"You honestly cannot take a break, can you, Lorenzo?" said the sergeant. "Why don't you leave it to the Feds?"

"This is important to me, Monroe. It's personal. Who is the Italian agent on the case?"

Sergeant Monroe coughed and cleared his throat. "Hold on, Lorenzo. I can't just—"

"Please."

Monroe paused. "Ugh, all right. Give me a sec." Lorenzo waited with clenched jaws, sitting on the edge of the love seat while Kate puttered in the kitchen.

"The agent is Francesco Colucci," Monroe said when he returned to the phone. "He's only been on the case since the Portland incident, but the file says the AISI has been following Alfonso's business off-and-on for years."

"Off-and-on," Lorenzo repeated. "What does that mean? They back off when bribed?"

"Could be. No proof. And you know, it always comes down to proof."

"Perhaps I could meet with this Colucci."

Monroe groaned. "Lorenzo, you have no jurisdiction there. You realize this, don't you?"

"I'm aware."

"And your friend?"

"She's aware. Again, sir, we have our own reasons for being here. Personal reasons."

"Jesus, what the hell are you up to, Lorenzo? Keep her the hell out of this. You got me?" Lorenzo looked across the room at Kate, who was rummaging for something in the kitchen. Monroe had no way of knowing, of course, but she was *already* part of this.

"Yes, sir." Lorenzo scratched his head. "Sergeant, Buddy was going to get the names of the drivers for me. You know, the guys who delivered the crate to the gallery?"

"Yeah, that's here . . . uh, okay. Gavin West and a guy calling himself Dario Donato. West came from Seattle, and the Donato kid is supposedly from New York—but he only spoke Italian, so draw your own conclusion." Sergeant Monroe sighed heavily, then gave Lorenzo the number for the Italian internal intelligence and security agency known as AISI. "Check your email. I sent you the report on the break-in at your apartment. Buddy handled it, but the FBI thinks you're right about the intimidation angle. Unfortunately—"

"There's no evidence. Yes. I see a trend here, sergeant. By the way, I have some information for Buddy about the university painting." Lorenzo moved to the open window and gazed across the park-like promenade to the many harbors strung up the coast.

"All right, send us a report. But that's it. You're on vacation, remember?"

"Mm-hmm." Lorenzo smelled Kate's sweet scent and noticed her standing beside him.

"Hey, Lorenzo—I don't want you getting out over your skis on this. I mean it. Be careful."

Lorenzo turned to Kate. "This could take longer than we think," he said, flipping his phone closed. "It may be weeks before we return to Portland."

"And Manarola? Have you forgotten?"

"Hmm," he said.

"You don't want to go?"

"Not that. Well, yes, that. It's been so long, Kate, I'm terrified of what I'll find." Lorenzo pressed his hand against the window and sighed with an air of resignation. There'd be triggers everywhere. How could he explain his fear of seeing Ella around every corner, or facing his estranged son and the family he'd turned away from when he needed them most?

Kate placed her hand over his against the window. An expression of solidarity, he thought. Or pity. Or, possibly—affection. He prayed it was the latter.

"Let's see where this case takes us, Kate. Then we can talk about Manarola."

Without thinking, he put his arm across her shoulders, and she leaned into him. *Keep her the hell out of this*, Monroe had said. But how?

Lorenzo called the AISI number in Rome and learned that Francesco Colucci wasn't in, so he left a message. The next morning, Lorenzo's phone rang.

Agent Colucci said he was in Genoa and agreed to meet Lorenzo unofficially on a local tour boat in the nearby harbor at 11 a.m. the next day.

An hour before their eleven o'clock meeting, Lorenzo noticed Alfonso's green Jaguar pass by the apartment and turn into the harbor parking lot further up the road.

"Looks like we have company," Lorenzo said.

"Think he's following us?" asked Kate, standing beside him.

"It wouldn't surprise me."

"We should leave for the meeting separately, just in case," Kate said.

"What? No. You're not going at all."

Kate stiffened. "Not an option."

They locked eyes, and Lorenzo turned away from the window, frustrated by her stubborn insistence to wave aside the danger he tried to shield her from. "I can't stop you," he said. "But could you at least wait until I cross the street? He might recognize me, and it'll give you time to turn back."

Lorenzo gave Kate the apartment keys with a firm reminder to lock the doors behind her. Then he headed down to the bookstore, where he picked up the daily newspaper. Finally, after a quick search for Alfonso's car, he crossed the hectic street to the promenade, which led to the harbor and the tour boat.

Blue plastic bench seats facing front and back lined each side of the rocking boat. Lorenzo searched for any man that might be Agent Colucci, but saw only tourists and couples, so he grabbed a booth near the back where he could watch for Kate. He spotted her as she approached, the hem of her coat flapping in the sea breeze. She caught Lorenzo's eye and smiled as she stepped onto the ramp. An older man in a faded black trench coat walked close behind her. His stringy black hair obscured half of his face. The other half revealed a swollen black eye.

Suddenly, the older man grabbed Kate's arm and pulled her back.

Lorenzo jumped from his seat, but there were too many people to push past, and he had to watch helplessly as the stranger studied Kate's face, then lowered his gaze. She yanked her arm from his grasp and hurried along the ramp, pushing past a young family and toward Lorenzo. The odd man's focus remained on her until she reached him —and then he met Lorenzo's glare.

"Did you see that guy?" Kate said, gasping for air. "He scared the *shit* out of me."

Lorenzo wrapped an arm across her shoulders and tilted his head toward hers. "Are you all right?" he asked breathlessly, leading her back to his seat. "What did he say?"

"I have no idea," Kate said, sitting back with a huff. "I *have* been trying, you know. I've been immersed in that damn phrase book like it's a best seller. But everyone speaks so fast, I can't tell one word from another."

Lorenzo looked past her toward the dock, but the man had vanished. "You'll be fine," he assured her. "Just keep your ears open and your mouth shut." She scowled, and he wanted to kick himself. Stupid! "I'm sorry," he said. "That came out wrong. What I mean is, it's important to listen closely; eventually, you'll catch the breaks in speech. I promise." Lorenzo handed her his newspaper, looking around for any sign of the intelligence agent.

"Admit it, Lorenzo; he looked sketchy. That black eye? Somebody else thinks he's a creep too." She opened the paper and noisily shook the kinks out of it.

"You're sure you understood nothing he said?"

"Not a word." Kate folded the newspaper and laid it on her lap, the front page dominated by a photo of Berlusconi and his beautiful wife. The bold caption beneath it referred to the newest changes to the Italian constitution. Whatever Lorenzo thought of George W.

Bush, nothing compared to the corrupt Berlusconi government and its threat to Italian democracy.

The overhead speaker squawked with announcements as the boat pushed off. "Hello and welcome. My name is . . ." The young couple sitting behind them were squabbling in Italian about their seat. She couldn't see. He couldn't hear. "I'll be your guide . . ." Lorenzo looked down at his phone.

"Expecting a call?" said Kate.

"Or a text—something, anything from our secret agent."

Just then, a man in a black leather jacket and tan slacks approached them, swaying to keep his balance as the rocking boat pulled away from the dock. He sat down on the bench directly across from them.

"*Che tempo, eh?*" he said, looking toward the clear blue sky.

"It's a lovely day," Lorenzo noted.

"English, is it?" The stranger smiled halfheartedly and held out his hand. "Francesco Colucci. Call me Frank."

"I'm Lorenzo Rotondo. This is Kate Noonan, an American journalist."

Frank's eyes lingered on Kate before turning to Lorenzo. "You have something for me?"

"I may." Lorenzo crossed his arms. "But I'm more interested in what you know."

Frank winked at Kate and said, "I think we can help each other, eh?"

"You're investigating Alfonso Robini?" asked Lorenzo, perturbed by the wink.

Frank nodded thoughtfully, apparently weighing his answer. "Not Alfonso exactly—his insurance business. But he's interesting to us. More interesting now with this recent development. You know what I'm saying?"

"Do you know how Alfonso's business ties in with the painting we discovered in Portland?" Lorenzo asked, pulling a fresh notebook from his breast pocket.

"Well, I'm working on that. But I need help, you know, on the inside. We need someone in his *confidenza*." He eyed Kate and grinned. "You would be perfect, *amore mio*."

Lorenzo glared and switched into Italian, so Frank would be sure to understand, and Kate would not. "Don't. She is not your love, and it's insulting."

"Stepping on toes, am I?" replied Frank in Italian, then switched back to English, unfazed. "The tax officials have no trouble with Alfonso's business. His profits are steady, and there has been nothing to alarm them."

"This isn't tax fraud we're talking about," Lorenzo said, scowling.

"Yes, well, this new complaint from the US changes things—but I have little to go on, *signore*," Frank said, his nostrils twitching, rabbit-like. Was it a tell? A signal that Frank was lying?

The boat ventured further into the harbor and the man sitting behind them cursed about his obstructed view.

"I might have something for you," Lorenzo said as Kate marked up her steno notepad with her illegible scrawl. "I won't know for sure until later, though."

"Yes? Interesting." Frank leaned across the gap between their seats and handed each of them his card. "I'll take any help I can get. Currently, I am staying in a small cottage near Alfonso's estate to get a better idea of the comings and goings." He swung a black leather bag from around his back and removed a hefty, professional-looking digital camera. "This is my cover." He snapped a picture of Kate and showed it to her. She waved it off and combed her fingers through her hair as the overhead speaker squawked something about Giovanni Ansaldo, who built the most beautiful ships in the world. At last, the couple behind them got up and moved to a vacant seat in the front of the boat, and Lorenzo felt emboldened by the sudden privacy.

Lorenzo did his best to ignore continuing interruptions from the speaker as he told Frank about the crate, the university painting, and their raid at the gallery. "This scheme has been going on for decades," said Lorenzo. "I discovered their hidden studio in '74." He told Frank about the farmhouse which led to the crate at the Port of Portland. Frank listened, nodded, and made agreeable sounds—but contributed nothing.

The boat cruised along the rocky coastline with views of ancient colorful buildings and hotels held in place by rock walls . . . and prayers.

Squawk. "The *Lanterna* is one of the oldest symbols of Genoa. This lighthouse is visible over thirty kilometers from the sea, and when . . ."

"You have proof of this crime?" said Frank.

Lorenzo noticed something peculiar about Frank—unprofessional for a federal agent. The overhead speaker squawked again, announcing Genoa as the busiest port in Italy. Lorenzo waited patiently for silence, then said, "I understand your office has been in touch with our FBI. Who is your contact there?"

"My contact? With the FBI?" Frank laughed. "We do not see this as an American issue, my friend." The nose twitched.

Lorenzo clenched his teeth and gazed into the water at the wake peeling from the hull. Not an American issue? Was Frank dismissing the *FBI?*

"There is a crate in the US filled with stolen art that leads directly to Alfonso and his insurance business. We've mapped it all out. All you have to do is work with the FBI. So why wouldn't you do that?" Lorenzo leaned in close. "I know this family. They're scum."

"*Alleged* stolen art, Lorenzo. Of course, I don't have your first-hand knowledge or history with the family. I don't know what you do. The FBI is a slow-moving machine, yes? But if I'm going to do my job, I'll need some help. I'm not kidding about needing you."

"Hmm. You don't know about the family? About Marco?"

Frank's nose twitched again. "Yes—um, how is this relevant?"

"Marco is Alfonso's cousin. He runs the foundation that funds the art school," Lorenzo said. "My theory is that Alfonso procures artwork for assessment by the art school where it's reproduced. The forgery then replaces the original artwork, which is sold to unscrupulous art collectors."

Frank took a couple more pictures as they passed an empty beach where colorful umbrellas, bound tight with rope and bungees, lay stacked like lumber against the seawall to wait out the winter until the inevitable onslaught of summer sunbathers.

"Where is this art school?" Frank finally asked.

"In Parma," Lorenzo said. *"La Scuola d'arte Bolognese.* Is this the first you've heard of it?" Lorenzo looked at Kate, her eyes narrowed in disbelief.

"I am late to the party, as you Americans say," Frank looked over at Kate and chuckled. "Parma, you said. I'll look into it."

When the tour boat turned back for the harbor, Frank pointed his camera toward the vast expanse of sea, where a couple of ships, a colorful buoy, and several sailboats dotted the sun-soaked horizon. Lorenzo followed Frank's gaze to a large yacht anchored just beyond the harbor, as their own boat moved toward the dock.

"Before we part, is there anything else?" Frank said. "Anything more you learned since arriving in *Genova?*"

"No," Kate said abruptly, catching Lorenzo's eye.

"Where are you staying?" asked Frank. "I'll meet you there after a rest, and we can talk over the finer details."

"We have some errands to run." Lorenzo patted the pocket where he'd put Frank's card. "I'll call you later if anything comes up."

Frank narrowed his eyes, then grinned at Lorenzo as if they shared a secret. "A little quiet time with your darling?" he said in Italian. "Understood." Lorenzo refused to respond.

"We should be off," Lorenzo said to Kate, then turned back to the agent. "Thank you for meeting us on such short notice, Frank."

"Anytime, my friend," Frank said, winking at Kate.

Lorenzo fumed. He knew how Italian men often admired beautiful women, and he'd expected Kate to get her share of attention. But Frank's gesture unnerved him just the same. Was he attracted to her?

The winks, the insinuations, the notion that Kate should befriend Alfonso—red flags, all of them.

Once the boat was tied off, Kate and Lorenzo held back as Frank disembarked ahead of them.

"What do you think of that guy?" asked Lorenzo.

Kate looked to where Frank stood at a harbor-side kiosk. "Not much. It appears we are his only lead. How is that possible? And it's as if he hasn't even *looked* at the file. He's not even trying. He wasn't even taking notes."

"What do you scribble on that notepad of yours when you already know what your source is telling you?"

Kate smirked. "Yeah, okay, so—maybe he knows more than he's letting on. Does this mean we should tell him about *Il Gatto*?"

Lorenzo stood and helped her up. "Not yet. We'll let this bit settle first. But I'm afraid we may be on our own here."

They were the last passengers off the boat. Once they reached the promenade, Lorenzo looked up and down the street, wondering if Alfonso lurked nearby. But the Jaguar wasn't there.

They approached the kiosk colorfully decorated with brand-name banners and advertisements for items like chocolate bars and disposable cameras.

Kate stepped back and gave the hem of Lorenzo's jacket a gentle tug. He followed her gaze and noticed the odd man with the black eye from the dock earlier. He walked toward the road, then stopped and glanced over his shoulder toward them.

Lorenzo took Kate's arm and led her along the promenade in the opposite direction of their apartment until he was sure they weren't being followed.

CHAPTER FOURTEEN

Kate

That evening, Kate and Lorenzo returned to the friendly restaurant on the piazza. Paulo jumped to find them a table, disregarding the other patrons waiting expectantly by the door.

"*Famiglia! Famiglia!*" he chanted, taking Kate by the hand, and excitedly leading her to a private booth. Lorenzo sat down across from her, grinning from ear to ear.

"Well, Signore Quixote, it appears they have adopted us." She returned his smile.

"It would seem so, Signorina Sancho. But for the record, my quest is very real. No windmills."

"I'm aware." Kate nodded firmly, still smiling, thinking of the boxer shorts she'd selected.

"And how does our new friend Frank fit into this scenario?"

Kate enjoyed their jesting, but the thought of Frank changed her tone. "He would be the dastardly innkeeper—not to be trusted. There's something weird about him, Lorenzo."

"I have some doubts myself," Lorenzo said. Something over her shoulder drew his attention, and he raised his brows in alarm just as Frank stepped up to their table, blocking Paulo from bringing a bottle of wine and two glasses.

"Mind if I join you?" Frank asked. Kate minded very much. So did Paulo, judging by the look on his face.

"Have a seat," said Lorenzo. Paulo poured their wine and went back for a third glass.

Kate popped up from her bench to sit beside Lorenzo, who squeezed her hand reassuringly under the table. It felt nice, like when he'd taken her hand on the plane to calm her.

"It appears I am late to the party again," joked Frank.

Lorenzo released Kate's hand. "Right on time," he said, displaying more class than Kate felt was necessary under the circumstances. Paulo poured Frank's wine, filling it short of the mark. Apparently, Frank was the black sheep of the *famiglia*. Kate smiled up at the waiter, sensing he understood her frustration.

"Did you finish your errands?" asked Frank, folding his jacket neatly beside him and laying it over his camera bag.

"Just about," said Lorenzo, leaning into Kate. She recalled how they'd spent their afternoon stretched out on the bed for a siesta. Neither had been sleeping well—Lorenzo buzzed and snorted through the night, while Kate traveled from one side of the bed to the other, crowding him or inadvertently stealing the covers. Still— neither had complained.

Lorenzo topped off his wine and added a splash to Kate's untouched glass.

"And you rested well, I hope," Kate said, remembering what Frank had mentioned on the promenade.

"I did not," said Frank, nose twitching. "A neighbor stopped by unannounced." Kate wondered whether he was lying.

"Where are you from, Frank?" she asked. "Do you get to Genoa often? And how long, exactly, have you been on the forgery assign-ment?" Kate hoped the rapid-fire questions would throw him off balance.

Frank's mouth dropped open, and his face colored as he took a moment to register what was going on. Then his eyes narrowed in on Kate, and he said, "I am from Salerno, *signorina*, but live now in *Roma*. I do not have the pleasure of visiting *Genova* often. I am a stranger here. The, um, *compito*, how do you say—*assignment* is new to me. Two weeks, maybe." Frank's piercing look made Kate uneasy, but she did not back down.

"Have you been with the agency long, Frank?" Kate's heart raced, fueled by adrenaline. "What is your plan for Alfonso?"

"Is this an interrogation, *signorina*?" Frank winked at her, then looked away.

Kate felt Lorenzo's knee nudge her under the table. Clearly, he wanted her to back off. She nudged back and sipped her wine. She wasn't going to back down. She had question and wanted answers. Lorenzo emptied the bottle between the three glasses and ordered another, along with some bread and cheese. Paulo dealt out their menus and disappeared.

"I noticed you brought your camera with you," Kate said. "Would you mind showing me some shots from today's outing?" She hoped the pictures would give her some insight into him. Maybe reveal other aspects of his investigation into Alfonso.

Frank shook his head. "I really—"

"Please?" Kate insisted. "I've never been good with a camera myself. I would love to see your work."

Frank grudgingly set his camera bag on the table and slowly unzipped it, nostrils twitching. Emboldened by the wine, Kate moved to his side of the table, where she could see the screen more easily while Frank scrolled through the pictures.

The first picture was of her. Kate sneered at the candid image. Shots of the harbor, coastline, and empty beaches followed, but the sailboats, industrial ports, and coastline in quick succession made it appear Frank was surveying the place. The last photo was a close-up of a luxury yacht, *Il Palazzo*. Kate playfully took the camera from Frank's hands and sidled back beside Lorenzo to share the last picture with him, scrolling back so he could see what she had. Without Frank noticing, Lorenzo deleted the photo of Kate. Nudge. Sip. Smile. Repeat. They were enjoying themselves.

"Those are quite nice," said Lorenzo. Frank retrieved the camera from Kate and lifted it to take their picture. "The two of you—what do you say, Lorenzo?"

"No." Lorenzo placed a hand on the lens.

"You know," Kate said, turning to Lorenzo, "I should pick up a camera. I saw an inexpensive one at the kiosk."

"No, no, no." Frank waved his arms. "Those are for tourists. The shop on Via Cipro, by the supermarket. They will have something for you."

But you said you were a stranger to Genoa, thought Kate. Had she caught him in a lie?

"Do you have any pictures of Alfonso?" asked Lorenzo.

"Of course."

"And Marco?" Kate sat back, hoping to appear relaxed, though she was on high alert for another lie.

Frank shrugged. "He is not in the picture, as you Americans say."

"He's the focal point of this picture," Lorenzo said, leaning in.

"And you're so sure of this?" Frank said, smirking.

"You're *not*?" Kate said. How had this man become an intelligence officer?

Frank exhaled heavily through his nose. "Marco is not under investigation for this case, *piccola*."

"He *is* the investigation!" said Lorenzo. "He's the purse. None of this is possible without him or the foundation."

"Yes, the foundation. You mentioned that earlier." Frank fussed with his shirt sleeve, avoiding eye contact.

The wine and cheese arrived, and Paulo waited for them to order.

"I haven't even looked at the menu," said Kate, opening it up and looking for a familiar word.

"Do you mind if I order for you?" Lorenzo asked.

"Please."

He took Kate's menu and launched into Italian with Paulo. Frank merely pointed to what he wanted. Paulo took the liberty of topping off Kate and Lorenzo's wine, leaving Frank to fend for himself.

Lorenzo inched closer to Kate and murmured, "I think you'll be happily surprised." She felt his knee knock against hers in a friendly nudge and her pulse quickened.

"Thank you, detective. I'll wait to be amazed." She tore her bread and slathered it in soft cheese, then looked across the table. "How long have you been with the agency, Frank?" she asked for the second time.

"Nearly eight years now, each one an adventure." Frank elaborated on his life in the agency and dangers he had faced, bouncing from English to Italian and back again. Then he returned to the subject at hand. "Tell you what, Kate—I have an idea to sort out this Alfonso business. Would you help me?"

"What do you have in mind?" asked Kate. Lorenzo took the wine and emptied it into his own glass.

Frank reached into his camera bag and pulled out what looked like a little black pill box. "I could use your help to get this into his office. It will be simple for you. Alfonso has an eye for beautiful women, so he would accept you without question. The closer we get to Alfonso, the more we'll learn. With your help we can be on the inside, maybe even get something on Marco. That should make you happy—eh, Lorenzo?" Frank flipped over his cocktail napkin and scribbled something, then slid it across the table. Lorenzo picked it up and looked at it.

"Alfonso's address? You're mad," Lorenzo said, his eyes fixed on Frank.

"Also, Alfonso's secretary's office and his car. He might even invite you into his home. Everywhere he takes you, leave one of these." Frank dropped the black box on the table.

Lorenzo leaned forward as if he were about to reach for Frank's throat. "What about the agency?"

"As I said on the boat today, Lorenzo, I have little support on this case. I need help."

"No!" Lorenzo gripped the table, his face burning with frustration. "She is my responsibility. No, Francesco. *Assolutamente no.*"

"I can speak for myself, Lorenzo," Kate murmured, resting a hand on his leg to reassure him. That she'd do anything so daring was unthinkable, in some respects giving credence to George's image of her, but she didn't want to give in to Lorenzo's fears, and she had no intention of putting her own life at risk. Frank's proposal was out of the question. "I'm flattered, Frank, but I couldn't possibly do that. There must be another way." Slowly, she removed her hand from Lorenzo's leg.

Lorenzo sighed with relief, tilting his head to hers, his warm lips brushing across her ear. "Thank you," he whispered.

"You need to trust me," she whispered back, feeling the bristles of his unshaven face against hers. It was the most intimate they'd been since that morning at her house when she'd held him in her arms.

"Am I interrupting something?" Frank said with a wry smile.

Their meals arrived—lamb chops for both of them, swimming in a mushroom sauce with small green salads on the side. Kate flashed back to the first meal they'd had together. It's what she had made that night, seemingly a lifetime ago. Nudge.

Lorenzo, visibly more relaxed, ordered another bottle of wine before splitting open the steamy loaf of bread, moaning in appreciative ecstasy, while Frank slurped his *cioppino*, picking out the mussels and tipping the sweet meat into his mouth with relish.

When they'd finished, Lorenzo laid a hand on Kate's arm. "I have a few questions still for Frank," he said. "It would be easier in Italian. If you like, you could go on home, and I'll be there soon."

Kate considered staying, if just for the language immersion, but some time alone to work on her story would be nice too. As she stepped away from the table, Kate looked back to see Lorenzo's sweet grin, wondering what he was up to.

Kate entered the piazza under a shower of golden light cast from the streetlamps overhead. It was just after nine and the city had shifted from the daytime crowd to nighttime revelers, but Genoa seemed to always be in a state of perpetual celebration, whatever the hour.

She passed performers playing for anyone willing to stop and watch, recalling her first day here nearly a week ago with Lorenzo, eating, drinking, and shopping their way through jet lag. Back then, facing the reality of their accommodations, Lorenzo had slept on the love seat rather than sharing the bed. She'd never known someone so chivalrous.

Sometimes, when she woke to the sound of sirens, train whistles, or Lorenzo's buzzing snore, she'd catch herself pressed against his back, or her arm draped over his chest. She'd think what it would be like if he woke right then—before she pulled away.

Pausing now in front of the bookstore, Kate touched her ear, remembering the feel of his warm breath against it at dinner. "Thank you," he'd whispered.

Kate looked up and caught her reflection in the window. As her focus shifted from the window glare to the display on the other side, she stared, stunned, and stumbled back, fumbling for the apartment keys in her pocket.

Alfonso Robini with a book in his hand, looking directly at her, grinning. He nodded, assessing her with the critical eye of a red-blooded Italian man. She forced a smile in return, worried that her wildly thumping heart would give her away, and race-walked past the apartment door, stepping out of the night into a gelato shop to hide and collect herself.

"*Gelato, per favore. Cioccolato.*" She panted, pulling a couple of bills from her purse, keeping her back to the window. The teenager behind the counter must have recognized the American accent—she went right into English. Kate felt a cold draft from the door.

"You want chocolate? How much?" The girl looked bored.

"The smallest you have—I only want a taste," Kate said, feeling every bit the stupid American.

"Ah, women and chocolate!" said a voice from behind her. "I prefer the cherry and vanilla combination myself." Kate glanced at the newcomer and her heart nearly stopped. Alfonso had followed her into the shop. He stepped up close, the bright ceiling light shining off his balding head. "Hello," he said. It was not the hello of a friendly stranger.

"Hello," answered Kate, turning back to the teenager busily scooping her gelato into a paper cup. Alfonso held a finger up to the teenager and ordered in Italian. His cologne overtook the sweet scent of the shop.

"You are from the US?" he asked. "I am familiar with America. What part are you from?"

Did he know who she was?

"Colorado," she said, thinking in the language of half-truth while struggling to breathe.

"Colorado. How nice. I understand it's beautiful there—great skiing."

"Um, yes." Though Kate stood taller than Alfonso in her heels, it didn't feel like an advantage.

The gelato arrived for each of them; a cup for her, a waffle cone for him. She wanted to get away but had nowhere to go. She couldn't return to the restaurant and risk leading Alfonso right to Lorenzo, and to go to the apartment would give away where she was living. "The skiing is nearly year-round," she said. "Do you ski?" She fought to control her quivering speech. *Not so confident now, are you, Sancho?*

He laughed. "No, I have not the body of an athlete, only a mind for business." He glanced at her hand as if checking for a ring and moaned as he wrapped his mouth over the top scoop. "What brings you to our beautiful *Genova?*"

Kate dipped her plastic spoon into her paper cup. "Oh, I'm just on my way down the coast. It's beautiful. You live here?" She was finding her voice.

"Out in the countryside amid olive groves and fertile pastures. I have an extensive stable with exquisite horses that could always use some exercise." He sounded as if he was trying to impress her. "Do you ride?" He circled his fat tongue around the rim of his cone and took a bite. The attempt at sensuality looked grotesque.

"I'm afraid not. Besides, my mother told me never to go home with strangers."

"What is so strange about a boring old man like me?" A guttural laugh bubbled up from his barrel chest.

Kate shook her head, unable to speak. Her nerves were making her ill. His pungent cologne didn't help.

"No? What a shame." He pulled his phone from his coat pocket and glanced at what looked like a text message. "Well, I must be on my way; I have some business to attend to." Alfonso tossed what remained of his cone and fastened his heavy wool overcoat around his round body, his stubby fingers pinching each button into place. "It has been a pleasure, *signorina*. Perhaps we'll meet again during your coastal exploration."

Kate said nothing.

He chuckled and pushed the door open, inviting a sudden gust that sent a chill up her spine.

Kate sat at the plastic table by the window, biding her time and collecting her wits. She stirred the chocolate pool on the bottom of her cup but had lost her appetite. Then, once she felt the coast was clear, she ducked out . . . and careened straight into Lorenzo.

"*There* you are!" he huffed. "You didn't answer the door, and I—"

Kate took his arm. "You will never believe what just happened." She looked over her shoulder and led him upstairs.

Once inside, Lorenzo poured some wine while Kate described her chance encounter with Alfonso.

"I shouldn't have sent you away on your own." Lorenzo took two deep swallows of wine. "I wasn't thinking."

"Do you think he's meeting with Frank?" Kate picked up her glass. "Because if you ask me, Frank is up to something. It wouldn't surprise me if he's using us."

Lorenzo shook his head. "I don't know." He topped off his wine. Kate wondered how much he'd had already that night.

"I'm sure my encounter with Alfonso *wasn't* a coincidence. The neighbor that stopped by Frank's place today? I'll bet anything it was Alfonso. I don't like this, Lorenzo. He isn't watching Marco. He hasn't even *spoken* to the FBI!"

Lorenzo placed a warm hand on her shoulder. "I hear you, Kate. I'm not disregarding you. But Frank is still my best hope of finding Marco."

"He doesn't even *know* Marco."

"Not true. Frank said he wasn't *concerned* with Marco, but I set him straight. He's going to look into the art foundation and promised to open a file into Ella's murder—but in return, we need to give him more." Lorenzo recapped his conversation with Frank—how he'd shared the *Il Gatto* plan. It was the key now to tracking the operation —from forgery to fraud and the sale of stolen art.

Kate cocked her head to the side. "Mm, okay, follow the cat. That was *our* plan."

"Yes, but now we have a partner."

Kate shook her head. *An unreliable partner.* "And Marco?"

"Frank said he'll find Marco." Lorenzo retrieved the cocktail napkin from his breast pocket and laid it on the counter. Alfonso Robini's name was printed across the top in neat block letters, his address below it. He finished his wine and poured another glass.

"I don't know how you can trust this guy." Kate pushed the bottle out of reach. "If Frank *is* working with Alfonso, he's probably working with Marco too." She wanted to validate Lorenzo's grand strategy, but she needed time to make sense of it all.

"I think it's worth the risk. And right now, Kate, it's all I've got."

Scowling, Kate tucked the napkin into her backpack, then squirmed onto one of the kitchen stools and opened her laptop to write about *Il Gatto*, the boat ride, the so-called intelligence agent, and his photos. Who *was* Frank? Why did he buddy up to Lorenzo so quickly? And did he have the power to open Ella's murder case, considering how ineffective he's been with the art fraud? It was overwhelming to have more questions than answers for the article that she was counting on to save her career.

Lorenzo plugged the cork back in the wine bottle and walked into the bedroom. He emerged a moment later with a clean shirt and his wool coat.

"Are you okay?" said Kate.

"Grab your coat," he said with a drunken smile. "We're going out."

Kate looked up from her notebook. "But what about Alfonso?" She didn't want to run into *him* again.

"Let me worry about him."

Lorenzo's purposeful gait had been replaced with the occasional stumble as he led her beyond the familiar piazza to a larger, busier one. The invigorating night air seemed to sober him up some by the time they heard the rhythmic *thump, thump, thump* reverberating from the club. Lorenzo pushed through the crowd at the door, heading straight to the bar, where he ordered two beers.

The band played passionately on a pair of slim keyboards, an electric guitar, and a set of drums. But it was the saxophone that stole the show. Kate felt the lively music through her whole body as the guitar player cried, "*Danza, danza, danza!*" to a dance floor packed with twentysomethings. Kate's beer tickled her tongue and trickled down her throat. Lorenzo grabbed her hand and pulled her onto the floor.

"I'm a terrible dancer!" she shouted over the music.

Lorenzo beamed. "So am I."

Kate felt like she was nineteen again, bouncing and flailing to the

Thompson Twins or Cyndi Lauper. She couldn't remember the last time she'd had so much fun. And the joy on Lorenzo's face added to her delight, vanquishing any thoughts of Frank or Alfonso.

Eventually, the rhythm slowed. Kate turned to retrieve her beer, but Lorenzo took her hand and pulled her back.

At first, he held her at a short distance, then drew her closer, the palm of his hand pressed firmly on her back. She rested her head on his shoulder, her cheek nestled against his neck, as they swayed to the music, feeling the rise and fall of their chests as their breathing synced with the slower tempo, their bodies warm and damp with sweat. Eventually, their dancing slowed until they stood almost motionless in one another's arms.

When the music stopped, Kate stepped back and gazed into Lorenzo's expressive eyes. She felt his fondness for her. He kissed her forehead tenderly before guiding her off the dance floor.

They stumbled home arm in arm, laughing and joking the entire way, without a thought of Alfonso, Frank, or *Il Gatto*. Alcohol still coursed through their veins as they fell into bed, exhausted.

Kate lay in the dark, the beautiful music still playing in her head, the memory of Lorenzo's warm body against hers. She wanted to feel that again. She wanted to feel *more*.

"Lorenzo?"

"Mm?" He rolled over to face her, his face visible in the sliver of moonlight slipping through the blinds. He was beautiful.

"I had fun tonight." She reached for his hand and brought it to her lips. It felt rough and warm and smelled of herbal soap.

He squeezed her hand and sighed, finally saying in a voice deep and drowsy, "*Buona notte*, Sancho." Then, slowly, he pulled his hand away.

"Goodnight," said Kate. The sharp stab of rejection was dwarfed by her embarrassment at having read the evening all wrong.

CHAPTER FIFTEEN

Lorenzo

Sylvia woke them early the next day when she called to say she'd left *Il Gatto* with Robini Property Insurance. Lorenzo pressed his fingers to his temple to ease his splitting headache, the aftereffects of every glass of wine and beer from the night before, propping himself up on one elbow as they spoke, while Kate clambered bashfully out of their warm bed, avoiding his steady gaze.

He recalled her warm lips on his hand the night before. He'd recognized the invitation. He'd come so close—his brain at odds with his body, imagining the feel of her naked skin and the taste of her mouth. What the *hell* was he waiting for? But they'd been drinking—heavily. He feared taking advantage.

"Lorenzo?" Sylvia brought him back from his thoughts. "Did you hear what I said?"

"Alfonso has *Il Gatto*. Yes. I understand." He heard the espresso maker at work in the kitchen while Kate hummed a tune from the previous night.

"And, he said this would be quick. Two weeks for an appraisal."

"Two weeks? Hmm." Lorenzo picked his watch off the night-stand. 8 a.m. "He's sending it to Parma?"

"Yes."

Lorenzo wrapped up the call with Sylvia and changed into his running gear. He needed to sweat out the overindulgence of alcohol and sort out his emotions.

Kate caught his eye as he reached for the door. "This is the last of the coffee," she said, handing him her cup.

"Keep it," he said. "I'll grab some on my way back." Lorenzo stood at the open door, locked in her gaze, wanting to say something reassuring about the night before, but not knowing how to begin.

"Have a nice run," she said. That let him off the hook, which only made him feel worse.

Lorenzo headed outside, where the bashful sun peeked out from behind its thin veil of clouds and warmed the streets, which had been dampened by an overnight shower. He'd jogged a mile or so up the promenade toward the more commercial wharves when, from the corner of one eye, he spotted Alfonso's Jaguar rolling slowly along, inching toward a traffic stop. Lorenzo turned away sharply but looked back once the car had moved on. It turned into the harbor parking lot with the window rolled down.

What are you up to? Lorenzo wondered, crossing the street to the cement pier where he could get a better look. The harbor buzzed with activity—trucks coming and going, boats of all sizes loading up for a day of fishing or leisure.

Alfonso parked his car and remained there until a van pulled up beside him, driver's side to driver's side, the van facing away. Lorenzo cursed as a family of tourists noisily barreled down the pier toward him, the youngest screaming at his mother. A pair of binoculars bounced off the father's chest. Focus, Lorenzo told himself, staring at the van, but unable to see the driver.

"Excuse me," Lorenzo called to the father. "Could I borrow your binoculars for a moment?" Surprised, the man stopped and pulled the small pair of binoculars from around his neck.

Lorenzo raised them to his eyes just as Alfonso stretched out an arm holding a small, white box. A hairy arm reached out of the van window and took it. The men spoke briefly. The driver leaned out the window. "Show me your face," Lorenzo murmured.

"Sir? Are you finished? We'd like to be on our way." The father looked impatient.

Lorenzo ignored him, but the man snatched the binoculars right out of his hands.

"Please, I'll just be a moment," said Lorenzo, glancing over his shoulder at the van.

"Brad! Hurry up, we're going to miss the tour!" screeched the man's wife.

"Twenty euro," Lorenzo said. The man hesitated. "Forty!" Lorenzo pulled two bills from a pocket in the lining of his shorts. The man looked at him as if he were mad but took the cash and handed over the binoculars. Lorenzo grabbed them and whipped around just as the van drove off.

"Where did those come from?" Kate asked, tugging at the binoculars draped over his neck.

Lorenzo removed the binoculars and hung them on the hook by the door. "You'll never believe who I just saw." He ducked into the kitchen and dropped a bag of fresh ground coffee and a paper sack of oranges onto the counter. Kate caught a renegade orange as it rolled toward her. She brought it to her nose and began peeling it over the sink. Lorenzo continued. "I think I saw Alfonso handing off *Il Gatto*."

"Really?" Juice trickled between Kate's fingers as she pulled a segment from the orange and stuffed it into her mouth. "Oh my God, Lorenzo," she mumbled, mouth full. "So juicy!"

Lorenzo handed her a towel. Kate swallowed and wiped her chin. Her eyes sparkled as she pulled the remaining segments apart and lined them up on the counter, each crescent nestled beside the other

—a conga line of orange pieces. She bit into another and held one out to him with juice dripping from her fingers, her eyes bright with joy.

Lorenzo found it hard to concentrate on Alfonso with this beauty standing before him. Last night, he'd stupidly rebuffed her advance. Now, he wanted more than anything to taste the juice from her lips. Impulsively, he lifted her fingers to his mouth, the sweetness of the orange flooding his senses. Her eyes met his as he held her hand to his chest and kissed the corner of her mouth—tasting it, and smelling her sweet breath. "Kate, I—"

Boom-boom-boom. Someone was pounding on the door. Lorenzo pulled away.

"Lorenzo, it's Frank," said a voice from outside. "Let me in!"

Lorenzo squeezed Kate's hand, then reluctantly went to the door and opened it. Frank pushed past him and stood, panicked and panting, in the center of their apartment.

"Come with me!" Frank's nose twitched nervously. "*Fretta!*" he screamed, fists clenched at his sides.

"What is it, Frank?"

"It's Marco!"

Lorenzo grabbed his coat and followed Frank to the door. Kate wasn't far behind them.

"Stay here," he said.

"She should come." Frank grasped her hand, but Lorenzo slapped it away.

"No. She'll stay," he said. If it had anything to do with Marco, he didn't want her anywhere near.

"Lorenzo!" Kate said.

His lips still tingled with the taste of sweet orange as he considered his need for vengeance. Kate and Marco, both within his grasp. He felt muddled and confused by competing emotions. He needed a minute. "Wait for me outside, will you, Frank?" Frank turned and stomped down the stairs.

Kate stood at the door, her coat securely wrapped around her.

"Stay here. It could be a setup."

Kate pulled her collar up and glared at him. "And what about you, hmm? If it's a setup, then you are walking right into it." Lorenzo bowed his head. She had him there.

"I have my phone," he said, "but if anything happens, call this number." He tore a piece off the paper bag and wrote the number for Sergeant Monroe in Portland.

Kate squared her shoulders and glared at him. Her cheeks flushed as red as the lips he'd tasted moments before Frank's untimely interruption. "That won't be necessary because I'm coming along."

Lorenzo admired her tenacity, but the risk in this case was too great. "Kate. Katie? Have I earned the honor?" He grinned and stepped closer—so close he could smell her orange-scented breath. Then he loosened the belt from her trench coat and pulled the garment from her shoulders.

"Lorenzo, we don't have all day!" shouted Frank from the bottom of the stairs.

Kate stared at him with anger and hurt in her eyes.

"I'm sorry," Lorenzo said dolefully, rubbing the nape of his neck. Kate reached for the binoculars from the counter.

"You might need these," she said.

He took them in one hand, touching her warm cheek with the other. "Lock the door," he said, before closing it behind him.

Frank and Lorenzo jogged up to the harbor, where Lorenzo spied Alfonso's green Jaguar still parked, but with no one in the driver's seat.

"There!" Frank pointed into the bay. Lorenzo focused his binoculars. *Il Palazzo.* The same boat from yesterday. "It's Marco Robini's yacht."

Lorenzo wondered if Frank had known that when he'd photographed it. "Is Marco on the boat?" Lorenzo asked.

"He is."

Lorenzo told Frank about Sylvia's call that morning, then about Alfonso and the mysterious van.

"I think that van is the courier. Probably taking the cat to the art school," said Lorenzo, looking at Frank and wondering how far he should trust him.

Frank shifted his glance to the yacht. "Call your girlfriend. She should join us."

"She is not my girlfriend. We're—" It was a reflex, but Lorenzo remembered the sweet taste from Kate's mouth seconds before Frank's interruption and looked over his shoulder toward the apartment. Was there a word for that space between friend and lover?

Frank laughed. "Just friends? Seriously? I saw you two last night, remember? Call her. We can all have lunch here at the harbor while we watch for Marco."

Lorenzo brushed him off. "She'll be fine, Frank. Leave her out of this."

Frank glanced toward the apartment. "Call her." This request sounded more insistent.

Why was he so interested in Kate? "Frank, how did you know where we're staying?"

"What?"

"And how did you get in the door from the street?"

"Uh, the door was unlocked."

Lorenzo raised his binoculars once again. That's when he saw two people on board *Il Palazzo*—the American with the mustache who Sergeant Monroe called Gavin West, and the black eye who'd stopped Kate on the dock. A third man stepped into view. He was white-haired, obese, and leaned heavily on a silver cane. Lorenzo recognized the gluttonous face from the art foundation's website.

"There!" said Frank. "See? It's Marco."

He suddenly felt as if his heart had stopped, and the blood in his veins had turned to ice. His ears rang so loudly that a bomb could have gone off and he wouldn't have heard it.

Frank gripped Lorenzo by the shoulders and shook him. It took a moment, but when the daze began to clear, Lorenzo heard, "I said I'd help you find him. Didn't I tell you? Well? Here he is."

"Yes, Marco. I see," Lorenzo said. He felt dizzy. *Marco.* But what could he do from here? "How is this supposed to help me, Frank? What's going on here?"

"Huh?" Frank's mouth dropped open as he glanced at the yacht. "I—I told you to bring her."

"Why?" Lorenzo said, then it hit him.

He'd left her alone. How could he have been so stupid!

Lorenzo darted across heavy traffic, sprinting back to the apartment at breakneck speed. That had been the plan all along, he thought as he barreled down the sidewalk. To get Kate alone. And Frank? Was he trying to protect her?

The blue door stood wide open. Panicked and winded, Lorenzo bounded up the stairs and turned the knob on the next door. Locked.

"Kate!" Lorenzo pounded on the door. "Kate!" There was no answer. "Katie!"

"Lorenzo?" Her voice sounded muffled.

"Yes, yes, it's me, Sancho. Please, open the door." Seconds ticked by as he waited for her to react. "Kate?" The lock clicked, and Lorenzo thrust the door open. Kate stood a foot away, her eyes open wide, her face white as a sheet. She glanced at the open door behind him. Lorenzo kicked it closed and locked it.

"Someone was here, Lorenzo," she gasped. "He said it was you. He pounded on the door and called my name just the way you did now." Kate's hands trembled at her sides.

Lorenzo pulled her close, clasping her quivering body so tightly against his that he could feel her heart fluttering like a frightened bird against his chest.

"Shh, it's fine now," he murmured in her ear.

Who could it have been? Did she see him? How long had she been in this condition? Lorenzo put his questions aside as he tightened his hold on her, waiting for her breathing to return to normal. Waiting for his own breathing to return to normal.

"I tried calling you," Kate said, "but my hands . . . useless . . . just couldn't stop . . . shaking."

They heard feet pounding up the steps, and she flinched.

"Lorenzo, it's Frank. Is everything all right?"

"Ignore him," Lorenzo murmured. "He'll go away." His arms remained firmly around her. "Shh." She nestled into him, her head on his shoulder, her soft hair against his neck.

"Lorenzo," Frank called again. "Look. It wasn't me. I just got caught in the middle. It's—hey, these people aren't messing around. You need to go home."

Kate wriggled in Lorenzo's arms, but he wasn't going to release her, not until the shaking stopped. After a few minutes, the footsteps descended, and he heard the door to the street open and close. Lorenzo would call him later. Right now, he simply needed to hold Kate.

"Too tight," Kate said. "You're hurting me."

Lorenzo flushed and relaxed his fierce embrace. "You should lie down. I'll bring you some tea."

She shook her head.

"Kate, you're in shock; please let me help you." Lorenzo led her by the hand into the bedroom. He closed the blinds and dragged the covers back.

When he turned for the door, she stopped him. "Don't go," she murmured. She'd already stripped down to her camisole and panties.

"I'll only be a minute," he said, longing to touch her.

She stepped closer and wrapped both arms around his neck, her breasts pressed against him, her lips parted. He lightly placed his hands on her hips, heart racing, unable to push her away as his desire mounted, heightened by the adrenaline from moments earlier, believing her harmed or taken from him forever. He couldn't bear it.

Santa Maria, Madre di Dio, he prayed, touching his lips to hers and hesitantly inching a hand up the silky camisole. Her nipple hardened beneath his thumb, and she kissed him more urgently. Lorenzo pulled his sweater and the T-shirt beneath it up and over his head. The vestiges of panic and fear mingled with lust as he ran his hands across her silken flesh—her body moving to his touch, her soft, full lips on his. They slid between the sheets where he took his time getting to know the landscape of her body, unhurriedly caressing each curve—as if committing her to memory. With his lips, he savored the taste of her mouth, her long neck, and her soft round breasts. Oh, how he'd longed for this moment.

Kate moaned with pleasure with each discovery, wrapping her legs around his waist, and without another moment's hesitation, he entered her, taking their passion to a whole new level until a setting sun fell on their own contented afterglow.

Kate laid her head on Lorenzo's chest, drumming out the rhythm of his heart. He was calmer now than when he'd burst through the door, believing Kate harmed in a way he'd never overcome.

Lorenzo stared at the ceiling, trying to work out why Frank had wanted Kate to join them when it seemed unnecessary. He'd said he got caught in the middle, likely coerced by Marco to get her alone, then reconsidered. Lorenzo pictured the man from the dock who'd stopped Kate on her way to meet Frank. Him, Marco, Frank, and the intruder from earlier. Who had that been? It had all been so organized.

Lorenzo stroked Kate's hair, savoring her warmth and attention. "You were right," he said. "It was a setup."

Lorenzo watched Kate reach for the blanket bunched up at their feet. She pulled it over them. "He told us to go home," she said, settling beneath the blanket.

He looked away. "I can't. Not yet." He wasn't through. He needed to get his revenge on Marco. "But *you* need to go," Lorenzo said, practically choking on the words.

Kate sate up, her mouth set in that stubborn pout he recognized. "We're doing this together, or we're not doing it at all."

Lorenzo sighed, weighing the risk of staying against his ardor as he gazed at Kate, recalling the passion they'd shared moments ago. "All right, but we have to get out of Genoa," he said.

"And go where?" she asked.

"We'll leave for Parma first thing in the morning. We need to find out if the school received *Il Gatto*, and what they've done with it."

Kate lay back down and nestled up close, satisfied with his reply. He put an arm around her and caressed her bare shoulder.

"Parma. Is it far?" she said.

"A few hours," he said lazily, preoccupied with the softness of her skin. "The train will take us down the coast first, then cut inland through Pisa."

"Should we check in with your family?"

Lorenzo sighed. "Not yet. I still don't think I'm ready for that."

"Hmm." Kate pushed a stray lock of hair from her face.

"Are you disappointed?"

"A little. But I understand you wanting to wait. It'll be better when you can take your time getting reacquainted with them."

Lorenzo pictured his homecoming. Would there be raised voices or tears? Rejection or hugs?

"So, our last night in Genoa," Kate said. "I'll miss this city."

"And our apartment," he added.

"And the bed?"

He kissed her tenderly. "Definitely the bed," said Lorenzo, thinking of that first morning, her nighttime kicks and shoves, the kiss she'd planted on his hand the night before, and, of course, their coupling that afternoon. He ran the back of his hand along the length of her arm while admiring her and felt like the luckiest man on earth.

Hoarfrost carpeted the coastal landscape as the train from Genoa barreled in and out of dark tunnels carved through rocks and cliffs. Lorenzo announced the approaching towns—always just before the conductor did—and pointed out specific details he remembered while the train waited to exchange passengers at each stop. The nervous flutter in his belly rose and fell as, one stop after another, the train shortened the distance between him and his home village, heightening his anxiety.

Though Lorenzo knew the landscape, some things had changed. Tagging and graffiti now spoiled the tunnels with messages telling Americans to go home, spray-painted in red, white, and blue. It was this damned war in Iraq. Lorenzo had been in Italy long enough to know that the average Italian was firmly against Berlusconi's support of George Bush's presence in Iraq—and even more against Italy's promise of troops. What was in it for Berlusconi? He did nothing that didn't benefit him personally. Lorenzo could say the same of Marco or any of the Robinis. But what exactly would Marco have to gain by going after Kate, for example? *Was he purely motivated by profit, or had it been a scare tactic?*

Lorenzo draped his arm across Kate's shoulders and noticed she'd fallen asleep. The night before, they'd stayed up late getting more familiar with one another under the sheets. He grinned, thinking of how he'd woken to her radiant smile that morning.

Shortsighted by lust and longing, he hadn't given birth control a single thought. Nor had she mentioned it. A glimmer of hope crossed his mind. A child. A second chance. He gazed at her as the train slowed to another stop. Her coat, which laid over her like a blanket, slipped off, so he pulled it back up, inadvertently waking her.

Kate opened her eyes and yawned. "Where are we?"

Lorenzo had arrived at this station hundreds of times in his life. Other than the modern train and the renovated platform, nothing had changed. But one memory was fixed. This was the last place he'd seen Ella alive.

"This is Manarola," said Lorenzo. *Home.* Kate sat up and looked out the window. He leaned across her and pointed. "It's that way." She looked behind them where rooftops and patches of colorful houses peeked over the tunnel.

"How are you feeling?" she asked.

"About being so close to my family, or about you?" He grinned.

"All of it." Kate wove her fingers through his.

"I'm nervous—about all of it."

She squeezed his hand. "Aren't you curious?"

Lorenzo was beyond curious to see the family he'd left behind—curious, anxious, and terrified of what awaited him.

"There is a beautiful hike down along there." He pointed beyond the tunnel. There was so much he wanted to show her, and that hike was the least of it. This was his home turf. He was proud.

Lorenzo followed her gaze beyond the trees and shrubs bordering the platform to the glittering sea as she considered his home village with the curiosity of a child. She looked down the coastline, then up toward town at the terra cotta patchwork of rooftops. Finally, her eyes rested on a young man staring down the length of the platform, waiting for someone. Half of his face was cast in shadow. The other half was lit by the early morning sun, giving him an angelic glow.

"Looks like that poor guy's been stood up," said Kate.

He was young and handsome, noted Lorenzo, with brown wavy hair just long enough to tuck behind his ears and eyes that squinted into crescents in the sun's glare. He looked familiar—old enough to be his son.

Lorenzo blinked.

Could it be? Was it possible? Lorenzo shook off the thought as the young lady stepped off the train and wrapped her arms around the waiting man. Lorenzo watched the pair walk away toward the underground tunnel leading into town. He envisioned himself and Ella. It felt like he'd stepped back in time.

"Are you sure you're all right?" asked Kate as their train lurched ahead.

"Mm-hmm, I'm fine." Lorenzo tugged on the soft blue scarf

around Kate's neck and looked into her eyes, thinking of what lay ahead.

Someday, life will give you a second chance. When that time comes, take it. That's what he'd said to everyone he arrested over the years, and now he believed it more than ever.

A half-hour later, their train stopped in La Spezia, a much larger city than his little village—with museums, a university, a naval base, and the police headquarters where he'd been working the day he answered that fateful call . . .

They'd found Ella's body on the cliff. She'd been raped and brutally beaten. Not ten minutes had passed before reporters swarmed the station, shouting over one another with intrusive questions and ugly insinuations.

"Do you have any witnesses? How many suspects? Murder or suicide? Are the police prepared to open a full investigation?"

Then the questions turned personal. "Where were you when your wife went missing?" *Missing?* "What was the nature of your marriage? Were you happy? Did she leave you? Are you worried the assailant will come after you or your family?" They'd followed him to the train station, his heart aching for the woman he'd loved more than life, his grief like an open gash in his chest, a severed artery spilling agony for all to see. Yet they couldn't see his pain—or, worse, they chose to ignore it. They suffocated him. That was the source of his disdain for the press.

It remained a mystery to him, after all the questioning, how little news there was about her murder—as if someone had swept the story under the rug.

CHAPTER SIXTEEN

Kate

The Parma hotel included amenities, like an outdoor pool—closed for the winter—and a fine restaurant. But Kate and Lorenzo skipped lunch and went right to their room at the end of the hall, focused on satisfying an entirely different appetite.

"If that's lunch, I can't wait to see what's for dinner," Kate said afterward. She was still tingling all over from Lorenzo's skillful attentions.

He looked at her lazily, bunching his pillow behind his head as Kate traced the outline of a birthmark on his chest. "We still have work to do," he said.

"What? *Now?*"

"*Il Gatto*, remember? The art school is a long way from town. We'll need to rent a car."

"Do a drive-by? Catch Marco red-handed handing off the pink kitty?"

"Heh. I don't think it's going to be quite so easy."

Kate wished he'd leave it to the police but understood his need to take Marco down himself. "Could we take the rest of the day off? Explore Parma? See the sights?"

Lorenzo shook his head, but she saw a grin tug at the corner of his mouth.

***

That afternoon, they toured the Glauco Lombardi Museum, where they perused the collection previously belonging to Napoleon's second wife, Marie-Louise of Austria. Kate oohed and aahed over marble busts, gilded china, gem-laden necklaces, and silk gowns.

"And I thought *my* shoes were ridiculous," she said, pointing out the tiny silk slippers. "It's a wonder she could stand at all."

Lorenzo leaned over her shoulder and murmured in her ear. "I doubt a woman of such leisure spent much time on her feet."

"Mm." Kate turned her head for a nuzzle, her pulse quickening with the vivid memory of his body pressed against hers earlier that day.

They left the museum for the rambling gardens of Parco Ducale along the west bank of the Parma River, where painters, photographers, and lovers gathered with their easels, cameras, and quilted blankets. They spent a good part of their afternoon wandering in the extensive park, until the clouds rolled in, and they felt the first drops of rain.

Kate ran for cover under the awning of a nearby kiosk and laughed as she wiped the rain from her face. Lorenzo snapped a photo of her with his phone.

"Don't! I look terrible."

"I want to remember you always just the way you look today." He showed her the picture. Kate cringed, ignoring the crack that ran along the left side of the screen. She looked wild, her face pink and damp, her hair disheveled—but her smile broader than she'd ever seen it.

"That's not me," she said, wondering what he saw that she did not.

He grinned. "That is exactly you."

It was full-on dark by the time they sat to dinner on the hotel patio. Raindrops danced a gentle pitter-pat on the glass overhang. Hidden garden lamps illuminated pink bougainvillea vines so that each blossom appeared magically suspended like tiny Chinese lanterns along the perimeter wall.

"What a beautiful day it's been," said Lorenzo, staring out into the starless night. "More wine?" He emptied the last of the bottle into Kate's glass.

"Are you trying to get me drunk, detective?"

"I don't think it would make a difference—do you, madam?"

Kate fussed with the blue scarf around her neck. "You think you know me so well."

"Every beautiful inch."

"Thank you. You're rather beautiful yourself." Kate laid her hand on his thigh and leaned in—her lips just shy of touching his. "I prefer you without the beard, though."

He grinned. "Noted."

The server interrupted their tête-à-tête to clear their plates.

"We'll take our coffee inside," said Lorenzo.

They chose a table by the window, away from the other patrons. Then relaxed over a shared slice of almond cake while Lorenzo told a story about being a police officer in Manarola, and the day he had arrested his next-door neighbor for tossing a rotten melon over the garden wall—and hitting Lorenzo's mother in the head with it.

"No!" Kate laughed.

"Yes! And she pressed charges purely to tick him off. It worked, too. He was livid. That's one of the hardest parts of the job; you always see people at their worst."

Something outside the window caught Kate's eye, but it was dark, and she couldn't be sure what she'd seen. It was close though. A dog —no—a face down low, where a dog might be.

"Your presence is either unwelcome or on the heels of someone's misfortune. Once—"

"Lorenzo, someone's watching us," Kate whispered, keeping her eyes on the image crouched outside the window then rising to its feet. A man. "Look."

"Sorry?"

She looked to Lorenzo for an instant and then pointed. But when she turned back, the figure was gone. "I'm sure they were there."

"A person?"

"A man—I'm sure of it."

Was it Frank? Was he following them? If not him, then who? Two other possibilities came to mind. The creep at the tour boat with the black eye, or the man who'd traumatized her two days ago. She felt butterflies stir in her chest, followed by a wave of nausea.

Lorenzo went outside to investigate while Kate waited nervously by the door. Thirty seconds ticked by. A minute. Two. After her traumatic incident at the apartment, she didn't like being separated from Lorenzo. Where *was* he?

The door swung open. "I looked everywhere," Lorenzo said, dripping wet. "There was no one. I'm sorry."

Kate led him back to their room, where he promptly locked the door and closed the blinds.

"Do you remember anything about him?" asked Lorenzo, peeling off his wet clothes. "Big or small? What was he wearing?"

"I don't know." She started pacing from the bed to the desk and back again. "He seemed big. I can't be sure." Kate tugged anxiously on her scarf. "Oh! He wore a hat. I think it was a hat. Might have been his hair. Oh crap! I don't know."

"Give it time," Lorenzo said. "It'll come to you when you least expect it." He fished a dry pair of pants from his suitcase, which was propped open outside the bathroom door.

"Do you think someone followed us from Genoa?" said Kate.

"I wish I knew. If there's one thing I've learned over the years, it's that anything is possible."

Kate stopped at the desk. "Frank?"

Lorenzo shrugged. How could he know? She was the one who'd seen the man. But at least, for now, they were safe in their room—just the two of them.

Kate picked through the brochures of nearby attractions laid out on the desk, including one for the Cinque Terre. She walked her fingers up the five villages on the map. "How big is Manarola? It was hard to tell from the train."

"Just over three hundred people." Lorenzo padded barefoot across the room to stand behind her. "Most can't stay; not enough jobs, not enough space, not enough houses." He rested his hands on her hips as he glanced over her shoulder at the brochure. "It's one reason Ella and I had to get creative and consider that old farm-house." He paused. "That damned farmhouse."

"Do you think it's still there?"

"Probably, but the Robinis cleared it out—after." He pushed the brochure aside. Kate recalled that from when Lorenzo had shared his story. Stripped all the evidence, so when the police finally went to investigate, there was nothing left. "I'm afraid I've painted a grim picture of Manarola for you, Kate. It's really a beautiful village." He leaned back against the desk while Kate sat on the edge of the bed, listening to Lorenzo talk about his hometown and family, giving her vivid descriptions of everyone with short anecdotes to flesh them out. She laughed as he mimicked his parents, scolding one another for everything from telling a story wrong to breathing too loud.

"True love," she said.

"You joke, but I believe it was. Their quarrels were harmless. We all knew my parents loved each other deeply. The love pats, stolen kisses, and eight children were proof enough."

"Sex is not love," said Kate, rising from the bed. Lorenzo cocked an eyebrow.

"Why is it called making love, then?" He ambled toward her.

"Sex is an *expression* of love, not love itself," Kate said, pulling the covers down on the bed with a playful grin.

He placed his hands on her hips and drew her close. "And exactly what do you think *we've* been up to, my dear Sancho?"

CHAPTER SEVENTEEN

Lorenzo

"*Buongiorno mia cara*," Lorenzo said, setting a steaming cup of coffee on the bedside table. He'd woken much earlier, troubled by the lack of planning. While Kate had continued sleeping, he'd mapped out a rudimentary way forward. First, get familiar with the art school. It would not be easy, but he hoped to walk in the front door rather than sneak in through the rear. And second? Well, he didn't have a second step yet.

"Good morning." Kate yawned and stretched her arms high above her head. She looked flush and glowing, gazing at him with a new smile that radiated sensuality—a smile he imagined reserved especially for him. He bent to kiss her, and she wrapped her arms around his neck. "I'm starving."

"Me too. Should I call room service?" He grinned.

"Later," she purred, pulling him to her.

While Kate showered, Lorenzo walked to the piazza down the street for coffee and pastry to surprise her. The neon sign in the cafe window blinked "free internet" and "fresh pastry." He hadn't reached the shop before noticing someone approaching from the center of the piazza.

Frank? It was. Had he followed them to Parma? *Had* it been Frank that Kate saw in the window last night? Lorenzo braced himself for the encounter.

Pop, pop, pop.

Lorenzo recognized the sound of gunfire instantly, of course, but could only watch helplessly as Frank staggered back, opened his mouth to speak, then toppled to the ground. He'd taken a bullet to the forehead and two to his chest. Lorenzo couldn't believe his eyes.

People nearby screamed, scattering to shield themselves behind benches, trees, or trash bins in the piazza. "*Pistolero!*" they cried. Some brave souls moved in closer. Others followed.

"What happened?" someone asked. "Who is that?" A baby's shrill cry echoed off the surrounding buildings.

Lorenzo looked around for the shooter. The shots had come from the north side of the piazza, but he saw only an older gentleman and his wife creeping out from behind a pillar outside a travel office. Quickly, he turned around to where Frank lay face up in a pool of blood with his legs twisted and one arm over his chest—as if he'd been pledging an oath, a slip of paper in his hand.

Lorenzo knew right away that Frank was dead, but knelt to take his pulse anyway, furtively removing the slip of paper while the crowd moved in. Women cried, shedding tears for a stranger, making the sign of the cross. Father, son, and holy spirit. Soon after, sirens blared.

It took everything Lorenzo had to remain calm and walk away, but he couldn't stick around and become the next victim.

Once he'd reached the other side of the piazza, Lorenzo looked over his shoulder to make sure the coast was clear and unfolded the note. "Cat at school. I'm going in. Leave at once." Wrapped in the note were two train tickets to Milan.

Leave at once? Was Frank worried about his safety or Kate's? Or was it something else altogether? The note left too many questions.

Sancho. *Why* had he agreed to let her come along? Professional courtesy had nothing to do with it, if he was honest with himself. She'd bewitched him at the opera long ago, and infatuated him since the morning he'd seen her in Thomas's office. The shared tears in her living room sealed his affection. And now, with their newfound intimacy, he needed her like a drug—which made what he had to do that much more difficult.

Cursing himself for not being more careful, Lorenzo returned to the hotel where Kate emerged from the bathroom in her bra and panties, smiling at him like he was the center of her world. It broke his heart. He wanted to wrap himself around her, feel her bare skin against his. Instead, he retrieved her jeans from the floor and held them out to her.

He swallowed hard, hoping it would help with the lump in his throat. "Get dressed."

"Where are we going?" she asked, filling one leg of her jeans.

"You—you're going home. The train leaves in a half-hour." Lorenzo's heart raced as if supercharged on caffeine and sugar. He was sweating with fevered worry, the palms of his hands clammy and slick.

Kate froze. "And you?"

Lorenzo held out her blouse, but she ignored him, her jeans still only half on, waiting for him to speak.

"Get d-dressed, and I'll explain." He could not think straight with her staring at him like that, mostly naked, flush with emotion. "Please."

"We're in this together. I'm going nowhere!" She pulled up her jeans and fastened them, then slipped the camisole over her head before snatching her blouse from his hand.

"Frank's been shot." The *pop, pop, pop* rang in his ears as he recalled the scene.

"What?"

"Frank was just shot and killed in the middle of the piazza." Lorenzo still couldn't believe it. He reached into his pocket for the note and handed it to her. "I need to finish this on my own, Kate. It's too dangerous for you. I cannot take that risk. I won't."

She read the note out loud. "Cat at school. I'm going in. Leave at once." She looked at him. "I'd say it's too dangerous for you too."

"I'm not finished here. I didn't come all this way to give up now, so I'm going to the school, and I'm going to get what I can to finish this off." He handed her one of the train tickets.

"I quit my job for this story!" She thrust the ticket back at him. "All you have is this—vendetta!

There was truth to her remark, and it stung as sharp as if she'd slapped him across the face. He stood, openmouthed, the ticket crumpled in his hand and an ache in his chest. "Is that what you think? Honestly?" Lorenzo took a cautious step toward her, and then, almost as an afterthought, added, "You quit your job?"

"Walker was going to demote me, but I couldn't give up on this story. It's everything. It *was* everything. Now there's you, and I'm not so sure about *anything*. I thought we were a team."

"You can be sure about me, but, please, Katie," he said. "You *need* to get on that train."

Kate fixed him with a steely glare. "No." He'd expected as much, and with a heavy sigh, he reconsidered.

"Manarola then. Find my sister but spare her the details. Tell her you are a friend of mine and wait for me."

Kate scowled. "A *friend*?" She shoved him with all her strength.

He steadied himself. "A very *close* friend."

"But I thought we—"

"Yes, yes. You thought right. You just can't say anything, understand? And your location *must* remain secret. No one can know where you are—*No one.* It's the only way." Lorenzo cringed. "If Marco or Alfonso get wind you're there, you're as good as dead."

"How will I know if something goes wrong? How will I know if you're okay?" Kate's voice cracked with emotion.

Lorenzo approached her cautiously, taking her trembling hands and drawing her close. He held her tightly, soaking up her pain, absorbing her passion as if it could sustain him.

"Hush, now. It will all be fine—trust me." His throat tightened. "It won't be too long." He shouldn't have promised, but he needed her on that train. Lorenzo ran his fingers through her damp curls, kissing her neck, her chin, her lips. She wriggled to free herself, but he held her tighter. "It's the only way. I must finish this alone."

Kate gathered her things quietly, tears streaming down her cheeks. She remained quiet as Lorenzo walked her to the train station, praying he wasn't making a huge mistake. Her eyes were dull and red around the edges, and her typically rosy lips had lost their color. The sight broke his heart.

"I'll call Muriel once I get settled. Let her know you're coming," said Lorenzo. The thought weighed on him. It had been years since he'd heard his sister's voice. Kate looked up at him, her eyes narrowed in . . . what? Anger? Disdain? Doubt? "I'm going to take care of this, Kate. Be patient."

When they reached the train, he stepped close and kissed her one last time. "One more thing." He was about to say he loved her. He wanted to say he needed her. But with clenched fists and an aching heart, he said, "Be careful."

Back at the hotel, Lorenzo took his suitcase to the concierge for safekeeping, then swung through a second-hand store. He needed a disguise. He picked out a faded black hoodie and an olive drab backpack, among other things. Now, dressed in humble garb and rubber-soled shoes, Lorenzo set off toward the local information stand, where he found a brochure for a bed and breakfast near the art school, and a regional road map. After a quick look at both, he tucked the brochure and map into his pack and began walking south along the two-lane highway.

Traffic sped by in a burst and taper fashion. One moment a torrent, loud and reeking of fumes, the next almost quiet enough to hear the wind blowing through the trees along the side of the road.

He'd gone about two miles, replaying the last few hours with Kate in a loop, when a white pickup truck with a canopy on back passed him and pulled over into the gravel.

"*Vuoi un passaggio?*" asked the driver through the open window. He was a muscular man with calloused hands and patchy stubble on his chin. A decal on the door read Gio's Laundry Service.

Lorenzo kicked the gravel beneath his feet. By his calculations, he had another seven miles to his destination.

"Seriously. It's no trouble. But I do need to get moving. Got a schedule to keep," said the driver, pointing back into the canopy with his thumb. "Where are you headed?"

Lorenzo handed him the brochure from his pack. "Maybe it's not too far out of your way?"

The driver took the brochure and looked it over. "I'm sure it's a nice place, but my sister rents rooms near there, and her food, ah, *bellissimo.*"

"Um." Lorenzo felt tired and wasn't in the mood for this, but agreed, provided it wasn't far from his original destination near the school.

"No problem." The man looked Lorenzo in the eye, then flipped open his phone to call his sister. "Pietra, it's me, Salvo." When the call ended, he said, "It's your lucky day, my vagabond friend. She has a bed for you."

They drove along a maze of rural roads and finally pulled up to a small dairy farm. Pietra Tarolli, Salvo's sister, met them at the door. She looked as if she'd worked hard on the farm her whole life. Weathered skin, thin graying hair, and callused hands were the price for self-sufficiency.

She introduced her son, Berto—a man of twenty-five or so who wore a shiny black leather jacket and a gray driving cap. He stood with his shoulders hunched and his hands stuffed into his pockets like a gangster ripped from the pages of a crime novel.

After some small talk and a healthy lunch in the family kitchen, Salvo said goodbye and made a hurried exit. "I'm in for it now," he cried, looking at his watch.

For the equivalent of twenty American dollars a day, Lorenzo would get full room and board if he paid up front for the week. Salvo hadn't exaggerated the quality of the food; the lunch was marvelous.

Berto led Lorenzo to a small plaster-walled room with a twin bed, a faded landscape painting over the dresser, and a caned rocker in the corner. After opening the blinds, he left the room, and Lorenzo retrieved his phone from his backpack and plugged it in beside the bed. He flipped it open and ran his thumb across the cracked screen. No new messages. He'd hoped to hear from Kate when she'd arrived —a text, an email. Perhaps she was still angry with him, or perhaps there was no cell service in the small village. Perhaps there was no service *here*. He checked. Sure enough. No bars.

Lorenzo studied his map and discovered the farm was less than a mile as the crow flies from the Bolognese School of Art. Except for the lack of cell service, Salvo had not steered him wrong.

"Pietra?" Lorenzo said, entering the kitchen. She was already prepping for dinner while the dishes from lunch dried beside the sink. "I'm looking for a signal," he said, holding up his phone.

"No signal," she said, then pointed to a cordless phone mounted to the wall.

"Internet?" he asked. She shook her head. "What about Berto?"

"No," she said. "No computer."

Lorenzo glanced at the phone, tempted to use it to call his sister's house, then imagined the awkward conversation to follow. Did he want Pietra overhearing that, and the delicate private details? No.

Lorenzo grabbed his binoculars and set off down the gravel road wearing the faded black hoodie he'd purchased at the secondhand store, his cell phone tucked into the pocket. With luck, he'd find a signal.

He set a course along the pasture where a dozen cows picked at green stubble on the other side of the fence, paying little attention to the passing stranger. A tractor rumbled slowly by, clumps of dirt spinning off its tires.

The walk was relaxing. If it wasn't for his need to find the school, he'd have taken his time. But as he came to the end of the woods on the other side of the pasture, he spotted a massive stone building in the distance. The school?

It appeared to be an old private estate with a circular drive. He raised his binoculars to have a closer look and noticed that the driveway branched off, leading to a small stone house set back and off to one side of the main house. He'd need to get closer, but the sun was sinking fast, and Pietra would be serving dinner soon, so it would have to wait.

Before heading back to Pietra's, Lorenzo pulled his phone from his pocket, hopeful for a signal. Nothing. "How will I know if something goes wrong?" Kate had asked. "How will I know if you're okay?"

That sentiment went both ways. He wondered whether it had been such a good idea to come here by himself after all. Kate might have loved it at the little dairy farm. They could have posed as husband and wife. He smiled to himself, imagining Kate beside him in the single bed.

That night, alone in his room, Lorenzo found his blinds closed, his bedding turned down, and the addition of a decorative nightlight plugged in beside the door. His pack remained untouched, propped against the wall where he'd left it. He felt grateful that in the time he'd spent with Pietra she had never once asked a personal question, other than what was needed to fill out a brief form for her records. Name, address, and telephone number. "Lorenzo Rossi," he'd told her. "I'll pay cash."

With the lights out, Lorenzo lay comfortably in bed, wondering about Kate's reception in Manarola. It would be, he imagined, challenging to navigate his family even in the best of circumstances, but his own absence and glaring lack of communication could make it worse. What would she find there? Muriel would surely become her friend. He'd counted on that—but what about the others?

Lorenzo worried most about Emilio—a man now, doubtless with a not-so-genial opinion of his absent father. Lorenzo had missed it all: Emilio's first words, steps, report card, job, and other milestones. He knew little about his son, except for the nuggets his sister added to her letters, usually imploring Lorenzo to reach out to him. But every time Lorenzo had tried, he'd ended up thinking of Ella, and his heart had broken all over again. Did Emilio look like her? Did he have her eyes?

Lorenzo closed his eyes and saw Ella in her satin-lined casket, moments before they had sealed it for eternal rest. How he wished he could forget that sight. Her black hair and rose bud lips burned in his memory. He closed his eyes tighter, trying to blot it out, to send it to darkness. He was so exhausted he thought his mind might be playing tricks on him. Was he really dreaming of Ella? The figure opened her eyes. They were as blue as the sea on a summer day.

It was Kate.

Lorenzo shuddered, feeling as if his heart would burst.

The next morning was the first day in over a week Lorenzo hadn't woken beside Kate, and it felt odd. She, too, would wake up alone in an unfamiliar bed. Was she thinking about him now as he thought about her?

Lorenzo retrieved his running shoes from the bottom of his pack and set off to see how close he could get to the old estate he'd seen the day before, taking his phone along in case he found a signal further from the farm.

He ran by the pasture—empty at this early hour, the cows still holed up in the barn. Gradually, Lorenzo increased his pace along the twisted rural roads, panting a white cloud of breath in the near-freezing temperature. Before long, his fingers and toes had warmed, and the old stone building came into view.

He stopped at the foot of the drive to catch his breath and glanced up at the sign posted prominently at the front gate: *Scuola d'Arte Bolognese*, engraved in flowing letters. Below it, a red three-legged stool.

CHAPTER EIGHTEEN

Kate

The train to Manarola traveled under a thickly clouded sky. Not a speck of blue in sight. Kate used the time to make sense of the events leading to their arrival in Parma and the cause of her departure.

Frank.

As much as she didn't care for the man, she was disturbed at the horrific way he'd died. His murder added yet another layer to the story—and it added to her fears. Was he the man she'd seen the night before in the window? Or was that another, more treacherous foe?

A terrible thought suddenly occurred to her. If someone had followed them to Parma, could they be tailing her now? She looked over her shoulder, paranoid. Three men sat behind her—one young, two older, staggered like chess pieces on a board. Two women about Kate's age sat together, whispering. It could be anyone. It could be no one. They could be following Lorenzo too. From what she understood of Marco, he would never let Lorenzo destroy his organization. But who ran the organization—and were these three seemingly unrelated businesses, in fact, a single organization? The three-legged stool she'd imagined?

They could have been on their way to Milan by now. Out of harm's way. Why couldn't Lorenzo let it go? Closure? Revenge? Vendetta, as she'd suggested so heatedly? But if Marco murdered Lorenzo's young wife, he would have no qualms about harming Lorenzo—especially if the family business was at stake.

Kate fought the impulse to return to Parma and drag Lorenzo out of the quagmire she believed he was stepping into. It was only with Lorenzo's confidence in his plan that she remained on the train and was rewarded with a blast of sunshine when it stopped in Manarola.

***

After hoisting her backpack over her shoulders and retrieving her roller-bag from overhead, Kate made her way off the train, knowing it was time to worm her way into Lorenzo's dearest sister's life with a flimsy cover story. Other than the few details he'd shared the night before, Kate knew very little about her. Muriel was kind, he'd said, and generous. She made friends easily. He described her as the peacemaker in the family, always breaking up fights—usually fights Lorenzo had started. That thought made Kate smile. She couldn't imagine him starting an argument.

She followed a handful of passengers through the tunnel from the station, the handle of her roller-bag gripped tight in her hand. Snippets of conversation—in Italian, of course—echoed off the walls. Two whispering women walked past the information boards at a ticket kiosk on the other side of the tunnel. Kate stopped and glanced at fliers offering lodging and dining. There was a Mass schedule for the local Catholic Church, San Lorenzo. It was this church's bell tower she was to locate. Lorenzo said the bakery would be easy to spot from there. She followed the winding path down the hill, flanked by colorful buildings that looked as old as the village itself, adorned with Christmas lights and decorations.

The bell tower across from the ancient Gothic-style church was simple enough to locate, but the bakery eluded her. The church bells tolled loud and clear, and seemed to go on forever. *Bong. Bong. Bong.* Kate checked her watch. Surely this didn't go on every hour? How would anyone get any peace?

She stepped up to the rail behind the tower. Looking down, she saw another road, where shop doors stood open to welcome patrons, and stairways made of thick stone slabs peeled off in multiple directions. The view beyond sent her heart racing. A mosaic of terracotta rooftops and terraced vineyards lined a narrow canyon twisting toward the bright blue sea where mammoth rocks were slammed by the incoming waves.

Bong. Bong. Bong. The deafening bells continued as men, women, and small children spilled from within the church and past its massive doors.

She sat down on her suitcase at the foot of the bell tower, waiting for the crowd to thin. Churchgoers filed past her; most didn't even notice her. A scrawny cat slinked between her legs and mewed, but Kate had nothing to give it but a pat on the head, so it moved on.

Kate finally stood, her backpack heavy with the weight of her laptop, and began making her way uncertainly down the street, trying to remember the Italian word for bakery. An older gentleman with an impressive white mustache and a wool blazer, worn thin at the elbows, stopped and spoke to her. She recognized the concerned tone in his voice but not the words. He nodded and waved down a young boy of about ten for help.

"*Parli italiano?*" asked the boy, looking back at the older man for approval. The old man nodded, hovering over the boy with a sweet yet curious expression.

"*Non parlo italiano. Lei parla inglese?*" Kate asked, carefully enunciating each syllable. The boy's laughter was answered with a gentle slap on the shoulder by the old man.

"I speak little English," said the boy proudly, then looked to the old man, who repeated his earlier concern. "He say you are lost sheep," the boy said.

Kate smiled. "I'm looking for the bakery. Mamma Rotondo's bakery. Um . . . *panti ficio*." The boy laughed again, joined by the old gentleman. Together they pointed to a canary-yellow house with a small wooden sign tacked above the door: *Panificio Rotondo*. How had she missed it? Kate blushed but joined in their laughter. They walked with her to the bakery door, where the old man poked his head in, bellowing, "Mamma! Mamma Rotondo!" There were colorful exclamations from the back room. The man winked at Kate, slapped the counter, and made a hasty exit.

"This is the *panificio*, thank you," said the boy.

"What is your name?" asked Kate.

"I am Luca. And you? What is your name?" He sounded like a good little student.

"*Mi chiamo*, Kate," she sputtered proudly, glad she'd been practicing.

"Thank you, Kate." Luca glanced past her. "Here is *nonna*. This is Mamma Rotondo."

Kate turned to face a small, sprightly woman with hair squeezed into a long braid down the center of her back. She gripped a faded blue apron tightly in one hand and scowled. Kate was already regretting the interruption.

Mamma carried on passionately for some time before the boy asked Kate, "What will you like? The woman take much to *mercato*, and you can have much luck there to find what you are look for."

"I am looking for Muriel."

"Zia Muriel?" the boy asked. "She is at *mercato*." He giggled. "*Nonna* think what you want is at *mercato* and she is all the time right." He prattled on to the old woman, who shooed them both out the door.

So *that* was Lorenzo's mother. Kate felt as if she'd just met a legend.

"*Nonna*." said Kate. "Your grandmother?"

"Yes. Grandmother." Luca grinned up at her. "Come with me, please. I take you to *mercato*," he said, then took off along the stone pavement further down the hill. Kate followed, dragging her little green roller-bag past narrow three- and four-story buildings painted in sun-bleached tones of gold, red, and orange. As they walked closer to the sea, private townhouses sporting narrow verandas and rooftop gardens gave way to shops and restaurants. Their journey ended at the piazza with a spectacular view of a tiny marina and the brilliant sea beyond it.

"Here," he said, pointing out three women standing beneath a light-green awning with a beautiful display of bread and pastry spread out on a table in front of them. But just as Luca began introducing Kate to the women, Lorenzo's mother hustled into the piazza in her threadbare apron and marched right up to the old gentleman from earlier—her arms flailing, rich with meaningful gestures. To Kate's amazement, the man did not back down; instead, he came back with his own passionate speech. Lorenzo's mother was a firecracker, but the old man proved a formidable opponent.

A woman behind the table peered over her rimless glasses. "*Come posso aiutarla?*" she asked with a smile. She had a mass of dark hair twisted tightly into a clam-shell clip.

Kate adjusted the straps of her backpack, which were digging into her shoulders, and smiled back. "Muriel?"

"*Sì.*" Muriel did not resemble Lorenzo—but looking into her vibrant eyes and candid smile, Kate instantly liked her.

"Could I speak with you alone?" Kate asked, praying Muriel spoke English at least as well as the boy, Luca.

Muriel tilted her head. "Eh?"

"It's important," Kate said. "Um, *importante.*"

"Over here." Muriel wiped her hands on her apron, then with a cautious look back at the other women, led Kate toward a nearby table with two folding chairs.

"*Mi chiamo* Kate. I'm a friend of Lorenzo's. From Portland."

"Enzo?" Muriel cocked her head as if in doubt. "My brother?"

"Yes, your brother."

Muriel's eyes opened wide. "You know my brother?" she asked, raising a hand to her mouth. Kate nodded. Muriel sat down and motioned for Kate to sit as well. "How is he? Where is he? Is he here?" She scanned the piazza as if she expected Lorenzo to saunter up to them. If only that were true.

"No, I'm sorry. I'm here alone. He didn't call you?"

"He did not," Muriel said. Kate's heart sank, realizing she was on her own.

"This is a big surprise, sorry," she said, glancing down at her hands knotted in her lap.

"Yes, a surprise." The lines on Muriel's forehead deepened. "I have not heard from Enzo in years."

Kate winced. "He mentioned that. I'm sorry," she said. "My showing up unannounced like this is probably hard for you. Honestly, I kind of expected you to—well, I don't know what I expected."

"There is nothing but love for Lorenzo here in Manarola." Muriel removed her glasses and dabbed at her eyes, smiling. "But we miss him terribly. If you could let him know this, I would be grateful. Tell me, Kate, how is he? Is he well?"

Kate nodded. "Lorenzo is fine. He's fine." She hoped.

"And he's happy?"

Kate reflected on the last few days and smiled. "He is." She sat up straight, lifting her chin and squaring her shoulders. "We work together," she blurted. "Work friends."

"Girlfriend?" Muriel's five-star smile could not have grown any larger.

Kate felt the heat rise to her face. "Um, no." Lie, lie, lie. She hated this. "When I mentioned I was coming to Italy, he insisted I visit you." Without a script for this moment, Kate feared her improvisation might sound unconvincing.

Muriel nodded and glanced over at the pastry stand. "I want to know so much more, Kate. Where are you staying? Here in the village?"

"Well, I don't have a place yet. I wanted to check in with you first."

"Oh, of course." Muriel smiled. "You can stay with me," she said, checking her watch. "We close the stand at one o'clock, but I'm busy in the bakery until four. Can you come to the bakery then? At four?" Though astonished by Muriel's ready hospitality. Kate didn't need to think about this long. Where else would she go? She had a place to stay with someone she trusted.

"Of course." Kate looked down at her roller bag.

"Luca will take it." With that, Muriel dragged Kate over to the others who were eagerly waiting in the booth. "Kate, this is my sister, Sofia. She's the baby of the family." Sofia appeared about as old as Kate, with a long braid down her back like her mother, and dark blue eyes, like Lorenzo. "That is Lydia Pasini, our dearest friend," Muriel said. Lydia nodded shyly. "And you know Luca."

"*Sono felice di conoscerti,*" Kate said, making eye contact with Sofia, who seemed particularly interested in the newcomer.

"Kate is Enzo's friend from America!" Muriel announced excitedly in English.

"*È amica di Enzo!*" Sofia jumped out from behind the booth and threw herself at Kate with an enthusiastic embrace. How old had Lorenzo said she was when he left? Ten years old? Yet she reacted with such unrestrained joy at the mention of him. Kate hadn't known what to expect, but this wasn't it, and she was relieved. She only hoped things went as well with Emilio when—or *if*—the time came.

Bong. Bong. Bong. The bells again.

"Do they ever stop?" Kate asked.

"You'll get used to it," said Muriel, glancing at the line queuing up at the stand. "We have to get back to work, though, Kate. I'm so sorry. We'll see you at four, yes?"

Sofia handed her a fat bun wrapped in waxed paper.

"Yes, um—*Sì.*" Kate slung her backpack over one shoulder and walked with Luca, who dragged her suitcase back up the bumpy road.

"You can wait at the *parco*." Luca pointed down a cliff side path. "It is *bellissimo* with much to see."

"Thank you, Luca. I'll start there." She waved goodbye, but he was already speeding up the hill with her roller bag bouncing behind him.

Her walk took her past colorful wooden boats, some no bigger than a rowboat, propped against buildings or resting on trailers, awaiting their fisherman owners along the side of the road. Kate wound her way to the park overlooking the sea and settled on a sunny patch beside a stubby palm tree, its fronds waving wildly as if greeting an old friend. Seagulls circled overhead. Shouts and snippets of conversation drifted up from the bluff. Children played nearby, giggling and squealing.

Kate turned her gaze toward the sea, recalling the last few days with Lorenzo—his warm embrace, the sound of his voice. It made their separation harder to bear and the prospect of meeting his family under a pretense more disturbing.

She'd said they were friends. But what should she have said? Obviously, they were more than friends. Good friends? Could she say, close friends? Dare she say, lovers? No, she wouldn't say lovers, though she wanted to. She wanted the world to know.

She removed the bun from its wax paper bag, pulled it apart, and inhaled its aroma like Lorenzo might. She ate the bun while taking in the surrounding activity until she succumbed to fatigue and rested her head on her backpack. Within minutes of closing her eyes, Kate was asleep.

She woke suddenly to two seagulls squabbling nearby and pulled her coat tighter against the chill.

When the church bells tolled four, she stood and shook life back into her legs, then strolled back down the hill to the bakery.

"Hello? Anyone home?" She waited, her hands braced against the counter.

Luca jumped out from the stairwell at the rear of the shop. "Come this way." They climbed the narrow staircase single file, then turned into a cozy sitting room with two well-worn recliners and a dim lamp in the corner, where two stools sat empty on either side of a chess table set for battle. The framed print of *Madonna and Child* hung above the table, exactly as Lorenzo had remembered.

He should be here.

Luca disappeared out the door and down the hall and returned with Muriel.

"Do you live here?" asked Kate.

"No, my house is up the hill. This is Mamma and Papa's house. My sister Sofia lives here with her daughter Marta and my nephew Emilio and his boy." Muriel laid a hand on Luca's head and ruffled his hair. "The evening meal is always here, though."

So, Luca was Emilio's child? Lorenzo's *grandson*? Kate blinked back her surprise and stared down at the boy, searching her memory for any mention of a grandson. There was none. Had it been deliberate, or was Lorenzo so removed from this family that he didn't know?

"Emilio!" called Muriel out the door.

"*Papà!*" Luca shouted. Emilio didn't answer, but the old man from earlier roared and stomped into the sitting room to see what was up. Once he saw Kate, he broke into a toothy smile, barely visible beneath his mustache, and he crossed the room to embrace her. He took Kate's face in his hands and spoke as he might to a child. His voice was soft. His words sounded kind. When Muriel told him Kate was Lorenzo's friend, he seemed to tingle with excitement and fired off a dozen questions. Sofia joined them with a few of her own. Muriel, fortunately, helped with the interpretation.

"Yes, he's happy. He is a police detective. Yes, he is healthy. Girl-friend?" Kate felt a tug at her heart. "No, I'm not his girlfriend." Mamma joined the crowd, her scowl now replaced with glee, and the entire process started all over again. "Yes, he's happy . . ."

Muriel did her best to keep up with her parents and sister as they all reminisced about Lorenzo and his silly antics as a child. Kate had feared Lorenzo's family would be angry with him, perhaps even discounting him after so many years absent. But what she saw proved the opposite. He was gone but surely not forgotten.

Sofia and Mamma left to prepare dinner. Kate asked to help, but they shooed her out almost as quickly as Papa, who was never welcome in the kitchen and made a stink about it to the point Kate was sure they could hear him in Genoa.

The meal was a feast fit for Lorenzo himself, with pasta, bread, sauces, and a nut-crusted cake that tasted like heaven. Kate, acting as his surrogate, did her best to sample everything till she nearly burst.

Muriel called the other siblings together. Matteo and Antonio arrived with their families in tow just as the dishes were being cleared. The children, including a handful of grandchildren, all delighted in competing for Kate's attention. There were moments when she felt more like a curiosity than a guest, as furtive glances passed her way.

Antonio and his wife seemed particularly keen on Kate's relation-ship with Lorenzo and how he could let her travel so far alone. "I'm not alone," Kate said, smiling. "I have you all." This earned her another glass of wine and a toast to Lorenzo.

"Remember the time Enzo took grandfather's boat out and father had to fish him out of the water?" said Matteo with a belly laugh.

"Or when he set fire to the bridge?" said Sofia.

"That was an accident," Muriel said. "Besides, you're too young to remember that."

"I was *not*!"

Where was Emilio? Had he deliberately avoided the party? Had he deliberately avoided *her*? At least his absence was overshadowed by the attention of his son, Luca—a bright and happy boy who was undeniably well-loved.

Once the table had been cleared and the wine ran out, Muriel took Kate by the hand.

"You must be tired," Muriel said.

Kate guessed it was past eleven. "Yes. It's been a long day." From waking in Lorenzo's arms to being loaded onto a train and arriving in the coastal hillside village of Manarola, Kate felt equally exhausted and exhilarated.

They said their goodnights, accompanied by warm embraces, and stepped out onto the cobbled street. The evening had been intense—with introductions, storytelling, smiling, and laughing at jokes she couldn't understand. But the fresh night air worked wonders to help Kate unwind.

"I'm sad Lorenzo missed this," said Kate as they walked. The quiet street looked like a movie set under the streetlamps.

"Ah, yes." Muriel slowed her pace, then took Kate's hand. "But we have the next best thing, yes?"

"Hmm." Kate shook her head. *Hardly.* They walked onward up the hill, a seemingly endless climb. "The children are adorable," she said.

"And intelligent. Marta will take her exams soon, and we all expect her to be accepted into the same school in Genoa that Emilio attended. They only take the brightest."

"Emilio went to school in *Genova*?" Kate said, trying on her Italian pronunciation.

"We all felt it was best."

"And Lorenzo?" They veered from the shops and cafés and entered a narrow stairwell with walls on either side interrupted by doorways decorated by potted plants and welcome mats.

"I wrote to him about it. He never answered." Muriel's pace slowed further. "We had to do what was best, Kate. I felt an obligation to Emilio in Lorenzo's absence. He's like a son to me. You understand?" Muriel pulled her sweater tight around her. "My daughter, Gina, and Emilio were more like sister and brother than cousins." She looked behind her as if she'd heard something. Then she turned her attention back to Kate. "I missed Emilio terribly, the sweet thing. He wrote nearly every day the first year until he made a few friends and took up sport. Our summers were lovely, though, with the family together. But by his last year, the letters were few, and he was always unavailable when my husband visited."

"He lives here now, right? Back in the fold?"

"Yes, and how thankful we are."

"He missed a lovely dinner," Kate said, noticing a gray tabby cat peeking at her from a dark doorway.

"Busy man," Muriel said. "Working, working. Always working. Like his father, no?"

"Hmm." Where would Lorenzo be sleeping tonight, why he hadn't called his sister, and how would Kate know if something was wrong? Kate cleared her throat. "I'm sure Marta will do well at the private school," said Kate. "Her parents must be proud of her."

"Sofia is, certainly. Her father . . . well, he's long gone." Kate hadn't noticed. It didn't seem important at the time—so many people, so many distractions. "He was a Sicilian tourist who didn't even leave a phone number. But Marta's a special girl and he'll never know what he's missing."

"And Luca?" Kate's curiosity about Emilio—and the fact that Lorenzo had a grandson—made it impossible not to ask.

"Ah, Luca—*un ragazzo dolce*. A sweet boy, no?"

"Lorenzo didn't mention that he has a grandson." Kate looked ahead at the next few steps, adjusting the straps of her heavy backpack. They'd been climbing the whole way, and after her explorations that afternoon, her legs felt like jelly.

"Emilio does not want him to know." Muriel looked Kate in the eye to make her point. Apparently, Kate was to keep this secret as well.

Finally, they arrived at a green door, adorned with a Christmas themed laurel wreath and lit on both sides by globe-shaped porch lights. Muriel pushed open the door and flicked a switch, lighting the front hall entrance and a stairwell beyond it where Luca had thoughtfully left her suitcase. Muriel turned on the kitchen light.

A man wearing a black wool jacket and faded jeans leaned against the counter, reaching high above his head for something on the shelf. Kate felt a sudden rush of adrenaline.

He was the good-looking man she'd seen waiting on the train platform only days earlier with Lorenzo.

"*Cazzo!*" He looked over his shoulder and turned to face them, his deep blue eyes shifting their focus from Kate to Muriel. "*Mi dispiace, Zia,*" he said, hastily tucking something into his jacket.

"*Va bene, Emilio. Non importa. Ha fame?*" Fine, not important, hungry. Kate recognized these simple words. But one stood out: Emilio. It seemed strange that he would be at Muriel's.

"Emilio, this is Kate, your father's friend from America," said Muriel cheerfully. Emilio stared impassively at Kate, and then, as if fleeing an emotion he did not want to feel, nodded abruptly before rushing out of the house.

Muriel turned to Kate with a shrug. "Don't worry. That's Emilio being Emilio. He'll come around." Though she understood how Emilio might be reproachful to be reminded of his father so suddenly, it still stung.

"I hope I'm not imposing. Lorenzo said this would be fine, but now I'm not so sure," said Kate, looking down at the tile floor, hoping Muriel wouldn't confirm the imposition.

"Impose? No. You are Enzo's friend, so you are my friend."

"It's just for a couple of weeks." Kate peeled off her backpack and set it at her feet. "He said he would call you," she said, rubbing the back of her neck.

Muriel turned toward a black box at the end of the counter. Kate wove her fingers together. The solid red light confirmed her fears. No messages. *Where are you, Lorenzo?*

She sighed and leaned back against the kitchen counter, where Emilio had stood moments earlier. Muriel stood across from her in the small kitchen. A bright bowl of lemons sat beside a wooden bowl of onions on the countertop.

"What do you think of Emilio?" Muriel said. "Good looking, *si?*"

Kate nodded. He was flawless—tall and lean, with beautiful hair and piercing eyes. "He looks so much like his father."

"Yes. I've always thought so. Such a sweet and quiet man, our Emilio. He would make a perfect husband. I tried to arrange something years ago, but he refused." Muriel held her hands up in defeat.

Kate squelched the impulse to ask about Luca's mother, deciding instead that, tired as she was, it was time for bed.

Muriel walked her up two flights of creaky stairs and opened the door to an attic bedroom. "I'm happy you'll be staying with me," she said, laying a tender hand on Kate's arm. She crossed the room and switched on a little lamp beside a single bed against the wall. "I've lived alone since April, when Gio, my husband, passed." Muriel sighed dolefully. "His heart failed him."

Kate followed Muriel into the room, a hand to her chest. "Oh, Muriel, I'm so sorry."

"I miss him like you can't imagine." Muriel began hastily clearing boxes and clutter from the bed.

"I guess now you and Lorenzo have that in common."

"You know about Ella?" Muriel turned toward Kate, a dusty stack of books in her hands. Kate nodded, blushing, wondering whether Lorenzo would approve of her talking about his late wife. "I could *never* compare my loss to his," Muriel said. "Ella was like a sister to me. We all suffered, but not like my brother. He loved Ella with every cell in his body. It was as if—as if a healthy vine had been snipped and left to die. We watched him wither before our eyes, becoming desperate, melancholy, bent on self-destruction." She shook her head. "I believe in my heart that leaving Manarola saved his life. Even without his correspondence, I am comforted knowing he is out there in the world."

"I'm sorry," said Kate, struck by a new awareness of the depth of Lorenzo's grief—and by how easy it was to stick her foot in her mouth when it came to him.

Muriel shook her head. "How could you know? This family is complicated." She laid the books on an antique sewing table behind the bed, then turned to the window and pulled the curtain aside. "In the daylight, you can see the Mediterranean from this window."

Kate gazed out into the night. The narrow village streets were lit by random streetlights.

"It's been a long time since I've had a guest," Muriel said. "Do you mind putting on your own bedding?"

"No, not at all. I'm thankful to you, Muriel."

Muriel took both of Kate's hands in hers and peered into her eyes. "We are thankful that our dear Enzo asked you to come to us. You are welcome for as long as you like. This is good." She nodded. "Very good." Muriel left but returned a few minutes later with fresh sheets and a comforter sealed in an airtight bag. Then she pushed the few boxes against the wall. She tapped her fingers on a brown box with a faded orange lid. "You might like this one. It has some old things of Lorenzo's."

"Thank you," Kate said, her heart racing a little at the thought of going through the box. "Muriel, before you go . . ."

"Yes?"

Kate crossed her fingers. "Do you have internet?"

"Yes!" Muriel answered excitedly. "My daughter set it up for me. The password is Misu2." She spelled it out carefully. "Tell Lorenzo we are all well." She winked at Kate and left the room.

First, Kate unpacked her computer and set it on the antique sewing table beside the books. Then she reached for her suitcase. She could still feel how her eyes had been blurred by rage and heartache when she'd packed it earlier that day. She heaved the suitcase onto the bed and opened it to find Lorenzo's brown sweater lying right on top.

A wave of emotion flowed through her as she clenched the sweater in her hands and brought it to her face. She wanted to sleep in it, wake up in it. The sweater was a poor substitute for her handsome Italian, but she loved that he had given it to her.

She laid the sweater on her pillow, then logged on to Misu2. There must have been a story behind that name, but as Kate typed it in, she couldn't help but see "Miss you too"—so that's how she began her email to Lorenzo.

November 30, 2004
    To: Det.RotondoPDX
    From: RockyMountaingirl546
    Subject: Miss You
    Dear Enzo,
    Yes, now I know your pet name. (Wink.)
    It's been a long day—for both of us, I imagine. I'm embarrassed about the way I acted this morning. You only had my safety in mind, but I hated the idea of being away from you. Damn the story. (It's pointless now, anyway, since I don't have a job.)
    I've met your family, at least as many as Muriel—who is incredible!—could drum up. Nearly all of them. Such a crowd! Your parents crack me up. I met your father on his way out of church this morning. I didn't know it was him at the time. He actually stopped me in the street. I must have looked lost, so he found a boy who spoke English to help me out.
    He led me to the bakery where I met your mother. (Mamma is so nearsighted; she had to get right in my face to look at me.) Muriel was at the market with Sofia. When I introduced myself, you would have thought I'd sat at the right hand of God, the way they and your entire family treated me. Lord Enzo of Manarola. I bow to you. Gladly.

I met Emilio later this evening—about twenty minutes ago. He was here at Muriel's. (I forgot to mention that Muriel has invited me to stay indefinitely. You knew that would happen, didn't you?) Emilio is a man of few words. Muriel thinks he walks on water. It makes sense, you being God and all. I will reserve thoughts on Emilio, so I don't influence your first impression when you meet him. And you will meet him. You will come to Manarola. If not to see your family, then to collect your lovely sweater.

When did you sneak that in there? I am so glad you did. Thank you. :)

P.S. Muriel asked me to tell you they are all well. She misses you, Lorenzo. They all do. That goes double for me. Come home soon.

—Kate, aka Katie, aka Sancho

At first light, Kate popped out of bed and immediately checked for a reply to her email, quickly culling through the usual messages from George and the targeted ads that missed their mark.

Nothing, though, from Lorenzo. It tugged at her heart as she slipped into her jeans and pulled her black turtleneck over her head.

It had only been eight hours, she told herself, closing her laptop. But she flipped open her phone, thinking a text might get his attention. "Good morning, detective," she wrote, then waited for a reply. Again, her heart sank when nothing happened. She consoled herself by topping off her outfit with Lorenzo's brown sweater. He was with her in spirit.

She found a note from Muriel lying beside a plate of breakfast pastries on the kitchen table. It said to make herself at home and suggested places to explore. After two espressos and a quick shower, Kate retraced her steps from the night before with a gooey, cheesy pastry in hand. She descended the narrow stairwell back to the main drag and passed the bakery, the piazza, and a dozen shops and restaurants until she reached the harbor. Here, she saw how Manarola connected to the rest of the world. Looking into the bay, she saw a dozen fishing boats like those parked along the side of the road the previous day. One- and two-man crews with nets and sturdy poles.

Kate sat on the jetty, shielding her eyes from the bright winter sun, and gazed at the ancient cliffs that defined the village with houses set into them as if they'd grown organically from the stones. White sea foam billowed from waves that crashed against the rocky outcrop behind her.

After a long walk to the top of the hill, she turned to admire the village below, with its colorful homes and businesses along narrow boat-lined streets. The absence of cars hadn't hit her until that moment. This was strictly a pedestrian village, as Lorenzo had said. It was exceptional and—quiet.

Cue the church bells. Kate had to laugh.

She collapsed onto an empty bench to rest her feet and imagined Lorenzo walking the same streets, listening to the same bells, perhaps even sitting on that very bench. Ella too. What had she been like? "He'd loved her with every cell in his body," Muriel had said. They were young, with raging hormones and, Kate assumed, beautiful bodies. It was that desire that created Emilio.

And what about Emilio? If first impressions were worth anything, Emilio struck Kate as arrogant. Muriel asked Kate to forgive his behavior, as if that was simply who he was, and everyone else had no choice but to deal with it. But if Emilio's treatment of Kate was any sign of how he'd treat Lorenzo, it would break his heart. Perhaps Lorenzo expected as much from the son who'd lost his mother and was abandoned by his father.

Abandoned.

"Oh, Lorenzo." Kate had to dig deep to fathom how Lorenzo could have stayed away for so long. She struggled to understand. Was his love for Ella so consuming? A wave of envy passed quickly as Kate thought of how Lorenzo had made love to her as if there had been no one else.

She wondered about the night he'd shown up out of the blue at her door. What if she had taken him upstairs? Once Megan had planted that seed, she wondered if she'd made the right choice. Would sleeping with him that first night have changed anything? Would she still be here in Manarola, sitting on this bench, waiting for Lorenzo's return?

With these unanswered questions, Kate began her descent back into the village, stopping briefly at the kiosk outside the tunnel to buy a phone card.

She also purchased a Cinque Terre visitor's card, which included train, bus, and boat rides to and from the five seaside villages, as well as a pass to walk the popular trail. She tucked both purchases into her pocket and walked down to the piazza where she found Muriel and Sofia loading a cart with the remaining bread and pastries.

"Closing shop so soon?" asked Kate.

"Good to see you, Kate." Muriel bent toward a black-and-white cat with a scrap of bread. "Short day today. You will join us for lunch?" The stray walked up to Kate and rubbed itself against her leg.

Kate smiled. "Yes, thank you." Sofia took hold of the cart and began walking up the hill with Kate and Muriel on either side.

"We'll be in Vernazza tomorrow. It's different every day," Muriel said.

"Lorenzo mentioned that you could only get here by train or boat," Kate said. "But I saw a bus schedule."

"There is parking and a bus up there," Muriel pointed up the hill, "but the train is still best."

"Yes," said Sofia. "Train is best."

Mamma Rotondo enlisted Kate's help after the midday meal. It was initially uncomfortable since Mamma didn't know a word of English, but they worked out a kind of pantomime to get the dishes cleared, cleaned, and put away. Then Mamma began preparations for dinner and assumed Kate's cooperation, leading her into the small, private garden behind the house to collect basil, oregano, sage, and rosemary. Empty tomato cages and bean trellises waited for spring planting. Artichoke stumps and tiny white nubs of asparagus lined the surrounding rock wall, shaded by a compact lemon tree. Kate grinned, recalling Lorenzo's story of his mother getting clunked with a rotten melon—and her spirited revenge.

Mamma pulled open a flimsy door to a makeshift garden shed. She pointed to a braid of garlic hanging to the right and a wire basket of onions to the left. *"Due e due,"* she ordered—so Kate grabbed two of each, proud as a kindergartner that she knew her numbers up to ten. She followed the old woman into the house, and there, Kate began cleaning and chopping the onions and garlic. Mamma nodded, grinning, and hummed an unfamiliar tune while they worked. There was no shouting or exchange of harsh words, as Kate had assumed was part and parcel of living here. Just the amicable clink and clatter of two women in the kitchen.

Once they'd finished, Mamma took Kate's hands in her own and squeezed hard. "Lorenzo, eh?"

"Si, Lorenzo," said Kate. Mamma grinned and nodded, then marched upstairs without looking back. Kate wondered what she'd just agreed to.

Alone now and free to do as she pleased, Kate returned to Muriel's. The first thing she did was open her email, hoping to see something from Lorenzo. He hadn't responded. No text reply either. A flutter of nerves nested in her chest as her worry mounted.

She clicked Refresh and a new email arrived from George. "Subject: What about the house?" The expletives that followed shouldn't have alarmed her—but in her current predicament, nerves worn thin by Lorenzo's silence, they did. She read on. He'd called a realtor to have the house assessed.

Kate snapped her laptop closed, grabbed her coat, and set off on foot to the neighboring village, Corniglia. Twenty minutes of foot-stomping therapy where she drilled down on George's email.

"You always do this," he'd said during his last visit. "You always give up before the race is over." His words had wormed their way in, and she couldn't help but break them down into the realization that she had indeed given up on many things. Important things—like her pregnancy, her marriage, her job, and the article she'd been so passionate about. *He's right. I'm a quitter.* In a huff, she did an about-face, backtracking down the trail to work on her story until realizing she'd done it again. "Argh!" she gasped and turned back for Corniglia.

That evening, Kate resurrected her notes on the art fraud story. Sorting truth from theory, she began with a recap of the painting discovered at the university, then tied it to Sylvia's, and how C. Robini Property insurance falsely certified others as well. Next, she linked the Bolognese School of Art with the National Art Foundation, citing familial ties with Alfonso Robini. Naming names, calling out fraud, exposing Alfonso, Marco, and the operation. It was a rush, but when she sat back and reviewed her work, all she saw were its weaknesses. She knew she lacked the proof to confirm her suspicions. For that, she'd need Lorenzo.

Or would she?

CHAPTER NINETEEN

Lorenzo

Lorenzo's heart quickened as he watched Marco emerge from a black sedan, leaning heavily on a silver cane as he had on the yacht, and hobble up the art school steps like a hippo on dry land. What was the nature of the visit? Lorenzo chomped at the bit like a horse at the starting gate, hoping to get inside that building and learn more about the operation.

He'd been scouting out the school on his last few morning runs, hoping to get a glimpse of anything of interest from the neighboring woods. In that time, he'd noted the comings and goings of students and staff, and an intermittent stream of visitors to the smaller house at the rear of the school.

Lorenzo raised his camera and snapped a picture of Marco. One more link tying the school together with the art foundation. But before tucking the phone back into the hoodie, he scrolled down to the candid picture he'd taken of Kate in Parma, and her beaming smile meant for him.

Lorenzo never dreamed he'd become so dependent on a cell

phone and internet service. How frustrating it was to be off the grid. Kate. Katie. Sancho. He missed her smile, her laugh, her lips, and every inch of her silky skin. He wanted to tell her how he felt about her, and how he missed lying beside her each night. That he'd found a good place with Pietra and was, for the time being, safe. How he longed for their reunion.

First, though, he would need to get into that school. He glanced at the building. The old man from earlier held the door open for Marco, then continued down the driveway toward the street. His slumped shoulders and weary gait told a tale of hard work and made Lorenzo aware of his own posture, stooped over his useless phone.

Lorenzo checked the time. He'd been gone too long from Pietra's, so he tucked his phone away and set a course for her farmhouse.

"You return late today," Pietra scolded. "Breakfast was served and cleared."

"I'm fine, Pietra. A piece of fruit is all I need." Lorenzo smiled, and Pietra plucked an apple from a bowl on the counter and handed it to him.

"Would you help me in the greenhouse?" she asked. "I'm laying gravel between the benches and Berto's off on one of his errands. I could use a pair of muscular arms." He nodded and removed his hoodie.

"Pietra," Lorenzo said, catching her eye. "What can you tell me about that marvelous estate up the way? I read a sign out front saying it was an art school."

"Oh, that. It's for troubled kids. You know the kind." She placed her hands firmly on her hips. "Their parents can't handle them and send them off to set them straight."

"A disciplinary program?" Lorenzo bit into his apple. The juice dripped onto his fingers, reminding him of Kate eating the orange in the Genoa apartment.

She nodded. "I've heard it works. They're culled each term. Those that make the grade stay on. Some become what they call masters. As if the next Botticelli or Caravaggio will come from *that* lot. There was an uproar when they opened. Talk of vandals and thieves living among us."

"When was this?"

"Seventy-three? No, no, it was seventy-five by the time they opened. Before that, it was home to a great family." Pietra smiled. "There's a wonderful sculpture garden in the back that's open to the public. When you get a chance, you should visit."

Lorenzo grinned. "Thank you. I think I will."

Laying gravel took the rest of the day. It was hard work. And though it was cool outside, there was little relief inside the sweltering greenhouse. Sweat dripped from Lorenzo's brow, down his back, and under his arms, despite the running fans and the open vents. His cotton T-shirt, grimy with dust, clung to him like a second skin. But the hard work felt good and allowed his mind to focus on his mission. The school, Marco, and the much-needed evidence.

Tomorrow, Lorenzo would make his move.

Lorenzo stopped to speak with Pietra again when he returned from his run the following morning. "I think I'll take your advice and visit that sculpture garden you spoke about yesterday," he said, mopping his brow.

"*Molto bene*, Lorenzo," Pietra said. "I'm sure you will love it."

Lorenzo sorted through his sparse wardrobe for something decent to wear. He wanted to make a good impression on the old man he'd spotted at the school. It always helped to engender trust when interviewing a witness, and, whether the old man knew it or not, he was a witness. Hopefully, a cooperative one.

Lorenzo cut across Pietra's open field and followed a narrow trail through the woods. The plan was to ask about the sculpture garden first, and only gradually work his way up to more pertinent information about the school, staff, and daily operations.

He passed by two cars parked in the driveway and approached

the massive doors to the old manor house, where he was greeted by a man well into his seventies, with a pockmarked face and fingers gnarled by arthritis. Just the day before, Lorenzo had seen this man hold the door for Marco Robini.

"Come in," the old man said, patting Lorenzo on the back as if they were old friends. "You are a welcome sight."

Lorenzo took half a step back. "Have we met?"

The man answered in the local Tuscan dialect. "Met? No. I don't believe so. But you're the first applicant who looks like he's qualified —and I've interviewed dozens."

"Excuse me?" Lorenzo said, wide-eyed.

The old man chuckled. "I am Franco Di Amati, the building manager. Follow me."

Lorenzo shelved his request to tour the sculpture garden and did as he was told. Franco guided him through the massive front hall. Light poured in through arched stained-glass windows above formal staircases on either side. The men continued down a dark flight of stairs into a musty basement dimly lit by two widely spaced fluorescent lights. Lorenzo slowed his pace, looking from side to side at the racks filled with cleaning supplies, and bins overflowing with random items like old doorknobs and hinges, or jars filled with nuts and bolts. *Was it a trap? Had Marco arranged this?*

Franco dropped into a chair on one side of an old, battered desk behind one of the racks and nodded at the vacant seat across from him. "Sit."

Lorenzo looked around the makeshift office and nodded, then removed his coat and draped it over the chair that creaked under his weight when he sat.

"First things first," said Franco, clicking on the tarnished desk lamp. "I'm not a young man." A self-deprecating grin exposed a row of discolored teeth. "This job has its share of heavy lifting. There is far more to custodial work than mopping floors."

Aha, thought Lorenzo, breathing a little easier. *This is about a job.* He could never have predicted this, but he was determined to adapt.

He'd take whatever position the man was offering and use it to his advantage in the investigation. He couldn't believe his good fortune. It was all he could do to suppress a grin.

Franco plucked a slip of paper from his pocket and placed it on the desk. Lorenzo looked over the list of responsibilities ranging from general maintenance to basic janitorial work.

"I would need you to answer the calls from teachers and staff." He laid a gnarled hand on the dusty cordless phone. "The students, too, from time to time. But the golden rule of service stands—remain invisible and keep your opinions to yourself."

"Of course." Lorenzo swept his gaze across the cluttered desk and the general disorganization of the so-called office, walled in by metal racks and a coffee cart. Then his eyes locked his eyes on a battered gray file cabinet covered in a thick layer of dust.

"So, young man, are you still interested?"

He'd begun the day only wanting to talk to the old man—to get some feedback on the operation of the school and look around at possible weak spots where he might gain access in the future. This was more than he'd hoped for—true *access*. Lorenzo beamed and held out his hand. "I appreciate your confidence, sir. Thank you for this opportunity."

Franco placed his arthritic hand in Lorenzo's, sealing the deal and pushing a list of that day's chores across the desk. "Let's get started." Franco rose slowly from his chair and shuffled to a coat rack behind him. "These should fit." The cherry-red coveralls would make it challenging to remain invisible, but Lorenzo accepted them with a polite nod. "I'll need this too," said Franco, laying a document on the desk.

Lorenzo hastily filled out the standard employment form, jotting down the same phony name, address, and telephone number he'd given Pietra.

"I should get a lay of things—learn my way around," he said eagerly, expecting he'd have everything he needed to condemn Marco by the end of the week. With luck, that would provide enough probable cause to re-open the investigation into Ella's murder.

The thought sent his heart racing.

"The first floor is administrative: instructors' offices, headmaster, and secretaries. That's *my* responsibility." He patted the set of keys fastened to his belt and grinned. "The second floor is all instruction: studios, workshops, and laboratories. The third floor is the dormitory. Girls on the east wing, boys on the west." Franco removed a key ring from his sagging pocket and placed it in Lorenzo's hand. "Those are for you."

"And the small house in the back—is that part of the school?"

"The masters studio. No one goes in there without a pass from the headmaster's office. Masters at work and all that."

"Masters?"

"Well, the best students are encouraged to stay on. They're paid well, but whatever they come up with in that studio belongs to the school. That's the arrangement as I understand it." Franco smiled and clapped his gnarled hands together, wincing from the effort. "That's all you need to know. Now let's get to work." He winked, then pointed to the first task on the list. "We'll start you off easy."

Lorenzo's mouth dropped open as he stared at Franco. "Now?"

"Of course."

He sent Lorenzo to the far corner of the boy's dormitory to clean toilets. The idea made Lorenzo cringe inside, but of course he couldn't refuse. Walking over, he remembered his own days in school. Boys were pigs.

Later, there was a desk to repair and a window to replace on the second floor. One in a classroom, the other in a ceramic studio— where, while installing the window, Lorenzo had a good look at the molds and found none matching *Il Gatto*. But would it need a mold? No, he thought—they needed a solid stone replica, something miles out of these novice students' ability. The masters, however, might pull it off.

It was not until he took his afternoon break in the basement that

Lorenzo had time to poke around the old filing cabinet. He wasn't sure what he was looking for. Names? Dates? Any little thing that might incriminate the school? All the good stuff was probably in the office, but to get in, he'd need Franco's keys.

Lorenzo wasn't sure how much time he'd have for this before Franco arrived, so he hurried. He drew his reading glasses from the breast pocket of his coveralls and got to work. The top drawer rumbled open, exposing the building plans, product manuals, and long-expired warranties. He closed it with a *click* and opened the next drawer—a dusty box of replacement parts for the water heater stacked atop an empty three-ring binder. Then Lorenzo opened the third drawer.

"Lorenzo!"

Lorenzo's head snapped up. Franco stood at the foot of the stairs. "There you are," the old man said. "Let's have a coffee, shall we?"

"Sure," Lorenzo said, as nonchalantly as he could—waiting for Franco to turn his attention to the drip coffee maker and then quietly closing the file drawer.

When quitting time rolled around, he lingered, hoping to get a look at the remaining two drawers. But the old man outwaited him.

"So, how did you like your first day?" Franco asked as they walked up the basement steps.

"Fine, fine. Thank you." Lorenzo cleared his throat. "Franco, I wonder if there is a computer here I could use. Internet, perhaps?"

"Internet—yes, of course. In the office. The students also have access in the computer lab."

"Excellent. Do you think they'd mind if—"

"Not for the likes of us, my friend." Franco shook his head. "Students and teaching staff only." Lorenzo's heart sank. He'd dared to hope but vowed to find another way.

Lorenzo walked back to Pietra's and found her waiting for him like a mother hen outside the greenhouse.

"So, you return to us," she said, wiping her dirty hands on her smock. "I thought perhaps we'd chased you off." Her half smile told Lorenzo she wasn't entirely serious.

"I seem to have snagged myself a job," he said, returning her smile. She raised an eyebrow.

Lorenzo explained that he was between jobs, and he'd only expected to be staying with her for a week or so to enjoy some free time before finding a new position.

"But the new position found you," Pietra said. "You'll be extending your stay, then?"

"For the time being, yes. If it's all right with you."

She seemed to take the news in stride—as if her guests often found themselves in this position.

CHAPTER TWENTY

The map at La Spezia train station showed Kate where she stood, with color-coded pictures depicting places of interest, and helpful English translations. She hoisted her pack over her shoulder and walked toward the central library. Unlike Manarola, La Spezia was a hustling, bustling city—metropolitan and thoroughly urban, complete with traffic and graffiti.

Kate found the library with no trouble and apologetically asked for archived newspapers in her broken Italian. The librarian spoke English, to Kate's great relief, and showed her to the records room. Seven-foot racks lined with fat binders and shallow boxes dominated this windowless chamber. One wall was dedicated to bulky computers and microfiche readers. She began there, searching for anything having to do with Robini in the past thirty years.

There were several articles, but no screaming headlines about corruption or murder. An obituary for Carlo Robini listed family members who'd survived him (a wife and six children) or preceded him (his parents and a young child). Kate found a few pieces about

Marco's charitable giving and Alfonso's prosperous insurance company. Marco had an older brother who'd died mysteriously. Alfonso's sister married a man from the regional government. That article was more about the politician than the sister. Kate printed off Carlo's obituary and left the rest for another day.

Eventually, she found a 1974 copy of the regional newspaper that mentioned Isabella Martina Fiore Rotondo's death. Her *death*, it said—not her murder. Kate made copies to take back to her room, where she would have time to translate them.

Originally, when Kate learned of Lorenzo's personal association with this case, she had intended to weave those details into her article. But now that felt like a violation of their relationship. Still, that link with the Robini's was vital.

It was late afternoon when Kate returned to Manarola. Muriel wouldn't be home for another hour, so she returned to her room with a hot cup of tea and sat on the edge of her squeaky bed with the day's work spread out around her. Then she got to work translating her copies.

Body found in a shallow grave near Manarola. The person who'd discovered Ella was a local man in his late teens. Cause of death—uncertain. The police investigation—inconclusive. Kate frowned and shook her head. No one knew anything about anything.

So much vagueness. "Near Manarola" was not a fixed location. Had Ella been beaten? Abused? What time of day was she found? A quote from *Commissario* Santos read something like, "We need to accept that sometimes there is no reasonable explanation." *That's crap.*

There was no byline. Right—because who would put a name to this shoddy piece of journalism? This story had holes all over it, just like Kate's first attempt to write about the Rossetti. No evidence. No proof. It wasn't so much the gory details of Ella's death Kate wanted, but how it tied in with the Robinis. They'd covered their tracks well, perhaps with Santos's help. Kate rubbed her stiff neck and sighed. Lorenzo mentioned Santos in his retelling of the story. He knew the investigation had been a sham. The article seemed intended to support what looked like a police cover-up.

She flipped open her notebook and added, *How did Santos fit into the Robini business?* Her list of unanswered questions grew frustratingly longer.

Funeral details followed on the next page, with a brief, impersonal obituary pasted in like an afterthought.

Survived by husband, Lorenzo Michele Rotondo, age twenty-two, and son, Emilio Lorenzo Rotondo, age six months. The obituary also listed Ella's parents and three siblings.

Kate studied the small grayscale photo of Lorenzo in a dark suit posed with his young bride in front of the church. Lorenzo's joyful face. His eyes. His smile. His proud posture. She had seen hints of that young Lorenzo in the man she knew now.

Ella was slim, with long black hair. Her bridal veil, anchored with a tiara, soared in the breeze. Lorenzo cupped her small hands in his as if he were keeping them warm. Her laughter, her joy, and her attention were all directed at him. This first look at Ella pulled at Kate's heart. So young and vibrant. So much to look forward to.

It took Kate some time to compose herself. There had to be more than this. How could a tight-knit community have such little regard for this beautiful woman and the families affected by her death?

Kate heard a tap at her door and hastily collected the photocopies. She didn't want to have to explain them to Muriel. But before she could stash them away, Emilio slipped into the room, his glance shifting from her to the floor beside her feet.

"You know my father."

Kate blinked, holding back the alarm she felt at seeing him. "Yes, I know your father." She watched his grim face as he pulled the stool out from under the sewing table and sat down facing her, their knees nearly touching. She held the photocopies on her lap and waited for him to speak while raised voices outside filtered in through her window. It was the same in Genoa and La Spezia—and likely every city, town, and village from Turin to Palermo. Italians were loud and expressive.

Most Italians, anyway. Maybe not the man sitting in front of her.

Emilio's eyes darted from the window to the sweater draped over the end of the bed, and then locked on the papers on her lap.

"Why are you *really* here?" he murmured. Kate shifted uncomfortably on her bed, crossing her arms.

"I'm simply taking some time off," she said, trying to sound lighthearted. "You know, *una vacanza.*" Emilio shook his head. Disappointment washed over his face as he rubbed the patchy stubble along his chin.

"Are you in trouble?" It wasn't so much a question as an accusation. Kate weighed the pros and cons of answering truthfully.

"Trouble? No. Why do you ask?"

"You tell me." His eyes narrowed. What could she possibly tell him? Emilio grumbled something under his breath. Kate stared at him blankly. He went on. "Who knows you are here?"

Kate blushed. "I'm on vacation. Your father asked me to look in on his family. That's all there is." She hated this lie, and the flutter in her stomach told her that Emilio intended to call her out on it.

"What are these?" he said. She flinched when his hand darted out to lift the top sheet from her lap. It was the article about his mother's death. Heat rushed to her face. She couldn't answer. Emilio shook his head, sneering, and then rose from the stool and left the room as quietly as he'd entered.

Kate felt unnerved by the tension he'd left behind. After a moment reflecting on the brief conversation, she went right to her notebook, adding another question to her growing list: *What does Emilio know?*

To her relief, Emilio did not show up for dinner that night. Sofia and Muriel sparred with their mother about cakes. The word *torta* popped up repeatedly. *Torta al limone, torta al cioccolato, torta . . .* It gave Kate more time to spend with young Luca and his more somber cousin, Marta, who rarely smiled and usually had her nose in a book, even at the dinner table.

Mamma served a lovely chocolate almond *torta* for dessert with ribbons of dark chocolate and an almond glaze. Kate wondered if this had been the root of the ladies' debate. After clearing the dishes, Marta and Luca challenged Kate to a chess game with each of them. She quickly and embarrassingly lost both.

"Dominoes?" offered Luca, pulling a wooden box from beneath the table.

"Why not?" Kate said. "Let's see all the ways the American can go down in flames." She smiled, and Luca thought it was funny, too—but Marta did not. Following Kate's predicted loss in dominoes, Luca suggested Scrabble, but Kate had to say goodnight.

"But we will play English!" Luca cried, following her out of the room and down the stairs. "You will surely win!"

"Don't be so sure, cowboy." Kate was not a sore loser—just a tired one.

Luca beamed with a satisfied nod. "Cowboy. *Mi piace.*"

Kate stepped from the warm house and turned toward Muriel's, still smiling from Luca's remark. *Mi piace*—I like it. She reveled in the minor triumph of understanding even the smallest bits of Italian. She'd enjoyed the boy's company. If only Lorenzo knew his wonderful grandson, too.

"Kate," called Muriel, catching up to her.

A mighty gust whipped up from the sea and seeped through every access point of Kate's trench coat. The two women battled the high winds as they walked swiftly up the hill, laughing as their hair whipped crazily about. They passed others in similar circumstances. One man struggled to hold his gray cap on his head. He looked at them, and then ducked behind a wall out of the wind.

Bursting into her house, Muriel said, "I'll put on some tea. We can chat." Kate rubbed her icy hands together and wandered into the sitting room. A tall, elegant floor lamp sanded to a silky-smooth finish cast the room in a golden light, bringing the furniture to life. A beautiful rocking chair, an ornately carved wooden chest, and the tall floor lamp were a few of the treasures Kate was admiring when Muriel walked in with a pot of steeping herbal tea and a pair of cups.

"You like them?" Muriel set down the tray.

"Are they family heirlooms?"

"*Heirlooms?*"

"Family treasure?"

"Ah, yes. Someday." Muriel laid a tender hand on the wooden chest. "Emilio made them. He has a gift." Kate picked up the teapot and poured herself a steaming cup, thinking of the man who'd stepped into her room and unnerved her that afternoon. Then she made herself comfortable in an overstuffed chair while Muriel sat down in the rocker. "We have had little time, you and me. How have you enjoyed our little village? People have been kind?"

"Yes, exceedingly kind. Especially your family. And to a stranger, no less! I'm so lucky Lorenzo pointed me in your direction." Kate noticed the ceramic nativity display on another chest under the window. Christmas was weeks away but would be upon them soon.

"We are the lucky ones." Muriel filled her own cup. "I think they want to hear more about his life—and I do, too. Has he emailed back?"

Kate's smile faded. "No."

"Typical. But don't worry, he'll write—eventually." She set down the teapot. "He knows you're here. I imagine he's curious about your visit."

"Yes, I'm sure he is. He told me about you all and asked me to seek *you* out, particularly. He misses you and your endearingly quarrelsome parents." Kate smiled and sat back in her chair while Muriel eased the rocker back and forth.

"Quarrelsome, yes." Muriel grinned. "Have you known Lorenzo long?"

Kate reached for the teapot and topped off her cup. She needed time before answering that question. "No. Not really. I'm a journalist, and we recently crossed paths on the same case. We've become friends." *Good friends. Intimate friends.* "Before that, we'd met at the opera. *La Traviata.* We sat next to each other, and he helped me with the translation. That was—years ago." Kate smiled, thinking back to that night.

"He likes opera?" Muriel laughed. "Lorenzo?"

"Yes. And music and art."

"You also like these things?" Muriel's smile grew into something Kate recognized as a family trait.

"Yes, but not like he does."

"Tell me more."

Kate's mind buzzed with thoughts of Lorenzo, still fresh. He could bake. He hated to shop for clothes but loved to shop for food. He could tend to a fire and was a perfect gentleman. He was handsome, intelligent, sensitive, and passionate.

"To be honest, we've only known one another a short while," Kate said, her cheeks burning.

"You have known him a short time, but he is important to you." Muriel topped off her own teacup.

Kate smiled. "Well, he's made an impression on me." Her mind drifted to Lorenzo's kisses and how it felt when he touched her —anywhere.

"Now, you know about Ella," Muriel said, leaning forward. "Does that frighten you?"

Kate wasn't sure what to make of that. Did it frighten her to know that Lorenzo had loved before? Or did it frighten her to know that Ella had died because that was the most potent message Marco could send?

And what if Kate was in the same danger?

"Lorenzo told me the story. It's horrific." Kate swept at a stray curl and tried tucking it behind her ear.

"Mmm. It was. It is." Muriel set her cup on the tray, then placed the tray on the handcrafted chest across the room. "Emilio wishes someday to have his work in a *galleria.*"

Kate appreciated Muriel's graceful way of changing the subject. "I think he'd do well, by the looks of this room." But Kate didn't want to talk about Emilio. She'd been trying to purge her encounter with him all afternoon. "Lorenzo mentioned that Emilio worked for the family business."

"He does some carpentry, but it's a waste of his talent." Muriel sighed and sipped her tea. "Manarola is no place for a man like him."

Kate drained her cup. "Thank you for the tea, Muriel. If you don't mind, I'll be off to bed."

"Goodnight, dear Kate. *Buonanotte.*"

"*Buonanotte.*" Kate bent to kiss Muriel on the cheek—then climbed the steps to the attic bedroom.

Lorenzo still hadn't replied, but Megan had emailed to say she'd found George snooping around the house. In fact, Thomas caught him trying to get in through the back door. "He's completely obsessed, Katie. So, when are you coming home? And how are things going with your gorgeous detective?"

Kate rolled her eyes. After George, she'd sworn to Megan that she'd never date again. "I'm fine all on my own." How shortsighted she'd been.

"Megan," wrote Kate, "My gorgeous detective is . . ." She paused. He'd said she couldn't reveal where they were. ". . . still busy tracking down the source of the forgeries. We've pulled away from the case, though, to enjoy some R&R." Kate smiled, recalling their day in Parma. "As for my return, I have no idea. A couple of weeks? Maybe longer. Don't worry about George. He has no power without my signature."

Kate hoped this was true.

She skipped past multiple messages from George and logged into her work email. Mr. Walker had asked for a truce. Ha! He wasn't asking her to return—merely to consider a freelance position. No regular paycheck. No benefits. No, thank you.

After spending a couple of days reviewing her notes and revising the outstanding questions—the who, what, when, where, and why of journalism 101—Kate boarded the train to La Spezia to visit the police station, hoping someone could tell her what had happened in Ella's murder investigation. If you could even call it that.

After arriving at the station, Kate approached the first of three cabs waiting outside and handed over the address she'd found online. The driver took the scenic route along the harbor, past a familiar landscape of ports, a sushi restaurant, and a McDonald's, then stopped a few blocks up from the waterfront.

A row of police vehicles—compact cars, motorcycles, and a small van—parked out front told her she was in the right place.

Kate combed her fingers through her hair and cleared her throat as she approached the building, hesitating as she reached for the door handle and swung it open. Inside, a half-dozen men loitered at their desks, some smoking cigarettes, some surfing the web. She stepped up to the worn laminate counter and asked, "Could one of you gentlemen help me with something?" It was clear they all spoke English when four uniformed men bounded from their chairs and were at her service. But when she told them she was a journalist, they all took a step back and rolled their eyes.

In the US, Kate knew, police and press were like oil and water— apparently it was no different here. But she persisted. "Who could I speak with about the Robini family?" She placed the photocopy of Carlo Robini's obituary on the counter. Three of the officers scattered like rats, and one actually laughed out loud.

"Never heard of them," said one officer.

"How about we have a few drinks and go dancing later?" said another, from his desk in the back. "You could try to loosen my tongue, and I could loosen yours." The other men laughed. One officer escorted Kate outside. She huffed at being kicked out of the building so quickly.

"I am Agente Claudio Casaro," the officer said, smugly, as if this name should mean something to her, but he had her attention. Casaro lit a cigarette and leaned back against the wall. He took a long draw while sizing Kate up. "Tell me," he said, exhaling. "Why is an American journalist interested in the Robini family? Don't you have enough to write about with your stupid war?"

Kate could barely understand Agente Casaro through his thick accent. He reminded her a little of George. Her heart fluttered with self-doubt, but she pulled her shoulders back and changed tack. She was done being pushed around.

"I had a tip that implied the Robini family has something to do with a story I'm writing," Kate said. "Do you remember Ella Rotondo's murder?"

"Ella?" Casaro took another draw from his cigarette and blew the smoke out the side of his mouth. The smell of his toxic plume turned her stomach. "Go home," he said. "There was no murder."

Kate glared at him, balling her hands into fists. "Show me what you have on her case and *prove* to me Marco Robini had nothing to do with it."

"Oh, now it's *Marco* you want to know about." He puffed. He blew. He scowled. But Kate waited him out. "Come with me," he said.

Casaro looked over his shoulder, then led her up the street to a piazza buzzing with business. He urged her to sit beside him at a bench overlooking a spectacular fountain, from which water spewed on all sides before splashing thunderously into the pool below. Clouds sailed overhead with the steady breeze—one moment sunlight glinted off the fountain's spray, and the next, a damp gray chill overtook them. Kate pulled her coat tight around Lorenzo's sweater and sat beside Casaro while he lit another cigarette.

"It's a beautiful city, isn't it?" he said. Kate looked at the fountain, the tall trees, and the elaborate architecture of the buildings surrounding the piazza. There were many pockets like this in La

Spezia, she'd noticed. And, as in Manarola, the Christmas season had cast a festive glow over the city.

"Yes, it is. Has it changed much since Ella's murder?"

Casaro sneered. "You should not be so nosy. It will get you into trouble. People here, they understand."

"You're still afraid of what Marco can do after all these years?" Kate blew on her fingers, trying to warm them up.

Casaro closed his eyes, exhaling smoke through his nose like a dragon. "If he's guilty, yes. And you should also be afraid."

"*If?*"

He leaned toward her, his sour breath on her face. "The Robini family has influence in high places. This accusation will get you killed. I saw with my own eyes what happened then. I was the one who found her body. Ella was raped, *signorina*. It was brutal." He paused. "I was a young cadet then. Not even a badge yet."

"The article said she was near Manarola, in a shallow grave," Kate said.

"She was lying in the grass. Her dress . . . well, I will not get into that. She was *not* in a grave. I saw her from the train platform and assumed it was a heap of trash. You know, the hikers can be so disrespectful. I went over to clean it up, but I knew it was her right away. Ella's husband was police here then. Poor man." Casaro shook his head. "He told us all that Marco had threatened him. He sent us to a farmhouse on Via Rosa for proof. Motive, you know?" Casaro shook his head and stared down at the ribbon of smoke spiraling from his cigarette. "Any evidence was long gone by the time we arrived."

Kate nodded and flipped open her notebook. "No evidence of the murder, or of the forgery operation?"

He glanced at her and smirked. "Nothing. Not even a simple fingerprint. And any evidence we collected from Ella's body is under lock and key in the archives. As for forgery—it's only that officer's word against Carlo Robini."

"Have you seen it? The evidence?"

"No." A police car sped by the park, its lights spinning, siren blaring. Kate waited for it to clear off before speaking.

"You believed the husband, though."

"It was a lot to swallow, but I believed him. Many did. You see, after the incident, Marco vanished. That sealed his guilt—or, at least, his culpability. I knew he was to blame, *signorina*."

"But the investigation ended there. The department could have done more," Kate said.

"Not with Carlo Robini hovering over the case. We had families too." He scowled. "Do you understand what I'm telling you? Ella Rotondo was an example to the rest of the village." Casaro wiped his runny nose with the cuff of his sleeve.

Kate glanced at her notes. "*Commissario* Santos—what was his role in all this?"

"Santos? Ah, I imagine it's like the others, eh? But—listen to me." He grabbed Kate by the elbow. "The Robinis are dangerous. They've always been. This thing with Ella was just one example of that. There are many more that I cannot get into right now. But such things are no longer under our noses. Carlo is dead. Marco is gone. The farmhouse is empty." Casaro flicked his hand as if to dismiss the whole thing. "Tell me about this story you're writing. What does it have to do with anything? What interest does it have with *Americani?*"

Kate pulled her arm from his grasp. "How do I know I can trust you?"

"You don't," Casaro said, dropping his cigarette on the ground and stomping it out. "But you wouldn't have come around asking about the Robinis unless you were prepared to take risks, no?"

Sure—she'd already taken risks. Did she want to take one more? Kate regarded Casaro's posture, his creepy grin, and his strange way of looking at her as if she owed him something. Without his help, she'd never get the answers she needed, and Lorenzo would never get closure. She did this for him as much as for herself.

Kate took a deep breath. "Lorenzo Rotondo is a detective in the

US," she said. Casaro raised his bushy eyebrows and nodded for her to go on. "We've been working together on a case involving possible stolen art imported by the Italian Art Foundation in Genoa, which is operated by Marco Robini. Lorenzo suspects fraud because of what he'd seen at the farmhouse."

"Ah. And there we are—the art! You should have said so." He tapped his fingers together. "You tell Lorenzo to relax. Tell him to leave Marco alone. What happened at the farmhouse is ancient history. Leave it alone. The Robinis are harmless as long as we leave him alone."

"So that's your strategy. Leave Marco alone." She glared at Casaro, fists clenched.

"I am sorry to tell you this. It is just the way it is here." He shrugged. "We police do our job, but it is best to look the other way sometimes."

"That's not doing your job. That's. . ." Kate searched for the word. Negligent? Lazy? Gutless? The fountain sparkled in a corona of rainbow colors as the cloud cover thinned.

"Lorenzo knows you are here poking around this hornet's nest? I cannot believe he would have let you come on your own. He, more than anyone, knows how dangerous Marco Robini can be." Casaro sucked his cigarette. "Tell me—has *Lorenzo* poked the hornet's nest?

Kate shook her head, but felt her blush betray her. Lorenzo had poked the hornet's nest the moment he'd accepted the case in Portland. Ransacking his apartment was nothing compared to what these people would do if he got any closer. Casaro had made himself clear. Back off.

Later that afternoon, back in the safety of Muriel's home, Kate emailed Lorenzo about her meeting, fleshing out Casaro's warning, and adding her own heartfelt concern. She needed to know that he was well. His silence worried her.

CHAPTER TWENTY-ONE

Lorenzo

Several days into his new job, Lorenzo glanced out one of the classroom windows and spied a truck approaching the master's studio with a canopy and a familiar decal on the door. Gio's Laundry. Salvo? He couldn't be sure at this distance and hurried downstairs to get a better look.

But as he reached the foot of the stairs, he saw Franco. The old man grimaced, rubbing his knee. Two boys stopped to see if he was all right but stepped back when Lorenzo arrived.

"Back to class," Lorenzo said to the boys, then approached the old man. Moments like this, Lorenzo wondered about his own aging father, and he felt a tug at his heart. Was it guilt, shame, or longing? Studying Franco, he spoke gently. "Why don't you get off your feet, sir? I can handle this."

Lorenzo glanced at the key ring swinging from Franco's pocket. Access to the office. Access to the master's studio. And access to the computer lab where he could get into his email.

Franko shook his head and narrowed his eyes at Lorenzo, rubbing his arthritic hands together. "No, no. I can manage," he said, stuffing his arthritic hands into his pockets.

"I understand a secretary asked to have a shelf hung. Do you want a hand with that?"

"Not today," Franco said. "There's no hurry. Maybe tomorrow." It wasn't what Lorenzo wanted to hear. There was nothing for him upstairs. He needed the office. He needed the master's studio.

Lorenzo spent the remainder of the day setting up the life-size nativity scene in the yard beside the driveway. It made him think of the massive hillside nativity they used to display in his own village. There was nothing in the world like it. He was sure the tradition had continued. He smiled, wondering what Kate thought of the spectacle.

***

As he approached Pietra's farmhouse that evening, Lorenzo noticed a white van in the driveway, but as he got closer, he saw it was Salvo's truck. He found Salvo speaking with Berto outside the greenhouse.

". . . not a thing," he overheard Berto saying. Berto glanced at Lorenzo, then promptly away. It was unsettling. There was something familiar about Berto, but Lorenzo couldn't place it. His manner? His build? What was it?

"Be patient," Salvo responded, then noticed Lorenzo. "*Ciao*, Lorenzo! It's good to see you again. How are you enjoying your stay? Is the food as I promised?" Salvo embraced Lorenzo as if they were old friends. An Italian characteristic Lorenzo appreciated.

"Better than you promised."

"I hear you got yourself a job!" Salvo said. Berto stepped back, stuffing his hands into the pockets of his leather coat.

"I did, yes. It's just temporary, though."

"That's what I said when I started driving that laundry truck fifteen years ago!" Salvo said with a laugh.

"Did I see your truck at the school this morning?"

"Me?" Salvo shook his head. "Afraid not, friend. My job takes me further afield." He chortled, scratching absentmindedly at the stubble on his chin.

Lorenzo thought back to what he'd actually seen. Gio's Laundry. The decal on the door. It *had* to have been Salvo. "My mistake. Sorry for interrupting." Lorenzo nodded. "Good to see you, Salvo."

With a quick wave, Lorenzo went inside. When he got to his bedroom, he found Pietra laying a short stack of freshly washed and folded clothes on the end of his bed.

"Those jeans and the few shirts you've brought won't do for long," she said.

Lorenzo noticed his backpack leaning against the wall by Pietra's feet. Hadn't he left it on the chair that morning?

He frowned and returned his attention to Pietra. "I hadn't planned to stay so long. Maybe I should go into town." He kicked himself for not thinking of that sooner. He'd have a cell signal and access to the internet. "Is there a bus line close by?"

She laughed. "A bus? No, but Berto goes into town almost every weekend. He can take you." *Ugh*, thought Lorenzo. He wasn't keen on Berto's company, but if it meant access to Kate, he'd do it.

After she'd gone, Lorenzo lifted his backpack onto his bed and opened it. He couldn't tell if it had been searched. To be safe, though, he decided to take it with him from now on.

Lorenzo preferred using the rear entrance each morning he arrived at the school because the walkway led past the master's studio. Ordinarily, he'd hear a steady hum of activity. But when he arrived the following day, the studio was unusually quiet. Lorenzo gripped the straps of his backpack as he stopped outside, pretending to admire the passing clouds above his head, and listened. Silence. After a quick glance for anyone approaching, he cautiously walked around to the rear of the studio and peeked in a window.

The room was dim, but he could make out sheet-covered easels, half-finished sculptures standing in fine dust, and a potter's wheel smudged with a tawny brown residue from the previous day's work. It was oddly reminiscent of the farmhouse on Via Rosa a lifetime ago.

He heard a squeal some distance behind him and tensed, but it was only a whirligig from the sculpture garden.

Emboldened, he checked the back door. Lorenzo turned the knob. The door opened—and standing there, filling the frame, was Franco, looking stooped and tired.

Franco scowled. "What are you doing here, Lorenzo? Do you have a slip?" A slip is what they called the pass issued by the administration office to gain access to the studio, the storage shed, and several workshops on the school's second floor for which Lorenzo had no key. One of those rooms, Lorenzo was sorry to learn, was the computer lab.

Lorenzo fought to hide his alarm. "Oh, well, no. I was looking for you. We were going to mount that shelf today," he said, stealing a glance through the door before stepping aside to let Franco pass. For an instant, he believed he saw Berto at the far end of the room and stepped back, his heart pounding. When he looked again, the man was gone.

Franco closed the door and took Lorenzo's arm. Then, slowly, they walked together to the main building, where Franco pointed down the hall toward the secretary's office.

"There, Lorenzo, room 104. You get the shelving from the basement. It's behind the red chest, you can't miss it. I'll wait for you there."

Lorenzo descended the stairs and stopped at Franco's desk. He looked across at the file cabinet, then slipped his backpack from his shoulders and set it on the floor.

Hurry, he told himself. Franco is waiting. He found a bundle of folders in the bottom drawer, creased and brittle with age—employee and student information dating back to 1981. He quickly stuffed them into his backpack, then lost no more time getting the shelving together.

It was unwieldy, but he tucked the boards under one arm and the brackets under the other. Franco was waiting for him when he walked into the office and winked up at Lorenzo from a chair beside the secretary's desk while Lorenzo set the shelves and brackets on the floor.

"Do you know Mira?" Franco said. The secretary blushed. Young and fair, her rose-colored cheeks reminded Lorenzo of Kate. Everything reminded him of Kate, of Genoa, of that little bed. "Mira, this is Lorenzo. He's new here. Single, I think. Am I right, Lorenzo?" Franco laughed. "Here I am, matchmaking. That's usually my wife's business."

"It's nice to meet you, Mira. Where do you need the shelves?" Lorenzo tried to sound friendly but professional.

He collected his things and followed Mira to an office in the farthest corner with a stately desk centered before two massive windows. A gold embossed nameplate read, *Preside Maximo Corta.*

"He would like the shelves there—see?" Mira pointed to a wall beside the desk with a collection of four framed photos of the Italian countryside. He removed the pictures and set them on the floor while Mira hovered in the doorway, watching.

"Thank you, Mira. I've got this."

When he was sure she'd left, Lorenzo closed the door most of the way, leaving it open a crack so he could hear if anyone was coming. He promptly donned his readers, then popped open the credenza doors and shuffled things around, looking for anything to help his cause. Nothing. He searched the file drawer on the right side of the desk and found a thick folder filled with correspondence from the Italian Art Foundation. After a glance at the door, he read through the first few documents, pocketing one to prove the connection.

The shelves went up quickly, and he had time to snoop further. Student rosters, employee reviews, bank records, and . . . *yes.* An accordion folder filled with shipping documents.

Mira tapped on the door. "Everything all right here?" she asked, easing it open.

Lorenzo quickly stepped away and removed his glasses. "Just fine. Almost there," he said, wiping his hands on his coveralls. "Ten more minutes."

She nodded, smiling, then turned away from the door. Lorenzo took a deep breath as he pried open the shipping folder to look for dates. 2004—July, August, September. "It should be here," he murmured, flipping through each document. October, November, December. He flipped through to the end.

There it was, laying loose at the back of the file. Shipped: September 8, 2004. Destination: The Robin's Nest Gallery c/o Monica Bower. He wanted to whoop in triumph. Finally, something substantial.

Lorenzo folded the paper over and tucked it into the breast pocket of his coveralls. He glanced nervously at the door, and then he reached for the bank statements. September, October, November deposits and withdrawals, with only numbers to identify each transaction. He needed names, but that would require more digging.

Just as he closed the cabinet, Mira tap tapped at the open door. "Ready?"

He smiled. "Just packing up."

CHAPTER TWENTY-TWO

Kate

A week had passed since Kate had spoken with Agent Casaro, and there was little for her to do but walk the town, work on her story, and dine with the Rotondos. The family usually conversed in English for Kate's sake—with Muriel, Marta, or Luca interpreting for Mamma and Papa. But tonight was different. Emilio was at the table, and the strictly Italian conversation promptly launched into a passionate argument. Kate understood nothing, but she kept noticing Emilio's dirty looks from across the table.

Lorenzo had suggested she listen carefully, and eventually, she'd start to sort out the words. She heard her name and the different tone it elicited. She heard *polizi*, and *famiglia*, and something that sounded like *casa*. Home? Emilio said, "*Questa non è casa sua.*" Kate understood—not her house. She looked around the table for the others' reactions. She'd overstayed her two weeks. Muriel had said she could stay indefinitely, but Kate didn't want to push her luck.

Kate went to her room that night thinking of the few words she'd understood, putting them together into a dozen different scenarios. She called Lorenzo, hoping for advice. Still no answer.

She wasn't surprised. He'd told her not to call—too risky. But where was he? Why couldn't he answer, or text, or email? Kate felt the stirrings of a primal scream. The nagging worry that occupied a dark place in her head had blossomed into full-blown fear.

It would do no good to hop a train to Parma. She wouldn't know where to look for him. She didn't even know if he was alive or dead. Holding onto the phone, Kate struggled with her conscience as she considered calling Agent Casaro. She frowned. And how would *that* go? She may have already done more harm than good by speaking with him.

Maybe she was making too much of Emilio's petulance.

Kate threw open her laptop and logged on to Misu02.

To: Det.RotondoPDX

From: RockyMountaingirl546

Subject: I'm going to lose my mind!

What is going on? What are you doing? Are you lying in a ditch somewhere—dead or dying? I'm tempted to call your Sergeant Monroe, tell him what's up so he can get the FBI to intervene on this crazy scheme. You and your windmills!

Sorry. That wasn't fair. You know I understand your motives. You need closure and throwing a monkey wrench into Marco's business will help with that.

But I'm afraid I'm running out of time. My "vacation" story is wearing thin. My name came up repeatedly tonight at dinner, most notably when Emilio said I didn't belong here. He wants me gone, Lorenzo.

I know I said I wouldn't write about him, but I have no one to talk to, and he's been a total *ass*. He scowls and grumbles at me, accuses me of lying (which I am). He asked me if I was in trouble, and if anyone knew I was in Manarola—as if this were all some plot against the family. I want to scream!

Okay, sorry about my rant. I'm just so frustrated that you have not written or even texted a simple note. Maybe I *should* go home. This trip is not working out the way I'd hoped, anyway. I can make a story out of what little I've learned without waiting for the Mighty Lorenzo to save the day.

Ranting—again. Sorry—again. Just write back! My phone is charged. Sancho is frustrated and terrified something has happened to you with no way to help.

Later that week, Muriel invited Kate to go for a short hike along a trail leading high atop the terraced cliffs. The trail was narrow, rocky, and overgrown with brush. Still, Kate wouldn't have minded, if not for the steep incline. It was a beautiful day, so Kate welcomed the invitation. She'd grown stir-crazy in the small town and had thoroughly explored the remaining four villages in the Cinque Terre. And besides, Emilio's comment the other night hit her between the eyes. What was she doing here? How much longer? The Rotondos must be asking themselves the same questions.

The previous day, during the tree lighting ceremony in the piazza, Kate stood with the family as they sang Christmas carols and school children decorated the tree. They treated her like family, but what were they *really* thinking?

What was she doing here? How much longer?

And still no word from Lorenzo.

"There—see that house?" asked Muriel. Kate gazed down a rocky path to a single-level home built of stacked stone and clay tile. "My dearest friends in the world live there. Would you mind if we stopped for a visit?"

"I would love that."

Once they'd arrived, Muriel pushed open the door and stepped across the threshold, calling, "*Ciao. C'è qualcuno a casa?*" Kate jumped at the clamor from beyond the front hall. Soon, an enthusiastic couple burst in, practically falling over one another to get to the visitors first.

The middle-aged woman was beautiful and effervescent, with wild black hair and gold bangles around her wrists. Her fire-engine red lipstick matched the silk blouse peeking out from the loose-fitting kimono that whirled about her as she greeted Muriel with a fervent embrace. "*La mia più cara amica!*"

A gray-haired man, dressed in baggy jeans and a fleece vest, playfully grabbed hold of his partner's arm.

"*No, Minni, mia dolce, Muriel è la* mia *più cara amica.*"

Minni's laughter bounced from the stone floors to the sturdy beams overhead as she pulled her arm from his grasp.

"This is my friend Kate," said Muriel, switching to English. "She's come to visit from the United States. Kate, this is Nikola and Minni. Minni has been my best friend since we played together as children, running circles around our mothers' market stands in the piazza."

"We roomed together at university," said Minni proudly.

"Nikola here grew up next door to me," Muriel continued, beaming. "A royal pest." She leaned over and kissed him on the cheek. "He promised to marry me someday."

"Someday, Muriel. I hold to that!" Nikola looked at Kate with a wide grin.

"Not if I have anything to do with it!" Minni laughed, wrapping her arms around him.

"Come, my love. It has been too long," said Nikola, taking Muriel by the hand.

Kate spun in the quick thread of conversation that followed. She heard her name sandwiched with Lorenzo's as the lively couple whisked her and Muriel through the house to a covered veranda overlooking a vineyard, the village, and the sea beyond that. The pillars surrounding the patio cast late-afternoon shadows extending into the garden like long, crooked fingers.

Another woman waited eagerly for them at the patio table, a near empty wineglass in one hand, a paper-thin slice of cured meat in the other. She sat pitched to the side and looked up at them with heavy-lidded eyes caked in blue eyeshadow and penciled-on eyebrows. A slender Doberman at her side hungrily eyed the meat dangling from her fingers.

Muriel pulled Kate close. "Brace yourself."

"Hmm?"

"*Ciao*, Estelle," said Muriel, her face suddenly losing its earlier glee.

"This is Kate," said Minni. "She's visiting from America."

"You two have some catching up to do," Estelle said, her words slurring. She stuffed the meat into her mouth, holding back a scrap for the dog.

"Kate, this is my sister, Estelle," said Minni. "She's visiting from Genoa."

"And this," Estelle patted the dog's head, "is my Pico." Like Pico, Estelle was long and lean—with big eyes, thin lips, and short hair. Her manicured fingernails glistened like Pico's claws, which clicked across the floor when the dog went to sniff shamelessly at Kate's crotch.

Kate looked down at the dog. A Doberman like the one she and Lorenzo had seen outside Alfonso's office. Then she was struck with a flash of recognition. The drag-queen makeup. Estelle's own painted face.

Kate swallowed hard in a failed attempt to remove the lump in her throat. "How l-long have you been visiting, Estelle?"

Nikola placed another two wine glasses on the table as Kate and Muriel sat down across from one another.

"I feel as if I practically live here," Estelle said, her penciled eyebrows rising and falling as she spoke. "And you, my new American friend, how long have you been in *Italia*?"

She *couldn't* be the woman from earlier. Just a crazy coincidence, Kate told herself, looking away, her face as hot and flush as she'd ever felt it. "Long enough to want to come back," she said. "You have a beautiful country." The harder Kate fought for composure, the more uncomfortable she felt. *I have to get out of here.*

"It's *paradise!*" Estelle said, her voice booming. "Isn't it, Minni? Simply paradise!" She pointed at Kate. "You will come to Genoa? Sure—then I will show you around. You will stay with us, of course." Estelle, like her Doberman, was overbearing to the point of alienation.

"Thank you." Kate knew a drunken promise when she heard one and hoped Estelle was drunk enough she'd forget their meeting. Muriel rolled her eyes and grumbled something under her breath.

"Everything all right, Muriel?" said Minni, her face sullen as if trying to apologize for her sister.

Kate picked up her glass and stepped away from the table to a railing overlooking the vineyard and garden, listening halfheartedly to the incomprehensible conversation / debate / argument she had come to know as Italian. Words spoken with such passion did not exist in Kate's world. It fascinated her, but it was also giving her a headache. Or was that the wine? More likely, it was Estelle.

Kate turned to Minni. "Would you mind if I explore the garden?"

"Not at all, my friend," said Minni.

Kate followed the stone steps to a garden path. A thin band of dark clouds formed on the horizon, but for now, the sun felt warm on her face as she stood at the picket fence, noticing the bare grape vines. Their long trellises descending in steep parallel terraces along the rocky coastline. She thought again of what it must have been like for Lorenzo to grow up amid such beauty.

She walked along the fence, then meandered through the garden, admiring the view. Several gulls swooped in and settled on a nearby rock pile. Their squawking reminded her wistfully of Lorenzo's parents.

Kate's heart skipped a beat at the sound of footsteps and noticed

Minni hustling down the garden path toward her. "I'm sorry, dear," she said, stepping up beside her. "I have been a terrible hostess."

"You've been wonderful. I'm just not feeling like myself today," said Kate, taking a sip from her glass in an attempt to tame the butterflies in her chest.

"Homesick, maybe?"

"Yes, something like that." *No, nothing like that.*

"A man?" Minni winked. "Lorenzo?"

"Well, uh, that's . . ." Kate fumbled for the word. "*Privata.*"

"Understood. My lips are sealed. Come, let me show you around." Minni hooked her arm through Kate's and led her through the herb garden, and down a vineyard row of bare vines pruned back to the woody main stem. "These vines are special to this area. Their grapes are used to make *Sciacchetrà*. Have you had it?"

Kate shook her head.

"We make it ourselves," Minni said. "Would you like to try?"

A sudden gust blew stiff fronds from stubby palm trees on either side of a weathered gate as the sun gave way to the expanding bank of clouds on the horizon. Minni led Kate up the steep slope away from the vineyards to the cellar behind the house.

They ducked into a dark cavern carved into the hill. It was filled with dozens of barrels stacked in twos along each side. "This vineyard has been in my family for ages," Minni said. "Nikola and I took it over in the 80s." She leaned in close. "And to be honest, our vintages are the best in the region."

Nikola and Muriel joined them as Kate's eyes adjusted to the dim incandescent bulbs dangling from the ceiling. Nikola set out four small glasses on an upturned barrel. He turned to a wooden box on the shelf behind him and pulled out a private label bottle of *Sciacchetrà*.

"*Cin-Cin,*" said Minni, holding her glass high, the broad sleeve of her kimono draping from her arm. "To friends; new and old."

Kate could not have agreed more. She tasted the wine and set down her glass. It was sweet and delicious, with notes of honey and something else she couldn't quite identify.

"Well, my dear, what do you think?" asked Nikola.

"It's delicious."

Minni handed Kate a bottle from that year's harvest. "Save this for a special occasion," she said, winking while Nikola refilled the empty glasses.

"*Salute*," said Kate.

"*Salute*," answered the others—but they were interrupted by barking, as Pico bounded into the wine cave, his cropped ears turning this way and that.

"Oh, I've missed the toast." Estelle's hand went to her face, accidentally smudging one eyebrow into a Vulcan peak.

"Shall I pour you a glass, sister?" Minni asked.

"*Naturalmente.*" Estelle staggered to where Minni stood at the barrel and dropped onto a short stool.

"We need to be heading off," said Muriel, with a sidelong glance at Estelle. "It gets dark so early, and by the looks of those clouds, I don't want to risk getting caught in the rain." Muriel drained her glass.

"Oh, so soon?" said Estelle, slowly rising from her stool. "It was delightful to meet you, Kate." She kissed Kate on both cheeks, her breath as noxious as it was flammable. "It *is* Kate, isn't it? I *must* remember that."

Muriel rushed Kate away from the house as a cold gust of wind whipped up from the sea. "We shouldn't have stayed," she said, panting as they race-walked down the path. "As soon as I saw Estelle, I knew it was a bad idea."

"You didn't seem to care for her much," said Kate hoping to learn more.

"I don't care for her *at all!*" Muriel said, panting. "How poor Minni puts up with that loudmouth lush, I'll never know."

They met a pair of police officers standing where the trail met up with the town. One of them smiled at Kate and wished her good evening. "*Buonasera, signorina.*" Not wanting to give away her American accent, Kate nodded and kept walking, wondering if their presence was merely coincidental or something more calculated. How well did she know Casaro?

Bong, bong, bong. They hurried past the clock tower and ducked into the house just as the first drops of rain fell.

That night, the family enjoyed anchovy-stuffed ravioli with pesto, fresh olive bread, and baked pears with homemade ice cream for dessert. Kate yearned for a simple meal without the fuss and frenzy that went into each evening.

"No Emilio?" she asked, somewhat relieved.

"He's working," said Muriel.

"Yes, working," chimed in Luca.

Mamma smiled at Kate from one end of the table. "Eat," she said. No one explained what Emilio did, and Kate was too self-conscious to ask.

Luca made Kate feel welcome, though. As usual, he sat beside her, still thinking of himself as her personal interpreter and instructor. When Kate said *gratsi*, he corrected her politely with, "No, Kate, like this: *grat-si-eh.*" *Scusi* became *scu sa mi*. He explained *amica* versus *amico*. "Both are friend—girl or boy. Like *Papà* Lorenzo is you *amico*, boyfriend."

"Not boyfriend," said Kate. Luca looked puzzled.

"*Man* friend," said Sofia, giggling. "*Fidanzato.*"

Mamma nearly fell out of her chair. "*Fidanzato?*"

Papà raised an eyebrow and smiled at Kate down the length of the table, his fork dangling from his fingers. Feeling lost, Kate looked to Muriel. But Lorenzo's sister merely grinned and patted Kate on the hand. "You might want to look that one up," she said.

Of course, when she'd returned to her room, Kate looked it up immediately. *Fidanzato.* Noun: Boyfriend. Fiancé. Implied romantic relationship. Adjective: Engaged.

Sofia's idea of a joke. No wonder they were all grinning.

<hr>

That night Kate lay in bed, listening to the house creak and groan as the storm intensified. Then, suddenly, the shutters snapped open, and rain slashed violently against her window. She threw it open and reached for the latch on the shutters, then locked it and closed the window tight. Kate felt wide awake now, but Muriel, her best companion, had gone to bed, so she would have to amuse herself.

She looked to the stack of boxes Muriel had left by the door and opened the one with the orange lid. Lorenzo's things. A collection of yearbooks and various memorabilia—like a ribbon with the name of his school. "Don't tell me you won the spelling bee," Kate said with a smile. There was a tarnished alarm clock and a ratty pair of sneakers. Perhaps he'd been a runner even back then. She relished the old photos and a newspaper clipping of Lorenzo posing with his mother in front of their bakery cart. He must have been about Luca's age at the time. She leafed through several cherished books, discovering small notes wedged between the pages. It wasn't his handwriting— maybe Muriel's or Ella's. Kate reached for her dictionary, then set it back down, preferring not to know. That tickle of envy at work again.

There's always the story, the article that lacked shape and direc- tion, continually morphing as new information came to light. Kate opened her laptop, then snapped it closed again. She didn't feel like working. The shutters rattled with a sudden gust of wind. Her mind felt as restless as the storm outside. Sleep would be impossible.

Sofia mentioned a hotel bar near the harbor that was popular with the tourists because it stayed open later than the rest. A glass of wine would help her sleep, she thought, so she got dressed and grabbed her coat, preferring to brave the storm rather than stare at the ceiling.

Kate scuttled through the downpour to the hotel bar and grappled with the door as a gust took hold. Once inside, she was met with the warmth radiating from a fireplace on the opposite wall. A guitar player sat on a chair in the corner, strumming and singing soulfully in Italian. Kate removed her trench coat—more stylish than substantive—and hung it by the door to dry. Then, rolling up the cuffs of Lorenzo's oversized sweater, she looked from face to face and settled onto an empty stool at the bar, draped with colorful blinking Christmas lights.

The bartender stood with his back to her, busily cutting limes into small wedges.

"*Scusami*," she called, and gasped when he turned to face her. "Oh!"

It was Emilio.

This was where he worked?

"What will you have, *signorina*?" he asked, stepping closer, his shirt sleeves rolled up past his elbows, his hair tucked back behind his ears. He wasn't wearing his typical scowl. In fact, he appeared amused by her surprise.

"Wine. Um—whatever you recommend."

Emilio poured a glass of *vino rosso*, then leaned back against the counter, wiping his hands on a fresh towel.

"On the house," he said.

"Thanks."

He stepped away to tend to another customer, leaving Kate to wonder why the family had been so tight-lipped that night at the dinner table when she'd asked where Emilio was. Was it something they were ashamed of? Was it something they wanted to keep from

Lorenzo the way they kept Luca a secret? The very idea felt disturbing.

Kate sipped her wine, wondering how Lorenzo would feel about this when he found out. It might only add to his pain.

The guitar player launched into a new song as Kate slipped her phone from her pocket. Still no messages. The wine did nothing to quell the sinking feeling in her gut—she was sure he was in danger. Was knowing such things a sixth sense couples had? Maybe. She'd been a miserable failure at knowing what George needed, wanted, or felt without some insulting rebuke. But Lorenzo was different.

Emilio returned to refill her glass, so Kate dug into her jeans and laid ten euros on the bar. He placed two fingers on the bill and pushed it back toward her.

"I can't drink for free all night."

Emilio grinned. "You plan to drink all night?"

"Well, no, of course not, but . . ." Kate sighed. Why couldn't she figure him out?

Once the guitarist packed up, the few patrons who'd braved the storm dwindled. There was an amorous couple at a table by the fireplace, and a drunk tourist sitting alone at the other end of the bar.

"Hey, you," the tourist said, waggling a finger at her.

In no mood for conversation, flirtation, or whatever that dope had in mind, Kate turned back to her drink. Somehow, she'd finished the second glass of wine. Or was that her third?

Emilio placed a tall glass of water in front of her and leaned in close. "It will help clear your head." After a few sips, he appeared satisfied that she would heed his advice and turned his attention to wiping the tables and putting the chairs on top.

She finished the water and stood to fetch her coat. Emilio stopped her before she reached the door. "Wait for me to close. I'll walk you home."

Not wanting to argue with him, Kate returned to her stool to wait as the other patrons left.

"The music was nice," Kate said.

"No one danced, though."

"It wasn't exactly dance music," Kate said with a smirk.

Emilio shrugged. "You'd be surprised what people dance to."

Kate recalled dancing with Lorenzo—the closeness and warmth of him. The music was irrelevant.

Emilio pushed two leather armchairs closer to the fireplace and poked the remaining embers to life.

Kate rose from her bar stool and joined him in the warmth of the rekindled flames. "Luca sure is fond of board games," she said, smiling.

Emilio's face softened at the mention of his son. "Yes." He grinned. "He wins every time."

"I thought it was just me."

"No, no, no. He's a clever boy." Emilio set the poker aside and sat down with a sigh.

Kate stood at the mantle and stared into the flames, listening to the steady crackle, thinking about Luca, about Briley, about the child she never had.

"So, you and my father are friends?" Emilio asked. "You know him well?"

She turned slowly to face him. "Fairly well."

"What is he like?"

She weighed her answer, folding her arms across the softness of Lorenzo's brown sweater. She realized that Emilio knew nothing of his father except the stories told and retold by his aunts.

"Well, um—he's quiet, like you." She smiled. "He would have loved the music tonight—maybe even danced to it."

"He likes music?"

"He loves music, wine, art, and good food—particularly bread." Kate grinned, thinking of how he'd savor the aroma of bread before it ever touched his mouth—as if it were a glass of fine wine. "He's serious about his work. He's a detective. Did you know that?"

Emilio shrugged, and Kate realized she wasn't saying what he wanted to hear.

"I've only known your father for a few months, but he confided in me. He told me of his pain at losing your mother and his—his shame for leaving you. He wants to make it right." Emilio grumbled something under his breath. Kate assumed it was derogatory. That was understandable, but she wanted Emilio to understand. "He simply doesn't know where to begin." She stepped closer to the mantle, tracing her fingers along a thin tendril of the engraved grapevine motif.

"He told you about me? He told you about my mother too?"

Kate nodded, thinking about the morning Lorenzo told her his story—the feel of his arms around her, and the tears he'd shed.

"Did he say how she died?"

"He did." Kate sat down in the empty chair beside him.

Emilio's eyes narrowed into thin, scrutinizing crescents.

"I'm a journalist," Kate said. "I'm working on a story that your father was investigating." She studied the embers, wondering how much to give away. "It's connected to the sale of stolen Italian art that turned up in Portland. I didn't know how personal the story was until your father told me about what happened at the farmhouse. The studio there." She was in deep now. "Did you know about the studio?"

"Is this *really* why you're here? For this story?" Emilio's icy stare told Kate his less-genial self had returned.

"Why did you ask me if I was in trouble?" she replied. "What did you mean?"

"Are you?" Emilio glared at her, his shoulders back. "I saw the papers on your lap. Did my father ask you to do this? Or someone else? I need to know." Kate regarded his scowl warily and leaned closer to him, feeling the warmth from the fireplace. He had so many questions. Was this why he'd plied her with free wine? Had he intended it as a truth serum?

"I am not your enemy, Emilio," she said. "I'm just trying to do my job. I don't understand why you *hate* me so much."

"I don't hate you," said Emilio abruptly, sounding very much like he hated her. "I just don't *know* you. I don't know if I should trust you." His irritation waned, and his face softened. "I *want* to trust you."

Kate stared at his fingers pressing into the leather of the chair, realizing she was doing the same. "All right." She took a deep breath, ready to tell him more. "You want the whole truth?"

"Yes. I *always* want the truth. Don't you?"

She twisted in her seat. "Your father is still on the case. He's here in Italy." Kate leaned back in her chair and sighed, relieved now that she had gotten this secret off her chest.

Emilio's jaw dropped. "Here?"

"In Parma. At least I *think* he's in Parma."

"Parma?" Emilio blinked, taking it in. "Why Parma? Why not *here*?" He stood, looking down at her, the glow of waning embers at his back.

"He's looking for proof. He wants to put Marco behind bars." Kate told him about the art foundation and its ties to Alfonso's insurance company and the art school in Parma. "There's a small sculpture in play: *Il Gatto*. It might be what the AISI needs to shut down Marco, Alfonso's insurance company, and whatever is going on at that school."

"My father works for the government?" asked Emilio.

"Not exactly. He's here—unofficially." She pulled at the hem of Lorenzo's sweater.

"We will go to Parma," Emilio said.

"No, we will stay put until he says otherwise." If he says anything at all, thought Kate, still worried about Lorenzo's silence.

"You will tell Zia Muriel. She will need to know."

Kate stood and nodded. She was done lying. "But that's it, okay? Just you and Muriel, all right?"

Emilio spread the few remaining coals and placed the screen in front of the fireplace. "All right," he said, stepping in front of Kate. He placed his hands on her shoulders. His cat-like eyes narrowed on hers. "You wanted to know why I thought you were in trouble?" Kate nodded. "Because you know my father, and if Marco knew you were here, he would kill you."

"That's exactly what your father said. It's why I'm here." Kate confessed she'd been traveling with Lorenzo until he felt it was too dangerous. "Lorenzo told me to stay with Muriel until he comes for me. I'm kind of—hiding out." She thought of Estelle—another potential danger. "The papers you saw were for my research into Marco's motivation and the Robini stronghold on this community. They're for my article."

"The police have been on patrol. You've seen them?" said Emilio.

"Yes, I've seen them. I assumed that was normal."

"One or two, that's normal. There are more. That is not normal. I was right. You are in trouble." Emilio reached for her coat.

Kate slipped her arms into the sleeves. "I'm sure I'll be all right." But she wasn't sure at all.

Emilio spread out the remaining coals among the ash in the fireplace, then nodded, satisfied they wouldn't pose a danger. The bar was quiet, and when he turned out the light, she felt his arm against hers as he opened the door. They stood, staring out at the driving rain before making a dash for Muriel's under a flimsy umbrella.

The tiny gray tabby was crouched in the doorway. "*Scacciare*, Misu," said Emilio, nudging it aside as he opened the door.

"Misu?" asked Kate thinking of the internet password, Misu2. "Is this Muriel's cat?"

"Village cat. A stray. They're everywhere."

"I've noticed," Kate said, entering the house. Emilio shook out the umbrella and stepped in behind her, leaving the door open to the rain splattered street.

He cleared his throat. "I hate Marco Robini, Kate. I don't hate you."

"Right—you just don't know me, says the bartender who greets strangers for a living."

Emilio grinned. "Exactly. I'm a terrible bartender." He kissed her on the cheek and turned to go.

Kate stood alone in the doorway, listening to his footsteps in the rain as he walked down the hill beneath his flimsy umbrella.

———

Kate closed her bedroom door and flipped open her laptop. Still nothing from Lorenzo. She started typing, filling him in on her eventful day.

To: Det.RotondoPDX

From: RockyMountaingirl546

Subject: Spilling the beans

Hey there, Quixote. Sancho, your steadfast partner here, tucked into her attic bedroom with a view of the Mediterranean. If only you could break away from your quest long enough to swing by, say hello—spend the night. Okay, on that note, assuming you will see this email, I have to say that I miss you like crazy. I wear your sweater, like, every day.

Kate paused, thinking about what he might say to that, and smiled.

Muriel took me to see some friends of hers today. Nikola and Minni. I guess Minni grew up next to you guys. But this is where things get weird. Her sister, Estelle, was there. She looked exactly like that lady we saw at Alfonso's. The one with the Doberman, remember?

I spoke with Emilio tonight. You're not going to like this, but I told him everything. Well, not *everything*. But everything about the art case in Portland and how you're in Italy to bring Marco and the Robinis down. He insisted I tell Muriel and I agree. She should know, Lorenzo. She loves you, and I know she'll want to protect you.

I don't plan to tell them about us—if there *is* an "us." Does a three-day love affair count as an "us"? I think of that time together constantly. It's not just an affair for me. I want you to know that in case you plan on dumping me. That way you'll feel like a total schmuck if you break my heart.

What has become of you, Lorenzo? You have me so worried I can hardly sleep. But I'm turning out my light now. You can be sure my thoughts will rest on you.

The following day, Kate rolled out of bed, slipped into her jeans, and pulled Lorenzo's sweater over her head with a sigh before opening her laptop to an endless string of emails from George, each one more disturbing than the last. She worried in earnest now whether she'd have a house to return to when this was over. Still, she couldn't bring herself to reply.

Megan had emailed, too. "George is practically camping out in front of the house and making a royal pest of himself," she'd written.

He's desperate, Kate. It would be sad if I didn't know what an ass he was. He went on a rant to Thomas about your detective. Like, "What is she *thinking?*" And, "She'll trust *anyone!*"

I know you say you're just working together, but you must have thought of—you know, more? I'm not joking.

Hope you're having a wonderful trip. By that, I mean memorable. And by *that* I mean, have some fun! I can't wait to hear all the juicy details.

Kate smiled, recalling some very juicy details before replying. "Since you asked," she wrote, "yes, I've thought of more. Juicy details to come upon my return. ETA still pending. I love Italy—everything about it."

Miles Walker had asked her to write back with her answer regarding freelancing for *The Oregonian*. She planned to write this story in any case—why not write it for Walker? Especially if it might mean a few bucks and a chance to get her position back—maybe even a promotion? Alternatively, she could submit the story elsewhere, on her own terms and in her own way. Katherine Noonan, freelance writer. She liked the sound of that.

Kate scrolled through the rest of her unopened emails. Junk. Junk. Junk. And still nothing from Lorenzo. Remembering last night's conversation with Emilio, she called Agent Casaro about the added patrol.

"Yes, a few more," said Casaro. "Does this bother you?"

"Is it for my sake?"

"Until you return home, *signorina*, which I recommend urgently."

"Can I trust that these men won't tell Marco?"

To this, Casaro laughed out loud, then reassured her she had nothing to worry about. She flinched, remembering how George had said she'd trust anybody. *Shut up, George.* What choice did she have?

After getting off the phone, she found Muriel in the kitchen, cracking eggs into a small clay bowl and whipping them into an airy froth. Kate leaned against the counter, her heart beating double time with a sudden nervousness.

"Muriel, there's something I need to tell you," she said. Muriel looked up, listening. "Lorenzo is in Italy."

Muriel immediately stopped whipping.

"He's *here*?" Her face flushed with excitement as she dropped the whisk, pulled off her apron, and patted her hair. "I'm a mess. How does the house look?"

"No. Not in town. Relax, Muriel."

"Why didn't he call? Oh! He's finally replied to your email, but—"

"No. No reply. Maybe we should sit." Kate led the way to the sitting room and waited for Muriel to settle into the rocking chair. "He's here on unofficial business. Robini business." Muriel gasped and covered her mouth. "Do you remember when I told you that he and I work together?" Kate continued, filling Muriel in on the details as she'd explained them to Emilio the night before. Kate leaned close. "No one must know. Understand?"

"Estelle!" said Muriel excitedly. "Estelle is Alfonso's wife! She's such a *chiacchierona*, Kate. What if she says something to Alfonso!"

Kate cringed. She'd assumed there was a connection. Now she knew how close that connection was. "I spoke with Agent Casaro in La Spezia," she said.

"You did? Why?"

Kate reminded her that she was a journalist, and while Lorenzo dug for evidence on his end, she was digging too. "Casaro doesn't know Lorenzo is nearby, but he knows I'm here, and he knows I'm curious about the Robini involvement in Ella's murder."

"The added police," Muriel said. "That's for you?"

"Yes, but I worry that one of them could tell Marco where I am. Casaro says the men are terrified of Marco. So why would they want him anywhere near here?"

"True enough." Muriel sat back with a sigh. "But Kate, you need to be careful, and not just of Marco. The Robinis are a dangerous family who wouldn't hesitate to punish Lorenzo again, and you are the perfect target."

Kate shifted awkwardly in her seat and swallowed hard, thinking of her encounter with Estelle Robini. "I'm aware."

CHAPTER TWENTY-THREE

Lorenzo

Saturday morning, Lorenzo waited outside for Berto. He was hitching a ride into town, but Berto was taking his time. It felt deliberate, and Lorenzo disliked the man more for it.

Finally, Berto opened the door and walked toward his little blue pickup. "Get in," he grumbled.

Berto held his tongue on the drive into Parma, emotionless but for the pout on his face. Lorenzo patted his pocket to make sure he'd remembered his phone. It vibrated beneath his hand. Good—he had a signal. He needed to speak with Kate—to hear her voice, be assured she was all right, and assure her in return.

Berto parked the truck in a public lot near the train station and pulled his gray cap from his back pocket. They agreed to meet after lunch. Lorenzo waited for Berto to set off on his own errand, then eagerly crossed the piazza to the café, passing the spot where he had seen Frank's lifeless body. A shiver ran up his spine.

Lorenzo grabbed a seat at an available computer in the café, his heart pounding as if he'd run a mile. Christmas music played overhead as he stared at the screen. *Comfort and joy,* he thought, collecting himself enough to log onto his email, eager to see what Kate had written—or even *if* she'd written.

Then, there they were.

One after the other, the string of emails struck him with her humor and her eyewitness accounts of life among his family, such as his sisters working together in the piazza, and his parents sneaking off to the sitting room for some peace and quiet. Typical. Sofia liked to tease and joke. Yes, he remembered that. Kate described the harbor and the view from the church precisely as he'd remembered it. And the bells! He grinned, recalling it all.

One email stood out. "If only you could break away from your quest long enough to swing by, say hello—spend the night." *If only.* He wished it was that easy.

On a more serious note, she'd confided in Emilio, and intended to tell Muriel everything. "Well, not *everything.*" Lorenzo's heart skipped when she asked, "*Is* there an 'us'?"

Kate's encounter with Estelle Robini concerned him most. Yes, he remembered her from his childhood, and remembered the woman with her Doberman in Genoa. That close connection to Alfonso terrified him. Lorenzo checked the date on the email. A week ago. *Damn!* He felt the squeeze of time closing in.

Lorenzo reread each email, relishing each personal detail and touchstone to their mutual affection. He imagined Kate wearing his sweater. *Enzo,* she'd called him. A name from his past.

It was time to write back.

To: RockyMountaingirl546
    From: Det.RotondoPDX
    Subject: Progress
    I'm back in Parma for a few hours, where I sit at a public computer near the train station. It is a rare opportunity because I've rented a room at a farmhouse near the art school with neither cell signal nor internet. It's frustrating beyond imagination.

I just read your many enlightening emails. You've been busy. Now, as for you not following my advice to keep a low profile—what will I do with you, my dear Sancho? Who is this man, Casaro? I don't remember him. Can you really trust him? I am afraid that the police (any of them) could have said something to Marco. Estelle could be a big problem. If word gets back to Alfonso, that could spell trouble for both of us. But I'm particularly concerned about *your* safety. I'm not paranoid. This is real. And I couldn't bear to see anything happen to you.

I'm relieved though a little apprehensive about you telling Emilio and Muriel about my whereabouts. I understand the difficult position I put you in, but now that they know, I can only hope it's for the best.

I've secured a position as a custodian at the art school. It's not the most distinguished job I've ever had—cleaning bathrooms and repairing broken windows—but I've run across some revealing files.

Il Gatto remains a mystery, but I may not need it now with everything else I've gathered. This will all be over soon. We're talking days now, Kate. Days.

I look forward to getting reacquainted with you, tucked into your attic bedroom with the Mediterranean view. (I'm smiling.)

I'll sign off here,

Not chasing windmills,

Lorenzo (Enzo—more on that when I see you)

P.S. I would like to assure you that there is an "us"—you and me. Sancho and the lovelorn knight, Quixote. Perhaps you should be my Desdemona because my quest has turned to our reunion. Forgive me if I'm overplaying this.

Lorenzo scratched his beard. He'd kept it short and well-groomed, but remembering Kate's preference, he decided right then that he'd greet her with a clean shave.

He returned to the piazza and sought out an empty bench in the sun. He had to call her. He dialed, listening to the ring with growing anxiety. Pick up, pick up—voicemail. Even the sound of her recorded voice brought him joy.

"Kate," he said, and then paused. "Where could you be, my Sancho? I imagine you as you were that day in Parma. Remember? Getting caught in the rain? You were so beautiful I didn't even need to take a picture. I've captured that image in my mind forever." Lorenzo closed his eyes to the bright sun overhead and felt the passing breeze brush across his face.

"I miss everything about you," he went on. "From your freckled nose to your freezing toes. I miss your smile. I miss you stealing the covers and nearly pushing me out of bed each night. Not that I minded when I'd wake and feel you pressed against me. You're so beautiful. Do you know that? I dream of that first night—your lips, your breath, how you'd pulled me into you." He grinned. "There is definitely an 'us.' It's what keeps me going. Thank you for trusting me in this crazy venture."

Lorenzo leaned back against the bench, with a heavy sigh, taking in the piazza and all it had to offer. A young family passed by. The father pushing the stroller. Lorenzo looked on with a winsome smile. Was this still a possibility for him?

Lorenzo dreaded the prospect of buying new clothes with only days left before leaving Pietra's, but he still needed to keep up appearances, so he returned to the second-hand store, making quick work of it so he could get back to Berto by noon.

As he came up behind the truck, he caught Berto watching him in the side-view mirror, his driving cap tipped low over his brow as he watched Lorenzo approach. The *coveralls*. The second man at the port who Lorenzo saw watching him through the side-view mirror? Dario Donato? That had to be a pseudonym. That was Berto! The sideways glance. The cap tipped low over skeptical eyes. Lorenzo had seen glimpses of that on the farm but hadn't been able to place his discomfort—until now. With an ache in his chest, Lorenzo looked sharply away to avoid Berto's stare.

There was nothing he could say, had he been able to speak, as they drove back to Pietra's farmhouse. But his thoughts swam with the ramifications of this suspected connection.

Berto ran off without a word right after lunch. To meet with Alfonso? Marco? Lorenzo remembered seeing him in the master's studio and kicked himself for not drawing the logical conclusion. It *must* have been him. Berto had been involved the whole time. And what about Pietra's brother, Salvo—or, for that matter, Pietra herself? Could he trust *anyone*?

Lorenzo decided he'd give it till Monday to find *Il Gatto*. Then, with or without it, he'd go back to Manarola—to Kate, his family, and his grown son.

Monday morning, Lorenzo signed into the logbook on Franco's desk for what he hoped would be the last time, then exited through the back door to head to the master's studio, where he intended to search for *Il Gatto*—thankful that Franco's bum leg had kept him at home, giving Lorenzo more liberty to poke around.

"Good morning, Lorenzo," said Mira, trotting up beside him in her high heels, a long wool coat draped over her snug dress, and tiny Christmas trees dangling from her ears.

Lorenzo acknowledged her with a disarming smile. He had nearly reached the studio.

"Where are you going?" Mira asked.

Lorenzo cursed his lousy timing. "Uh, to the garden shed—for more holiday lights."

"You'll need a slip for that. Come with me." Mira led him back into the school and down the hall to the office. He waited at her desk as she rummaged for her pen. "Ugh, it's wandered off again. Would you duck into Signore Corta's office and see if it is on his desk? He's always walking off with my pens. It's blue and white with a soft grip."

"Absolutely," said Lorenzo, though he was at best halfhearted about the task. He found Corta's office vacant. A collection of new books and a pair of beautiful bookends filled the shelves he'd recently installed. The window stood open a crack, and through it, Lorenzo heard the far-off rumble of a passing truck. He turned to the desk, bare but for a jumble of pens in a coffee cup and an open day planner. Quickly, he read:

December 20, 2004: AR 8 am. Lunch AR. Staff mtg AR

AR? Alfonso Robini? Lorenzo heard Mira chatting animatedly with another woman in the office and flipped back a few pages.

December 17, 2004: Prepare shipment / Set date for AR / MR arrival.

December 11, 2004: BT Studio

December 9—

He heard the *click-click* of Mira's high heels outside the door.

"Aha!" Lorenzo cried when Mira entered the office, plucking a blue and white pen from the cup. "Recognize any others?" He laughed and smiled charmingly. Mira returned his smile with a coy grin. Lorenzo broke eye contact and focused on the slip in her hand and a pair of silver keys dangling from her finger. "Could I look around the studio too?" he asked with a boyish smile, hoping to take advantage of her apparent attraction to him. "I've been so curious."

"I really shouldn't." Mira glanced down at the keys with a devilish grin. Lorenzo turned to the open window at the sound of a car coming up the driveway. "But the studio is vacant today, so—come, I'll take you."

Alfonso and someone he didn't recognize stepped from the green Jaguar and approached the steps. Lorenzo needed to make himself scarce in case Alfonso recognized him.

Mira took his hand and pulled him around to an adjacent office with its own exit to the hall. "I don't want the headmaster to see me leaving," she whispered, her breath hot on his neck as if she meant to bite it. Lorenzo could only think of the keys in her hand. They slipped out onto the walkway where they'd met that morning.

At the studio, she unlocked the door and entered first, smiling at Lorenzo as she closed the door behind him. Lorenzo wasn't blind to her pretty face, beautiful figure, and sparkling personality, but these features did not affect him. All he wanted was access to the studio so he could finish this business and get back to Kate. So, when Mira pressed herself against him, he reflexively pushed her away.

"What's wrong?" she asked.

"Hold on," he said, his eyes darting this way and that among the veiled projects in the room, looking for *Il Gatto* or anything that could seal his case. Where would it be? Finally, he looked at the stairs.

"Good idea," said Mira, her heels already clicking across the room. It wasn't what he meant, but it would get her out of the way for a few minutes while he explored.

"Right behind you," said Lorenzo, stepping deeper into the studio. This room held three potter's wheels and a workbench with a neatly organized tool rack. He noticed a lathe in the corner, a bookshelf beside it.

"Lorenzo," called Mira. She was already upstairs.

He plodded upstairs and down the hall, briefly poking his head into each room, hoping to see the pink cat. Instead, he found Mira stretched out naked on a velvet sofa, posing as if he might paint her.

"Ah, Mira. You are a beautiful woman," he said, feeling a twinge of shame at leading her on.

"Thank you." She shifted her pose, trying for something even more provocative.

"But . . ." Lorenzo scanned the room. A collection of easels—some empty, some draped with sheets to protect the oil. And then—the sharp scent of old plaster and turpentine—vividly returning him to memories of the farmhouse in Manarola. He felt as if the earth had shifted beneath his feet.

"But what?" Mira said, her eyes lowered, her lips pouting.

"I have work to do," Lorenzo murmured, looking away. "I'm on the clock."

Mira tilted her chin and relaxed her bent leg. "Then we'd better get on with it," she said, giggling. She couldn't have looked more accessible. But she wasn't Kate.

"There's no time," he said.

"You're not serious." It was the whine of a teenage girl. "It won't take long." But Lorenzo left her and returned downstairs to explore further, ignoring Mira's curses.

Like the farmhouse on Via Rosa, the studio had been a home once. Lorenzo walked past the potter's wheels and into a back room, peeking under sheets and admiring the finished art on the walls. Some pieces possessed the small vanity initial or symbol he'd seen on the forgeries. Others lacked them.

Lorenzo ducked into the next room—an office with a roll-top desk stacked high with books and a wire basket, half-filled. He listened for Mira, then picked through the basket. Invoices for art materials, a chart showing who was working on what, and future work orders. A productive day, he thought, folding and pocketing what he could.

"I thought you were in a hurry," Mira said, leaning against the door in her snug dress as she slipped into her heels.

Lorenzo turned to face her. "Guess I got distracted."

"Oh, *this* distracts you?" She threw up her arms, then stomped toward the front door. When Lorenzo caught up to her, she stuffed the slip into his hand. "Christmas lights," she said. "Remember?" She threw open the door.

"Yes, Mira, I remember. Eh, sorry about all that, really." Lorenzo followed her outside and watched as she locked the door behind him, then waited while she stomped back to the main building, reminding him of the vexatious Monica Bower.

Lorenzo heard voices approaching and quickly stepped around the corner of the studio.

". . . another truck after Christmas. The team is ready." The voice was high-pitched. It cracked as if speaking were an effort.

The men stopped on the walkway in front of the studio.

"Who's keeping watch on Rotondo?" someone said. Lorenzo recognized Alfonso's voice and his heart raced at hearing his own name.

"Berto's got an eye on him. How much time do we have?" said the first man. Was it Corta, the headmaster?

"Time's up. Berto found the American in Manarola. My wife confirmed it."

Lorenzo fell back against the building, panic mounting in his chest.

"Now what?" said Corta. "Is Berto going to take her? That is the plan, right? Get this Rotondo off our backs once and for all?"

"It was, but Berto failed to stop Rotondo in Portland," said Alfonso.

"Do you trust him with the American, then?"

"No, I don't. Neither does Marco and this is Marco's deal. He'll handle it himself—tonight."

Tonight? Lorenzo broke into a cold sweat, hands trembling and breathless. What now? Stay and listen further, or run?

Lorenzo remained hidden until the men cleared off, then returned to the main house to collect his backpack and stole away. He knew the back roads well now, having run them over the past couple of weeks, and wove through the woods to the far end of Pietra's farm. From here, he could hitch a ride into Parma.

Lorenzo drew the receipt he'd found in the studio from his pocket. He hadn't had time to look closely, but it was stamped December 16. Last week. The laundry truck at the masters studio— that *was* Salvo, come to collect the latest shipment. Berto's mysterious errands were his effort to find Kate. He'd succeeded, apparently, and now Marco intended to dispose of Kate the way he had with Ella. Now, despite Lorenzo's effort in exposing the forgery operation, he was back at square one.

Damn Berto. Damn Alfonso. And damn you, Marco Robini.

CHAPTER TWENTY-FOUR

Kate

After speaking with Muriel, Kate returned to her room feeling unburdened in one respect. The secret was shared now, and she felt like she had partners in Muriel and Emilio. She was coming to terms with her own role in bringing the whole Robini mess back into the picture, though.

She should have left Lorenzo to do his work without poking her nose where it didn't belong. Why did she speak with the police? Why couldn't she have stuck to the plan?

Kate reached for her phone and flipped it open. She expected nothing—she'd been conditioned to that. But to her amazement, there was a voicemail from Lorenzo.

"Ah, Kate, where could you be?" He began. Oh, how she missed him. She played it twice through before opening her email and reading his explanation for being out of touch. A matter of days? She could hardly wait that long. She tugged on the hem of his sweater, recalling the day they bought it. How she'd ignored his stubborn "leave me be" attitude.

Kate sat on the edge of her bed, remembering his soft touch, his tender kisses, his hesitation. She thought of his round shoulders and muscular arms and how beautiful he looked in the moonlight. Kate jumped to her feet when she heard footsteps outside her door.

"Kate?" It was Emilio's voice. He nudged the door open. "Did you speak with Zia?"

"I did. She took it well, but she's concerned." Kate watched his eyes dart about the room as he entered, then settle on the open laptop and the phone clutched in her hand. Then he moved past her to the window.

"You've seen the police? Those two?"

He pointed. Kate stood and peered over his shoulder. She recognized the same two policemen from the previous day standing in the street and shook her head. "I spoke with Agent Casaro this morning. He said not to worry. I believe him."

Emilio turned from the window, shaking his head. "How can you be sure?"

Kate thought back to her original conversation with Casaro when he warned her off and urged her to return to the states. She didn't like the man, but she did believe he had her safety at heart.

"I'm sure," Kate said.

Emilio glanced past her to the open door. She turned and saw Muriel standing there. She must have heard them speaking.

"Lorenzo just emailed," Kate said.

Muriel's mouth fell open. "Is he safe?" she asked, looking from Kate to Emilio before entering the room.

"He's renting a room near the art school. As for safe, I have no idea."

"How does he expect to solve anything from there?" said Emilio. Kate ignored Emilio's judgmental dig, just as she'd done with George over the years.

"He got a job at the school. A custodian." Kate recognized Muriel's blank expression. "A cleaner. He's found evidence to incriminate Alfonso's insurance company, the foundation, and the school."

"So that's it?" said Emilio excitedly. "It's done?"

"Not quite, but close. Days, he said. But he doesn't have regular access to a computer, so we'll have to sit tight until we hear from him again."

"*Days?*" asked Muriel, excitedly. "Can we call him?"

Kate realized she still held the phone in her hand. "No signal where he's staying. He was in town this morning, though, and—"

"He called?" Emilio's eyes locked on her. It occurred to Kate that Emilio hadn't heard his father's voice since he was a baby. Muriel stared open-mouthed as if about to speak.

"He didn't have much time, but he left a quick message," said Kate, tucking the phone into her front pocket. There was no way in hell she was playing that message for them.

Early the next morning Kate passed Emilio on her way to the bakery.

"Are you busy today?" Emilio asked. "Would you like to see the farmhouse?"

The farmhouse? The place where Lorenzo's life changed forever. Likely the place his wife had been murdered. Kate felt a shudder up her spine and tightened her coat around her.

"Yes," she said, her voice wavering. "I would like that."

Together, they slogged up the hill and cut off the road to a narrow, overgrown trail. Kate envisioned Lorenzo and Ella taking the same path that day so long ago—the field, the car, and Marco were all within steps of where Kate and Emilio stood now.

Emilio pointed through heavy brush to the weathered, gray house. A corner of the roof had caved in, and the porch had rotted through. "Watch your step," he said, pushing a low-hanging branch out of her way.

They climbed over a fallen tree and rounded the corner to the back, where Kate tripped over a fallen shutter from an upstairs window. Emilio caught her by the arm, and she leaned on him until she had her balance. He drew her closer and stared into her eyes as if weighing his next move.

Kate glared at him and pulled away. "When were you here last?"

Emilio stuffed his hands into his jacket pockets. "I haven't been up here in a long time. It's too sad, you know? Thinking about that day. Nobody won here but Marco."

"Don't count your father out. Marco is at the end of his freedom."

"We'll see," Emilio said. "My father has let us down before."

Kate stopped and turned to face him. "Don't *say* that!"

"Why? It's true. He had his chance to end this, ages ago. You blame the police. I blame my father."

"He was twenty-two, not much more than a child himself! Don't you remember being that age? Still so much to learn, still so much to do?"

"I was a father at that age," Emilio said.

"So was *he*."

Kate stomped up to the back door and whipped it open so it slammed against the house with a *bang*. It was childish, but she didn't care. She knew Emilio had been through a lot, but he wasn't being fair. She stepped through, and he followed, dragging his feet through the layers of dust, and grumbling something in Italian.

The air was rank with the odor of mildew, and Kate pulled her sweater up over her nose to cover it. Emilio coughed. "I'm having second thoughts," he said, looking up into the rotting beams. "We should go." He burrowed his nose into the crook of his arm.

"Not yet." Kate stepped deeper into the house. "Lorenzo said this room was full of art when he saw it. But everything was carted off before the police arrived. No evidence."

Emilio walked past an old, tattered chair lying on its back. He entered the small kitchen, its rotten floorboards black with mold. Kate turned toward the creaky stairs and motioned for him to follow her.

A sense of déjà vu came over Kate as she climbed the stairs and walked down the hall. It was exactly as Lorenzo had described. At the end of the hall, she slipped past a door hanging from broken hinges, then entered the room. Cautiously, she crossed to a grimy window and gazed out. Emilio remained standing in the doorway, unable or unwilling to enter—as if he'd sensed this was where his mother took her last breath.

Kate pulled the sweater down from her nose and mouth. "Your father stood where you are now," she murmured. "He saw a woman sitting here, copying a painting from another easel." Kate pointed to the other side of the room. "Marco stood there."

Emilio warily entered the room. Slowly, he stepped up to the window, the wood frame rotted and moldy. The exposed ceiling over-head revealed a broken lath through the cracked plaster and a hint of blue sky.

"Your parents wanted to buy this place," Kate said, thoughtfully, her voice sounding distant. Emilio stared out the window and shook his head. "They were going to fix it up. Can you imagine? But Marco scared them off, and then—well, we know what happened then." Kate heard Emilio's feet shuffle through the dust as he said something in Italian that sounded like a prayer. She laid a hand on his shoulder, wondering if coming here was a good idea after all, given the emotional triggers.

Kate poked her head into the other rooms on their way back down the hall, hoping something pertinent had been left behind. But she found nothing except old forgotten furniture, dusty or rusted with age and neglect.

"I wonder where they could have hidden the evidence on such short notice?" Kate said as they walked back down the stairs.

"The art?"

"Yes, and maybe other things—I don't know, like a weapon?"

Emilio's brows furrowed thoughtfully. "There's an old church near Volastra, but I don't think anyone would be stupid enough to hide anything there. Or—hey, there's a house out by the main road. Some crazy guy lived there until about two years ago. His barn is full of old stuff. I used to go up there to get material for my furniture."

"See anything of value?"

"Like a masterpiece just lying around? Are you crazy? But if you want to go, I'll take you."

Emilio walked her to the parking lot above the village, where visitors parked their cars and trucks, and residents kept their vehicles.

Kate shook her head as he led her to a small motorcycle. "Oh no. I'm not getting on that."

"It's easy."

She mounted the seat, uncomfortably straddling Emilio's backside. Emilio took her hands and wrapped her arms tight around his waist. "When I lean, you lean, okay? It's like dancing." With that, Emilio took off for the vacant house while Kate held on as if her life depended on it.

"Slow down!" she hollered. Emilio sped up, passing cars when he could, the engine squealing and sputtering like a chainsaw, *ring-ning-ning*, as signs flashed past too quickly to be read. Then, without warning, he turned onto a dirt road and stopped.

"I was just starting to like you," Kate said, slapping his shoulder and dismounting clumsily. She felt rattled and a little ill, then dusted herself off and jogged after Emilio, who'd already forced open the door to a forgotten machine shed.

Kate stepped past Emilio and blinked, allowing her eyes to adjust to the dim light. On one side of the shed, she noticed a rusted old tractor with metal scraps scattered nearby. She crossed the crumbling concrete floor to a sheet of warped plywood that leaned against the far wall beside a collection of oil drums and a busted wooden shelf. She took hold of the plywood and tipped it back—nothing. The oil drums were all empty.

"Ugh," Kate said. "Sorry to drag you all the way out here."

"This is great!" Emilio said. "Look!" He held up a set of hinges and a tarnished silver drawer pull.

"So happy for you." She turned to go, but a flash of white behind the tractor caught her eye, and she leaned over the seat for a closer look.

"What is it?" Emilio said, approaching.

"Help me with this."

Together they removed a dusty blanket from a two-foot-tall statue of a naked woman. Emilio whistled provocatively, but where he merely saw a naked woman, Kate saw art. Her heart raced.

She pulled her sweater sleeve down over her hand and clambered over the tractor seat to pick up the statue. She carefully carried the sculpture toward the light from the open door and set it down again. Kate admired the detail of the statue's feet and hands—right down to her tiny fingernails and the loose hair cascading over her shoulders. She was pure white, but for three streaks from a brown smudge at her heel.

Was that . . . blood?

A thin crack ran from the statue's knee to her foot. *TCalo* was etched into the chipped base. The signature? If so, it was unfinished. Or was it flawed?

Kate covered the statue with the blanket and set it against the tractor, then called Agent Casaro.

There were no raised voices or glowering looks at dinner that night. Instead, Emilio was charming, joking with his son and laughing with his aunts.

"Will you play games with me tonight, Zia Kate?" asked Luca.

"Zia Kate?" Emilio grinned, shaking his head.

"I would love to, Luca," Kate said. "It's such a pleasure to lose to you and Marta." She winked at the boy.

"Heh-heh," he said, in a way that reminded her of Lorenzo.

After multiple rounds of checkers and gin rummy—Kate actually triumphed in one round—Muriel invited Kate, Sofia, and Emilio to the hotel bar for some after-dinner drinks and dancing.

The place rocked with a four-piece band and a well-lubricated weekend crowd of out-of-towners. Sofia didn't waste a moment before grabbing Kate and dragging her onto the dance floor. Emilio made a beeline for the bar and returned with a tray of shots.

The party was well underway when Kate felt a tug on her blouse. Emilio pointed across the room to a man sitting alone at a table by the door. "Do you know him?" he shouted over the music. Kate glanced at the man and shook her head. Emilio frowned. "He's been watching you."

"I'm not interested, Emilio." Kate grinned. She was punchy from the two shots and the signature cocktail he'd mixed for her.

"Not what I meant." Just then, the man noticed them looking his way. He swiped his gray cap from the table and bolted. Emilio went after him.

"No!" said Kate. But he couldn't hear her over the dance music, so she ran after him. "Emilio!"

Outside, the streetlamp cast a blurry halo as she stepped out into the cobbled street. "Emilio!" she hollered again.

An arm slipped around her waist. "Shh!" Emilio put his finger to her lips.

Kate backed away. "Did you see him?"

"He just vanished," said Emilio. Kate kept thinking of how Lorenzo had searched for the man she'd seen in the window at the hotel. She felt queasy. She'd believed it was Frank in the window, but what if it wasn't? And what if that man had followed her *here*?

Kate returned to the bar, unnerved by the man's disappearance. She felt disconnected from the festivities, as if she'd disappeared herself. Muriel slid up beside her, plucking out the remaining olive from her empty martini glass. She leaned in close, speaking over the loud music and nearby conversation. "Lorenzo should be here!"

Kate looked around at the bar's smiling faces, then focused on the door, wondering if the man would return. Had he really been watching her? Who was he? She considered telling Muriel what had happened, but let it rest—for now. Kate didn't want to spoil Muriel's evening.

"I know," Kate shouted back. "He would love this." She noticed

Emilio at the other end of the bar, crouched over a shot glass, then downed the clear liquid in one go.

Muriel bent her head to Kate's. "Tell me, Zia Kate," she said, still grinning. "Are you in love with my brother?"

Kate flushed. In love. How wonderful it sounded. How intoxicating. She sipped her drink. "Listen, Muriel, I will never be to Lorenzo what Ella was."

"No? If he sees you through the eyes of a man who has known such love and trusted his family to protect you, I believe his heart is telling us all that you are as dear to him as Ella was."

Kate and Emilio stumbled up the road an hour after Sofia and Muriel had called it a night. The streets were empty but for the shuffle of approaching footsteps. *The man from the bar?* Kate turned cautiously but saw no one.

They stood in Muriel's open door as Emilio leaned in to say goodnight with a kiss on the cheek. He'd kissed her that way before—it was customary, and Kate thought nothing of it. But then he kissed her on the lips. Kate pulled away and stared at him in stunned silence— but she hesitated a moment too long, and their lips met for a second time. Kate placed a hand on his chest, burning with indignation.

"Goodnight, Emilio." She pushed him out the door and closed it, the feel of his unwelcome kiss still on her lips.

Kate woke late the following day with a mild headache and a terrible thirst. Emilio had seemed bent on getting her drunk, she realized, and Kate hadn't turned down a single glass of beer, or wine, or whatever had been in that shot glass. So of course she was hung over.

Suddenly she remembered his kiss in the open doorway. So brazen.

Trying to shake off the memory, Kate focused on the fact that Christmas was only five days away—in Manarola, that could not help but lift one's spirits. The hills glowed with the town's annual display —a spectacular manger scene among dozens of bright stars set into the terraced hillside, compliments of the village's own Mario Andreoli.

As Kate got dressed, she thought about the torchlight procession Muriel had described. She also looked forward to the fireworks display afterward—though that excited Luca more than anyone.

Kate pried open her laptop, hopeful that Lorenzo had written, but found nothing worthwhile. Then she removed her phone from the charger and flipped it open. There was nothing new, but she replayed Lorenzo's earlier voicemail. *There is an "us"* had become a kind of mantra. The phone slipped from her fingers, landing with a *thunk*. "Ugh," she groaned, leaning over the side of the bed to retrieve it—but it lay just out of her reach. She bent further, but it made her head throb. "Later," she grumbled. "After coffee."

She padded downstairs through the quiet house. According to the note on the counter, Muriel had gone to the bakery, but it would be a short day. The market closed the week of Christmas, while the house bakery kept a stock of favorites for the locals.

Kate cranked up the espresso maker, proud of her new skill, and dug around for a plain slice of bread or a box of saltines to settle her stomach. Not a saltine in sight, but she found a half loaf of bread and lopped off a fat slice. Mmm. Plain bread never tasted so good.

Muriel's kitchen was full of goodies meant for the family Christmas Eve party. Mamma's Christmas menu included roast lamb, swordfish, ravioli, and *baccalà* to follow the ample antipasti. There was panettone, pandoro, and Italian cream cake for dessert. Feeding the whole Rotondo family, apparently, was like feeding a small army—a very friendly and lively army. It took weeks of planning and today Kate was excited to help with the prep work—though it would have to wait until she finished her coffee and took a long, hot shower.

Luca met Kate at the door when she arrived at the family home. He said a quick hello then disappeared to the piazza to kick the soccer ball around with his friends. "*Calcio*," Kate murmured to herself, as she entered the bakery, picturing Lorenzo on the train from Milan to Genoa. She smiled, then froze when she saw Emilio at the foot of the stairs. She felt butterflies in her stomach unrelated to her hangover. They were alone.

"*Mi dispiace molto*," he said—looking at the floor, the ceiling, up the stairs, and finally at her.

She watched this uncomfortable display, feeling as if she too should apologize. But for what? Rejecting him?

"Emilio—"

Mamma charged in from the opposite end of the room, her hands flailing as if shooing flies.

"*Uscire, uscire!*" she cried, pushing Emilio out the door, leaving Kate alone with Mamma Rotondo for the second time since arriving in Manarola. "*Avanti*," Mamma said, pulling at Kate's elbow. Kate followed her back into the kitchen, where Mamma set a naked cream cake in front of her, with a bowl of whipped frosting and a spatula.

Muriel and Sofia joined the prep team soon after. The women bantered passionately—mostly in Italian, but they used enough English that Kate felt included.

At one point, Muriel smiled at Kate and wiped her hands on her apron. "Look over there," she whispered, nodding toward Mamma, who winked at them. "I heard her call you daughter this morning." Kate felt suddenly warm. She fanned herself with a recipe card. Muriel leaned closer, their arms touching. "Tell me, what are your plans from here? What will you do when Lorenzo arrives?"

"What do you mean?" Kate felt the seed of a "what are your intentions" conversation, which was certainly within Muriel's rights. She wished her father had sat George down and done the same.

"What will you do if Enzo stays here in Manarola? In *Italia*? Would you stay, too?"

Would she stay? Kate's first impulse was to say yes, without a doubt. But that question could go both ways. If she left, would he go with her? Was this Muriel's way of determining how committed she was?

"If he asked me to stay, I would stay," she said.

Muriel smiled. "That's what I thought—sister."

CHAPTER TWENTY-FIVE

Lorenzo

Lorenzo walked a mile up the rural road before a flatbed hay truck stopped to give him a ride. The driver's boots were crusted over with dried mud, his hands callused. He wasn't one for conversation, which suited Lorenzo fine. But he wasn't going all the way into Parma. So Lorenzo would have to walk the rest of the way.

Shortly after Lorenzo's phone buzzed, alerting him to a signal, the driver pulled over and let him out. Lorenzo looked up and down the two-lane highway, waiting for a string of traffic to pass before crossing and jumping a rough-hewn fence to a dirt road. He lost no time. He dialed Kate's number, his heart hammering as he waited for her to answer.

"Hey, this is Kate. Leave a message after the . . ."

Cazzo! Voicemail. Lorenzo spoke quickly. "Kate, ugh! Listen, Marco is coming for you," he gasped into the receiver. "Stay inside. Lock the door. I'm on my way, but it could be hours. Oh, holy God, please be safe!" He was panting, his anguish palpable. Did Marco already have her? No! "Please," he said, choked with emotion.

He called Muriel—but there, too, there was no answer, so he repeated his concerns to the machine, feeling sick to his stomach for leading Marco back to his family. "For God's sake, don't leave the house!" He prayed she'd hear his message in time.

Then he called La Spezia Police. "I need to speak with Agent Casaro. It's urgent." Lorenzo was breathless.

"Casaro? Who is calling?"

"Just *get* him." The phone went quiet while they placed him on hold. Then it crackled, and another voice came on.

"*Sovrintendente* Casaro." The line crackled again.

"Casaro, you don't know me. My name is Lorenzo Rotondo, and—"

"Yes, of course. I know who you are. I remember you, Lorenzo. It's Raoul. Raoul Casaro. I'm the one who—I'm the one . . ."

"You found my wife. Yes. I remember now, sergeant. You've come up in the world." Lorenzo was still breathing fast. "Listen, I have a favor to ask."

"Does it have anything to do with a certain American?"

"It does. I've just learned that Marco Robini is on his way to Manarola. He may be there now. He's focused on Kate." He nearly choked on his words. "Could your men check on her? Make sure she's safe?" There was a long pause on the end of the line and Lorenzo's temper flared. "This is urgent!"

"Of course," Casaro said. "Sorry. I was just remembering, you know, the last time. I'll radio the men. Where are you?"

"Near Parma. It'll be hours before I can get there." He checked his watch. 2 p.m. "You *must* help me!"

"Yes, yes. I'll be waiting for you at the station. Relax."

The winter sun hung low by the time Lorenzo boarded his train. He looked out his window along the platform to be sure he was in the clear—and he spotted Berto looking this way and that. Lorenzo gasped. Before he could obscure himself, Berto saw him and darted toward the train's open doors. *God no*, Lorenzo thought—wondering if there even *was* a God. But the doors closed tight, and the train lurched ahead before Berto could board.

Once the train was underway, Lorenzo reached for his phone to redial Kate and shuddered with panic when he realized the battery had died. He looked at his watch. He was running out of time.

Lorenzo finally arrived in Manarola at ten thirty. Night had overtaken the village, but the platform was well-lit despite the incoming fog, and Casaro was there waiting for him, as promised.

"Agent Rotondo, I'd know you anywhere." A handshake. An embrace. As if they were long-lost friends. Lorenzo barely knew the man, but now he was a lifeline.

"Kate," Lorenzo gasped. Two more police stepped up behind Casaro.

"She's locked down at your sister's. There's a man at the door." He patted Lorenzo on the shoulder. "Do you have a weapon?"

Lorenzo shook his head.

Casaro's radio squawked as he placed a police-issue pistol in Lorenzo's hand. "Here. Welcome to the team. I sent a couple of men ahead by boat. They spotted a yacht moored beyond the coastline—*Il Palazzo*." Casaro turned to Lorenzo. "Do you know it?"

"Marco's boat," Lorenzo said, turning the Beretta 92FS pistol over in his hand, then popping the clip. He reloaded it and checked the chamber—an exercise he could do blindfolded.

He'd carried a Beretta back in 1974, but a less reliable model with a sticky magazine. Usually, Lorenzo would have to reload his clip if he wanted to fire the gun, so he'd simply made a habit of it. Where was that gun now? He was supposed to turn it in with the badge that lay in the tin box with the other touchstones to his past life.

They all walked silently through the fog down the dark and twisted road into town and toward Lorenzo's parents' home, skirting along the narrow streets lit by the warm glow of porch lights. Lorenzo was gripped by the sight and smell of his old village. He'd feared this moment, haunted by the dreaded notion that Ella's spirit lurked behind every corner. An ache burned deep in his chest as he wrestled with guilt and his inability to protect her from Marco. It made this moment that much more important. He needed to focus on protecting Kate from Marco now.

Finally, his childhood home was in sight. Lorenzo stopped beside the bell tower and gazed at it. Golden light spilled from the windows, and bright holiday lights decorated the door. He heard music playing, and it reminded him of the thousand times his father's booming voice had yelled for him to turn it down when he was a teenager. He grinned, tempted to saunter in the door as if the past thirty years had never happened.

Someone stepped out of the shadows and Lorenzo reached for the pistol—but it was just an officer keeping watch over his parents' home. That reunion would have to wait. He had no time to spare. Marco was too close, and Lorenzo needed to be sure Kate was safe.

Casaro laid a hand on his shoulder. "Muriel's place is right up there," he said. Lorenzo followed his gaze. "Let's make it quick, though."

When they arrived, the door opened immediately, and Kate stood there as bright and beautiful as Lorenzo remembered her. Her freckled face turned crimson, her lips—ruby red. She wore his sweater, which meant more to him than he could express.

Behind her stood Muriel and the man he'd seen on the train platform weeks ago. Emilio? He should have known, though he'd had a sense at the time.

Kate grabbed him around the waist. Lorenzo wanted more than anything to ignore the mess they were in and whisk her to where no one could find them.

Lorenzo barely heard the door slam shut behind him, or the footsteps pass them by in the front hall as they clung to one another.

"Give them a minute," someone whispered.

"Is that really him?" said another. More murmurs followed, but Lorenzo couldn't let Kate go. Muriel finally broke the spell.

"Hello, brother," she said in Italian.

"Muriel." Lorenzo met her tearful gaze with his own and held out his hand, reluctant to leave Kate but exhilarated to reunite with his beloved sister.

"How I've missed you," he murmured with a loving embrace.

"We've all missed you." Her voice cracked with emotion. "But me the most," she added, with that wry grin she'd inherited from their father. "You've brought us a gift, though, with that one." Muriel nodded toward Kate.

"I'm glad you think so." Lorenzo took a step back. "Sorry—you know—about all this."

Emilio cleared his throat. "*Padre*," he said. But he sounded hesitant and guarded.

Father and son took each other in. Lorenzo studied Emilio's face, looking for any resemblance to Ella—to himself. They embraced awkwardly, kissing each other on the cheek—but formally, as if meeting a new acquaintance. They could never recapture the past thirty years, but Lorenzo looked into his son's eyes and prayed for redemption. He imagined the hard work ahead to repair this relationship and the many others he'd walked away from.

"We have business!" Casaro called from the kitchen. "Everyone to the table." More chairs materialized, and Muriel expanded the table by propping open two leaves on either end. "Lorenzo!" Back to reality. Lorenzo and Kate took their seats at the table. "Marco and five others have come ashore," Casaro said.

"Is there a plan?" asked Emilio, sitting opposite his father.

"I only have five men. Six, counting you, Lorenzo."

"Seven," Emilio said.

"No, Emilio," Lorenzo said. "Stay out of this." Saying his son's name aloud sent a shudder up Lorenzo's spine. He turned to Casaro. "It's most important we keep Kate and my family safe. Clear?"

"Clear," said Casaro.

"Has Marco come ashore yet?" asked Lorenzo.

"My man at the harbor says a Zodiac is headed for the dock. Marco's on it."

"Good. We have a chance to corner him. I'll go down first and bring him into the open. I'll bait him until he gives a confession. You all"—he nodded at Casaro and his junior delegation—"will stay hidden and be my witnesses. When Marco talks, you'll come in for the arrest."

"You're going to *confront* him?" said Kate.

"I am."

"No!" Kate said. "There are lab tests that will prove Marco's guilt and more evidence that can put them all behind bars for fraud. You don't have to put yourself out there." She placed her hand on his thigh. He covered it with his own.

"Don't be ridiculous, Lorenzo." Casaro said.

Lorenzo narrowed his eyes on Casaro. "You know I'm right."

"Who cares about the forgeries?" said Emilio. "It's Marco we want. Only Marco."

"I hear what you're saying, Emilio," Lorenzo said. "I do. But this is far greater than one man. Removing only him would solve nothing."

"He should pay for what he did to mother. He's a murderer!" Lorenzo reached for Emilio's hand across the table, but Emilio wasn't done, and quickly pulled away. "What if you don't succeed in baiting him? What of Kate? She will never be safe."

Kate winced. Lorenzo looked at his son, wondering about his concern for Kate's well-being.

"Failure isn't an option," Lorenzo said, standing. He patted the pistol under his raincoat and walked toward the door. Kate went after him.

Muriel held Emilio back. "Give them some privacy, dear."

Lorenzo pulled Kate to the side, out of his sister's field of vision and the piercing eyes of the son he did not know. He tugged at the two ends of the scarf draped over her shoulders. The blue matched the color of her eyes, the weave matched the softness of her skin.

"*Tesoro mio,*" he whispered.

"*Tesoro?*"

"My treasure," Lorenzo said gazing down at her.

Kate placed a hand on his still-bearded cheek. "*Tesoro,*" she answered.

"Heh," he laughed softly. "You're not such a terrible student, after all." He brushed the hair from her face and looked into her clear blue eyes, thinking about the weeks apart and what lay ahead for them. He kissed her neck, inhaling her scent, then kissed her mouth, relishing her taste. "Now," he said, taking a step back, and clutching both of her hands in his. "Lock the door behind us." Kate's eyes narrowed in defiance. "I'm serious. This is life or death. Marco's whole reason for being here is to get you."

"There is another way, Lorenzo."

"Not tonight, there isn't." Lorenzo needed closure. He needed to do what he should have done thirty years ago. He kissed Kate again and opened the door, waiting for Casaro and his men to join him.

"I can have one of my men take her to the police station. She'll be safe there," Casaro said.

"Maybe . . ." Lorenzo looked at Kate, thinking about the offer.

"I won't go," she said, resolute. "I want to be right here when you get back."

Her refusal didn't surprise him. "All right. But lock that door."

Lorenzo left the house, comforted in part that Casaro left one of his officers behind to watch the door. He followed Casaro into the quiet street, lit by strings of Christmas lights ringed by tiny golden coronas in the thick fog. They could see only six or seven feet in front of them. Casaro flinched as a pedestrian rushed past in the opposite direction.

"Jumpy?" said Lorenzo.

Casaro glared at him. "You're not?"

When they reached the harbor, Lorenzo stopped, his senses sharp. Waves licked the rocky shore, and he felt the icy cold sea spray sting his face as he looked around for the other officers, who had scattered to nearby posts.

"Listen," Lorenzo whispered to Casaro. There were voices down on the dock. An officer jogged on ahead and returned, holding up three fingers. Lorenzo nodded. Casaro and his men stepped out of sight. Three of Marco's men remained with the Zodiac that had brought them ashore.

Then, there he was.

Marco stepped out of the fog from the boat ramp thirty feet away, relying heavily on his cane, a burly bodyguard only a few paces behind him. He glanced around and grinned when his eyes settled on Lorenzo. "Well, look who's here!" Marco said, hobbling closer. "It's been a long time, Lorenzo. You're looking good."

Lorenzo widened his stance and felt for his pistol. "I can't say the same for you, Marco." Casaro remained hidden as the three men Lorenzo had been warned about stepped into view. "You've brought some friends, I see."

Marco smirked. "These men? Yes, I suppose you could call them friends." He looked over his shoulder at the closest one. "The most loyal friends a man could have. Wouldn't you agree?" Marco looked up and over Lorenzo's shoulder, his broad grin only made him look more porcine. "Well, now. Look who's joined the party."

Lorenzo looked behind him and his breath caught in his throat—he saw Kate twisting violently to free herself from the grip of a man twice her size, who was wrangling her toward them. What had happened? This was exactly what he'd feared! Where was the officer on watch?

Lorenzo eased the pistol from under his jacket and released the safety, holding it at his side. "Let her go."

"Or what?" Marco said. "You'll shoot me? Go ahead. What will that prove, Lorenzo? Ella is still dead. Killing me will not change that, except then you will also have blood on your hands."

Lorenzo looked around for Casaro, this was the confession he'd been waiting for. He turned back to Marco. "It's over. We have everything we need to make an arrest. The AISI is already on its way to the school. You and your operation are finished. Now let her go." He glanced at Kate—her eyes wide in terror. Lorenzo tensed, feeling his blood pulse in his sweaty hand as he clutched the textured grip of his gun.

"Not so quick," Marco said, motioning to Kate with his gun.

Casaro's man stumbled down the hill, clutching his arm, a strained look of defeat on his face. Emilio followed close behind. Had he come to rescue Kate? This couldn't have gone any worse.

Kate squirmed. Her captor pulled her arms tighter behind her—but with a violent twist and an anguished cry, she struck a blow to his ribs with her elbow and jumped away.

Instantly, Marco drew his pistol, but held it at his side.

"*Run!*" shouted Lorenzo. Kate stared at Marco's gun, unmoving. Marco released the safety. What was she waiting for? "Run. *Now!*" It dawned on Lorenzo that Kate was worried for *his* safety. Kate's scarf slipped from her shoulders when Emilio burst forward and pulled her back.

"Ah, there we are!" Marco said, nudging her scarf to the side. "The two young lovers trying to make a run for it." The verbal blow felt like a sledgehammer to the chest. "You didn't know, did you, Lorenzo? Your son stole your girl when you weren't looking." *No, impossible.* Marco's laugh gurgled from his throat. "Berto, you see. My eyes and ears."

Lorenzo's finger slipped from the trigger. Kate must have seen the hurt in his face because she pulled away from Emilio.

Kate rushed to Lorenzo. "Don't believe him," she gasped. "He's baiting you!" Lorenzo looked from Kate to Emilio, feeling the fiery blade of jealousy plunged through his heart, irrational as it was. "Lorenzo!" Kate said again. She'd nearly reached him when Marco raised his pistol.

Where the hell was Casaro? What had happened to the police? Kate stood directly in Marco's line of fire. Lorenzo pushed her back—and then, with a mixture of thrill and dread, aimed his rage at Marco's stony heart, and pulled the trigger.

Pa-*Pam*!

Kate's scream was the last thing Lorenzo heard before his world went black.

CHAPTER TWENTY-SIX

Kate

"**S**omebody, call an ambulance!" Kate screamed as blood oozed from a gash on Lorenzo's head. She noticed blood on his pants, then put her fingers to his throat and found a pulse. "Lorenzo, can you hear me? Lorenzo?"

"*Prendi l'americana!*" someone yelled.

Kate heard quick footsteps approach from behind and felt an arm grab her around the waist and hoist her over a sturdy shoulder.

"Let *go* of me!" Kate's feet flailed as she shrieked, her head bouncing against her captor's back as he ran from the scene. "Let *go!*" Finally, he dropped her. Panicked, Kate rolled to her feet, but in the commotion couldn't recover fast enough to see who it had been. She heard other men shouting and ran through the fog toward their voices. When she reached the spot where Lorenzo had been lying, he was gone.

No!

"Lorenzo!" she screamed. But instead of Lorenzo, she saw Emilio. She ran to catch up to him—then pushed past him to the dock, where the Zodiac waited, lit by a single lamp swinging from a rope. Marco was already clambering in with the grace of a three-legged dog while his guards blocked any approach from Casaro's men. It was madness. A horrific display of police incompetence.

"*Alfonso saprà cosa fare,*" Marco said as the boat shoved off with three of his men. And then—*there*. Kate's heart sank as she saw Lorenzo slumped over in the hull.

She spotted Casaro at the other end of the dock, wrestling one of Marco's men into handcuffs. "Well? Go after him!" Kate hollered. Casaro nodded to the officers, who jumped into their patrol boat. Kate climbed in with them.

"What do you think you're doing!" Emilio cried from the dock. But when Kate glared at him, he climbed into the boat, too.

With no time to lose, one officer tossed each of them a life vest as the police boat sped after the Zodiac, a spotlight carving a path through the thick fog. The Zodiac soared up at the bow with each wave, then slammed back against the sea. Kate held on for dear life, her teeth rattling with the impact. Drenched and numb with cold, Kate braced herself against Emilio who stare straight ahead, tracking the spotlight. Finally, they spotted the yacht and Kate's heart soared with triumph as they narrowed the gap. Then, just as their little boat caught up to the yacht, she heard the faint roar of *Il Palazzo's* engines. It was underway.

The Zodiac slowed. Kate rose to her feet. "Closer!" she screamed, intending to leap.

"*Pazza! È un suicidio!*" said the officer at the helm, steering away. Another officer leaned down to speak with Emilio, who nodded and turned to Kate.

"They'll follow the boat as far as they can. There's nothing else they can do." But as the yacht ventured further out to sea, the officers lost it in the fog, and the men turned back.

"No!" Kate wailed. Emilio took her hand, and she jerked it away. But he doubled down—wrestling her into a tight hold the way

Lorenzo had done when he'd found her in shock in their Genoa apartment.

"Don't touch me!" she said.

"They know what they're doing, Kate." Emilio held her tightly until the boat reached the dock.

When they arrived, Casaro offered Kate a hand getting out of the boat, but she rejected it. If Casaro had done as Lorenzo had asked, they wouldn't be in this mess. Kate was furious and she couldn't find the words to hurt him enough. Grief and frustration surged through her veins as she gazed down at the trail of blood Lorenzo had left on the dock. Emilio placed a hand on her back to comfort her, but she shook it off. Then Muriel stepped forward with a welcome embrace.

"What do we do now?" Kate said, her throat raw from screaming.

"Hush, sister," Muriel said. "Relax." Both women sobbed as Muriel smoothed Kate's damp, tangled curls. Arm in arm, they trudged back up the hill to Muriel's home, Emilio at their side.

The house was warm, but Kate shivered on the sofa, feeling alone despite the all the people—not just Muriel and Emilio, but a police contingent of eight or nine men, not counting Casaro, who seemed to occupy the whole house.

"We have two of Marco's men and a bulletin out for *Il Palazzo*," Casaro said. His voice was raw and tired, as if he'd been screaming frantically, too. "I'll let you know when it's spotted." He held out two cups of espresso to her and Muriel. "It's going to be a long night."

The strong coffee reminded Kate of Lorenzo—the first morning they'd woken up together in their little bed, and his shock when he'd realized where he was. She'd puzzled out how to operate the espresso maker in their tiny kitchen while he was in the shower and greeted him with a cup when he'd emerged. A peace offering. Is that what Casaro was doing now?

Casaro was right—it *was* a long night. He worked the phone between the AISI and multiple police outposts along the coast, from Genoa to Amalfi. Kate finally retreated to her room around 4 a.m. She wasn't ready to sleep, but she needed to shut her eyes for a bit.

As she lay back on her pillow, an image came to mind of Lorenzo lying unconscious on the pavement. It was her fault. He'd told her to lock the door behind him, and she did. But when she'd heard a loud bang outside the door, she had to check if it was him. Had he already returned? Then she noticed Casaro's agent staggering to his feet, holding his hand to his eye. Someone grabbed hold of her and dragged her down to the harbor, her cries muffled by his thick hand over her mouth.

Kate woke to the sound of muffled voices from downstairs and reached for her phone. It wasn't quite six. The floorboards creaked outside her room.

She heard a soft tap at her bedroom door. "Kate? Are you awake?" It was Emilio.

Kate sat up. "They found him?" She leaped out of bed.

The door opened slowly and Emilio stepped into the room. "They spotted the yacht this morning in Genoa. But . . . it was empty."

Kate picked her jeans up off the floor and slipped them on, annoyed by Emilio's habit of walking in uninvited. "You said Genoa?" She felt Emilio's stare as she pulled the sweater over her head.

"It arrived in the harbor two hours ago. The Genoa police are searching the streets."

"He won't be on the streets," said Kate, searching her backpack for the napkin. She held it out to him.

"What's this?" he asked.

"Alfonso's address," she said. "He has an estate in Genoa." Emilio shook his head and grinned. In that moment, he looked so much like his father that all Kate could think about was tracking her dear Lorenzo down and bringing him home.

They found Muriel in the sitting room, nervously sipping a cup of tea. She looked up when they entered.

"You heard?" Muriel asked.

"Yes." Kate looked around the room. "Where's Casaro?"

"Outside—cigarette."

"Ah. Right." Without waiting to say more, Kate headed for the front door and went outside. She walked right into Casaro's smoke cloud. "I know where Lorenzo is," she said.

"Do you?" Casaro dropped his cigarette and crushed it beneath his boot. "Where?"

Kate repeated what she'd heard on the dock the night before. "*Alfonso saprà*, Marco said." She searched her brain for the rest but came up blank.

"Alfonso will know?" Casaro shrugged.

She showed him the address in Genoa. "The yacht is in Genoa. Where else would they take him? Alfonso has stables—the perfect hiding place."

"Stables in Genoa." Casaro picked at a scab on the back of his hand. "I'll make a call."

They went back inside, where Casaro requested a search of Alfonso's estate. After a two-hour wait, the Genoa police came up with nothing.

"Nothing? Did they look everywhere?" Kate said.

Casaro smirked. "Are you the expert now?"

Rage burned in her chest, and she lashed out. "I'm no expert, but . . ."

"There is nothing more I can do." He pulled his coat from the back of the kitchen chair.

"What is *wrong* with you? Don't you *want* to find him?"

Casaro flinched. She'd gone too far—feeling the sting in her own words.

"I'm tired. The men are tired. There is a meeting later today with the *commissario*. I have your number. I'll call when I have news." He turned to go. "Oh, one more thing. Do you recognize this?" He fished something out of his jacket pocket and handed it to her. "They found it on the dock this morning."

Kate held the phone in her hand and noticed the cracked screen. "Yes. It's Lorenzo's," she said, handing it back. Casaro nodded and dropped the phone back into his pocket, then let himself out.

Kate stood at the foot of the stairs, fists clenched at her sides, breathing so heavily, she might have hyperventilated had she not shaken herself into action. She ran upstairs, retrieved her phone from under the bed, and tossed it, the charger, and her wallet into her backpack. Emilio appeared in her doorway.

"Grab your coat," she said. "We're going to Genoa."

He grinned. "The next train leaves in thirty minutes. We need to hurry."

<hr>

The train was early, but they boarded in the nick of time. Kate watched anxiously from her seat for anyone that could be following them, mentally urging the train up the coast. Emilio clutched a faded blue duffle bag on his lap, his fingers wrapped tightly in the straps.

She looked over his shoulder at three men, one with a brown leather fedora, another with a black knit hat. The third, wearing a gray driving cap and black leather jacket, looked sharply away and toward the window, as if admiring the sea view. She recalled that the man from the bar also had such a cap. Could it be? Was it him?

Kate leaned into Emilio and gave a subtle nod toward the man.

Emilio glanced back, then nodded.

The man rose from his seat and sat down right behind them. A nauseating waft of body odor surrounded him.

"*Signora*," he said. Kate turned away, terrified and repulsed. Emilio took her hand.

When the train entered the next tunnel, Emilio pulled her out of her seat. Then he nudged her along to the breezeway between cars. She looked back through the window in the sliding door as the man in the gray cap rose from his seat, his eyes focused on them through the little window. There was nowhere to hide.

A blast of icy cold air nearly knocked Kate over when Emilio opened the emergency exit door. She shifted her weight from one leg to the other, struggling to keep her balance.

"What are we doing?" she asked.

"Wait for my signal," he said.

"What signal? What are you up to?" The man was coming closer, a menacing grin on his face.

When the train slowed into the next bend, Emilio pulled Kate to him and counted. "*Uno, due, tre!*" Just as the man reached the connecting door, Emilio pushed her from the train.

She landed hard on the gravel along the side of the tracks and felt a searing pain in her arm. Before she could register what was going on, Emilio, who'd jumped too, quickly dragged her into the shrubs.

The previous night's fog had materialized into a sleet-like drizzle that sent a shiver up Kate's spine. "Are you *crazy?*" she said, looking down the tracks where the train disappeared around the bend, on its way to Genoa without them. "You are. You're certifiable!" Emilio stood and brushed the dust and bits of foliage from his pants, and then helped her up.

"That man from the bar the other night," he said. "I think he followed us to Zia Muriel's." Kate recalled the footsteps she'd heard that night. "I think he's a spy for Marco."

Okay, so *that's* what Marco meant, thought Kate. His eyes and ears. That man saw Emilio kissing her in the doorway that night and Marco used that knowledge as a weapon.

"But jumping from a moving train?" But even as the words left her mouth, Kate knew there had been nowhere else to go. The man would have followed them through to the next car and the one after that. At some point, they would have been trapped.

She pulled up her sleeve and examined her arm. The skin was

broken in patches from her wrist to her elbow. It stung, and ached. Had she broken it?

Emilio ducked into the brush and retrieved his duffle bag. "This way," he said.

Kate could hear waves crashing nearby, but he led her in the opposite direction, across the tracks. They tripped and stumbled up a steep bank through thick brush. Kate's fury was the only thing keeping her warm.

Finally, Emilio stopped. "Here we are," he said, clapping his hands together.

"Where?" Kate said, wrapping her coat tighter around her. It was torn down the side where her hip landed, and the sleeve was smudged with dirt.

"I'm not sure exactly—but I think this is the main trail."

"Oh, for Pete's sake! We're *walking* to Genoa? That is just brilliant." Kate pulled her collar up and tightened her backpack.

Emilio hoisted his duffle bag up and over his shoulder. "Don't worry. We'll catch the next train up the way."

"How far is that?" Kate was not an unaccustomed hiker, but she lacked the gear for this surprise expedition. No boots, no hat, no rain poncho, or the first aid kit, thermal sheet, and hand warmers she usually packed for emergencies.

"A couple of miles."

Two miles, she thought. *In hiking language, that's an hour.* But after an hour of clambering over exposed roots and slogging through mud and damp forest debris that soaked her tennis shoes through, it seemed they were no closer to the next town than where they'd begun.

"Could we take a break?" she asked. The bruises on her rear ached, and her arm throbbed.

"Um—okay. A quick one, though." Emilio threw down the duffle bag, then knelt beside it. Kate slipped into the brush to relieve herself and returned to see him rummaging through the duffle.

"What are you looking for?" she asked.

Emilio held up a bottle of wine from the duffle and kissed it, grinning at the unlikelihood of its survival. "*Salute!*" He set aside two cheese sandwiches that weren't so lucky and handed her an apple that, like her behind, had a giant bruise on one side.

She bit into her apple—grateful for the calories, the sweetness, and Muriel, who'd tucked a lunch into Emilio's bag before they left.

Emilio collected his things and systematically repacked his bag, then patted his pocket and smiled.

"What's so funny?"

Emilio reached into his pocket and pulled out a pistol. Kate shuddered. How much worse could this get? "It's my father's from before he left. When I first saw you in Zia's kitchen, this is what I was looking for."

"Why?" Kate adjusted the straps on her backpack.

"I didn't know why you were there. I thought—never mind." Emilio started walking away.

"No, tell me," said Kate, stomping along behind him.

Emilio stopped and turned to her. "I thought you were a spy."

Kate laughed. "A what?"

"Spy . . . like, you know." He marched ahead. "Like for Marco or —whoever. Never mind, it seems stupid now."

"Not stupid. I want to know."

Emilio walked on in silence, then finally said, "When I was a teenager, a teacher asked me where my papa was. I said I didn't know. We kids were told to say that. Grandfather insisted. Each time, it was the same question with the same answer." His pace slowed, and he glanced back to be sure she was listening. "Then this teacher began giving me presents. A watch, a radio, a gold ring. The gifts kept coming. Then he asked me again about my papa. I still said I didn't know. Then he told me I would fail his class if I didn't say. I was a kid. Fifteen. Grandfather expected excellent grades. All I could think about was how the family sacrificed to pay for that school. I could not fail, so—I told him."

"What did you tell him?"

"That he was in America," said Emilio. "In Oregon. He looked relieved, actually. But I felt like shit."

"Relieved? Like since your father was in the states, he was no longer a threat to them?"

"I told you, I was a kid." Emilio stopped and turned to face her. "I gambled my life as I knew it for my father's. So when you showed up, I assumed your visit wasn't an accident. You thought I hated you, remember? There was something about your story that didn't seem right. I thought you were a spy."

Kate nodded, thinking about Emilio's story and the guilt he'd been packing around, guarding it like Lorenzo guarded his own. Both fates provoked by Lorenzo's emotional impulse to flee.

"I'm sorry, Emilio. It must have been awful," she said, rubbing her hands together for warmth. They walked on a while longer before she said, "So, what's the plan here? How far is this next town? How long will this take?" She pulled her sleeve to check her watch, but it was just as banged up as her arm.

"You ask too many questions."

"Emilio, this is urgent! We can't lose any more time." Kate pictured Lorenzo stooped and unconscious in the Zodiac. What had they done with him? She tried not to worry that they'd finished him off, but it was a hard thought to avoid.

"I'm doing the best I can," Emilio said.

Kate felt the sting of icy sea mist against her face. "How much farther?"

"I'm not exactly sure, but we have to keep going."

Kate followed along, tripping over roots and stones on the slick trail. Her shoes resembled two mud bricks, and her feet were numb with cold. Her discomfort was all she could think about. That and how this unexpected detour postponed finding Lorenzo.

Emilio was not interested in chit-chat, so Kate filled the void with a monologue that included her impression of the weather compared to the Oregon Coast, a brief story about Megan and Briley, and her feelings about her ex-husband's latest attempt to get a locksmith to open the house. Occasionally, Emilio looked over his shoulder with a glower.

"A couple of miles," she grumbled under her breath. They'd been walking for ages, but she held her tongue, afraid to ask how much longer one more time and risk sounding like a whiney child. Keep your mouth shut. Stop complaining. Be a good girl. And just like that, she was back in George's grip. "Stop your crying!" the doctor had said during her procedure. She shook it off and kept walking.

Kate asked for an umbrella—and that reminded her of when she and Lorenzo had toured the Portland Art Museum. So, she shared that with Emilio, too. It was the only story he seemed to appreciate—he nodded his head, suggesting that at least he was listening.

"Yes, that picture in the sitting room," said Emilio, checking his watch. "I know it." He stopped suddenly and looked ahead to where the trail broke off toward the sea. "Follow me."

It was a slippery path, twisting down the bank, back across the tracks, and onward to the beach. Kate fell once and had a few other close calls. She marveled that she reached the bottom without serious injury.

"But I thought you said we were going to the next station," she said, wiping the mud from her coat and jeans.

"It's miles still. We need to rest, and I know a place. Come."

They slogged ahead in the wet sand for ten or fifteen minutes, backtracking to a stack of fallen logs from the cliff above. "I know it's around here somewhere," Emilio said, walking slower now. Kate watched the pounding surf and wondered if they were safe from the rising tide.

What Emilio found, eventually, was a tiny cave tucked into the rocky bluff. They crawled through the soft sand on their hands and knees—it proved difficult with Kate's injured arm, but the discomfort was well worth the shelter.

"We're *sleeping* here?" she asked. Emilio nodded. "Aren't you in the least bit worried about your father? We could have been in Genoa by now, on our way to Alfonso's, but you had to go all *Die Hard* and leap from a moving train."

He shrugged and retrieved the bottle of wine from his bag. He opened it clumsily with a pocketknife and passed it to Kate, who swigged gratefully, feeling its warmth course through her body. It was like entering a hot bath.

"Of course I'm worried about my father. I'm also looking out for you, in case you haven't noticed." Emilio leaned back against the cave wall.

Kate rubbed her arm. "How did you know about this cave?" she asked, peeling off her shoes and socks and examining the water-filled blister on the ball of her foot.

"I just knew."

"Never at a loss for words, are you?"

Emilio sighed. "I went to high school in Genoa. A boarding school. Sometimes we'd come down this way to party. It's far enough away that we weren't bothered, but close enough we could come every weekend if we wanted."

"Bonfires on the beach?" she asked.

"Exactly."

Kate poked her head out of the cave to shake the mud off her Nikes. Thick clouds and a gentle rain muted any worthwhile sunset and dashed any notion of making a fire to warm themselves. She ducked back into the cramped grotto.

"Emilio, why do you suppose they took Lorenzo when they'd come for me?" Emilio handed her the bottle. She took a drink and handed it back.

"Hmm?"

"That's what your father said at Muriel's. Marco had come for me, but they dropped me and took him instead. It makes no sense."

"After the gunfire, everything went crazy. Don't you remember? Casaro pulled you out of the way, but when those goons took off with Father, he dropped you and went after them."

"That was *Casaro?*" Kate didn't want to acknowledge it but felt she owed the man an apology.

"Let me look at your arm."

Kate pushed up her sleeve. Scabs had begun to form in patches. Emilio moved closer and wrapped his hands gently around her forearm. It felt warm and comforting, and she appreciated the gesture, but her arm still hurt.

"Better?" he asked, as if he thought he had the healing touch "A little," she said, easing her arm away and resting it in her lap.

"You don't trust me," he said.

"You're a little too handsy for me. It makes me uncomfortable."

"I'm sorry." He didn't move, though. She felt the warmth from his body beside her. "But you let me kiss you."

"No, I didn't. You did that all on your own." Kate's cheeks flushed. That and so many other similar encounters before and since. She inched back against the cave wall. Emilio reached for the wine, took a swig, and handed her the bottle.

"Pretty sure you kissed me back," he said.

"Men will always think that. They'll say we wanted it. They'll say they read our signals. But trust me, Emilio—if a woman wants to be kissed, you'll know it. Otherwise, ask. Got it?"

Emilio sniggered. "Men are pigs."

"My ex-husband was, anyway."

"But you married him."

"Ugh, yes." She hated to admit it, but it was true. She had chosen to marry George. "If I could go back and change the past, believe me, I would." There was a pause while the wine bottle passed between them.

"My father is good to you?"

"Your father is kind and gentle, and he treats me with respect. He's the best man I've ever known, Emilio."

"You love him."

Kate bowed her head, her hands knitted together on her lap. "I do, yes."

"All right. I understand. Cheers to that." Emilio took one last swig and let Kate polish off the bottle.

"And now he thinks *we're* together," Kate murmured, thinking of the look on Lorenzo's face when Marco had dropped that bomb. Had he heard her protest before he fell? Did he believe it?

Kate felt suddenly ill and needed to lie down. Was it the wine? She tucked her backpack under her head and stretched out on the sandy floor.

"Emilio?"

"*Sì?*"

"Will you tell me about Luca's mother?"

"Hmm, Luca's mother, eh?"

"I'm sorry. If you'd rather not talk about it . . ."

"No. It's okay." He sighed as if he'd known the subject would come up, eventually. "Giovanna was my best friend's sister when we were at university. I met her on a visit to his home during a school break. I immediately knew she was trouble—but oh, she was so beautiful. I longed to have her." Emilio hmphed. Not quite a laugh, but nearly. "To my surprise, she let me. Eight weeks later, I get this call. She's pregnant and wanted money to end it. I said no. It was an ugly fight, but in the end, I won. She had Luca, but I would raise him. That was the deal—and isn't Luca worth it?"

Sofia with Marta, Emilio with Luca. Kate recognized the importance the Rotondo family placed on life. She thought of Lorenzo's strong position on abortion, and it made Kate sick to think of how little consideration she'd given her own choice. What life might have been for her—how it could have been so different. It didn't change her beliefs about choice, but it did give her insight into Lorenzo.

"Let's try to get some sleep." Emilio tucked himself close beside her for warmth. "No funny business. I promise."

"Thank you." Kate closed her eyes and thought of Lorenzo's strength and determination, hoping it was enough to keep him safe and alive until they found him.

By morning, Kate's arm resembled one of her mother's more abstract paintings—a color spectrum from creamy yellow to brilliant purple.

After packing their gear, Kate and Emilio left their little grotto and set off on empty stomachs to the closest town, an additional mile down the main road, where they got lost in the morning hustle as the boutiques opened their doors for last-minute Christmas shoppers.

Emilio pushed open the door to a corner restaurant and took a table against the back wall. Kate removed her coat, tattered and soiled from their trek, and draped it over the next chair. They ordered two espressos and a plate of bread with a great selection of cheese, cured meats, and jam, on the side—as Lorenzo often pointed out, there was no such thing as plain old bread in Italy. Kate pried open a warm roll and spread a healthy portion of jam on one side. She brought it to her mouth, but—ugh, the smell. Like a barn stall late in the day. She set it down and pushed the plate away.

"What's wrong?" asked Emilio, scratching at the black stubble on his chin.

"It smells—off. The jam. I think it's spoiled." Kate suppressed a passing wave of nausea.

"It's fine. Look." Emilio picked up her roll and stuffed half of it into his mouth. "Delicious," he mumbled.

She sipped the espresso and put it down, too. "I'm just not hungry. Nerves, I guess."

"More for me," Emilio said, spreading a thick layer of creamy white cheese on the other half of her roll. He grabbed the other and stuck it in his pocket before they left, then led the way up the road to the train platform and checked the schedule.

Kate glanced at the map on the board, surprised to see that Genoa was west from where they stood, not north like she'd assumed. It was only a few more stops up the line, but if they'd been going by car . . . Kate followed the highway route and realized now why everyone took the train down the coast. She sat down to kick her shoes off and lay them in the sun to dry—but with a sudden urgency, Emilio stopped her.

"Get up," he insisted. "He's here."

"He?"

"Right over there." Emilio pulled her behind the platform, where she spied the man in the gray cap through the signboards. He must have gotten off the train, *expecting* them to show up at the next stop.

Kate and Emilio slipped past the parking lot, ducking behind cars and vans until they reached the other side. From there, they wandered uphill through dense brush until they found a trail that Emilio vaguely remembered as passable. It turned out to be only vaguely passable, but they followed it as far as they could before it vanished. Kate looked behind them at the twisting overgrown trail and recalled a similar situation twenty years ago with her college friends. They'd been backpacking for two days before they realized they'd deviated from the main trail onto a deer path. They'd needed to backtrack eight miles. It was the smart thing to do, but she and Emilio didn't have time for that.

Kate recalled the map at the train station. "Follow me," she said, tightening the clips on her backpack.

They bushwhacked for twenty minutes and emerged on a hillside vineyard high on the bluff.

If it wasn't for the heavily pruned vines, leafless and dormant, they wouldn't have seen the man working on his tractor at the other end of the row. Kate waved him down, hoping he'd give them a lift the rest of the way.

"*Buongiorno!*" she called. Emilio smiled.

The man looked up from his task and took a few tentative steps toward them.

Kate nudged Emilio. "Ask him if we can get a ride to Genoa." But before Emilio could get out a word, the man charged at them with a shotgun, forcing them to take off running, heading for the country road beyond the vineyard.

"Exactly what does that guy think we're going to *do*?" asked Kate.

"Um, you look, well . . ." Emilio cringed. Kate shoved her fingers through her tangled curls. She looked down at her muddy shoes and grubby jeans. Her coat was ripped from when she'd jumped from the train, and it was smudged with dirt and grime.

Kate noted the dark rings under Emilio's eyes and his two-day beard that had trapped bits of brush and debris. "You don't look much better. And don't get me started on how bad you smell."

"Me?" Emilio grunted and quickened his pace, while lifting his arm for a sniff. "Hmph."

They walked along the road until they read the next sign: *GENOVA 30km.*

"Thirty kilometers," Kate said. "What is that in miles?"

"Twenty?" said Emilio after some rough math.

Kate wanted to scream. She wanted to cry. "I can't do it, Emilio. I'm hungry. I'm thirsty, and my legs are shot."

They were long past the vineyard now and approached a small village. Emilio stopped at a convenience store, leaving Kate at a café table outside. He emerged with two bottles of water and a pair of sandwiches wrapped in cellophane.

"There's a hostel two miles up," he said, handing her a water bottle.

Kate rose to her feet and glared. "*Hostel?* Have you lost your mind? Emilio, we don't have time for this! We've already lost a day since jumping off the train!"

"We have to get off the road," Emilio said, peeling the cellophane from his sandwich.

Kate looked behind her, wondering which passing truck or car could be Marco or one of his men. Emilio was right. It wasn't safe.

"We just need to keep going."

"Walk?"

"*Argh!* You're not *listening!*" She stormed into the shop and up to the clerk. Looking him directly in the eyes, she said the only words she could muster: "*Genova. Adesso.*" The clerk handed her a bus schedule and gesticulated directions to the *stazione.* It wasn't much farther, and the tickets were cheap enough.

***

Though the bus got them to Genoa, the traffic in the city slowed their progress. Kate's stomach wrenched with anxiety, and she clutched the seat in front of her.

"Relax," Emilio muttered ineffectually. "Take it easy."

"I don't feel well."

"Drink your water," Emilio said, as if caring for Luca. She put the water bottle to her lips but couldn't drink. Emilio unfolded the bus schedule and examined the color-coded map on the other side. He tapped Kate on the shoulder. "The address?"

She dug into her pocket for the crumpled napkin and handed it over. After a minute or so, Emilio looked up from the map.

"Okay, look here," he said, showing her the map that divided Genoa into multiple zones. He pointed to a spot beyond all of them. *"That's Alfonso's."*

Crap.

When they finally arrived at the transit center near the harbor, she leaped off the bus, glad for the fresh air. They stepped over to the map on the board, marked with a sun-bleached arrow. *You are here.*

"The next bus will get us closer," Kate said with a heavy sigh. She gazed out at the harbor, scanning it for *Il Palazzo* and the man who owned it. Then her eyes drifted down the coastline toward the kiosk, and she thought of the blue door, the tiny kitchen, and the bed she'd shared with Lorenzo.

Emilio nudged her, pulling her from her thoughts.

The next bus arrived at the transit center twenty minutes later and dropped them off in the small community where Frank must have been staying when she and Lorenzo met him on the tour boat. She and Emilio would need to walk again, but this time with a redoubled sense of urgency as the sun began to set.

CHAPTER TWENTY-SEVEN

Lorenzo dreamed he was flying, coasting on thermals high above rocky bluffs and sandy beaches. The odd sensation abruptly stopped when he opened his eyes.

He lay in a comfortable room on a comfortable bed, but his head pounded with such pain as he had never felt. Gradually, he recalled shooting at Marco in the piazza, but he realized, touching the sticky mess on his skull, that he'd heard more than one shot.

As much as Lorenzo's head hurt, his throbbing leg concerned him more. Slowly, he sat up and regarded his thigh, wrapped tightly in a blood-soaked bandage.

Was he rocking? Or was that the room?

Lorenzo limped to a small porthole beside the bed and set his eyes upon miles of dark blue sea under stars fading in the morning light. He tried to check his watch, but it was gone. His clothes were gone, too, except for a pair of white boxers with tiny windmills, compliments of his mischievous Sancho. He didn't know whether to laugh or cry.

A sharp pang of terror struck him like a sudden freight train. Kate! Was she safe?

What about Muriel and Emilio?

Or his parents? How much did they know—if anything?

He heard footfalls overhead and the chatter of voices over the hum of what sounded like a motor or generator. Grunting, Lorenzo sat back down and ran his fingers through his matted hair. How had he gotten himself into this mess? Where had it all gone wrong? It was easy to point a finger—the AISI, Frank, the police. But the brutal truth was that it was his own damn fault. All of it. In his fervor to catch Marco, he'd acted recklessly. His go-it-alone mission to the school: stupid. His vigilante march through Manarola: shortsighted. What did he expect? He should have listened to Kate. Take that, George. She knew all along how foolish it was.

Argh! His head pounded, like a wooden beam with spikes through it. Lorenzo tugged at the bandage on his leg. It was too tight, and the wound burned deep. Was it infected? Does infection happen that fast? He'd never been shot in all his years of policing. This was all new.

He lay back on the bed and closed his eyes tight against the searing pain in his leg and his splitting headache. Eventually, he lost his grip on wakefulness.

He woke what felt like hours later to the backlit figure of a visitor standing at the open door holding a bundle. With effort, he recognized the curvaceous body.

"Cat got your tongue, detective?" Monica didn't wait for him to sit up before setting a hand on his knee and sliding it along his injured leg—only stopping when she reached the boxers. "I figured a clever man like yourself would have avoided such an embarrassing situation." Laughing, Monica laid a plush terry robe and Japanese sandals at the foot of the bed. "Make yourself presentable, will you?" she said before leaving the room.

Humiliated, Lorenzo hobbled into a tiny bathroom—about the size of what you'd find on a Boeing 737—and ran warm water into the small basin to wash up. Then he wrapped himself in the robe and sat back on the side of the bed to await his fate.

Lorenzo gripped the headboard to steady himself when the boat surged. Forward or aft? He didn't know. Where was he? He didn't know. And where were they headed? Again, he didn't know.

His meal finally arrived—but it wasn't Monica holding the platter.

"Glad to see you're up and about," said Marco, dressed all in white, with a navy-blue ascot knotted around his neck. "In case you hadn't noticed, we are underway."

"Where to?" asked Lorenzo. He tried to stand, but he still hadn't found his sea legs.

"Where you won't be a bother." A smirk spread across Marco's fleshy face, distorting his cheeks into two large pouches. Marco laid the tray on the bedside table. Then he circled the room. "Tell me, Lorenzo—what have I ever done to deserve this annoyance, eh?" He smiled and leaned back against the wall. "Ah, yes, Ella. Such a beauty, that one. I wanted her from the start. I suppose I owe you for sending her my way."

"I didn't."

"That's not what she said." Marco stopped and grabbed his crotch, his mouth twisting into a monstrous grin. "What do I need to do?" he said in a mock female voice. "She got more than she expected, but exactly what I'd promised, eh?"

Lorenzo gripped the quilted blanket in his sweaty fists. "*Zitto!*" he shouted, just wanting Marco to shut up.

Since hearing the Robini name in Portland and discovering the crate, his dreams had been filled with visions of what he imagined happened to Ella. That was bad enough, but to hear the details from her rapist, her murderer—it was more than he could bear.

"And this Kate. Yes, Kate Noonan—American journalist." A drop of spittle flew from Marco's mouth.

"Stay away from her."

"Oh, you poor, poor man. Duped by a pretty face. Your boy can't keep his hands off her."

"You're lying." Lorenzo felt dizzy—his brain muddled by misery, pain, and Marco's sick mind games.

"You simply couldn't leave me alone, could you? You had to push. Now, look what you've done. First Ella, now the American." Lorenzo picked up the tray and threw it against the wall. *Crash!* Marco laughed. "Was that intended for me? Heh—you throw like you shoot."

"I hit you dead-on."

"Ah, do you forget? I cheat." Marco tapped his chest. "Bullet-proof vest."

Hours later, gagged and blindfolded, with his hands tied behind his back, Lorenzo was jerked from a car wearing nothing but the robe and sandals Monica had given him on the boat and shoved into a cold, empty room. Alfonso removed the blindfold and untied the scarf that bound his wrists behind him.

"Tsk, tsk, Lorenzo. What have you gotten yourself into now?" said Alfonso with a chortle. Then he closed and locked the door behind him, leaving Lorenzo alone in a room that smelled of fresh lumber and drywall.

Lorenzo picked up the blue scarf and brought it to his nose. It smelled of Kate. He stumbled, then collapsed onto the bare concrete floor.

Not much later, he heard the pop and crunch of a vehicle rolling through gravel outside his door. Sitting up was difficult. He ached all over. Car doors opened and closed, and several voices chattered briefly. He called out, but no one came.

There was a cot against one wall, a short stool beside it. Lorenzo struggled to his feet and crossed to an unfinished washroom. *What is this place?*

With effort, he climbed onto the toilet seat, hoping to glean what he could through the mottled window near the top of the wall. The most he could tell was that it was daylight, and the lack of activity meant—what? What was he looking at?

He stepped awkwardly off the toilet and stumbled to the cot. Blood leaked from his bandage down his leg, soiling his robe. But that didn't concern him. They had Kate. He had failed yet again. Lorenzo pictured Kate greeting him at Muriel's open door. Her joy and excitement had been sincere. Hadn't they?

How well did he actually know her?

"Shut up!" he said to himself. Then he heard a crunch of footsteps outside his door. It opened, and Alfonso stood in the frame, his lip curled in disgust, a paper sack in one hand. He dropped the sack and left, locking the door behind him.

Lorenzo picked up the sack and peered in—a loaf of bread, a block of cheese, a spotty banana, and materials to dress his wound. If given a chance, he would have asked for a cup of coffee and some aspirin.

He fell into the musty cot and leaned against the wall. Exhausted, he tore into the stale bread. Dressing his wound was more problematic—he had two thin squares of gauze and a roll of tape, old and yellowed, that wouldn't stick. He did what he could to reuse the tape from the previous bandage, but it kept peeling back up. In the end, he tied two lengths of tape around his leg to fasten the gauze, then reclined on the cot, closed his eyes against the pain, and wiped his cheek of sweat.

Or maybe it was tears. He didn't know the difference anymore.

Lorenzo roused to voices outside his door. "Yes," said one man, "they came earlier. Shouldn't be a problem."

"They won't be back? What if—"

"Hello?" called Lorenzo from his cot. "Hello? Can you hear me?"

But the men's voices were already distant. He rose to his feet and limped across the room. "Hello? Hey!" He pressed his ear to the door, then pounded on it. But the effort nearly made him pass out. "Hello?" he murmured. Nothing.

The following day, Lorenzo woke when the door groaned open wide enough to toss in a paper bag. Then it slammed shut again. He looked away, disgusted by his lack of power. Had he been on his game, he'd have challenged Alfonso for doling out scraps like he was an animal in a cage. But Lorenzo could barely stand, or even lift his aching head from his cot. *Pathetic: adj. Arousing pity, especially through vulnerability or sadness.* It had been Lorenzo's word of the day once. Before his reunion with Kate. Before paintings lifted from a wooden crate tore open his deep wounds and sent him on a wild goose chase for Marco Robini.

He'd had his moment with Marco in the piazza. He'd shot to kill. Lorenzo had never wanted to hurt anyone more than at that moment. Maybe that's what blinded him to the weapon aimed at him.

Or maybe he'd been blinded by Kate. Yes—Kate, and the possibility that she was in love with Emilio.

What'd become of Kate? He imagined Marco in his whites with the blue scarf around his neck, Kate trapped beneath his girth, fighting for her life. Lorenzo shivered—paralyzing chills and sweat weeping from every pore. He slept a little that afternoon but kept having dreams flooded with pain and heartbreak. While awake, he listened for any hint that his captor would put him out of his misery. What were they waiting for?

In his fevered state, Lorenzo felt forsaken. He abandoned his will for liberty, contenting himself to eat handouts, as if he was a dog— unable to even tend to his own injury, which grew uglier by the hour.

Lorenzo surrendered to these facts with little chance for escape and less for rescue. He gave up hope of seeing a friendly face again—much less a loving one.

How long had it been since they had taken him? Two days? Three? He couldn't think straight.

What could they want with Kate other than to torture Lorenzo with the knowledge? Was that the plan—to make him suffer her pain? Lorenzo wanted to scream, but lacked the strength, alone in his confinement. He kept picturing Kate dragged off to some remote location, raped and tortured by Marco. No, she was too quick for him. Lorenzo envisioned Berto stripping Kate naked, and his mind fogged over. What of Muriel? What of Emilio? A walnut-sized lump lodged in his throat as he contemplated the tragic consequences of his capture.

"You fool!" he rasped. Here he was again, responsible for the suffering of others. Another death. Perhaps several. Overcome by self-pity, Lorenzo curled up in the cot and blacked out.

He woke sometime later to find another sack of food beside the first. With his stomach twisted in knots, Lorenzo couldn't eat. But while he had no appetite, his thirst raged, so he limped to the bathroom and watched the iron-laden water spill from the tap until it ran clear, then drank from his cupped hands. Thirst quenched, he glanced at the murky window. It had grown dark outside. Instinctively, he checked his wrist for the time.

"Half past a freckle." He giggled hysterically at his father's old joke until tears streamed down his face. Would he ever see his father again? His family?

Being the oldest child of eight came with its responsibilities. Expectations. Lorenzo and Muriel were as close as two siblings could be. She knew him and loved him unconditionally. But his brothers, his younger sisters, his son—what did he represent to them? Certainly not a role model. Not a poster boy for Italian traditional living. Lorenzo had tried the traditional lifestyle. Then, when his wife died, he fled. But where did that get him? Decades of loneliness, two-dimensional relationships, and dead-end romances. Was Kate just another notch on the belt?

Anguished, he pushed the thought aside and returned to his cot. Since being holed up, he'd divided his time between the smelly cot and the tiny stool, where he sat slumped in front of the door for most of the day, waiting for something to happen. He remained in the robe, now crusted with dried blood and puss. The sandals had drifted out of reach under the cot.

What was outside the bathroom window? A field? A forest? A place to hide, supposing he found a way out? Lorenzo dreamed of strangling his captor with the scarf and running for the void—but he knew it was a fantasy. He lacked the strength and fortitude to follow through and wasn't too deluded to know when he was beaten.

So it was, as Lorenzo sat at the door, or stared through the window, or lay on the cot staring up at the drywall ceiling, that he picked apart his pathetic life and waited for death. He envisioned Ella's beaming face on their wedding day—undoubtedly the high point of his life. Then he envisioned her lifeless body in the satin-lined casket—undoubtedly the low point. He mulled over his move to Portland—exciting at first, then overshadowed by guilt. Then there was Kate, who, thanks to his incompetence, was now captured—or worse. He kept her scarf wrapped around his neck, but her scent had faded, corrupted by his own stench.

Lorenzo remembered seeing Kate in Thomas Klein's office. How had he fallen for her so quickly, so completely?

He thought of her with Emilio, the man from the train platform. Lorenzo knew him the moment he saw him at Muriel's. The look he'd given Lorenzo—resentment for being away for thirty years? Or the look of a man bent on stealing his girlfriend? He had no notion of what his son was capable of. Would he go so far to hurt the man who had abandoned him?

And Kate—he'd barely known her before allowing her into his heart. Would she turn from him so easily?

No. Stop. It was unthinkable.

"Kate," he said aloud, as if she were in the room. "My Sancho." Lorenzo closed his eyes and imagined the feel of her skin against his. Her scent, her voice. He longed to lie beside her again, hear her sigh in her sleep, her moans while making love. She'd dropped everything to come with him on this fool's errand. She'd quit her job rather than disobey his order to wait until the next day. She'd risked losing a house she loved just to be with him. Not only smart, funny, and beautiful—she was loyal to a fault. Lorenzo refused to give in to petty jealousy.

For that reason, and the prospect of reuniting with his estranged family, Lorenzo decided it was time to pick himself up and get the hell out of his prison. He could not give up. Not now.

***

Speed and strength were in short supply, but Lorenzo would need both to get the jump on Alfonso the next time the door opened.

He stood back against the wall beside the door with each end of Kate's scarf wound tightly around his hands. He waited, imagining the scarf cinched around Alfonso's thick neck. But the room grew dim as evening fell and Alfonso still hadn't come. Was this the end? Now that Lorenzo had committed himself to freedom, had Alfonso given up?

Agh! The pain. Lorenzo glanced longingly at the stool. He wouldn't be able to stand much longer.

Finally, he heard the familiar footsteps in the gravel. Lorenzo's rage peaked. The door opened, but not wide enough for what he had in mind. The paper sack landed at his feet and the door began to close. Lorenzo released one end of the scarf and, with a flick, wedged it between the latch and the frame just as the door closed.

He waited as the footsteps retreated. No one had detected him. He'd done it. He looked down at an apple rolling away from the sack, knowing his own escape was imminent.

CHAPTER TWENTY-EIGHT

Kate

It was dusk when Kate and Emilio left the bus stop in the village to make their slow progress toward Alfonso's estate. But now a brilliant crescent moon hung low in the sky. Kate tried to block the sting of a burst blister, the sharp pain in her arm, and the bruise that throbbed on her backside as she focused on finding and freeing Lorenzo. But self-doubt began seeping through the cracks in her resolve.

"What if he's not here?" she said.

Emilio glanced at her. "Huh?"

"I mean, what if I'm wrong?" She felt a wave of nausea. Nerves doing their worst to remind her how far out of her depth she was.

"Then we leave it to the experts," Emilio said. "Maybe they already found him. Did you think of that?"

Yes, she'd thought of that. But she'd also imagined Lorenzo tossed overboard from *Il Palazzo*.

Kate squeezed her fists tight and pushed the worry away, focusing on the only solution she'd come up with on her own. She prayed she was right. She couldn't entertain a life without Lorenzo, the sound of his voice, the safety of his arms, and the tenderness in his eyes when he looked at her.

"You know," she said as they turned off onto a gravel road. "I was tempting fate for the first time in my life when I was on that volcano this fall. The risk never struck me until this moment. There I was, sleeping in the shadow of death—where people had been smothered or cooked twenty-some years earlier. It's disturbing to think that, at any moment, the mountain could have blown up again, and my charred remains would have been left smoldering in some hole."

"Would you be quiet?" Emilio blurted.

"Just throw me a bone, Emilio. You act as if you know what to do. We both know that neither of us knows what we are doing. That's the problem with this whole thing. That's how the Robinis have gotten away with murder and more—nobody knows what the hell to do. Even the police. Jeez Louise, what was that all about? They've had thirty years to get this right, but they did nothing. Then finally, Lorenzo served Marco up to them on a silver platter, and they failed."

Kate looked over at Emilio, his face half-lit by moonlight.

"Do you have a better idea?" he said. "You have been in Italy for *how* long now? And *how* far have you gotten? You put my entire family at risk and got my father captured."

Kate saw red. She had all she could do to not wring Emilio's neck at that moment. Instead, she stopped and got into his face with a pointed finger.

"That's enough, Emilio. I have no idea how you're feeling right now. I can guess, but I don't know. That does not entitle you to put me down. I am a journalist. Not a detective, or a spy, or an assassin. I have taken my share of degradation from men in my life, and I will not tolerate this from you. Do you hear me? Shut your self-righteous mouth and let's focus on finding your father."

Kate took off down the road. Emilio rushed to keep up with her.

"I'm sorry," he panted, "You're right."

Kate stopped and pointed ahead of them. "I think this is the place." They'd come upon a large house and beyond that was another building, long and narrow, with a jumble of construction material laid out neatly to the side. The whole place lit up like a park with spotlights and decorative lanterns. "There, see? Stables."

She withdrew her arm quickly when she heard a buzz. A loud click followed, and an iron gate opened to the side. They ducked for cover in the ditch beside the driveway and held their breath as a small blue pickup truck approached with its high beams on.

"It's him," said Emilio as the truck passed by. "The man from the bar, the train." Kate saw the brim of his cap in the moonlight and nodded. She looked back down the road, then up the wooded slope to her right.

"This way." They scrambled up the steep hill, crouched low, grasping at rocks and branches along the way. When they reached the top, she edged around to where they had a full view of the estate —house, stables, paddock, and all.

Multiple bundles of lumber lay scattered, and lengths of pipe and tile waited on wooden pallets. The unfinished addition was small—perhaps two more stalls, with an outbuilding to the side backing up to the woods. Somebody walked through the light to meet the truck.

"It's Alfonso," said Kate, recognizing the rounded profile. He stopped to talk to the man in the pickup, then turned and looked up into the trees.

"Duck!" Kate said, pulling Emilio to the ground with her. They heard raised voices and peeked over the shrubs.

The pickup sped out of the driveway and headed back out the gate as Alfonso stormed down a stone path leading to the house and disappeared through a side door.

"What was *that* all about?" asked Emilio.

"Give him a minute, then we'll go down and explore, all right?" Kate sat back and pulled off her shoes to rub her feet. She was cold and tired, and she hurt all over. Emilio pulled the gun out of his pocket. "Do you know how to use that thing?" asked Kate, watching him struggle to insert the clip. The gun was thirty years old. Was it even functional?

"I know enough."

Then the lights surrounding the stables went dark. Kate eased back into her shoes and they slid down the bank to the gravel drive.

As they neared the stables, Emilio lost his footing and cursed. One horse snorted, and another stomped and shuffled around in its stall. The door to the house opened, and out dashed Pico, the Doberman, running swiftly to investigate the commotion, barking at anything in his path.

Quickly, Kate and Emilio ducked into a nearby horse trailer, and Emilio hastily fumbled to swing the door closed behind them. They heard a single bark at the door, and then Pico sniffing. Then it was quiet. Kate stood on tiptoe and peeked out of a small window to see the scrawny dog racing back to the house.

"You think Father's here?" asked Emilio again.

Kate cringed. "I told you before, I don't know. But it's my best guess. Come on." She jumped from the trailer and ran in quick steps to the first stable door. A bright light suddenly switched on overhead, and she froze.

"A motion sensor," whispered Emilio, pulling her into the shadows. Desperately, he looked ahead for more, but they were hard to avoid.

"Back here," Kate said, darting behind the stable where there weren't any lights. Emilio followed. She knocked in soft thumps along the back wall. "Lorenzo. Lorenzo, are you here?" she murmured. "Can you hear me?"

"*Papà,*" Emilio said. "*Mi senti?*"

They knocked and listened until Kate heard a rustle in the woods behind them. She froze and signaled to Emilio to be quiet, wondering if the Italian equivalent of a coyote, bobcat, or cougar were any less threatening.

It was Pico again—this time he appeared out of nowhere with a nose-to-crotch greeting. He seemed almost friendly until he discovered Emilio. Then he barked and growled, only stopping when Emilio won him over with a pat on the head and some kind words. Finally, the Doberman bounded away, then barked again at something near the other end of the stables.

Kate followed the dog, hoping to shut him up, and afraid Alfonso would come investigate.

"Don't move," said Emilio. "The lights."

"I'll be careful," Kate said as the light popped back on again. *Damn.*

"Hold still, or the light won't turn off," said Emilio.

A man's voice called, "Pico!" Kate and Emilio backed into the darkness. Kate's heart pounded. Had Alfonso seen them?

"Kate." The voice was deep and raspy. Kate turned to Emilio. He shook his head—someone else was there in the dark. The voice sounded again. "Sancho."

Kate turned toward the voice. "Lorenzo?"

Lorenzo staggered out of the brush and into the halo of light. Kate gasped. She hardly recognized him. He was barefoot and wore a light-colored bathrobe that hung off one shoulder and Kate's scarf draped around his neck. She started running to him but stopped when she heard footsteps behind her.

"Well, isn't this adorable," said Alfonso, gripping Kate's sore arm. "All the way from . . . where was it? Colorado?"

"Let her go, Alfonso," Lorenzo said, stumbling forward.

Kate kicked Alfonso's shin, but it wasn't hard enough to do any real damage. He pushed her hard against the stable wall and held her there while Pico bounced back and forth between them and Lorenzo.

Emilio stepped into the light, holding his father's old pistol.

"Ah, the lover's triangle," said Alfonso. "I heard about this." Kate kicked him again, harder this time. He slapped her hard across the face—but in doing so, released his grip. She ducked into the brush where Lorenzo stood. "Lean on me," she said. He accepted, laboring for breath.

Emilio remained in Alfonso's path, the gun now pointed straight ahead. Alfonso laughed as he approached Emilio cautiously.

"Come, boy. Hand over your little *pistola*." He stepped closer. Closer still.

Hand trembling, Emilio pulled the trigger.

Click.

"Ha!" Alfonso said. "Perhaps it *is* a toy. Or did you forget your ammunition?"

Emilio pulled the trigger again. Nothing. He tossed the gun aside and made a run at Alfonso. The two men couldn't have been more mismatched—the aging, overweight Alfonso with arms flailing versus the young, nimble Emilio, who knew how to throw a punch.

As they fought, Kate realized she couldn't hold Lorenzo's weight any longer. "Sit down," she murmured. He wobbled and fell forward onto the gun.

"Emilio, get back," Lorenzo rasped. Kate reached to help him up, but he pushed her away. "I said, *get back*." Kate jumped back, confused.

Emilio turned, then stepped away from Alfonso. Lorenzo rolled over—groaning and clutching his leg.

Alfonso grunted and rose to his knees with Pico dancing all around him, whining and whimpering. Lorenzo struggled to sit up, so Kate moved toward him—but stopped when she saw his steely glare. He had the gun. He deftly released the clip, then snapped it back into place as if he'd done it a thousand times.

"*Casso!*" Alfonso rose to his feet, his eyes widening as Lorenzo lifted the gun and squeezed the trigger. *Pang!*

With a jolt, Alfonso fell back against the stable. The horses neighed and thumped behind the wall. Lorenzo fired again. Alfonso jumped, but his leg buckled beneath him, and he stumbled to the ground.

Kate ran to Lorenzo, still on the ground, and pulled him to her, holding his shivering body tight. Emilio took the scarf and fastened Alfonso's wrists behind him, then called the police.

By morning, the hall outside Lorenzo's hospital room buzzed with uniformed men waiting for the team of doctors to clear him for visitors. But the police, secret service, and press took a backseat to the swarm of Rotondo family members.

His mother was all kisses, her embrace so strong he seemed to struggle for breath. His father cried. One by one, his siblings came forward, introducing their spouses, children, and grandchildren. Lorenzo basked in the love and attention of his parents, brothers, and sisters. This was the first time he'd seen any of them for thirty years.

Kate stood close by while Emilio introduced Luca. Lorenzo's love for the young boy was obvious.

Then his eyes rested on Emilio, and Kate noticed a shift. Suspicion. Her heart ached to think he still believed there was anything between her and Emilio.

"I need to get some air," she told Muriel.

"Are you all right? You're not ill, are you?"

"I'm fine."

"You're white as a ghost."

Muriel went to find a nurse, who ushered Kate into an examination room. She took a close look at the bruising around Kate's arm.

Muriel translated for the nurse. "She's going to call for a doctor to look at you. He'll probably want an x-ray. You're not pregnant, are you?"

"Um." The possibility was too much to consider.

Muriel gave Kate's hand an understanding squeeze and nodded to the nurse, who went off to find the doctor.

Emilio stood in the doorway, with his torn shirt, filthy jeans, and a beard that had grown shaggy over the last few days.

"I'll just be down the hall," Muriel reassured Kate before leaving the room, patting Emilio tenderly on the shoulder as she passed.

"*Stai bene?*" Emilio stepped into her room and pulled a chair up to the examination table.

"I'm fine." She smiled. "You stink."

Emilio laughed. "You don't smell so sweet yourself," he said, winking.

Kate squeezed his hand and gazed into his face. "We make quite a team," she said. But she knew there was more to say. "Um, Emilio," she began, puzzling thoughts into words that were difficult to speak.

"What is it?"

She released his hand. "I think your father believes there was some truth to Marco's insinuation."

He glanced toward the door with a heavy sigh. "I think you're right," he said, shaking his head. "But there *was* something, wasn't there? I mean, if things had been different, we might have—"

"No, Emilio, there was nothing."

The doctor tapped on the door and entered the room. Emilio patted Kate's knee. "I need to get back, anyway," he said.

An hour later, Kate returned to Lorenzo's room—past the whole Rotondo clan, who was now assembled in the waiting area. They'd been banished while the Genoa police spoke with Lorenzo. But Kate was allowed to enter.

"How's the patient?" she asked, reaching for his outstretched hand. Lorenzo beamed, giving her hand a firm squeeze.

"This review won't take long, *signorina*," said the lead officer.

Kate was happy to learn about the AISI's headway with local police cooperation. They'd raided the insurance agency and found the remaining shipping receipts from the art school. They'd also raided the school, confiscating multiple paintings and sculptures tracked from the insurance office.

"And the foundation?" asked Kate.

"No foundation," said one officer. "Not really. It's a sham. The website is a facade. The addresses on all the shipping documents correspond with the auto shop in Genoa they used to warehouse outgoing cargo."

The investigators had already made several arrests, but asked Kate and Lorenzo to sort through a set of mug shots anyway. Some were easy, like Alfonso, who'd been arrested at his estate and was recovering in another part of the hospital. The police captured both Maximo Corta and the fellow with the black eye from the tour boat. A shiver ran up Kate's spine at the realization that the confrontation had been deliberate. They both recognized Berto, even without his gray driving cap.

"Agent Colucci was one of ours. We lost faith when he went off course to follow you."

"His killer?" asked Lorenzo.

"Unknown, but we have our suspicions. As a member of the Italian Secret Service, Colucci had access to places and people the Robini family did not. He made himself useful, as it turned out, to no one."

"Did the forensics lab get the results they were looking for?" asked Kate, remembering Casaro's claim that he would resubmit the evidence.

"They did," said one investigator. "It confirmed what you'd told us, Lorenzo. And that smudge on the statuette—Ella's blood. Marco's fingerprints were all over it, as well as Ella's."

"Have you arrested Marco?" Kate asked, squeezing Lorenzo's hand.

"Um, no *signorina*. Not yet. We're still looking for him."

Lorenzo spent Christmas Eve and Christmas Day in the care of the hospital's compassionate medical staff. Two days later, he was allowed to board the train back to Manarola. The Rotondo family dominated a whole train car with hugs, kisses, laughter, and singing. They all made Kate feel like part of the family.

Papa fussed over her, declaring that she was Lorenzo's special friend from "The United States of America"—which he pronounced as clearly as anyone who had never spoken a word in English. Kate felt such affection for the old man.

Kate and Emilio received ample attention for having saved Lorenzo from certain death.

"He freed himself," Kate told them, glancing at Lorenzo.

"I couldn't have made it on my own," said Lorenzo, nudging Kate with his good leg as Muriel looked over her seat, her brow set into deep valleys.

"Are you comfortable, brother?"

"Why did I stay away for so long?" he asked her.

"We all have our own way, Lorenzo. Yours just took a few—detours." They shared a laugh.

The party continued after the train arrived in the village, with the entire community pouring into the piazza. There was music, dancing, and generous quantities of wine and food. It was like Lorenzo's very own feast day. Kate smiled till her cheeks hurt and laughed until her belly ached.

Neighbors and friends, including Nikola and Minni, greeted Lorenzo with hugs and tears. The once broken man had returned a hero. Kate looked on, wondering if he could leave this for his life in Portland.

She watched as Lorenzo approached his son, Emilio tensing the closer Lorenzo came. Kate couldn't hear it, but Lorenzo said something that made his son smile. His glance at Luca suggested it was about the boy. Good, thought Kate—Emilio was warming to his father. How could he leave now?

Mamma Rotondo, smiling ear to ear, took Kate's face in her hands, looked into her eyes, and winked. Then she pulled Kate toward Lorenzo, grabbed her hand, and waggled it in front of him, smiling through her harsh words—one of which Kate understood. *Fidanzato.* Sophia had suggested it at dinner one night. Lorenzo laughed and hugged his mother tightly.

Muriel put her arm around Kate and steered her toward the woman Emilio had greeted at the platform so long ago.

"Kate, this is my daughter, Gina."

"So this is the woman who brought our uncle back to us," said Gina. "We owe you. Emilio owes you."

Muriel glanced over Kate's shoulder and smiled. "Lorenzo owes you."

Kate felt Lorenzo's warm hand slip around her waist. He pulled her close and cradled her gently in his arms—and she felt the weight of the past few weeks lifted.

CHAPTER TWENTY-NINE

Lorenzo

Lorenzo looked around the piazza, where his family and the whole village had gathered after his homecoming.

He'd rejected the wheelchair at the train platform, preferring to show strength, but that strength was flagging as the pain medication wore off.

"I'm tired," Lorenzo murmured to Kate. She hadn't been more than two feet away since the hospital, and he couldn't have been more grateful.

Kate looked him over. "I'll take you back to the house."

Lorenzo recalled too well the condition he was in when Kate found him. A sorry sight, reeking of rotten flesh and human filth. She hadn't batted an eye.

Muriel went ahead and waited for them at the door as they made their slow progress up the street from the piazza.

"I've made up Gina's room." she said when they arrived. "It should be nice and quiet back there." She led them up the first flight of stairs and down the hall past the bathroom and Muriel's own room.

She had the bed made up with flannel sheets and a heavy quilt. He looked around and smiled.

"There's a lot of pink," he said flatly.

Gina seldom used this room since she lived a quick train ride away, but Muriel maintained it as it had been on the day she moved out. The one thing out of sync with the feminine decor was the handcrafted desk beneath the window. Lorenzo leaned heavily on it as he studied the room. Muriel had thoughtfully tucked his luggage beside the dresser, after the local police collected it from the Parma hotel.

"We'll be fine from here, sister, thank you."

"You're sure?" Muriel said, hovering.

"I've got this, Muriel," Kate said. Muriel cocked her head and nodded before closing the door.

"Oof," Lorenzo said, sitting on the side of the bed and looking up at Kate. She sat down beside him and reached for his sore leg.

"Does it hurt?"

Lorenzo grinned. "Yes." It had healed significantly, but he remembered the red, inflamed flesh around the wound, with pus oozing from the cracked scabs. After removing the bullet, the hospital pumped him with antibiotics and sent him home with a prescription for painkillers he refused to take—Italian machismo.

"You should never have come after me," he scolded. Kate waved off the reprimand.

"We're a team, remember?"

"Who says?" asked Lorenzo. But he enjoyed her attention. He put his arm around her and nuzzled her ear. "I missed you."

Kate leaned into him. "I missed you too."

She wore the brown sweater. It looked as frumpy on her now as it had back in their tiny apartment over the bookstore. Lorenzo tugged at the sleeve.

"Don't tell me you want it back," she said. "I *love* this sweater."

Lorenzo leaned into her, shoulder to shoulder, in a familiar nudge. "I love *you*."

"Ah—well, I knew that when I found this sweater in my suitcase," Kate said, grinning.

Lorenzo shook his head. "I loved you long before that."

"*I* knew I loved *you* the night you showed up at my doorstep."

"It's a competition now?" he said, laughing.

"Okay, well—maybe not that night. But once I tasted your sweetbread the next morning, that was it. I was a goner."

"Heh. Ah, yes—the sweetbread. Works every time." Kate gawped and playfully punched his arm.

Lorenzo recalled how his heart leaped when he'd seen her behind the stables. The thrill of the moment affirmed his feelings for her. He'd immediately searched for her when he woke in the hospital to a roomful of strangers, who he quickly realized were not strangers at all. Emilio and Kate stood together in the corner of his hospital room, looking like a couple, whispering, laughing, and greeting family members.

Marco had implied the two were intimate. But being with her now put that fear to rest.

Kate doled out his medicine and encouraged him to take it, saying, "Don't even think about toughing it out, mister. It's not worth it." Two pills down the hatch with a cold-water chaser. Lorenzo set down the water and gazed into her freckled face as she undressed him.

"I could get used to this," he said, longing to pull her into bed. He brushed his thumb across her lips, and she kissed it, then kissed the palm of his hand the way she had after their night at the jazz club.

"You smell so sweet," he whispered.

Kate grinned. "Hotel soap. I splurged on a room in Genoa while you were in the hospital."

"Soft pillows and Italian television?"

"Twenty-minute showers and room service. It was decadent." She laughed, and he kissed her open mouth, weaving his fingers through her hair, which had grown past her shoulders since leaving Portland.

"There's room for two," he said, patting the double bed. The drugs were potent. He could hear himself slurring his words.

"Lay back, Lorenzo. Yes. There you go." He heard her voice drift into a drug-induced haze. She lifted the sheet and quilt up to his chin. He felt her lips on his. "Sleep well."

He watched, blearily, as she turned out the light and closed the door—then listened, heartbroken, as she walked down the hall.

Long after midnight, his room lit by what little moonlight could seep through the clouds, Lorenzo woke to an angel at the foot of his bed.

He was groggy, and his vision was blurred by painkillers, but he was sure: he saw Ella's spirit. At first, he was comforted. Then he was terrified. He wanted the image to go away. Maybe the apparition was drug-induced? But no—the covers pulled away enough for the fantasy to climb in bed beside him.

She pressed her naked flesh against him, wrapped her arms around him, and sought out his mouth in the dark. Lorenzo felt no pain as she continued her delicate exploration.

He woke the next day to the church bells of his youth. *Bong, Bong, Bong!*

"Are you hungry?" asked Kate lying naked beside him. He reached out for her, grinning widely. His stomach growled. "I'll be right back," she said, kissing him lightly on the forehead. She pulled on some clothes and slipped out of the room. He used the opportunity to visit the bathroom, shave, and brush his teeth. Kate was waiting for him with a tray full of provisions and his next dose of pain medication as he hobbled back to bed.

"Thank you," he said, picking up a slice of pear and using it to push the pills aside. He'd had enough hallucinations for now.

As they ate, he told her how he had planned to strangle Alfonso with the scarf. "I should have done that the first night—before I was so bad off. But I thought I would never see you again if I didn't make it out of there. It was the motivation I needed."

Kate picked up the empty tray and set it on the floor. "Adrenaline is a powerful drug."

"It wouldn't have been enough to strangle Alfonso. I was out of my head and so weak." He took her hand. "Marco told me he had you. The scarf that tied my hands was your scarf. I had nothing else to go on."

Kate wove her fingers through his. "How is your arm?" he said, holding it up and studying the faded bruising.

"Arm's fine."

"Muriel said they ran a blood test—that you weren't well."

"Oh, that." Kate squirmed. "They wouldn't do an X-ray without a pregnancy test." Lorenzo dared to hope, but Kate looked down into her lap, and his heart sank. "We'd tried—George and I, but at some point, we gave up. *I* gave up. Then this test brought it all back. I figured I was past it all, but . . ." Lorenzo put his arm around her and pulled her close. He tried to kiss her, but she pulled away. "Lorenzo, there's something I need to tell you—want to tell you." She shook her head. It wasn't a good something. Emilio?

Don't say it. He'd put it behind him and didn't want to hear more.

Kate looked off toward the corner of the room. "I barely knew him."

Lorenzo fought the butterflies in his chest. "Who? What are you saying?"

She turned to him, but he couldn't meet her eyes. "I didn't want to tell you. Your views on abortion and—"

Lorenzo straightened, throwing his shoulders back. "*Abortion?*"

"It was ages ago. College. Please—don't hate me."

Lorenzo swallowed hard, still feeling the cramp in his throat as he struggled to respond. The anguish in her face broke his heart. "Oh, Kate, I could *never* hate you."

They ate, slept, and cuddled until finally leaving their sanctuary to be sociable. Emilio rose from the table and gave his father a superficial hug, superseded by Luca's tight embrace.

"*Buongiorno, Nonno. Buongiorno, Zia* Kate."

"*Buongiorno,* Cowboy," said Kate.

Lorenzo smiled. "*Zia?*"

Emilio pulled a chair back from the kitchen table. "Off you go now, Luca. I need to speak with *Nonno.*" Luca gave Lorenzo another hug, then bounced down the hall to the front door.

"He's a beautiful boy, Emilio," said Lorenzo easing into the chair.

"Yes." Emilio smiled and sat down beside him. "You slept well?"

"Very well." Lorenzo looked over at Kate in the kitchen, busily fixing coffee. He thought of the vision slipping under the covers, at first imagining it was Ella's spirit until their lips met. Kate's mouth tasted so sweet he could have swallowed her whole.

Emilio leaned on the table; his forearms crossed in front of him. He took a deep breath. Whatever he had to say, it was important, and Lorenzo's heart raced in anticipation.

"This isn't easy," Emilio said in Italian. "I have a million things I want to say and I can't seem to come up with a single one."

"Me too," Lorenzo said, continuing in Italian. "Perhaps I should start with an apology, no?" Kate set two espresso cups in front of them and disappeared up the stairs. "I can think of so many times I picked up the phone to call, or put pen to paper to write, but—I don't know why. I just couldn't open that door. You see, I loved your mother so deeply and when she was stripped from me, I had to pull away. I convinced myself that it was for the good of the family, but it wasn't fair to you, and I feel the weight of it and how much I've missed of your growing up. You have a son, for God's sake!" His thoughts were tumbling out, and he wondered if he was making any sense.

"I've tried putting myself in your shoes," Emilio said. He sipped his espresso. "I've tried to imagine walking away from Luca, and every time I just feel rage. The unfairness of it all."

"Yes, yes. I'm sorry." Lorenzo reached for Emilio's hand and was surprised when he didn't pull away.

"When Kate arrived, I wasn't sure what to make of her," Emilio said. Lorenzo nodded for him to go on, eager to hear more, and to get the truth. "This smart, beautiful woman who blushed when anyone said your name. A friend of yours, she'd said."

Lorenzo took a deep breath. "She is very special to me, Emilio."

"I understand that now, *Papà*."

CHAPTER THIRTY

Kate

Kate spent a week attending to Lorenzo before opening her laptop. She discovered an email from Mr. Walker, insisting on her prompt reply and an ETA for her return to Portland. He said he was worried about her. But the anger in her belly hadn't quelled enough to accept his offer. Not yet.

George emailed stating his intention to take possession of the house if he did not hear from her that day, claiming abandonment. Was that even legal? Her mortgage payment was late, and without a steady job, she feared that a "for sale" sign was the only way out.

Megan asked about Kate's return, too. But she didn't have an answer for any of them.

Lorenzo also fielded calls from Portland. His landlord billed him for the new lock on his door. Buddy practically begged him to come back—the workload was mounting. Sergeant Monroe's request was more diplomatic but no less urgent. Finally, Casaro offered Lorenzo a position at the La Spezia station—an offer that took him entirely by surprise.

Not a day passed without debate from the Rotondo family and their friends, who frequently popped in unannounced. Did Lorenzo intend to stay, or would he return to the States? Kate, too, had contemplated the pros and cons of staying in Italy. She'd formed a bond with her host family and the village of Manarola. But she had a career and treasured relationships back home with Megan, Thomas, and Briley. On the other hand, staying here would take care of the homeowner issue.

Kate wrote Mr. Walker with an outline for her article and explained her intention to sell it to the highest bidder.

She spread everything she'd collected since arriving in Italy out in her attic bedroom, which she used now solely as an office. She began piecing her story together. It wasn't easy. The activity in the house distracted her, as did George's odd behavior. She needed some time to clear her head.

One day, Kate found Lorenzo reading the newspaper in the sitting room—a new pair of reading glasses perched on the end of his nose. "Let's go for a walk," she said. "I need some air."

"I'll get my coat," he said.

They walked down the hill and followed the path leading past the park she'd visited on her first day in Manarola.

"Would you mind a little detour?" Lorenzo asked, nodding toward the ornate gates of the local cemetery.

"Of course not." Kate had passed these gates often on her exploratory walks. When they entered, she'd expected to see rows of gravestones, but this cemetery was different. It consisted of above-ground corridors of high marble walls inset with what he called *loculos*—vaults large enough for a casket.

Lorenzo led Kate to Ella's *loculo*—pink asters filled the sconces on either side of her tomb, and her name was engraved above a laminated photograph of her and Lorenzo. He touched the photo.

"My family chose that picture as if I'd died with her—which, in a way, I had. A piece of me, anyway." Lorenzo sat on the bench opposite the wall. Kate settled beside him and took his hand as a seagull landed on the wall—then two, then five. All lined up six inches apart. They turned in a way that looked staged. Lorenzo gazed up at the birds. "The last time I saw her, I was on my way to work. She'd walked me to the train all dressed up like she was going to a party."

"What a beautiful memory," Kate said.

Lorenzo shook his head, cringing. "She came to ask me a favor. She wanted me to try for the farmhouse again. I told her it was out of the question. No discussion. She said our house was too crowded, and with another baby on the way . . ."

"Oh, Lorenzo." Kate laid a hand on his back, and he leaned into her.

"That was the first I'd heard about it. I didn't know what to say, so when the train pulled up, I got on. Then Ella walked back to town to take matters into her own hands." Lorenzo cleared his throat. "I remember the day of her funeral—the walk from the church to this spot. My mind was gone. I could hardly stand. My father held me up on one side and Muriel on the other while my mother held little Emilio. He was wailing away like he knew what was happening. That was when I made my decision to leave it all behind. To run away—like a coward." He crossed to Ella's *loculo*. "I couldn't handle the weight of it all."

Kate remained on the bench, thinking Lorenzo would rather be alone. But he turned around and held out his hand. She rose and took it.

"I never really had closure," he said. "I never said goodbye." He pulled the photo from the *loculo*, then replaced it with a photograph of Ella alone—her head cocked to one side, smiling for the camera. He kissed his fingers and touched the new photo. "*Arrivederci, fiore mio.*"

CHAPTER THIRTY-ONE

Lorenzo

Three weeks into his recovery, the house was quiet at last. The parade of visitors and family shrank to the few who lived in town. Muriel spent her days at the bakery, as Kate finished her article up in her office. They were alone on this rainy afternoon. With a grin, Lorenzo climbed the stairs and tapped at her open door.

Kate looked up at him from the sewing table she used as a desk. "Hey."

He smiled, closing the door behind him, then eyed the single bed. At fifty-two, he felt like a twenty-year-old pulling the sheets down. She grinned, looked at the bed, and blushed, then rose from the wicker stool and came to him, unbuttoning her shirt.

"I've thought of this a hundred times," she said, kicking her jeans aside and slipping between the sheets.

"Just a hundred?" Lorenzo stripped and slid in beside her. Kate shivered under the cold sheets and he pulled her closer into his warmth. Then they heard footsteps outside the door. Tap, tap. Kate giggled, and Lorenzo put a finger to her lips.

"Ignore it." He pulled the blanket up and over their heads.

"*Papà?*" It was Emilio.

Lorenzo sighed and peeked out from under the covers. "Yes?"

"Agent Casaro is here to see you."

Kate's warm body wriggled beside him. "I wonder what Casaro wants?"

Lorenzo grinned and kissed her bare shoulder. "I have no idea, but his timing couldn't be worse."

"Hello, my friend," Lorenzo said, greeting Casaro in the front hall downstairs. "I'll make some coffee."

"This isn't a social call, Lorenzo," Casaro said, removing his dripping hat and tucking it under his arm. "I've come for your help."

"What can I do for you?"

"We can't find Marco anywhere. It's exhausting. The AISI went through everything you gave them, adding what little they knew. He's vanished."

Kate stepped into the front hall and nodded to Casaro.

"Come. Sit down." Lorenzo walked with Emilio to the sitting room while Kate fired up the espresso maker.

"We've confiscated his boat," Casaro said. "We've revoked his passport and searched his home. We don't know where to look next."

"Have you searched the art school?" asked Kate from the kitchen.

"Yes. Nothing." Casaro made himself comfortable in the rocking chair while Lorenzo and Emilio settled onto the sofa.

"There is much more to that school than meets the eye," said Lorenzo. "The dormitories and classrooms are nothing compared to all the dusty chambers in the basement. Plus, the offices and a full kitchen. I could go on. That place is enormous."

Casaro rocked back and sighed. "We've scoured the place, Lorenzo. There's no trace of Marco anywhere."

Kate handed Agent Casaro his coffee. "A private jet?" she asked, sitting beside Lorenzo. "He wouldn't need a passport for that, would he?"

"Yes, he would," Casaro sipped from the small cup. "But he knows people in high places. It wouldn't surprise me if he sneaked out of the country that way. Lorenzo? Where would he go?"

Lorenzo scowled. "How should *I* know?" he said. "I'm sorry, but it's not like I knew him well. Have you asked Alfonso? How about Berto or Salvo? Any of them know Marco better than I." He stared reflectively at a spot on the carpet. If he were Marco, where would he hide?

"Give it some thought," Casaro said. "We could use your help."

Casaro emptied his cup and rose from the rocker, gazing at the polished wooden chest. "This is lovely."

"My son built that," Lorenzo said. "The lamp, too." He noticed Emilio's proud smile.

Lorenzo walked Casaro to the door and watched him dodge puddles as he made his way up the road and disappear around the corner. Rain dripped from the eave and trickled into pencil-thin rivulets down the stony road toward the sea. Lorenzo's thoughts collected in much the same way.

He had one idea where Marco could be hiding.

Lorenzo woke before dawn the following day while Kate slept soundly, one leg sticking out of the covers and an arm stretched to his side of the mattress. *Bed hog*, he thought affectionately. He eased past her, then pulled the covers over her bare shoulders and silently closed the door behind him.

Sunrise hid behind dark clouds closing in from the sea, and the wind kicked up an imminent winter storm. Wearing his running shoes and black hoodie, Lorenzo left the house, and walked as far as the trail that split off uphill through brush and bracken. It was a shortcut he remembered from childhood that led to the main road. Once he hit the pavement, he ran.

All the miles he'd walked over the past weeks hadn't prepared him for the heart-pounding release he felt as he approached Via Rosa. The farmhouse was barely visible through the overgrown brush and wild roses. Thunder rumbled from miles away as he slowed his pace, snaking up toward the house.

He was now at the rear of the farmhouse, standing in front of the door he'd entered decades earlier. But this was different. He reached for the gun he'd reclaimed from Emilio and secured the clip.

"Slowly," Lorenzo said, trying to control his racing heart. Then, with a steady hand, he turned the knob.

Marco waited at the door, looking disheveled, wearing a moth-eaten and tattered woolen coat. He had a pair of black rubber boots on his feet, a chunk of crusty bread in his fist, and a self-satisfied grin on his whiskered face.

"Why am I not surprised?" Marco said, breadcrumbs falling from his mouth.

Lorenzo looked over Marco's shoulder. "Are you alone?"

"No, there's a harem of young darlings waiting for me upstairs. Plenty to go around." He let out a deep-throated laugh, tossing the bread aside. "Ah, yes, how is that threesome working out for you? Did they make any room for you in their bed?" He continued laughing, louder. "And that leg? Seems you're getting around."

With his pistol firmly in hand, Lorenzo crossed the room into what served as a kitchen. There was no water or electricity, but Lorenzo saw a propane stove and a clear plastic box of food stashed against the wall. Marco approached him, but Lorenzo held him off with the gun, listening for signs of others in the house.

He considered the state of the place and Marco's disheveled appearance. "How long have you been here?"

"Too long," Marco said.

"Turning yourself in, then?"

"You'd like that, wouldn't you?"

"The alternative?" Lorenzo said.

Marco's lip curled in an ugly sneer as he took a small step toward Lorenzo. "Oh, just shoot me. Go ahead," he said, opening his coat. "See? No vest."

It would have been satisfying to shoot Marco with the very pistol he'd worn way back when he'd done nothing to avenge Ella's murder. But Lorenzo wanted a fight. He *needed* a fight.

"And your threat?" asked Lorenzo.

"A *warning*," said Marco. "To a *friend*. Carlo wanted you gone that night. *I* talked him out of it."

"Gone? As in dead?" asked Lorenzo.

"Yes—dead."

"Then why Ella?" he asked. But did he really want to know? Would it make any difference at all?

Marco shook his head. "I found her coming out of the tunnel that morning. She said, 'You're just the man I want to see.' I had no idea what she had in mind until she said she wanted the house and wouldn't take no for an answer. I gotta admit she had guts. We walked up here. She practically ran. I didn't expect what happened next. It wasn't my plan—but there she was, so willing. But you know the farmhouse wasn't mine to sell. It belonged to Carlo. I told her this —after, you know, and she flipped out. Went completely out of her head. 'What have I done?' she screamed over and over. I was simply trying to shut her up—to stop her from demolishing the place. Christ, what a temper! Then she came at me with the statuette. I snatched it from her, and . . . I don't know why. It was just a reflex, but she just wouldn't *shut up*!"

Fury burned beneath Lorenzo's skin. He longed to feel Marco's jaw crack under his fist. Lorenzo glanced at the back door as a sudden gust of wind forced it open. It swung wildly on its rusty hinges, squealing open and slamming shut. Open, shut. Open, shut.

"You cleaned up the crime scene," Lorenzo said.

"Carlo got a head's up from Santos, our illustrious, but dirty *commissario*." The door slammed shut again. "But you did him a favor. After we moved everything out of here, Carlo got this brilliant idea. He merged his insurance business with the school where his forgery artists studied, then put me in charge of the family's languishing art foundation. The program changed dramatically after that. He went from selling the fakes to selling the original art for more money. Greedy bastard."

None of this surprised Lorenzo, though he had believed Marco more culpable than he was letting on.

"What was your role?" Lorenzo heard the first drops of rain hit the kitchen window. The storm was upon them.

"I was the laundryman. All the money flowed through the foundation, and I distributed it." Marco winked. "Not without my fair share, of course. Yachts like *Il Palazzo* don't come cheap."

The door rattled violently, then swung wide open as rain slashed across the threshold.

"How about Monica Bower?" Lorenzo asked, testing his luck, since Marco seemed willing to talk.

Marco pulled his coat tighter around him and laughed. "That whore? Her little gallery was useful, though, like so many galleries before hers. It was only dumb luck you came upon that crate. I blame Alfonso."

"An elephant without tusks," said Lorenzo.

"Yes! You remember!"

"And Frank?"

Marco wiped a string of snot from his nose. "What can I say about that moron? He just didn't know how to play the game. Berto, though, knew how to keep me happy. He nailed Frank. But we could have avoided all this if he'd removed you back in Portland."

"You were going to take Kate."

"In *Genova*? Yes—Berto botched it again. And Frank—don't get me started. The worthless shit. But we were watching for you in here in Manarola. Your reunion."

"You could have killed me then."

"I didn't *want* you. I wanted *her*. And we had her until Casaro pulled her out. Probably the most policing he's done in twenty years. What a night that was, eh? I took the next best thing, hoping she'd come after you and allow Berto to redeem himself. But then came your son. Such a knight, that one."

Lorenzo wouldn't let Marco plant that seed again. "And the job at the school?" he asked.

"With limited access, as you may recall, but it kept you out of our hair until Berto found your American."

"What about Pietra?"

"She's clueless, but her brother reeled you in nicely. Don't you agree?"

"His truck. I saw it at the school. He makes your deliveries." Lorenzo had mistaken Salvo's truck for a van when he'd seen it in Genoa beside Alfonso's Jaguar.

"I'm tired of this." Marco took another step toward Lorenzo and made a grab for the pistol, but Lorenzo held it high out of reach. "Coward," Marco said, "just fucking shoot me."

Tempting. The floor creaked beneath Lorenzo's feet as he stepped back and took his phone from his back pocket.

"Lorenzo Rotondo calling for *Agente* Casaro. I have a gift for him."

PART 3

PORTLAND, OREGON— SPRING, 2005

CHAPTER THIRTY-TWO

Kate

Kate and Lorenzo sat at a table in the Italian café. There was a sign in the gallery window across the street. *NEW OWNER-SHIP*, it read.

Emilio and Luca sat across from them. Emilio looked as proud could be as they all toasted to his new venture—building and selling his handcrafted furniture. He and Luca had moved in with Kate and Lorenzo after Lorenzo bought George's share of the house, and they worked on filling it with the furnishings that made it a home. Kate's story about the art fraud scheme had successfully gained international attention and earned her the promotion she'd longed for. She now had a new editor to guide her. She'd never been so happy.

The young server from Salerno stood ready to take their orders—Kate noticed she wouldn't take her eyes off Emilio. Of course, with Emilio working right across the street, they would see a lot of one another in the future.

The bells chimed from the café door, and in walked Megan and Thomas. Briley bounced over to Luca.

"Hello, cousin!" Luca shouted, hugging the preschooler. They had become fast friends. Thomas cradled little Shaina—a chubby three-month-old now—and handed her off to Kate's outstretched arms.

Lorenzo squeezed Kate's hand under the table. She grinned and nudged his knee with hers. He knew how much she'd wanted a family of her own. He, too, had missed out on that experience. Both appreciated their second chance, with Emilio and Luca under their roof.

They'd spent an entire week in Burton after returning from Italy. Lorenzo wanted to see every corner of the quirky community and to meet the residents who made it successful. Kate's parents adored him. Her dad even said, "Now, this is what I was talking about," as he patted Lorenzo on the back.

The fact Kate didn't have a ring on her finger didn't seem to bother anyone except Mamma Rotondo, who remained adamant that her son needed to make an honest woman of Zia Kate. But it was Kate who opted out of marriage. It was enough that they owned the house together and shared a deep and binding love—for all the right reasons.

ACKNOWLEDGMENTS

Novels require the honest feedback and support of friends, family, and professionals. In my case, I would like to thank my mother, Sandy Hinkes, for her relentless enthusiasm for books and my passion for writing; my sister, Eileen Fitzpatrick, who read early drafts that streamlined the direction of this heartfelt story; and my sister-in-law, Linnea Fitzpatrick, for her help and support. I would also like to thank author Stephanie Butland for her valued assessment and mentorship on this project. And a special thank you goes out to Andrew Durkin of Yellow Bike Press for his eagle-eyed edits, constructive feedback, book design, and publishing advice, which helped launch this novel into the universe. Thank you all.

DEAR READER

Thank you so much for choosing this book!

You are cordially invited to leave an honest review on Goodreads, or the online store or reader website of your choice. Reader reviews are the lifeblood of independent publishing, and your opinion is valued!

For updates, please join the mailing list at maureenhartman.com.

Authors are nothing without readers! Thank you again.

ABOUT THE AUTHOR

Maureen Hartman is an Oregonian with midwestern roots. Besides writing, she enjoys gardening, hiking, and spending time with the people she loves.

For more, visit maureenhartman.com.

ALSO BY MAUREEN HARTMAN

SPIRIT (2020)